Praise for H

'*In the Shadow of the Hill* is a th
explodes into a finale which I
style is smoo

Roger Hutchison, Author

'Helen Forbes has hit the ground running. The page-turning
climax has more twists and turns than the Road to the Isles,
making it impossible to put down.'

Press and Journal

'*Madness Lies* is a murky tale, Forbes twisting her noose ever tighter
around some sympathetic characters. Gritty and ominous, Forbes's
brand of 'Highland Noir' is shaping up to be a good series.'

Sunday Herald

'*Unravelling* was definitely an unputdownable, engrossing read,
and I highly recommend this book.'

Caron Allan, Author and Blogger

'I devoured *Unravelling* in one sitting. It is tense, intense, well
plotted, beautifully written and constructed with cleverly drawn
characters who are vivid and alive.'

Margot McCuaig, Author

'*Unravelling* is beautifully written and cleverly plotted, by a
writer who knows exactly what she's doing, but it's much more
than that. Meticulously researched, the exploration of mental
illness is nuanced and compassionate, the setting and characters
captured with an authenticity that will instantly speak to
anyone with a knowledge of the area.'

Margaret Kirk, Author

Also by Helen Forbes

In the Shadow of the Hill

Madness Lies

Unravelling

Deception

Helen Forbes

Scolpaig Press

Copyright © 2021 by Scolpaig Press

First paperback edition 2021

ISBN (paperback): 978-1-9168883-2-6

ISBN (e-book): 978-1-9168883-3-3

www.helenforbes.co.uk

Book design by Hannah Linder Designs

For my Auld Reekie pals: Clare, Carole, Teresa, David and Mads.
Thank you. It was a blast.

And in memory of Olive Smith, a good friend who left too soon.

Chapter 1

LILY

THEY WERE BEATING Lily on the back of her head. Sharp, vicious words. They were much worse than blows. Bruises faded. Words stayed. She had a little box of them hidden away in her head. She kept it locked, mostly, just opening it every now and again to put in new words. It must be overflowing by now, ready to explode. She imagined the words ricocheting around in her head. Maybe she wouldn't accept them a second time. Perhaps she'd finally face up to the fact that love didn't speak those words, and she was living the wrong life.

But these sick, stomach-churning words were not aimed at her. She might have ignored them, kept her eyes front, if it wasn't for a sudden loud groan of fear that tugged at her heart. As the bus took a right onto Corstorphine Road, she turned.

The man had a big moon face, like an overgrown child who shouldn't be out on his own. His shoulders were hunched, eyes closed tight, as thick lines of Buckfast tonic wine dribbled over his head, soaking into his odd little tufts of hair.

Lily got up from her seat and crossed the aisle to sit beside him. He opened his eyes, and his pupils were huge and dark, tears and tonic wine pooling above his lower eyelids as he shrank from her.

She smiled and put her hand on his arm. 'Hey, it's okay. Which is your stop?'

His stumbling sounds made little sense.

'Next one?'

He nodded. Lily rang the bell and stood. Her hand on the man's arm, she guided him out of the seat. There was laughter behind her. 'Time to get off, guys.'

Lily turned, blocking the passageway. 'No, it's not.'

There were three of them. The tallest had broken black teeth and dead eyes. 'That right, pal? What's it got to do with you?' He brandished the empty Buckfast bottle. It smelled of cough syrup and paint thinner.

The second one had narrowed bloodshot eyes. 'Do her, Malky. Glass her.'

The bus stopped. Malky dropped the bottle and pushed Lily onto the seat. 'Out of my way, bitch.'

The third one had good teeth, she noticed, as his spittle just missed her and hit the window. Lily sat up and saw the man cross the road and go into a shop. The bus pulled off, and she smiled. He was safe.

She wasn't. They hadn't got off in time. They gave up arguing with the driver in his perspex cage and came back for her. The blank faces of the other passengers stared ahead, willing the bus on to their stop. They'd talk about it afterwards in the safety of the shop or their home, but for now, if they didn't look, it wasn't happening.

*

IT WAS THAT policeman. The one with the grey eyes that made Lily's heart beat a little faster.

'Lily Andersen. Again?' His soft, island accent chased the darkness away. He leafed backwards in his notebook. 'Not even two months since we last met. The beggar on Princes Street. You got a black eye.'

She smiled and nodded. 'Sorry. PC Gunn, isn't it?'

His eyes widened, as if surprised she'd remembered. 'That's right. I know you think you're doing good, but you're putting yourself in danger. You were lucky today.'

She had been lucky. Two workmen in donkey jackets had got on when the bus stopped. She hadn't noticed them sit across from her. The neds barely got two insults out before one of the guys was on his feet.

'Excuse me, boys.' He was enormous, great calloused hands bunched at his sides. 'No talking to the lady like that, eh? Think you should sit down the front.'

His companion was huge, too. He didn't stand or speak; he just nodded towards the front of the bus. Heads down, Malky and Co. had shuffled to the front seats, where they sat in silence until the police got on at the next stop.

PC Gunn frowned. 'The other passengers saw and heard nothing. Though the driver radioed it in, all he and the men heard was a bit of swearing. Not enough to take it further.'

Lily nodded. She saw the bus moving off, the neds leaving, people passing, seeing nothing and no one. 'I couldn't just ignore it. It wouldn't be fair. What would you have done?'

He smiled. 'Same as you, but that's what I'm paid to do. And you're right; it's not fair. Life is not fair. You couldn't just accept that and stop trying to make it better for every poor soul you meet? Make your life easier. And mine.'

She frowned. 'But if I did nothing, I'd just end up thinking about it all the time and beating myself up, so the end result would be the same.'

'Without the bruises.'

Lily shrugged. 'No bruises today. Anyway, they disappear.'

He nodded and put his notebook in his pocket. 'Please stay out of trouble.'

Chapter 2

SAM

FEET. SO MANY sizes and shapes. They fascinate Sam, telling him so much when his head is clear. And when it's not, when the fog comes down and his thoughts aren't even his own, the never-ending feet make him dizzy. Sometimes desire has made him reach out for a slim ankle or a pointy-toed shoe. It's not sexual. It's interest, a need to know, to read their story. Not the best way to go about it, as the two twisted fingers on his right hand remind him. That stamp had sobered him up, replacing the fog in his head with a burst of pain. And she had looked so genteel.

The head's clear today. That man's feet may be flat and his shoes worn, but he's optimistic. He's smiling. Sam knows, without looking up. And those little feet encased in white socks and expensive patent shoes: they're nervous. Bullied at school, perhaps. Or at home. These high pointy-toed shoes: she's a force to be reckoned with. A corporate lawyer in a big firm. She'll not be heading home yet. Just out to grab a wrap and a latte to keep her going into the early hours. He doesn't need to look up to know she's carrying the food and drink in one hand, and texting with the other. Ooh, nice brogues; soft Italian leather. A lazy walk, self-assured, handsome. And generous.

'Thank you, sir.' Sam grabs the fiver from the cup on the pavement and sticks it in his inside pocket. Sam looks up, and Lily's on the other side of the street, passing the Central Library. Gliding through the tourists and the tired workers, her blonde hair is gleaming. That smile. And her boy, a little prince in a carriage. He's laughing with excitement, his arms waving as he swats the plebs out of his way with majestic flourish.

Sam smiles and whispers: 'Hold on to that, little boy. The self-assurance, the self-importance, the self-confidence. Don't let them take it from you with their rules and their regimentation. Don't listen when they say you're less than you are.'

He shouts her name and waves. Lily waves back, and they're gone into the crowd. Through a gap in the legs and the traffic, he sees her crossing towards Deacon Brodies. The boy's still bouncing, still turning. Though he can't see their faces, he knows they're smiling.

So is Sam. Until a sudden surge of pain shoots through his hand. He cries out and tries to pull his hand away, but it's held by a black size twelve magnum boot. A pig. The pig.

'Officer?' He doesn't look up. Doesn't want to see those eyes.

The pig presses harder. 'What have I told you about perving?'

'I wasn't perving. She's my friend.'

The pig kneels. He's not in uniform, and his jacket is hiding what his foot is doing. 'Is that why you sit here? So you can see up their skirts?'

'On the other side of the street? My eyesight's good, but it's not that good.'

Sam swallows a scream as the pig grinds his hand into the pavement. He leans forward, his words hissing against Sam's ear. 'Smelly, cheeky, alky bastard. If you don't leave this city soon, I'm going to make sure everyone hears about you and your sordid past. Do you know what vigilantes do to people like you? And when they're done, I'll be right here to finish you off.'

'I've never told anyone what I saw.' Sam hates the whining desperation in his voice. 'I swear. I never will.'

'Too right, you won't.' The pig shrugs. 'But it's not as if anyone would believe you.' He smiles, straightens up, and lifts his foot. 'Have a nice day, now.'

Sam's hand is in his oxter, blood seeping into bruised flesh. At least the pig didn't leave him anything. He's been generous in the past. Urine, a used condom, dog shit, a lit firework. Too many people about for that right now. But not at night. That's when he'll come back. The thought terrifies Sam, but he won't be moved. He saw off a couple of Romanians and more than a few neds to keep this pitch. He's not leaving now.

Chapter 3

LILY

THE LAWNMARKET WAS hoaching, tourists spilling off the pavements onto the cobbled street, in the shadow of the tall medieval buildings. Lurking in the mouths of the narrow closes on each side of the road. Squeezing in and out of souvenir shops. Stopping for photos, selfie sticks extended. Standing in the middle of the road, oblivious to the taxis and buses. Chattering and exclaiming and making a nuisance of themselves. Though there was never a quiet time in Edinburgh's Old Town, Lily usually tried to avoid the late afternoon. It would get so much worse in the summer, during the festivals. Each journey home would mean running the gauntlet of buskers and fire-eaters, artists and living statues, amid the constant thrust of flyers for the very best shows on earth. Several times last summer, she'd vowed to reach the apartment without accepting a single flyer. It was impossible. Though she'd tried not to make eye contact, the desperate students wouldn't let her be, so she'd smiled and given in.

She turned into Ramsay Lane, leaving most of the tourists behind. Not all of them. There were always a few hanging around Ramsay Garden, breathing in the charm of the cobbled courtyard. They'd spot the complex of iconic apartments from Princes Street as they gazed across the valley of ornamental gardens. They'd see the splendour of Edinburgh Castle, clinging to black volcanic rock, and then Ramsay Garden, etched into the skyline. Oriels and turrets, balconies and balustrades, steep-pitched roofs, white harling and red masonry, epitomising the medieval character of the Old Town.

As the pushchair trundled over the cobbles, Lily wondered how many of the tourists knew that Princes Street Gardens was once a sewer, and, far from being medieval, most of the Ramsay Garden complex was built in the late nineteenth century. Still, it was beautiful, and there was nowhere else in the city she'd rather live.

When she stopped to unlock the main door to the block of apartments, Ronan strained against the straps of the pushchair. 'Out, Mama.'

She lifted him, and he wrapped his arms around her neck. How she'd missed him. It had been his first day at nursery. He'd cried. She'd cried. And then she'd left him, forcing herself to walk away, her heart breaking into sharp little pieces. He was only eighteen months old, but Nathan said he had to learn to socialise. The day had been so long without him. She'd wandered round the Old Town for a while, then she'd taken a bus to the Gyle Shopping Centre. Wandered some more, and then a bus back, and the neds and PC Gunn. She was exhausted.

She collapsed the pushchair with one hand and tucked it into the alcove under the common stair. Half way up to the second floor, she stopped to catch her breath. Ronan tickled her nose. She laughed 'You better walk soon, little one, or this is going to kill me.'

After he'd eaten, it was time for Ronan's bath. Fingers splayed, his wee hands hit the water, sending droplets high into the air. The squeal of his laughter made Lily laugh too. She pulled off her clothes, and she was in the bath with him. Sitting him between her legs, she slid back and fore, until waves threatened to spill over. She spoke in her first language, the language of her heart, tales of sea maidens, whales and selkies. He listened and laughed, his little hands trying to capture the growing waves.

Downstairs, she heard Nathan's key turning in the door, and she scrambled from the bath. Ronan's lower lip quivered while she struggled into her clothes, fighting against wet, unwilling skin. She made a funny face, and he giggled. Her clothes on, she tickled his tummy, and he laughed. She was kneeling at the side of the bath when Nathan poked his head round the door.

'Hi guys. How are you doing?'

Lily smiled. 'We're fine. You?'

He nodded. 'Okay. Could see tonight far enough.'

So could she. The thought of leaving Ronan again, even if he was asleep, tore at her heart. And leaving him with Rebecca? She wasn't sure Nathan's sister even liked Ronan, but Nathan had insisted on both counts. It was a retirement dinner for a colleague and he needed Lily there. It would be good to involve Rebecca more, he'd said, especially with the wedding coming up.

*

IN THE FULL-LENGTH mirror in the reception area, there was a stunning couple. He was in a kilt and she was in a knee-length silk shift dress in duck-egg blue. Her hair was curled and pinned up, her legs so long. He was tall and fair, with blue eyes and perfect teeth. He had a look of the late American actor, Paul Walker. Lily almost turned and looked behind her, just to check. Nathan squeezed her hand and whispered in her ear. 'Looking good, aren't we?'

She smiled. 'Not bad.'

A waiter passed with champagne on a tray, and Nathan gave her a glass.

'You not having any?' Lily asked. 'You could leave the car.'

He shook his head. He introduced her to two of his male colleagues. She didn't catch their names in the buzz of conversation around her. The younger one congratulated her on their engagement. The older one asked after 'the wee one'. And then it was all work talk.

Stats and markers and complaints. Moans about the government and the ministers, them upstairs and her downstairs.

Lily's champagne was soon gone. Her glass was whisked from her hand by a passing waiter, replaced with another, and then another. At the third glass, Nathan frowned. She almost put the glass down, but the champagne was bubbling through her, making her head light. She needed that light after today.

They sat in the shadow of the top table. The man on her right didn't return her smile, his watery, narrow eyes surveying the room with disapproval. When he deigned to speak, he trashed Edinburgh's trams, the Scottish Parliament building, devolution, Scottish independence. Despite disagreeing with everything he said, Lily stayed silent. Nathan commented occasionally, but the man wasn't interested in anyone else's opinion.

The starters came, and the man attacked his soup. His missus spoke to him, and he sprayed her with pulverised bread and carrot. It stuck to her specs in little pointy mounds. As she took them off and wiped them with her napkin, Lily felt a burst of laughter coming. She quashed it with the last of her champagne.

A hovering waiter. 'Wine?'

She nodded and heard Nathan sigh, so she ran her hand up his thigh. He almost choked on his smoked salmon, then he smiled. 'Maybe the wine's not such a bad idea after all.'

*

PLUSH LOOS. CANDELABRAS and soft rolled-up towels. Expensive soap and deep pile carpet. In the end cubicle, Lily checked her phone. Nothing from Rebecca. She thought of calling, but Ronan rarely woke before morning. If Rebecca was struggling, she'd get in touch. She heard the door opening. Giggly voices. Cubicle doors slamming shut. A volley of gossip. Dresses and shoes; hair and make-up; lookers and mingers.

'What about the blonde? She's so young. Not what I expected.'

'Nor me. Thought she must be a right heifer when no one had met her.'

Lily held her breath. She'd never met Nathan's colleagues socially. Were they talking about her?

'What's a heifer? A baby horse?'

Lily smothered her laughter with a fistful of toilet roll.

'Shut up. A heifer's a cow. A baby horse is a foal.'

'Whatever. Our Bruce is a dark horse.'

They weren't talking about her and Nathan. Lily felt a rush of relief.

'Sophia's not looking too happy about it.'

'Ever seen her look happy? She was all over Jake when we left the table, trying to make Bruce jealous. Seriously, though, why is he shagging that cold-hearted Polish bitch when his fiancée looks like that?'

Lily heard them unlock the cubicle doors and wash their hands. She stayed where she was. As they opened the toilet door to leave, one of them spoke. 'Sophia, how you doing?'

They got a grunt in response. Maybe Sophia had overheard them miscalling her. The woman didn't turn when Lily came out of the cubicle. She had long glossy black hair, a very short dress, high-heeled sandals, and a mobile phone clamped to her ear. She spoke in another language. Polish, presumably. Though Lily couldn't understand a word, the irritation in her harsh voice was unmistakable. She went into a cubicle, leaving behind a lingering scent that tugged at Lily's memory.

Chapter 4

LILY

Nathan looked as bored as Lily. Hopefully, she could persuade him to leave soon. She asked him which one was Bruce. He shook his head. 'I don't know everyone here.'

'He's having an affair with Sophia.'

Nathan raised his eyebrows. 'I very much doubt that. Probably isn't a man in this room, except me, of course, that doesn't fantasise about Sophia.'

'Even him?' Lily nodded at her neighbour. He was ranting at a woman across the table.

Nathan laughed. 'Maybe not.' He picked up the wine bottle. 'More?'

Jeez. One minute, he acted like she was a drunk. The next, he was encouraging her. But then, consistency had never been Nathan's forte. She put her hand over her glass. 'No thanks.'

'You sure? The speeches are about to start.' He yawned. 'You'll need something to keep you awake.'

He wasn't kidding. By the third speech, Lily was back on the wine. It didn't help. At last, the speeches were over, and Nathan said he was going to the toilet. Lily's eyes were not the only ones that watched him cross the floor, kilt hugging his low, shapely hips, the heavy cloth swinging around his long legs. He looked gorgeous.

While she waited for his return, in the hope he'd be ready to leave, Lily fiddled with the stem of her glass. Beside her, the ranter was bludgeoning the European Union to death, while his wife nodded, her eyes glazed. Lily's glass was almost full. The wine was warm, and she'd had enough, but it seemed a shame to waste it. She stood, the back of her hand nudging the glass. The wine spilled into the man's lap, and he shrieked like a child.

'I'm so sorry,' Lily said. 'Let me –'

He swatted her hand away. 'Leave it. Napkins, Mary. Napkins!'

His wife produced a bunch of napkins and dabbed at his crotch. Lily resisted the urge to give her a wink as she left the table. She'd get some fresh air, then she'd go look for Nathan.

She didn't have to look far. He was standing outside the hotel with two women. Sophia had her back to Lily, and she was talking to a female with a mass of short, dark curls, sallow skin, and brown eyes. She looked about fifteen. Her skirt barely covered her backside, and her high heels made her skinny legs look ridiculous. She was wearing a miniscule vest and her midriff was bare. On her shoulder, there was a small tattoo. She was glaring at Nathan, tears on her cheeks. His eyes were narrowed, his mouth set in a tight line. He reached for the girl's wrist.

'Nathan,' Lily said. 'Is everything okay?'

He dropped his hand. The girl's eyes widened as she stared at Lily. She muttered something. Was that bruising on her cheek? Sophia gripped the girl's shoulders and tried to turn her round. The girl shrugged the hands away and glared at Nathan. 'You … you look stupid … in lady skirt.'

Nathan laughed and took Lily's hand. 'Ready to go?'

The night air was rich with malted barley from the breweries and distilleries. It was Edinburgh's signature scent. Nathan was quiet as they walked to the car. There were a dozen questions in Lily's head. She sorted through them, weeding out the ones he wouldn't like. When they reached the car, he came round to open her door.

'Who was the girl?' she asked.

'Sophia's sister. She was half cut. Should have heard the abuse coming from her.'

'She looked about fifteen.'

Nathan laughed. 'Not close up, she didn't. You've had too much wine.' He moved towards her, his hand sliding up her thigh, his breath warm against her neck. 'Forget her. Did you see how they were looking at you in there? They all wanted you. The men. And probably half the women.'

Lily laughed. 'Hardly.'

*

A BARRAGE OF ugly snores escaped Rebecca's gaping mouth. If Lily had been alone, she'd have taken a video on her mobile phone. Not to show anyone else. She wasn't that mean. She'd just have used it to remind herself, when necessary, that Nathan's elegant sister was human too. When she suggested covering Rebecca with a blanket and leaving her to sleep, Nathan whispered that his parents would worry if she didn't come home. Besides, knowing she was in the room below might put him off.

Lily smirked. 'Put you off what?'

His hands were on her waist as he backed her out of the room, pulling the door closed behind him. He kissed her neck. 'Tease.' He swivelled his sporran to the side, then he pressed his hips against hers. 'You've been doing that all night. Driving me mad.'

The snoring stopped. They held their breath. Rebecca snuffled and shuffled, groaned and yawned.

'I'll see her down to her car.' Nathan twisted his sporran back into place. 'Don't take anything off. Not even an earring.' He pushed the door open. 'Hey Rebecca. How did you get on?'

Rebecca sat up. Her hair was all over the place, her eyes bleary.

'Thanks for babysitting,' Lily said, with a smile that wasn't returned. 'I'm going up to check on Ronan.'

Her son was sleeping on his back, a contended smile on his face. Lily waited until she heard them leave. She pulled the door over and went back downstairs. The front door was open, and she could hear their muffled voices in the stairwell. Were they arguing? Nothing new there.

From the balcony in the lounge, Edinburgh was drenched in moonlight. Church spires and monuments pierced the darkness. Some were floodlit, others black and threatening. Edinburgh Castle squatted on its rocky plinth, illuminated by soft glowing floodlights. She'd only been inside once. It was before Ronan was born. In the prisons of war and the dungeons, she'd shivered and felt as if all the anguish of the past had seeped into the ancient walls and was pouring into her. She'd found sanctuary in St Margaret's Chapel, the oldest building in Edinburgh. The sunlight had streamed through the stained-glass windows, chasing the gloom away. She'd whispered a prayer to St Margaret that everything would work out for her and Nathan; that their child would bring them closer; that they'd be happy. She was still waiting for an answer.

There was a slight chill in the breeze that stirred Lily's dress against her bare legs. And he was there, his hands on her breasts, lips on the nape of her neck. 'I want you right here. Now.'

She twisted round to face him. There were lights in the apartment next door, someone at the window. 'Better not.'

He carried her inside and up the stairs.

Chapter 5

SAM

It's Tuesday. No nursery for wee Prince Ronan, and he's sleeping. Though Sam loves the little one, he likes when he's asleep and Lily can talk without interruption. She's hungover today, she tells him, and embarrassed about her behaviour last night, spilling a glass of wine on the man next to her. Sam wants to know every detail. Hah, he scoffs. The fellow was lucky to get away with a wee drop of wine. Sounds like he deserved an Exocet missile shoved where the sun don't shine. It's good to see her laugh. They're off to the beach at Portobello, to blow the cobwebs away. She loves the sea, Lily. He waves her off, his mind on the day they met.

There had been confidence in her steps that first day, but something heavy too. When she stopped beside him, he'd seen soft leather boots on slender feet, a dress of delicate fabric falling around her ankles. He'd looked up and seen in her swollen belly the reason for her heaviness. Not long to go. She'd brought him two pies and a bottle of water, handing them over with an apology. 'Don't feel you have to eat them. Maybe half a dozen interfering busybodies have given you food already.'

He laughed. 'I've had two lit fag ends, five South African rand, twenty-three pence, and yesterday's Sun. Will you have one?'

'No, thank you. I've eaten. Pastry gives me heartburn.' Her hands spread over her swollen abdomen. 'It's temporary, I hope. I love a good pie.'

There was a hint of an accent in her soft tones, but he couldn't place it. He waved the Sun newspaper. 'Do you want to sit? Might as well put this rag to good use. Wouldn't be seen dead reading it.'

She'd never get up again, she said, and they both laughed. She'd appeared twice again before she gave birth, bringing food and drink, and that smile. He felt as if life had finally given him something special. Silly bugger.

After the boy came, she passed most days. Sometimes on his side of the street, sometimes on the other, but never without a wave. And more. Before that, he'd barely had a sensible conversation in years. People stopped and chatted, but they didn't sit with him and discuss current affairs or literature.

Lily was an enigma. Sometimes she glowed as bright as the stars, light and laughter bubbling from her. And other days, there was a lost quality. A sadness, maybe. He could never quite define it, probably because of the effort she made to hide it. She never spoke of her home life, and he'd figured she was on her own. And then one day, she was wearing an engagement ring with a rock of a diamond, and he'd laughed at himself. What had he imagined? Immaculate conception?

The ring, the expensive clothes, the fact that she lived somewhere on the Royal Mile: they suggested a rich partner. Sam never asked. He'd tried not to imagine, because he knew he'd fail. Who could be good enough for her?

By the time they pass again, a few hours later, Sam's half-cut and glad they're on the other side of the road. Lily looks healthier and Ronan's laughing and waving. Sam waves back, waits until they've passed the library, then he opens another can of super lager.

*

SEVERAL CANS LATER, in the dark of the night, Sam's shivering beneath his blanket inside the Robert Burn mausoleum in the Old Calton Burial Ground. He was lucky to get in first. This tomb has a roof and no gate, so it's in demand. He usually knows when he's about to fall asleep. He gets a prickling feeling in his limbs, a lightness in his body. His mind wanders as if he's starting out on the path to a dream. Hypnagogic hallucinations, apparently. They're not always pleasant. Sometimes he sees things. A leering face or something dark and sub-human. He rarely has auditory hallucinations, but that's what's happening now. At least he hopes it is.

'Samuel. Wake up, Samuel.'

He turns over. Snuggles down.

'Samuel. Wake up, you manky bastard.'

No thanks. I'll just be getting off to sleep, if it's all the same with you.

Whack.

He clutches his head, turns and sits up. The moon is shining through the entrance of the tomb. He stares at the sub-human thing before him, and he wishes it was a hallucination. The pig's wearing a hoodie, but there's no hiding those eyes. 'Fucking alky bastard.' Kick. Punch. Kick. Kick. If it wasn't for the newspapers stuffed down Sam's trousers to keep him warm, his legs would be in bits. Pain shoots through his hand and his arm. He cries out.

'Shut the fuck up, you stupid, stupid bastard. I'll kill you.'

And he means it. The hatred, the madness, they're shining in his eyes as he launches himself at Sam. A head-butt, followed by gouging fingers in his eyes. Sam screams, a high scream that echoes across the cemetery, falling on the graves. Fat lot of use the dead will be.

'Hey!'

Maybe he's misjudged his fellow occupants. Through streaming eyes, in the entrance to the mausoleum, he sees two slim figures. He can smell them. Aftershave and illicit sex. They're not dead yet. They rush towards him.

'Are you all right?' One of them is crouching beside Sam.

The other's on his mobile phone. 'Police and ambulance, please.'

And the pig is pulling his hood up, and hot-footing it from the scene of the crime.

Sam pleads with the boys. He doesn't want any fuss.

'But there's a police car at the gates.' The younger one leans close. 'They must be in the area.'

He's taken aback when Sam laughs. 'They're in the area all right, son. They certainly are.'

Chapter 6

LILY

THE WIND WAS shoving Lily and the pushchair along George IV Bridge. There was no sign of Sam. It was Friday, and she hadn't seen him since Tuesday. He'd never been gone so long. Perhaps he was ill. She thought of the wheeze in his chest, and the other pains he tried to hide. She shivered and stopped, tucking the blanket around Ronan's legs. He laughed and kicked until the blanket was loose again, then he swayed back and fore, trying to propel the pushchair onwards. Lily smiled and carried on.

She wasn't smiling on her return. Ronan hadn't wanted to stay at nursery. He'd be fine, the staff had told her, as they took him from her, his arms flailing and his crying loud. He'd really enjoyed his first day once she was gone. Soon, he'd not even notice her leaving. Lily wasn't sure she'd like that any better.

There was a huddle of ragged men with white scabbed faces and filthy clothes at the entrance to Greyfriars Kirkyard. She scanned the group, but Sam wasn't there.

'Hey, gorgeous.' A grin of black stumps and putrid breath. She couldn't remember his name, but Sam had warned her to keep away from him. 'Got anything for us?'

'Have you seen Sam?' Lily asked.

The grin was gone. He shrugged. 'Depends.'

'On what?'

'How much you're willing to pay?'

The others laughed. Lily smiled. 'Forget it.'

At Sam's pitch, there was only a crumpled Costa cup and two fag ends. Lily knew he sometimes slept in the closes and courtyards off the Royal Mile. She checked each one between his pitch and Ramsay Garden, on both sides of the street. There was no sign of him. Maybe she should keep looking, walk down towards Holyrood. But it was cold, and she had a lot to do. They were having dinner guests.

*

NATHAN AND REBECCA were arguing again, always arguing in their loud, harsh way. It was the fault of their Italian great-grandfather, Luca Collesso, apparently. They couldn't help it. Nonno Luca had a lot to answer for. The empty wine bottles, the insults and accusations, the gesticulations and protestations, delivered in tones that Lily feared might waken Ronan. Handy to have a dead ancestor you could blame for all your faults. And one that had made enough money to leave the family with this apartment, a mansion in the Grange, and a wine importing business that brought in more money than they knew what to do with.

There were photos of Luca Collesso all over the apartment. He didn't look the argumentative type. He looked kind, standing outside his first ice cream shop, shortly after his arrival in Scotland in the early 1900s, pride in his dark eyes, a smile on his handsome face. Lily wondered what he'd have made of his great-grandchildren. Nathan's eyes were glazed, his mouth slack, as he stared at his sister's pointing finger. Lily didn't hear the words that slammed between them, just the tone, mostly Rebecca's. The mother, Rita, had thrown in a few random jibes earlier. Lily wasn't sure who they were directed at, and no one seemed to care. Now, glasses perched on the end of her nose, Rita was sorting the photos on her iPad and breaking Lily's heart. Ronan with snot or drool or food on his face – deleted. Sticky up hair and sleepy eyes – gone. Dirty knees – binned. Only perfect grandchildren allowed.

The father, Jonathon Collesso, came in from the balcony, followed by the scent of cigar. Lily liked Jonathon. He had a kind smile and a good sense of humour, attributes that the rest of the family lacked. 'You still arguing? Poor Lily. She's bored stiff.'

A scowl from Rebecca, and some muttered words aimed at Lily. They didn't reach her. She'd shut Rebecca out soon after they met. There had been a time when she'd hoped they'd be friends. Lily had known no one in Edinburgh but Nathan, and she'd been excited about meeting his sister.

'She's gorgeous,' Lily had said when Nathan showed her a photo. Rebecca was the only one in the family that showed a touch of their Italian ancestry. She was tall and elegant, with dark brown hair and eyes that were almost black. In the photo, she looked serious, pensive. Lily would soon discover it was Rebecca's default expression. Moody, disinterested, and dismissive, especially around Lily.

'More, please.' Rita held up her wine glass, eyes still fixed on her iPad. 'Tomorrow, Lily. Ten o'clock. You won't put it off again, will you? We only have four months. A bride should start looking at least twelve –'

'She'll be there.' Nathan yawned. He looked at his watch and scratched his oxter.

'And tomorrow night?' Scroll, scroll. Peer. Delete. 'Nathan said it was fine.'

Lily frowned. He had mentioned nothing to her. Surely they weren't meeting up again so soon?

'It's fine, Mum.' Nathan yawned again. 'You can come for him at three. I'll collect him about five on Sunday.'

Lily's heart disintegrated. It wasn't enough to force her baby into nursery two days a week. 'Nathan …'

Nathan shook his head, his eyes narrowing a little. 'It's fine, Lily. You'll get some time to yourself. It'll be good for you both.'

Jonathon was perched on the arm of the settee. He squeezed Lily's forearm. She looked up at him, and there was a touch of concern on his face, as if he understood. Still, he wouldn't go against his wife and son. 'Don't you worry about Ronan. He'll be fine. Spoilt, but fine.'

Lily said nothing.

After they'd left, and the table was cleared, Lily stared out the kitchen window. Beyond Princes Street Gardens and the New Town, the moon was high over the Firth of Forth. She felt the familiar ache. A surge of longing for sea and salt, breaking surf and crying gulls. The memory of a cold sea-shell pressed to her ear, and the echo of ancient, distant waves, captured forever in a spiral of pearl. A longing for home. She wanted to sweep the dishes and glasses from the draining board, hear them smash on the ceramic floor. Take her sleeping child and run.

But Nathan was behind her with his drunk, groping hands and grinding hips. Only his mind was willing; his body was having none of it. He nibbled at her ear. 'You don't mind Ronan going for a sleepover, do you?'

Lily kept her mouth closed to stop the angry words from jumping out. It was too late for a fight, and he was so drunk. She sorted through the words until she found something palatable. Her weakness taunted her as she spoke. 'I'd rather he didn't. He's so young. You could have discussed it with me.'

'It's done now. You coming up?' The grinding had stopped. 'Don't think I'll be much use to you tonight, love. Sorry.'

'No worries.'

None whatsoever.

*

IT WASN'T THE done thing to take your illegitimate son with you to buy a wedding dress, apparently. Rita didn't say as much. She didn't have to. She wrenched the pushchair from Lily's hands and thrust it at Rebecca. 'Take him. Go for a walk.'

The disgust on Rebecca's perfectly made-up face was almost comical. 'But I babysat on Monday.'

'Go.'

The sound of Ronan crying and Rebecca's feet stomping along the pavement followed Lily and Rita into the shop. It was all downhill from there. At every suggestion of Rita's, Lily shook her head. 'No. No. Never.'

Rita apologised to Susan, the shop assistant. 'We have four months. Can she even get a dress in four months?'

Susan nodded, her face serious. 'It's tight, but it's possible.' She smiled at Lily. 'What did you have in mind?'

'Something tasteful. No big net skirts; no meringues; nothing strapless or off the shoulder.'

'Something simple?'

She nodded, and Rita rolled her eyes. 'Simple, all right.'

Lily laughed at Rita's muttered insult. Susan looked appalled. She placed a sympathetic hand on Lily's arm. 'There's a small selection in the back. Why don't you come and have a look?' She thrust a magazine at Rita. 'Read that. We won't be long.'

Behind the curtain, Susan sighed. 'I'm sure your mother means well, but they have a way of taking over.'

Lily smiled. 'She's not my mother. She's his. I'm sorry I'm so difficult.'

Susan patted her shoulder. 'Don't apologise. You take as long as you like. It's your day. You've got to be sure about everything.'

Sure about everything? Lily wanted to laugh out loud.

'I have some here.' There were half a dozen dresses on a rail. 'They're from last year's collection. Small sizes. They might not need much alteration. I think you might like this one.'

It was gorgeous. White with a lace cap-sleeved sweetheart bodice, fitted at the hips, and flaring out in soft satin. Lily tried it on. She twirled, and the skirt was an enormous circle, rippling like the wind around her legs. If there had to be one, this was it.

'You look stunning,' Susan said. 'It hardly needs altered. Just a little tuck at the waist. It was made for you. Will we show her?'

The bell on the shop door rang, and Lily heard Ronan's babbling voice.

'He wouldn't stop squawking, Mum,' Rebecca said. 'People were staring as if I'd kidnapped him. The chocolate didn't even keep him quiet.'

Chocolate? Ronan had never had chocolate. Lily peeped through the curtains. His face was all slavers and snotters and brown streaks.

'Ronan, stay still.' Rita seemed desperate to salvage a morsel of respectability. If she had to have a bastard grandson, at least let him be clean. And then Ronan saw Lily. His arms started flailing, his feet kicking. 'Mama. Mama.'

'Hey, gorgeous.' She came out, but she didn't dare go too close. Rita and Rebecca were silent. Mouths open. Eyes narrowed. It must be the right dress.

Chapter 7

SAM

THE LAST TIME Sam was in hospital, ten or eleven years ago, the nurses had drawn straws to see who would have to touch him. The loser had kitted herself out like she was handling waste from Dounreay. They'd incinerated his clothes and discharged him in enormous trousers and a tiny pink t-shirt. It was winter. No one had asked where he was going or how he was going to get there.

It's different now. There are protocols. Early intervention, assessments and questionnaires. They want him to speak to people, fill in forms, be referred. There's talk of a case conference, joint approaches, multi-agency working. It's terrifying. All he wants is a bit of rest, his clothes laundered, and some good grub. The nurse brings him another form to complete, so he tells her he's moving to a room in a friend's flat in Dalkeith. There's doubt in her eyes, and he feels bad. It's not a total lie. There is an acquaintance in Dalkeith with a spare room, but Sam tried that before. The first two nights were good. Running water, electricity, television, a comfy bed. Heaven. On the third night, after a drinking binge, it was hell. His kind friend had turned into a slavering eighteen stone groper in the middle of the night. Sam had to smash the bed-side lamp over his head, and run.

The nurse smiles. 'The police are here to see you.'

There's two uniformed coppers. The inspector's standing at the end of the bed, arms crossed, smirking. The constable's a gentleman, with grey eyes that can't hide his concern. Sam's seen him a few times, on and off duty. He knows his walk. Self-assured. Solid. A good man.

'Can you remember anything about your attacker?' The soft Hebridean tones make Sam smile. 'There's CCTV in the area. If you can give us a good description, we might get this guy.'

Sam nods, his eyes fixed on the silent inspector. There's a sudden alien rush of fire in his veins. 'He looked a bit like your colleague. Same build and hair colour. About the same age. Looks respectable, but he's not. He may come across as charming and articulate, but he'll be a loner, an inadequate. An evil bastard.'

The inspector laughs. 'Didn't know you had a psychology degree, Samuel. Are you a closet poet, too? Is that why you were sleeping in Robbie Burns' mausoleum? Hoping his talent might rub off on you?'

The constable's trying not to smile at the stupidity of his superior. Sam's not so diplomatic. 'If I was sleeping with the bard, I'd be in Dumfries, Inspector. Robert Burn, not Burns, was an architect.'

The inspector's face is puce as he closes in. 'What exactly were you up to with those two lads? Maybe the guy that attacked you took exception to your depraved practices.'

Sam looks at the constable. He's turned his head away from the inspector, as if to hide the rage that's burning in his grey eyes. Sam laughs and shakes his head. 'Your inspector has a fine imagination, Constable. It happened just as I told you.'

'And have you seen this man before?'

Sam is silent. The inspector shakes his head. A warning. The constable's eyes are on his notebook, so Sam winks at the inspector. 'I think I have seen him skulking around. If I see him again, I'll be in touch. This man has to be stopped before he kills someone.'

He closes his eyes and listens to the retreating feet. Both angry, for different reasons. Has he just signed his own death warrant?

He'd hoped the pig might take this as a warning, but maybe it will push him over the edge. Sam isn't one for regrets or for fighting, but how he wishes he'd made his mark. Preferably on the pig's face, so he'd have something to explain to his colleagues and anyone else unfortunate enough to be involved with him. Wouldn't make up for the concussion, the sprained ankle, three broken fingers and multiple cuts and bruises, but he'd feel a little better.

*

FOUR NIGHTS IN the hospital. They're nice to him, the nurses. They bring in clothes and blankets. He gets a cracking pair of waterproof trousers and a cagoule, and a lovely wee lass from Cumbria gives him a leather suitcase and some books. Straight to his pitch on Saturday morning, and no one has taken it over. Hallelujah. He tucks his suitcase in behind the bikes, and it's business as usual. The strapped-up fingers and the black eyes are a bonus. He doesn't see Lily coming. Smells her first, that lovely clean smell. He looks up and her face scares him a little, her eyes fierce and her jaw sharp. 'Sam, who did this to you?'

'Lily, I'm fine. Better than fine. I've had a few days in hospital, and look what I've got.' He points to the suitcase. 'Good waterproofs and books. Couldn't ask for more.'

'Just tell me who did this. I'll get it sorted.'

He holds up his hand. 'The police are sorting it. There's no need to do anything.'

'Did the doctors check your chest and your legs?'

'They gave me a good going over. Don't you worry.'

'Are you still sleeping at Calton Hill?'

He shakes his head. 'No way. Not going back there.'

'You should never have been sleeping in a cemetery.'

He shrugs. 'Dead can't hurt you, can they? Mind you, there was all that nonsense along at Greyfriars Kirk.' He leans towards her and lowers his voice. 'It's mayhem when the ghosts of Bloody

MacKenzie and all the massacred Covenanters get started. Those poor visitors …'

Her face softens, as he knew it would. She smiles and sits. 'Tell me more. I love a good ghost story.'

'For an angel, you're such a ghoul. MacKenzie was Lord Advocate in the mid-17th century, responsible for persecuting the Presbyterian Covenanters. Back in the late nineteen nineties, loads of visitors were attacked beside MacKenzie's mausoleum, the Black Tomb. Hot spots and cold spots. Cuts and bruises. Grabbing and hitting. Fainted, some of them. Others knocked unconscious. Mostly attacked by unseen forces, though one or two say they saw something vague and dark.

'It all started when a homeless man tried to break into the tomb, looking for something he could sell. The floor gave way, and he fell into a pit of decomposing plague victims. Set off a right commotion. Sudden fires in adjacent properties. A priest who tried to carry out an exorcism died of a heart attack. They had to lock up the Covenanters' prison, where MacKenzie's victims are buried.

'Then a couple of lads, twelve or thirteen years ago, broke into the tomb. Didn't fall through the floor, but they took the head off a corpse and kicked it around a bit. First people to be convicted of violation of sepulchre in over a hundred years. There's been no excitement like that in my cemetery.'

Lily puts her hand on his arm. 'You couldn't just find yourself a shelter?'

'They're only open in the winter, except for the dry one in the Cowgate, but can you see me in a dry shelter?' He smiles. 'Don't worry. I'll find somewhere safe.'

She looks at her watch. 'I better get off.' She waves a carrier bag. 'Don't want to be late with Ronan's lunch.' She stands, brushing dust off the arse of her jeans.

'How long until the wedding?' Sam asks.

'Four months. I chose my dress today.'

She doesn't sound excited about it. 'Is he good enough for you, Lily?'

'Hardly. Who is?'

Sam laughs. 'That's the spirit. Bring the wee one next time. Is he with his dad?'

She nods. There's a sudden darkness in her eyes, a shadow of pain. 'He's … he's going to stay with his grandparents tonight.'

He can see how much that hurts. She forces a smile. 'What did you say is in the case?'

'Clothes and books.' He pulls the case towards him and opens it. 'Isn't it exciting?'

She rifles through the books and looks at him with a smile. 'Wouldn't have had you down as a fan of hospital romance or zombie apocalypse. And definitely not chick lit.'

'A starving man is not fussy. I love a book to read at night.'

'I'll get you a torch. Wouldn't want you ruining your eyes on those literary masterpieces. It won't be easy dragging that thing around. Do you want me to take it home? You can tell me when you need something from it.'

He smiles. 'Lily, you're a darling.'

Chapter 8

LILY

THE SHEETS WERE tangled, the afternoon sun shining in the bedroom window. Nathan whispered in an intimate tone, his hand caressing Lily's leg. An observer might have thought they were exchanging words of affection, the whispers of satisfied lovers. But no. He was telling her he was going out now. He was meeting a friend for a meal before work. He wanted to know what she was going to do with herself. Where was she going? When would she be home?

She didn't have any inclination to do anything. Not with Ronan's cries still ringing in her head. He'd yelled all the way down the stairs as his father carried him to the waiting car. Going back to bed with Nathan was an attempt to avoid thinking about it. It hadn't worked.

'I'll phone Julie. Maybe go and see her.'

'Text me and let me know. I'll phone around ten. Make sure you got home safe.' He frowned. 'Listen, about Julie – have you thought how the wedding photos will look? We're not exactly unattractive. And you're going to have a fat forty-something bridesmaid.'

Lily kept her voice even. She was good at that. 'Julie's not fat, and certainly not unattractive.'

'What about her occupation? A bit of a conversation stopper. You won't sit her next to my mother, will you?'

She shook her head.

'Why don't you ask Rebecca to be a bridesmaid?'

She bit her tongue to stop a burst of laughter. As if she'd let Rebecca ruin her photos with that scowl.

'I wish you guys got on better. I wish … Lily, are we all right?'

'We're fine. Course we are.'

He ran a finger down her cheek. 'I'd do anything for you.'

She nodded. Doing anything for her included arranging nursery and giving Ronan to his parents without asking her.

He frowned. 'It's going to be strange at the wedding with none of your family there. No friends, except Julie. Are you sure? We could contact your mother and stepfather.'

'Contact my mother? And tell her what?'

Nathan's eyes widened at the ice in Lily's voice. 'I'd … I'd speak to her. Tell her the truth.'

Lily shoved the quilt away and sat up. 'I don't want them there.'

*

IN THE SOFT light of the late afternoon, a breeze swayed the flowers and swept bursts of laughter and music through Princes Street Gardens. The sounds took Lily to the carousel, where she watched and wished. The children captivated her and the mothers taunted her. There were fathers too, the kind that spent time with their children. The kind that didn't take their son from his mother. A child fell, and she almost pushed past his parents to reach him and soothe him. Time to get a grip.

An hour later, she was at Julie's door in Sciennes, with a bottle of Swedish vodka, two large pizzas and some ice cream. Though Julie had sounded pleased to hear Lily was coming over, her friend looked a little preoccupied. Something was going on. A few vodkas, and Lily was certain Julie would spill.

A couple of drinks, and they both relaxed. A bottle of wine with their pizza, and the chat and laughter came easily, the final fragments of Lily's tension floating away. It *was* good to have time to herself, and Ronan would be fine.

When the food was done, Lily curled up on the sofa, and reached for her wine glass. 'So, Ms Ross, you going to tell me what you've been up to?'

Julie shrugged. 'Don't know what you mean.'

'The sexy Ralph Lauren robe hanging in the bathroom. Two bath towels. Two toothbrushes. Packaging from fancy new bedding in the recycling bag in the pantry.'

Julie shook her head. 'Did you check the rubbish bins, Inspector Clouseau?'

Lily laughed. 'Not yet.'

Julie's cat, Cleo, jumped on the sofa and shoved her head under Lily's hand. She put her wine glass on the table and stroked the cat. 'So?'

The room was darkening, but in the evening sun that shone through the living room window, Lily saw the slight flush on Julie's face. To the loud sound of Cleo's purring, Julie spilled.

Philip was a psychologist, and no, she hadn't met him in a professional capacity. He was a friend of a friend. They'd met at a party, and they'd chatted all night, ignoring interruptions and distractions. It had been effortless. Romance hadn't crossed her mind then or after she left the party, but she'd awoken in the night and found herself unable to get back to sleep for thinking about him. She'd asked her friend for his email address and contacted him the next day. Nothing heavy. Just saying it was nice to meet him and she'd enjoyed their chat.

No response. She'd seethed a little and shrugged it off. Forgotten. Until the next party and his friendly face, so obviously pleased to see her. This time he asked for her phone number, and he called her the next day. It turned out he'd changed his email address months before.

'And?'

'A few dates. A walk or two. Lots of talking.'

'And last night?'

Julie smiled. 'I'll leave that to your imagination.'

'Are you happy?'

She nodded. 'And nervous. That's why I didn't say anything. Scared of hexing it.' She drained the last of her wine. 'I didn't expect this. Not now.'

'Why not? You're gorgeous.'

Julie blushed. 'Thank you.' She shrugged. 'I'm used to being on my own. Time will tell. Another vodka?'

Lily nodded. 'One more.'

One became two. 'Definitely the last one,' Lily said. 'How did it go at Bonnyrigg yesterday?'

Julie raised her eyebrows. 'Okay. A bit weird. I found six jars of nail clippings. Fancy jars. Lined up on the bathroom shelf like ornaments. Must have taken years to fill them.'

'What? Why?'

Julie shrugged. 'God knows –'

Lily's phone rang. She looked at the screen and frowned before answering. 'Nathan.' She held the phone away from her ear while he ranted. 'Yeah. Sorry. Just leaving. No, I'm not drunk. Yes, I'll get a taxi. Yes, I'll be careful. See you in the morning.' She rolled her eyes as she cut the call. 'He's been phoning the flat. Worried I'd been abducted, raped, murdered, transported to another universe.' She drained her vodka glass. 'Or worse. I might just be having a good time.'

'Is everything all right with you two?'

Lily shrugged. 'Dunno. He's been odd lately.' She smiled. 'Odder. It'll be fine. I better go.'

'Do you want to come to work with me on Monday, if Ronan's going to be at nursery? I could do with a hand. I'll pay you.'

'Will there be nail clippings?'

'It's a different house. Morningside. The woman sounds posh, but I can't guarantee there won't be grossness involved. Do you think Nathan would mind?'

'Too bad if he does,' Lily said. 'I'd like that. Text me tomorrow.'

Outside, the moon was high and full, the air heavy with the smell of cut grass and malted barley. Clerk Street was busy with students and drinkers. No sign of a taxi or a bus, so Lily started walking. Ten minutes later, she heard her phone ping.

U home yet?

She still had a bit to go, but Nathan didn't need to know that.

Just in. Night night xx

Fifteen minutes later, she turned on to the High Street. It was quiet, but there were distant sounds in the air. Laughter and shouting. They could mean fun or fear, and she shivered as she remembered a night of both. Her first night in Edinburgh. She shoved the memory away, and kept walking.

Chapter 9

DAVID

DAVID GUNN WAS standing just inside the mouth of Anchor Close, listening to the voice on the phone, hearing the frustration and barely concealed implication that it was his fault things weren't going as planned. Yes, he agreed; he might as well get off home. He cut the call and put the phone in his pocket. On the other side of the street, the dark bulk of St Giles Cathedral loomed, a subtle glow radiating from the top of its crown steeple. He was about to head for the nearest taxi rank when she passed by. He didn't see her face, but he knew. The way she walked, her hair, her height, her scent. He knew. He should let her go, but he couldn't.

'Hello Ms Andersen.'

She turned and smiled. 'It's Lily, PC Gunn. How are you doing?'

He nodded. 'Fine, thanks. Are you okay after the bus incident? These things can cause … maybe delayed shock … or something?' Shut up, he told himself.

'I'm fine. It's kind of you to ask. You had a good night? You're obviously not on duty.'

'Okay night, thanks. Just heading home.' He wanted to ask her if she fancied going for a drink. Fool.

A sudden burst of swearing and shouting split the still night.

A rabble of youths was coming up the other side of the street, pushing and shoving each other, looking around for an easy target. He slipped further into the close. 'Do you want to wait in here until they're gone? It's safer.'

Anchor Close was lit by wall-mounted lanterns that cast a yellow glow down the steps that led to Cockburn Street. They sat on the steps and waited for the youths to pass.

'There was a printing house in here.' Lily's voice was hushed. 'They printed some works of Robbie Burns.'

He smiled. 'I'm impressed. Do you know the history of all the closes?'

'Only the ones with a plaque on the wall.' She nodded towards the information plaque at the entrance.

He looked over his shoulder and laughed. His phone beeped. He took it out of his pocket, read the screen, and texted a quick reply.

'Do you like Edinburgh?' he asked.

Lily nodded. 'I love it now. I wasn't sure at first. What about you?'

'I haven't been here long. I was in London before. Been there a few years.'

Lily smiled. 'Do you miss home?'

'A bit.'

'Tell me about it.'

He told her he came from North Tolsta, a village fifteen miles from Stornoway, on the Isle of Lewis. The beaches – Garry Beach and *Traigh Mhòr* – were just a short walk from his house. As a child, he was warned away from the high cliffs, and the caves and sea stacks below. It hadn't worked. He and his friends had outdone one another in their exploits. Their favourite time was when the mist came down and transformed the land until they could see nothing around them. They could hear the sea roaring below, but they couldn't see the cliff edge. How close were they? How far did they dare go? Too far, probably, but they lost no one.

On the beach, they'd climb the stacks and hide in the caves

while the tide was out, waiting, daring each other to stay there until the tide rose. His father had to rescue him and a friend from a cave one night, the sand blasting off the beach and scouring their skin as they struggled home.

Lily leaned towards him. 'It sounds beautiful. I'm envious, PC –' She frowned. 'I can't keep calling you that.'

'David.'

'I like that name.'

Her approval made something glow deep inside. 'I was called after my father. It made for a lot of confusion in our house. He's gone now, but I'm still *Wee Davie*. My mother will probably be calling me that when I'm sixty.'

Lily smiled, but there was sadness in her eyes. 'I lost my father, too. It was cancer.'

'I'm sorry,' David said. 'Tough, isn't it? My dad's fishing boat went down off the Shiants thirteen years ago.'

She looked devastated. 'That's so sad.'

He longed to see her smile again, so he told her of the pods of playful dolphins he watched from his bedroom window. The guillemots and cormorants, the red-throated divers and gannets. She smiled and gazed at him as if he was telling her the most magical tale ever. He leaned towards her, wanting so much to …

She jumped to her feet. 'It's been lovely talking to you. Better go.'

Chapter 10

LILY

FOR A MOMENT, Lily had imagined David was going to kiss her. He'd be gentler than Nathan; she was certain of it. The thought of her fiancé had broken the spell. And yet, even as she walked away, she wanted to turn back, sit and listen to that voice that felt like home. She wanted to hear more about his father. Maybe tell him about her father, and how much she missed him. David would understand. There had been a connection between them. She laughed and told herself she was a fool.

There was a couple entwined at the entrance to Milne's Court. The female was against the wall, all skinny legs and high heels. The male was groping and wriggling and moaning. Over his shoulder, Lily recognised the female's face. It was Sophia's sister, from outside the hotel, the night of the retirement dinner. She wasn't as young as she'd looked that night; maybe eighteen or nineteen. She saw Lily, and her face darkened into a scowl. She shouted something in Polish. It didn't sound like a compliment. Lily waved and carried on.

In the kitchen, she ran the cold tap and filled a glass. She took it upstairs, stopping on the landing to close the sky-light. There was an unpleasant scent in the air. Something dark and bitter. Before she could turn, a hand covered her mouth, another grabbing her hair. The glass dropped to the floor.

Was it David Gunn? Had she misread him? She was certain she'd closed the entrance door at the bottom of the common stair and locked the front door. Maybe not. Perhaps he'd slipped in while she was in the kitchen. Come to collect what he thought he was going to get in the close. She was pulled away from the wall and pushed towards the bedroom.

'No. Please.' The words couldn't pass the hand that covered her mouth. Her feet stumbled as she was shoved face-down onto the bed. She felt the weight of a body sitting astride her, one hand forcing her head into the pillow, the other twisting and pulling at her engagement ring. If she could breathe and speak, she'd tell her attacker he could have the ring, gladly.

He gave up on the ring and pressed with both hands on the back of her head. Memories came to her from her first year of medical school, from that wondrous time of knowing and expansion and promise. A new world, exciting possibilities mapped out in blue and red on a full-sized body on the wall. New words. Asphyxia. Hypoxia. Hypercapnia. Acidosis. The blood pumping round her body, carrying no oxygen to her cells and organs. They wouldn't last long. There was dizziness in her head and pain in her chest. A passing thought that freedom was only moments away. And then the weight was gone and her body was being rolled over.

She wanted to laugh at the fleeting hope that the attacker was a stranger. Anything to avoid the dismal reality of her life. A wedding dress, a diamond ring, a luxury apartment. They meant nothing. She wished she could stop her fickle chest from gasping for air. Let Nathan think she was dead, that he'd killed her. He might kill her yet, for his face was contorted with rage. 'Who were you with?'

She shook her head. It ached as oxygenated blood rushed into her brain. 'No one.'

'You lying bitch. You said you were home.'

'I … I was, but I was feeling sick, and I knew I wouldn't sleep, so I went for a walk.'

He stared at her, and she wondered how long he'd been here. If he'd come home just after she texted, he'd know she was lying. He gripped her upper arms. 'Why would you do that in the dark?'

'I had too much to drink.'

He punched the pillow, just missing her head. If he'd hit her with that force, he'd have knocked her out. Or worse. As if he realised how close he'd come to really hurting her, his face softened, and he pulled her into his arms, whispering her name over and over. She caught a hint of perfume from his shirt. It wasn't the first time she'd smelled it on him, and now she matched it with the musky scent in the bathroom at the retirement dinner. It was Sophia's perfume.

'I'm sorry,' he said. 'You know that, don't you? I would never hurt you. I just can't bear the thought of you with someone else.' He held her away from him. 'You weren't, were you? Swear on Ronan's life.'

Nothing would make her do that. 'I wasn't with anyone.'

'Why won't you swear it, Lily? Why?'

In his eyes, she saw just how tenuous his remorse was. It would take nothing for him to erupt again. And then his phone rang.

*

NEXT BUS. THAT was the one for her, no matter where it was going. Lily stuck her hand out and pulled it back again. Craigmillar. Maybe not. She mouthed an apology to the driver, then she sat in the bus shelter and thought of places she'd been meaning to visit. Rosslyn Chapel. Vogrie Country Park. Ikea.

Not today. Her head and her body felt as grey as the clouds that threatened rain. She wandered back towards home. Where North and South Bridge met, she turned on to the High Street, but her feet refused to go any further than Cockburn Street. Down to Waverley Bridge, through the Gardens and along towards the West End.

Her phone kept pinging, but she didn't take it from her bag.

She didn't want to know what Nathan had to say. The phone call in the night had taken him back to work. He hadn't been home when she'd left, though he should have been. Maybe he was with Sophia. She remembered his words from the night of the dinner. *Probably isn't a man in this room, except me, of course, that doesn't fantasise about Sophia.* For once, he was being honest; he didn't need to fantasise. Though she knew she should feel hurt, angry, vengeful, she felt nothing. She'd left him a note saying she was meeting Julie for lunch. It was a lie.

She sat on the grass opposite the Ross Fountain, her knees hugged tight. There was an ache in her chest, and she couldn't tell if it was physical or emotional. She didn't really want to know. Much easier, safer, not to examine things too much. Box them up, shut them away. The usual strategy. It mostly worked, unless things came creeping out of the boxes, taunting her, like the moonlit memory of his fist descending. With a groan, she lay back on the grass and watched the clouds. She didn't want to think about him and how much he had changed over recent months. Didn't want to think about last night. Time to move.

In Waterstones, she browsed for a while, then she bought a book of Celtic mythology. She was hungry, at last, so she ate in the café and lost herself in the tales of the Irish hero, *Cu Chulainn*.

*

AT THE TOP of Castle Wynd North steps, Lily stopped to get her breath. She looked at her phone. Ten texts from Nathan. Two from Julie. She texted a quick reply to her friend to say she was still coming to work tomorrow, then she deleted their texts. She didn't read Nathan's. A figure standing by the restaurant on the corner caught her eye. Mobile phone to his ear, he had his back to her, but she recognised David Gunn. Seeing him again made her shiver. It wasn't him; it was what Nathan would have done if he'd known why she was late home last night. She pulled up her hood and put her head down as she crossed the Esplanade, making for the gardens below the Castle. The land there was rough and overgrown, and there was a bench with a small metal plaque that read 'Rest and Dream'. Lily had often done just that in the early days, when life with Nathan seemed to hold such promise. She'd go there now, read some more, until it was time for Ronan to come home. A sudden shriek made her look up. 'Mama!'

Rebecca was standing by the railings, a look of panic on her face. Lily ran towards them. She crouched and opened the harness and lifted her son from the pushchair. She held him tight, then she twirled him round. 'My darling, how I missed you.'

He put a hand on each side of her face and stared into her eyes, then he sank against her neck, his breath so warm and his smell wonderful.

Lily smiled at Rebecca. 'Thanks for bringing him home. You're early. Did you walk? I thought Nathan was collecting him.'

Rebecca shook her head. 'He's hardly stopped crying all day. Mum and Dad went out, and I couldn't stand it any longer. I thought a walk might help. It didn't. How do you put up with that?'

Lily laughed. 'He never cries. Not with me. Is Nathan not in?'

Rebecca shrugged. 'No answer, but his car's there.'

'He'll be in bed, with earplugs. Or maybe he's gone out. Are you coming up?'

The very idea made Rebecca's eyes widen. 'Eh ... I have to ... I've got to ... No.'

Result.

'Ronan, say bye-bye to Rebecca.'

His head was still buried in her neck, a wee whisper warm against her skin. 'No, Mama.'

'He's sleepy.' She took the bag from Rebecca and thanked her again. She watched her walk down Castlehill, past the Camera Obscura and David Gunn. He was staring at Lily. When she got closer, he smiled, nodded, and walked away.

Chapter 11

DAVID

DAVID WAS USED to long walks. If it wasn't the beaches at home, it was the moors. As children, he and his friends would cross the Bridge to Nowhere, an abandoned arched concrete bridge, left behind by the soap baron and philanthropist, Lord Leverhulme. He'd bought the Isle of Lewis in 1918. Among the many schemes and ideas he had for the island was a plan to link David's home village of North Tolsta to Ness, on the northernmost tip of Lewis, a distance of twelve miles across the moor. His plan came to nothing, leaving the bridge as a constant reminder of what might have been. To those with no imagination, the bridge went nowhere, but it could take the local children to places far and wide, real and imagined. David and a friend once walked across the moors to Ness. Seven hours it took them, and they were so proud of themselves. He'd phoned his mother to come round by the road and pick them up. She'd refused, told them to walk back or get the bus. But they had no money and their feet were sore, he'd said. Too bad. She had better things to do with her time than drive thirty-six and a half miles to pick up two boys that should have been home hours ago. Thirty-six and a half miles by road? He understood then why Leverhulme had wanted to build a road across the moor. His friend's mother was a little kinder. She came for them, then berated them all the way home. He'd learned some new Gaelic words that day.

Though his job sometimes involved walking the city streets, much of his time was spent in the station or in a car. Pounding pavements at speed on a Sunday afternoon was something else. Everything ached. He'd been certain Lily had seen him in the Gardens, sitting on a bench close to the fountain, in sunglasses and a baseball cap, nose buried in *The Herald on Sunday*. He'd hoped for the comfort of a broadsheet to hide behind, but it seemed all the decent newspapers had gone compact. If he was to be seen, he certainly wouldn't be seen with the *Sunday Telegraph*. Enjoying the rest, he'd hoped she'd stay on the grass for a while, but she'd suddenly shot to her feet and scarpered, a look of fear on her face. The impression that she was trying to outrun something had been there all day, in the hunch of her shoulders and the timid feet that didn't seem to know where they wanted to go. It was such a contrast to her usual demeanour. He wondered if something had happened after she got home the previous night. The thought of her at home with Nathan Collesso wasn't something David cared to dwell on. All he wanted now was to get home himself, a long soak in the bath, a curry, and some television. But it wasn't to be. He had orders and he couldn't disobey them.

It wasn't far to the high-rise block in Dumbiedykes. The council housing scheme had benefitted from its proximity to the Scottish Parliament, but it was still an impoverished estate, with high unemployment and significant drug and alcohol problems. Not somewhere he'd be too keen to walk at night. The block of flats was well kept, with a secure entry system and a clean lift. Probably factored by the local authority. The flat was on the top floor. He tapped on the door and waited. When it opened, the eyes that peered through the gap were suspicious. A nod of a head, and David slipped inside, breathing in the pungent smell of cannabis. And more. Perfume and booze and lust. Beyond the smells, there was an aura of something dark and evil. It made David's skin crawl.

There were three men in the living room, sprawled on the couch, playing cards. There was a single mattress in the corner of the room, and a grubby sleeping bag. Music blared from the television. The man that had opened the door sat at a small table. He barked an order, and the music was gone.

'I am Jakub,' the man said. He was older than the others. Late forties, with hunched shoulders, a shaved head and the shadow of a beard. Dark, intelligent eyes studied David. He lifted a bottle of Polish vodka, tipping it towards David, eyebrows raised.

David nodded, and Jakub poured the vodka into a chipped mug, then he kicked out a chair. David sat and knocked the vodka back in one, suppressing a shudder as it burned his throat and gullet. Jakub poured another. 'Our friend tell you what we need?'

David nodded.

'And what we pay?'

Another nod.

'We have special pay for you today. Bonus, I think you call this. I let you have it first, then we talk.'

David's heart sank. He'd been told all about the bonuses. Jakub said something in Polish to the men on the couch. There was a ripple of laughter. One of them put his cards face down on the table and stood.

'Come.'

David threw back the second vodka and followed him. There were three doors off the hall, and he knew exactly what was behind each one. He shook his head when the man opened the first one. And the second. As the man reached for the third door, David prayed to a God he didn't believe in that this one would be different.

She was.

Chapter 12

LILY

THE HOUSE IN Morningside looked well kept. It would be nice to live somewhere like that, Lily thought, without the incessant summer noise of the Tattoo, the fireworks and the live bands on the Castle Esplanade. Though she loved Ramsay Garden, she dreaded the start of festival season.

The front door opened. The woman was in her mid-sixties. She was well-dressed, with short fair hair. She tried to smile at Julie and Lily, but tears glistened in her eyes.

'Mrs Rutherford?' Julie offered her hand. 'I'm Julie from *Neatspace*. This is my colleague, Lily.'

'It's Miss,' the woman said, ignoring the outstretched hand. 'Miss Rutherford. Are you the ... the clutter busters?'

Julie smiled and let her hand drop to her side. 'That's one way of describing us. In fact, I've been trying to think of a new name for the business. *Neatspace* is a little boring. *The Clutter Busters*? I like that.'

Miss Rutherford frowned. 'Might give the game away if you had that on the side of your van.' She peered out into the street.

'It's okay,' Julie said. 'There's nothing on my van. As far as the neighbours know, we're here to unblock your drains or put up shelves.'

'Nothing wrong with my drains, and I don't need any shelves. I keep a clean house.'

'Would you like us to come in?'

'Not really.' She nodded towards a bench. 'Can we just sit in the garden?'

'You and Lily have a seat,' Julie said. 'I'm going to the van to get some things.'

They sat, and the woman studied Lily. 'You don't look like cleaners. Are you sure you're not here to scam me out of something? I know all about those scams. People that prey on the elderly.'

Lily smiled. 'Do we look like scammers?'

Miss Rutherford shrugged. 'Probably not, but isn't that the point? Wouldn't fool many people if you looked the part.'

'We're professional de-clutterers. Well, Julie is. I'm just helping her out today.'

A frenzy of tiny sparrows flitted around a bird table and feeders, perching and pecking and fighting each other.

'I love my wee birds,' Miss Rutherford said. 'There was a cat next door.' She gestured toward a bungalow that looked neglected. 'A skinny black shadow that flitted through my garden, hiding in the bushes and trying to catch my wee friends. Its owner was a horrible old man, Lily. A stalking horse. Is that what you call them, those people that won't leave you alone?'

'Do you mean a stalker?'

'That's it. Always phoning and asking me if I'd like to come and sit with him. I'd tell him to leave me alone. He'd get people to put flowers and chocolates on the doorstep. I put them in the bin. There was a bottle of wine once, and I kept it, though I hardly ever take alcohol. I thought I might have it on Christmas Day or on a special occasion. I opened it three weeks ago yesterday. I had two glasses, and I felt quite squiffy, but I thought it was important to toast him on his way.'

'On his way where?'

Miss Rutherford looked up to the sky, then she shrugged and

pointed at the ground. 'Who knows? I'm putting my money on down below.'

Their laughter chased a blue tit from the bird table.

'The moggy went soon after him. I think the SSPCA took it away.' Miss Rutherford frowned. 'I don't mean to be nasty, but he was so old, and he made me uncomfortable. I think he was looking for a free nurse.'

'Were you a nurse?'

She shook her head. 'I was never anything. Just plain Margaret Joan Rutherford. Lived here all my life. Never worked, never married, never did anything. Such a dull life.' The tears were back.

Lily put her hand on the woman's arm. 'It's all right, Miss Rutherford. We'll get it all sorted. I promise.'

'Really?' She shrugged. 'I don't know what to believe, but you look trustworthy enough. You can call me Margaret.'

Julie was back. She had black bags, plastic aprons and a storage caddy with cleaning supplies. 'Will we go in?'

'I have my own cleaning products,' Margaret said. 'You'll not be needing any of that in my house. And I'm not mad, you know. Just because the meter man couldn't reach the cupboard, they said it was a health and safety risk. They've made me go for this counselling. Said I had to get you people in. I don't think it's going to help.'

Lily had heard enough from Julie about hoarders to know what to expect. The hall didn't look too bad. There were boxes stacked against the wall, and a couple of free-standing gas radiators. On a small table by the door, there was a pile of unopened mail. They'd soon get this sorted out. And then Margaret showed them the bedrooms.

The biggest room, where Margaret slept, was stacked with boxes and newspapers and books. There was a narrow path from the door to the bed. Apart from a small bedside cabinet, it was impossible to see if there was any other bedroom furniture. The heavy curtains were closed.

'Father was a solicitor.' Margaret was wringing her hands. 'He often worked from home. His business partner came after he died and he went through the papers and took some away. I didn't know what to do with the rest.'

In the second bedroom, there were two ancient electric fires, several toasters, three sewing machines, a jumble of kettles and irons, and a range of vintage swivelling office chairs. 'Father could never find a comfortable chair. He was always ordering new chairs. My brother and I had fun playing on the ones he didn't want. But we were careful; they have some life left in them. And the other things, they could all be fixed. They're not rubbish. It's wasteful to throw them out.'

Margaret's face was grave as she opened the door to the third bedroom. It was piled high with paper and books, boxes and crates, clothing and pictures. In the boxroom, there were more electrical appliances. Margaret picked up a hairdryer. 'These are all in working order. Bargains. I had to buy them. Someone might need them.'

Julie smiled. 'Indeed. Do you need them?'

'Not at all.' She shook her head. 'I have what I need. But someone might.'

'We could help you with that. There are charities and initiatives to help people in need. I'll get you some leaflets. Will we make a start?'

'A start?' Margaret's eyes widened, and she held a hand to her chest. 'But where?'

'The back bedroom?' Julie said. 'We could do a first pass.'

Margaret frowned. 'What's that?'

'Sorting out. We put the same things together. Clothes with clothes. Photos with photos. Electrics with electrics. No throwing out. Just organising.'

'No throwing out? I like the sound of that.'

When the room was organised, so that the electrical appliances were in one corner, the clothes neatly folded on the bed, the papers stacked against one wall, boxes and crates against another, and pictures against the third wall, Margaret stood at the window. 'This was my room until mother got sick. I used to open the curtains early in the morning and watch the birds in the trees. There was a squirrel that stole our plums. Father threatened to poison it, but I begged him not to. I was so happy in here. I don't know why I didn't come back when Mother passed away.' She gestured to the single bed, covered with a pink candlewick bedspread. 'That was a new bed. I got it just before Mother became ill. I never enjoyed sleeping in my parents' room. It just didn't seem right.'

'Why don't you sleep here tonight?' Julie asked. 'We can clear everything else out.'

Margaret's eyes widened, and she smiled. Her face lost a decade. 'That would be marvellous.'

Chapter 13

LILY

THE RADIO WAS on and Julie was singing along to "Rolling in the Deep". Lily stared ahead and remembered. She could have had it all. Until Nathan. When the memories threatened to overwhelm her, she swallowed them and zoned out.

'You were great with Margaret,' Julie said as she pulled up in front of Ronan's nursery. 'Thanks for offering to work on Friday. I don't think she'd have had us back otherwise. Do you want to make it a regular thing? Mondays and Fridays? I could do with the help. I've been meaning to get someone else.'

'Can I think about it?'

'Course you can.'

As she walked home, Lily considered Julie's offer. Working a couple of days a week while Ronan was at nursery might be good for her. She hadn't planned on getting a job. But then, she hadn't planned on getting pregnant. If that hadn't happened, she'd be in Aberdeen, finishing her last year of medical school now, about to start the two years of postgraduate training as a junior doctor. She had no regrets about Ronan; how could she have? She couldn't say the same about medical school. It wasn't too late, Julie often told her. She could do her last two years in Edinburgh. Lily couldn't see it working out. The life of a junior doctor wasn't really compatible with having children, unless you had a very supportive, preferably stay-at-home, partner. Nathan would never be either of those things. Maybe being a clutter buster would suit her just fine.

*

NATHAN'S FOOTSTEPS WERE fast and light on the stairs. He pushed open the bathroom door. 'Hey, guys. How are you doing?'

In a fraction of a second, Lily had checked his eyes, his mouth, his stance. All okay. His hands were behind his back. Another present? There had been chocolates and champagne waiting for her when she got home the previous day. And a sheepish Nathan, full of apologies and promises.

She smiled. 'We're fine, thanks. You?'

'I'm good.' One hand still behind his back, he waved at Ronan. 'Hey, wee man, guess what I've got for your beautiful mummy?'

The smell of death was in her nostrils, her eyes watering, a headache hovering.

'Lilies for my Lily.'

They were in her hands, the hideous scent choking her. Lily forced a smile. 'Thank you.'

'And this.' He pulled a flat box out of his pocket and opened the lid. 'It's an infinity bracelet.' He crouched and slipped the delicate gold bangle onto her wrist. 'I'll love you forever, Lily.'

Later, they settled down to watch a film, but Nathan's phone kept ringing. Each call took him to the kitchen, and every time he returned, his mood was a little gloomier.

'Everything okay?' Lily asked after the fourth call.

He nodded and tried to smile. 'Just work.' He looked at the clock. 'Will we give up on the film?'

Lily yawned. 'Might as well.'

He lifted the mugs off the coffee table. 'You go up. I'll take these through.'

As Lily passed the kitchen door, she heard his phone ring again. She crept closer to the door, and she could smell the lilies.

'I said I'll get it sorted. Believe me.' He sounded scared. 'I have to go.'

She had to go too, before he came out and caught her. She was on the third step when his voice rose. 'How do you know I'm at home? Are you watching me? I said I'll sort it.'

From the en-suite, she heard his steps on the stairs and then the ping of a text or an email, followed by muttering and swearing. When she came out, he was sitting on the bed, staring at his phone, shaking his head. 'I don't believe this.'

Probably best not to ask. She sat at the dressing table to take off her jewellery and she could see him in the mirror, his eyes still fixed on the screen.

'Lily?'

'Yeah?' She kept her voice light, glanced in the mirror and saw him looking up, frowning, standing.

He was behind her. 'What did you do today when Ronan was at nursery?'

The ice in his voice made the temperature in the room plummet.

'Eh … did I not say?'

'I don't believe you did.'

'I … Julie and I, we spent the day together.'

'Uh huh. What did you do?'

She shrugged. 'Just hanging out.'

He dragged her by the hair from the stool and threw her on the bed. His hand was over her mouth, his nails digging into her cheek. She could feel the skin breaking.

'Lying bitch. I know exactly what you were doing. A cleaner? My fiancée? How long has this been going on?'

She shook her head, and he took his hand away. 'Just once, I promise. I was … I had nothing else to do.'

'Nothing to do? You couldn't spend my money? Or lunch with a friend? Oh no, you only have one friend and she's a cleaner. You didn't get enough of her company yesterday?' His grin was vicious as he pulled away from her and stood. 'Another lie. You didn't go anywhere near Julie yesterday.'

In the en-suite, she heard him filling the sink. She looked to the bedroom door, and thought of running, but he was back. He dragged her off the bed, her feet stumbling on the wooden floor. He plunged her head under the water. It was icy cold, stinging her nose and her throat. As she held her breath, a desperate pain rising in her chest, she wondered if this would be the last time.

Apparently not. He pulled her up by the hair. She gave a shuddering gasp and heard the drip, drip, drip of water. He pushed her to the floor. 'Bitch. I try so hard with you, over and over, and this is how you repay me.'

Lily clasped the edge of the sink and pulled herself up. In the mirror, she saw deep bloody gouges in her cheek. There would be scars. Always.

In the bedroom, he had his back to her as he took off his clothes and pulled on a t-shirt. 'Tomorrow, you're leaving. Ronan will soon toughen up without you petting and pampering him. He'd have walked long ago with a normal mother, instead of a freak.'

Lily had never hit him back. But now, everything he'd ever said and done since the day they met, the day he stole her life and all of its promise, raced through her head. There was metal glinting under the bed. She bent and grasped the small dumbbell and pulled it out. It felt good in her hand. Solid and heavy. He turned and his eyes seemed as big as the moon that shone through the thin curtains. He raised his hands to protect himself, crying out as the dumbbell hit the knuckles of his left hand, splitting them open.

Rage contorted his face into something terrifying. He pulled the dumbbell from her and pushed her onto the bed. He stood over her, dumbbell raised. And then he shook his head and laughed. 'You're not worth it.'

The dumbbell clanged to the floor. He pulled the bangle from her wrist, then he grabbed his phone from the bedside table, and his clothes from the chair. 'I'll sleep in my son's room.'

Chapter 14

LILY

As Lily lay in the dark, his words went round and round in her head. He'd never threatened to throw her out before, or to take Ronan from her. They'd have to leave. But where would they go? How would they survive? So many questions, and no answers. She stuck in her earphones and listened to music. It was hours before she slept.

She awoke at seven. The city was coming to life, with the buzz of street cleaning machines and car horns. In the en-suite, she saw the vivid nail marks on her cheek. She was supposed to meet Julie for lunch. She'd have to text her and put it off. Or maybe … maybe she should text her and ask her to come round. Tell her. Ask for help. It was a terrifying thought.

And then she discovered the decision had been made for her. She couldn't contact Julie or anyone else. Her mobile phone was gone, along with the landline handsets. No netbook or iPad on the kitchen table. Her keys were missing from her bag, and the spare keys were no longer hanging by the door. She was locked in.

The pillows on the single bed in Ronan's room were dented, and the quilt was trailing on the floor. The cot quilt was all bunched up. It made her smile. He'd get himself into the oddest contortions while he slept. The floorboards creaked, and she stopped and held her breath, waiting for that little tousled head to poke up above the bumper. Eyes heavy with sleep, yet still he'd smile.

But not today. He wasn't there.

She remembered a folktale from home of a bloody cot and a missing baby. Whispers of the harm that might befall an unbaptised child. A piece of steel attached to the nappy to ward off evil. Infants taken and fairy changelings left in their place. But nothing had been left in place of her boy, except smudges and smears of blood on the bedding and the door handle. Nathan's blood. It had to be Nathan's blood.

Lily sat on the balcony, breathing, calming, telling herself he wouldn't hurt Ronan. But would he bring him back? She went into the lounge and saw Nathan's laptop on the floor. If she could get into her email, she'd contact Julie. Together, they could decide what to do.

Lily had caught Nathan looking at her iPad a few times. He hadn't really hidden what he was doing, but she hadn't made a fuss. She had nothing to hide. She'd never thought of checking up on him. Turned out, he'd password-protected his laptop. She tried all the family names and schools and birth places. When she tried *Bruce,* she told herself off for being neurotic. It seemed neurosis was the best bet. The password was *Sophia*.

There were three emails from Sophia in his inbox. They'd been read. Before she could open them, the intercom buzzed. Lily lifted the handset and pressed the button to open the downstairs door. The footsteps were faster and lighter than the postie. No stopping off at other doors. The doorbell rang. Through the peephole, Julie looked funny, her nose huge and her eyes tiny. Though Lily had wanted to contact her friend, she hadn't envisaged talking through the letterbox. What the hell would she say?

The downstairs door opened again. Heavier footsteps. No stopping. And Ronan's laughter. Her hands over her mouth, Lily backed away from the door, relief cascading through her. In the lounge, she closed down the laptop. She could hear Nathan. He sounded so sincere. 'Hi. Are you Julie? It's great to meet you at last. Is she not answering? Probably still asleep.' She heard him unlock the door. Ronan squealed. Nathan lied. 'We were out last night. Just picked Ronan up from my folks. Is Lily expecting you?'

'No. We're meeting for lunch, but I was in the area, so I thought I'd pop round and make plans. I sent her a text, but she didn't answer. Maybe she's still asleep.'

'Maybe. You hold him. I'll go up and check.'

'I'm in here.'

Julie came in first, holding Ronan. Lily grabbed him from her. Turning away, she held him tight. She would never let him go again. She took a deep breath, desperate for his scent. All she got was the smell of Sophia's perfume.

'Coffee, Julie?' Nathan sounded so normal. So convincing.

Say yes, Julie; say yes. Please stay.

But.

No. Say no. And leave.

'Em … yeah. That'd be nice.'

Lily felt a hand on her shoulder and she flinched. It was Julie. 'What's wrong? What happened to your face?'

A shout from the kitchen. 'Can you give me a hand, love?'

Julie reached for Ronan. 'Will I take him?'

'Never.'

The phones and her netbook and iPad were on the kitchen table. He was pouring coffee, plasters on three of his knuckles. 'Lily, why didn't you tell me you were going to work with Julie? Could have avoided all this.' He took a step towards her. She backed away and knocked against a chair. She clutched Ronan tighter.

He frowned. 'What's wrong? You know how much I love you. I wouldn't hurt you.'

She shook her head. 'Are you for real?'

He shrugged and held up his injured hand. 'Works both ways. It's just how we are. We fight sometimes.'

'You took Ronan. You locked me in.' Conscious of Julie in the lounge, Lily lowered her voice. 'You only came back because Julie texted me. You were scared she'd find out. Who told you what I was doing yesterday and Sunday?'

He didn't answer. He looked at the bin; the lilies stuffed in upside down. 'That's childish.'

'Not really. I hate lilies; always have.'

'And I thought we knew each other.'

She followed him into the lounge. He put the coffee mugs down, then he lifted his laptop. 'It was nice to meet you, Julie.' He kissed Lily on the cheek, her good cheek. 'See you later, love.'

Chapter 15

JULIE

JULIE WANTED TO keep driving, put as much distance as possible between Lily and Nathan Collesso. And yet. Part of her wanted to race back to Edinburgh, confront him and his family, his boss and his workmates. Show them Lily. Show them what he'd done. And then kill him.

She remembered a boyfriend when she was in her early twenties. She'd quite liked him. Until the night of his best friend's 21st birthday party, when she dared to dance with another guy. She'd laughed at his huffiness, tried to coax him out of it. It didn't work. On the way home, he dragged her into a wooded area and pinned her against a tree, his hands squeezing her throat. She was a tart, he said, and he wasn't having it. She was his. From now on, she'd do and wear what she was told. Did she understand? She'd nodded, waited until he'd turned away, and then whacked him on the back of the head with a rock. Knocked him out and left him. It was a frosty night. She didn't sleep much, waiting for the knock on the door, the handcuffs, prison. Nothing happened. Six weeks later, she bumped into him at a party. He made the sign of the cross, called her something rude, and backed away. Sorted. That was what you did to bullies. She'd have put money on Lily doing the same.

Julie had always had her doubts about Nathan. Though she hadn't met him until today, it was obvious he was extremely controlling. There was a sadness about Lily sometimes, but her private nature had stopped Julie from probing. Lily scarcely spoke of him or the wedding, and they rarely went out together. Julie had offered to babysit, but Lily hadn't taken her up on it. She suspected Lily hadn't told her the half of it this morning after Nathan left. Just enough to explain the gouge marks on her face and the bruising on her ring finger. A hint of previous incidents. Enough to send Julie's blood pressure soaring through the roof. She'd taken over then, hurrying Lily into packing some things, ushering her and Ronan out before Nathan returned. There was a constant wee niggle in her head, whispering that maybe Lily wouldn't have left of her own accord.

They'd gone straight to Julie's house, but Lily couldn't settle. 'We can't stay here. He'll find us. He'll take Ronan again. I can't risk it.'

There had been a loud yowl from behind the sofa. Cleo bolted out from one end; Ronan's grinning face appearing from the other. Lily had scooped him off the floor and held him tight. 'I'm sorry; we're just going to cause you trouble.'

'Come on,' Julie said. 'We need to get out.'

'Can we go to the sea?'

*

AT BELHAVEN BAY, while Ronan laughed and threw soft sand into the air, Julie watched Lily walk barefoot down to the shore. Her shoulders were slumped, toes scuffing the sand, leaving tiny trails. She stood at the edge of the water, head back, eyes closed, face lifted to the sun that sparkled gold through her hair. The soft foam of the tide rolled over her feet. On the horizon, a tiny white wind-filled sail glided through the blue water.

When, at last, Lily turned, she looked like a different person, as if the sun and the sea had restored her. She was smiling as she walked towards them. Surely it meant she wasn't going back.

Nathan's texts and calls punctuated their journey home until Lily switched off her phone. Back at Julie's, after they'd eaten, Lily bathed Ronan and brought him down to the living room for his bottle. As Ronan sucked, he struggled to keep his eyes open, but they kept falling closed. In minutes, the sucking stopped, and his head lolled back against Lily's arm. 'I'll just put him up.'

Her phone was on the arm of the sofa. When she reached for it and slipped it into her pocket, Julie's heart began to race.

Chapter 16

LILY

LILY PULLED OVER the bedroom door, then she sat on the top step of the stairs and listened to the voicemails. Nathan sounded about ten years old as he begged her not to leave. He couldn't bear losing them both, he said; it'd kill him. The phone rang. Lily silenced it and stared at the screen, her eyes shifting between the options. *Decline? Accept?* She wasn't accepting Nathan, she told herself, as she chose that option. Just accepting that she had to speak to him, eventually. She'd never heard him cry before. It was horrible.

'Nathan, I can't make out what you're saying.'

She heard him take a deep, shuddering breath. There was a pause, and she was determined not to fill it.

'I'm sorry, Lily,' he said, at last. 'I'm … I'm scared I'm having a breakdown.'

She said nothing.

'Remember how good it was?' He spoke of their holidays in Barcelona and Rome, the weekend trips to spas and luxury hotels. The Paris rooftop where he'd proposed. 'It can be like that again. I know I've changed, Lily. It's work … I'm struggling, but it'll get better. I've got a meeting with my boss tomorrow, and I think some things will get sorted. Please, Lily; give me another chance.

Tell me what you want. I'll do anything.'

Memories and thoughts cascaded through her head. Boxes opening and closing. Words creeping out. Sneaking and taunting. This was not right. It had never been right, no matter what she'd told herself. It wasn't normal. Her sanity would not survive. From the bedroom, she heard Ronan cry. 'I'll phone you back.'

Maybe it was the travel cot that was unsettling Ronan. The mattress was thin and firmer than he was used to. She got a soft blanket from the airing cupboard and placed it over the mattress, then she stroked his cheek and sang a lullaby. As his eyes drifted closed, he whispered: 'Where Dada?'

*

JULIE TURNED AWAY, but not before Lily saw the anger on her face. She couldn't blame her friend. She waited, leaning against the kitchen worktop, until Julie looked at her. The anger was gone; she just looked perplexed. 'Will we have some wine in the garden?'

They sat on the patio below the room where Ronan was sleeping. Lily lifted her feet onto the chair and hugged her knees as she sipped at her wine. Julie's words were hushed. 'Do you love him?'

Lily stared across the garden. 'I … I'm not sure.'

'But you still want to marry him?'

Lily shrugged. 'I don't want Ronan growing up without his father.'

'He needn't. Lots of parents separate and the children cope with it.'

'I don't want him to have to cope. I want him to be part of a happy family. I owe it to Ronan to try again.'

'Is this because you lost your father? Because you hated your stepfather?'

Lily hesitated. Julie might be close to the truth, but it wasn't something she wanted to talk about. 'I didn't hate him,' she said, at last. 'I just didn't like him very much.'

'Two attacks in three days, Lily.'

Lily nodded. 'I know. That hasn't happened before. And it's never been like … like this.' Her hand rubbed at her scarred face. 'There's something going on at his work; I don't know what. Maybe if he gets past that. Who knows? He said he'd do anything, whatever I wanted.'

'And what did you tell him?'

Lily smiled. 'I probably should have asked him to stop seeing Sophia, get help with anger management, work less. Instead, I told him Ronan won't be staying overnight with anyone until he's older. If this happens again, we're gone. And I'm going to be working with you on Mondays and Fridays.' She put her glass down. 'If the offer's still open. I'd understand if you didn't want …'

Julie laughed. 'The offer is very much still open, not least so I can keep an eye on you. If he touches you again, I'll kill him.'

Chapter 17

SAM

You'd think in a city the size of Edinburgh, there'd be plenty of places to sleep, but Sam can't find them. There's none more territorial than the homeless. A sheltered, hidden space, with undisturbed and regular sleep is as precious as a mansion. When you find somewhere safe, you want to keep it, and keep it to yourself. Most of the sheltered doorways in the closes and courtyards are taken, and their occupants don't welcome a roommate. And if you find one that's vacant, you're no sooner settled for the night than an amorous couple comes along. It's one thing being wakened by the dawn chorus; quite another to be brought round by the cries and promises and lies of a copulating couple.

You want to keep off the main routes. Too many youngsters whose favourite night time sport is to find a tramp and give him a good kicking, or worse. Vulnerable when you're awake, and a sitting target when you're asleep, it's no wonder so many homeless people are addicts. How else can they get through the night? But the booze hasn't helped Sam lately. He hasn't had a good sleep for ages. Last night, he ended up in a bin store. He knows he's not fragrant at the best of times, but today he can hardly stand the stink himself.

He doesn't see Lily coming. He smiles up at her, and then he sees the marks on her cheek. Vicious gouges, she's tried to hide them with a coating of hideous make-up. His heart is beating like crazy. It's going to explode. Who would do this to her?

'Lily …'

Her eyes won't meet his. And now he realises why he didn't hear her coming. Her steps were not her own. They were weak, faltering, dragging steps. The steps of someone who wants to hide away from the world. She's only out for the wee one's sake. He's fast asleep, wrapped in a soft cocoon of blankets.

Sam smiles through the fear in his stomach, the pounding heart. 'How are you doing?'

'I'm fine. Are you enjoying the book you started?'

'It's pish.' He frowns. 'Sorry. It's not very good. Will you bring me another from the case?'

She nods. 'I could bring one of my own. I've got a few you might like. We could talk about them.'

'Our own wee book group?'

'Yeah.'

'Lily, are you all right?' He tries not to focus on the marks, doesn't want to embarrass her or force her to lie.

That smile. 'I'm fine, Sam. Better get him home. I'll look out a book for you for tomorrow.'

He watches her walk away, forcing herself forward, her head held high, shoulders back. If he had just one ounce of her strength, his life would have turned out so differently.

Chapter 18

DAVID

SOMETIMES DAVID DREAMT he was sinking with his father. As gulls wailed overhead, the little fishing boat was tossed by the ocean, swamped by the waves. Water gushed into his mouth as he reached for his father's hand. Fingers almost touching. Almost. And slipping away. Swallowing and coughing and choking, as he woke with the taste of salt on his lips. Was it the sea or his tears?

Other images haunted his dreams. A grim room in a flat in Dumbiedykes. Eyes as big as the moon, as black as coal. Dark curls. Fragile shoulder bones with a tattooed tracing of a delicate rose. Sallow skin shadowed with bruising. The smell, the forced laughter, the hopelessness.

He'd wake and race from his bed, hoping if he moved fast enough, the memories wouldn't catch him. In the shower, he'd scour his skin, trying to wash it all away. Sometimes, though he tried to stop them, thoughts of Lily Andersen would replace the tortured dreams. Flawless skin, that smile, her gleaming hair. The spark of interest and the light of laughter in her eyes. Brightness for a moment. Then he'd remember what he was doing, and how she'd hate him if she knew.

On a day when he was so tired, he wanted to phone in sick and stay in bed, David forced himself into the shower, then into the station. It was better to be there, he told himself, doing something useful. He was sent out in the patrol car with Eva Hunter, a young PC, and they got a call over the radio. The sudden death of a baby, just a couple of streets away. David hoped the ambulance would get there first, but it didn't. They found a young mother clutching her baby, pacing and babbling, while the father sat in a chair and sobbed. Every so often, he'd lift his head and howl out one word. A word that would probably remain unanswered forever. *Why?*

With compassion way beyond her years, Eva persuaded the mother to let her take the baby. Clasping the little boy as if he was the most precious thing she had ever held, Eva took him to the nursery and placed him in his cot while they awaited the ambulance. The parents were taken to the station to be questioned separately, while crime scene officers searched and measured and photographed, bagging bottles and blankets and clothes. David had to question the neighbours. Did they know the couple? Had they heard anything unusual? Had they ever been concerned about anything? He hated having to do that. The parents were so obviously innocent, it seemed a travesty to go through this procedure. It was necessary. He knew that, but it didn't help him any.

At the end of the shift, he took his colleagues up on the suggestion of a few drinks. Some of them went home to shower and change and try to transform themselves into ordinary people. It never really worked, for there was always someone in the pub who guessed they were police officers, no matter how they dressed or behaved. David could never put his finger on what exactly gave them away. Tonight, he didn't care. He wasn't going home, because he knew he wouldn't come out again, and he needed this.

David and two other male officers went straight to the pub. They'd had a few by the time the rest of the crew turned up. Eva Hunter's efforts to transform herself had worked, and David was certain no one would guess she was a police officer. He'd hardly recognised her when she came in, wearing a short dress, high heels and perfect make-up. She looked glittery and gorgeous and completely out of place among the dull plods. Her eyes caught his, and he saw the pain beyond her smile. He turned away and took up his pool cue. Another game with Rob, the dog handler, and their glasses were empty again.

'Another pint?' Rob asked.

'Yes, please.' David wasn't anywhere near as drunk as he wanted to be.

'You sure?'

'Aye. Why?'

Rob smiled. 'Over my shoulder. At two o'clock.'

Eva was leaning against the bar, a cocktail in each hand, laughing at one of Billy Bain's notoriously bad jokes, and throwing sly glances David's way.

David blushed. 'Maybe it's you she's looking at.'

Rob's laughter was loud. 'I wish.' He put his hand on David's shoulder. 'Son, you must be the only person in the station that hasn't noticed the way she looks at you.'

Really? David had been involved with colleagues before, and he'd decided not to do it again, not when things were so awkward afterwards. Though it hadn't happened to him, as far as he was aware, there was always a risk of intimate details, or even intimate photos, being shared around the station for revenge. Shitting on your own doorstep was best avoided.

And yet … he glanced at Eva again. She wasn't listening to Billy Bain now. She was staring at David. He felt something shimmer between them, a tentative bond forged from the day's shared heartache.

'Eh … just a half pint, then.'

In her bed, in a tiny flat in Haymarket, he touched Eva as if she was made of glass, as fragile as the infant. Afterwards, she cried, and he held her until she slept. He lay awake, scared to close his eyes for fear he'd dream and cry out. It wasn't just his father or the room in the Dumbiedykes flat. Now, there was another little spectre to haunt his dreams. An infant with blue skin and glassy eyes. As dawn filtered through the thin curtains, he crept from the bed and gathered up his clothes. Eva stirred as he dressed, but she didn't open her eyes. He kissed her cheek and left.

Chapter 19

SAM

In a certain light, Sam can see the faintest marks on Lily's cheek. It's been a couple of months, and it can still set his heart racing. If only he knew who had done it. He'd kill for her, if he had to. But hopefully it won't come to that, for she's brighter and stronger and happier than Sam has ever seen her. Her steps are more certain, her strides longer. The boy has settled at nursery, and she's enjoying her work. It's not what he'd have expected for her, but it makes her happy. When she's happy, he's happy, even though the pig is pursuing him without mercy, even though he's slipping into the downward spiral that happens every summer, when visitors are aplenty and generous. He's been told of an influx of Romanian women, and they do a good line in begging. On their knees on Princes Street, hands clasped in prayer. Shivering and shaking with tremors, some with missing limbs. Poor souls. Doesn't matter to him where they came from, but others aren't pleased, worried there might not be enough takings to go round. Just last week at the soup van, he overheard Old Geordie having a rant about the foreigners. They're not even homeless, he'd said. Gangs coming over from Eastern Europe, making a fortune on the streets, and sending it home so their families can live in mansions. It wasn't just the foreigners that had rattled Geordie. Youngsters were letting the side down too, with their dogs and their fags. These were luxuries the donating public shouldn't see. There were standards to be upheld.

Sam would like a dog. Something to cuddle, to warm his bones at night. He read an article last week in a newspaper someone gave him. Stroking a pet has significant health benefits. Lowers your blood pressure. Reduces anxiety. Provides a refuge in times of stress. He'd like a refuge. The pig came by the other day and said if he didn't move out of the Old Town, he'd be found dead one of these mornings. Being dead might not be so bad, but he's determined not to die at the hands of the pig. He's been killing himself for a long time, anyway. Every mouthful of poison takes another few minutes off his life expectancy. It's early, and the street is quiet, so he takes out the half-bottle and toasts that thought. And again.

Save it, he tells himself; save it for later. If he passes out during the day, someone will help themselves to his takings. And it's good to have some poison left for night time. If he drinks enough, he doesn't dream of the pig, or wake up hating himself because he's never had the guts to report the truth about that animal. It's not just the attack in the cemetery; that doesn't really matter. It's the other things he's seen, the things the pig knows he's seen. He should have said something long ago, and he hates himself for that. But he can't risk bringing himself to the attention of the police again. They didn't believe him before, and they won't believe him now.

Chapter 20

LILY

HAD NATHAN LOST more weight? If he had, Lily had found it. She pushed away her second slice of toast. No more biscuits, cakes or crisps. If she wasn't careful, the wedding dress wouldn't fit.

'I'm not going.' Nathan's voice was listless. 'Next week, the course. I don't want to leave you guys.'

Lily didn't show her disappointment. 'It's only a week. We'll be fine. We've managed before.'

Nathan twirled the car keys round his finger. 'I don't want to go.' There was a whine in his voice these days. A petulance that hadn't been there before. A lack of confidence. Self-doubt. Whatever was going on at his work, it hadn't been sorted out.

The phone rang. Lily held the handset away from her ear until Nathan's mother stopped screeching. Something about centrepieces for the tables, flowers that wouldn't be available, colours that wouldn't match. The whole thing was a disaster. When the noise died down, Lily spoke. 'It'll be fine. Don't worry about it.'

'Don't worry? If I don't worry about it, who will?'

Nathan signalled he was leaving. Lily nodded. 'See you later.'

Rita's roar nearly deafened her. 'You will not see me later! You will stay on the phone and take some interest in the plans for your wedding.'

'I was talking to Nathan.'

'And he's another one. I'm the only person who's interested in this wedding. I'm not sure why I'm bothering.'

Ten excruciating minutes later, the buzzer went. 'Sorry, Rita; there's someone at the door. I really have to go. Email me. Let me know what you need me to do.'

'Chance would be a fine thing. Goodbye.'

Lily opened the door. The Polish girl, the one Nathan had said was Sophia's sister, was leaning against the wall. She looked drunk, and she smelled bad. Stale perfume, alcohol, sweat and more. Her top had slipped off one shoulder. The tattoo Lily had noticed the first night was a small rose. In the sunlight that flooded the common stair, Lily could see the faint remnants of a black eye, through layers of heavy foundation.

'I need speak to him.'

Lily smiled. 'Who?'

'Tony.'

Lily shook her head. 'Sorry; there's no Tony here.'

The girl's mouth twisted into a sneer, revealing a daub of claret coloured lipstick on her front teeth. 'I think yes.'

Lily shrugged. 'It must be another address.'

From upstairs, Ronan yelled. 'Mama. Up. Now.'

The girl's eyes widened. Her mouth dropped open. Above her head, a spider dangled from a long thread of silk. Someone opened the door downstairs, and the spider was taken this way and that by the breeze that swept up the stairs. 'Sorry,' Lily said. 'I have to go.'

The girl shook her head, then she spat on the ground. She glared at Lily, hatred in her dark eyes. 'He don't love you, Tony. You will see.'

The spider landed on the girl's head and left with her. Lily closed the door and leaned against it. She could hear the high heels clacking down the stairs, and the harsh bang of the door.

They met Julie at a café in the Grassmarket. Lily's appetite had left her, along with the Polish girl. She ordered a coffee. When Julie's pizza came, Lily refused a slice. 'I need to lose some weight. The dress will be too tight. No more of your lunches for me. I'll bring something for myself on Friday. I can bring yours too, if you like.'

Julie shook her head. 'You're all right, thanks. I've seen your sandwiches. So, what's up? Is it him?'

Lily smiled. 'Nothing gets past you. It's not Nathan. Just a strange girl that came to the door looking for someone called Tony. She unsettled me.'

Lily didn't mention the thing that had unsettled her most: the rose tattoo. It was exactly like a tattoo Nathan had asked her to get, not long after they met. She stirred her coffee and glanced at Ronan. He was smiling and munching his cheese and carrot sticks, happy as ever. 'Nathan announced today he's not going on the course next week. Doesn't want to leave us alone. I was really looking forward to it. He's not a lot of fun lately.'

'Was he ever?'

Lily shrugged. 'Occasionally. It wasn't all bad.'

'Do you think he's seeing Sophia?'

'No sign of her perfume.'

Julie was staring over Lily's shoulder. Lily followed her gaze. David Gunn was standing in the doorway of the shop next to the café. He smiled and turned away.

'Who's that?'

Lily felt her face redden. 'David. He's a policeman. We've spoken a couple of times.' She hadn't seen him for a while. She'd sensed him sometimes, turned, thinking he was there, but he wasn't.

'Interesting. He's been watching you for ages.'

'Maybe he was watching you.'

Julie laughed. 'I've had my share of younger guys, but not that young, and certainly not that hot. It was definitely you. Anything you want to tell me?'

'No. Would you mind having Ronan for a wee while? It's nothing to do with David. I won't be long.'

Julie nodded. 'Take as long as you like. We'll go to the Museum of Childhood.'

Chapter 21

SAM

EYE CONTACT. WHAT's so difficult about it? So, you don't have any spare change, or you do, and you don't want to part with it, for whatever reason, and said reason is none of my business. That's fine. But why pretend you can't see me? Are you scared I'll get into your head? Eye contact will form a contract between us? If you look, you'll have to give? Maybe it's not just me. Maybe you give no one eye contact.

But, wait. What's this? A wee glance. A nod. I like a nod. And a God bless you. I appreciate that. Doesn't mean I believe, but if you do, and you want to bestow some mythical divine goodwill upon me, go for it. Oh, a smile. Lovely. Sometimes a smile is even better than money.

Sam laughs aloud. He's quite the philosopher today. The sober philosopher. He's going to stay that way. Can't just be giving in to the urge whenever it takes him. If he drinks morning, noon and night, there'll be no pleasure left in it. It's been a good morning. The sun's shining. A lovely lady brought him a sandwich. He's got a card in his pocket that's making him think. He got it last night, down the Grassmarket at the soup van, from Peter, who works at the dry hostel. They had quite a chat. No pressure, no preaching. Just sensible talk about life on the streets. It took a while to dawn on Sam that Peter had been there, too. The way he described the negatives: boredom, lack of privacy and toilet facilities, vulnerability, territoriality. And the positives: living life entirely in the moment, having only basic survival necessities to worry about, and answering to no one. Peter knew, and it wasn't just from talking to others. He'd nodded when Sam asked if he'd been on the streets. He'd shrugged at the question of what had changed that, and said he'd tell Sam another time. Hah. A cunning ruse. Sam can't resist a good story.

He squints up at the sun, feels it seep through his outer shell, warming him to his heart. Life's not so bad. Not really. And then he sees Lily on the other side of the street, tension weighing her down. Her steps are fast and timid, her confidence gone. She waves, but there's no smile. And the day is spoilt.

Someone stops beside him. Black boots. His heart dances, but the feet are a little longer and broader than the pig's. Sam looks up and sees PC Gunn. He's not in uniform and he's staring after Lily, his gaze heavy with longing, and more than a little concern. He shakes his head, then he smiles at Sam, a weary smile.

'How are you doing?'

Sam grins. 'Very well, thank you. Do you know my friend, Lily?'

A flush creeps up the constable's neck. He nods. 'We've met a couple of times. Have you recovered from your injuries?'

Sam nods and holds up his left hand. 'Look at the good job they did. You'd never know. Not like these two.' He holds up his right hand with the twisted fingers.

'You didn't get those seen to, though, did you?'

'No. It was pride, mostly. Didn't want to admit I'd been attacked by a size six stiletto.'

PC Gunn nods. 'That's understandable. The room in Dalkeith, in your friend's flat – it didn't come to anything?'

Sam could listen to his accent all day. He shrugs. 'Wasn't to be. Are you from Lewis, Constable?'

'Aye, how did you guess?'

'I had a… I knew someone from Ness. He and I were … ach, never mind what we were. He was a fine man. I loved to hear him speak the Gaelic. *Mach à seo*, he used to say. I can't remember what it means.'

PC Gunn smiles. 'It means 'let's go', or, literally, 'out of here'.'

Sam nods. 'I'll remember that.'

Such intensity in the constable's eyes. 'The man that attacked you – if you ever want to tell me anything about him, you can. On or off the record.'

Sam nods. 'I appreciate that.'

PC Gunn squats and tucks something into Sam's jacket pocket. He groans as he pushes himself to his feet.

Sam waves. *'Mach à seo.'*

The constable laughs. 'Take care.'

When he's gone, Sam checks his pocket. Ten pounds. It's a kindness and a curse. He had wanted so much to keep a clear head until tomorrow. Now, his mouth waters and his heart beats just a little faster.

Chapter 22

LILY

LILY HADN'T BEEN sure if she'd recognise Sophia again, having only seen her from behind, but there was no mistaking that hair or the attitude. She came out of her workplace with her phone to her ear, her right hand gesticulating. Lily crossed the road and followed her. Sophia was angry and loud. People were staring and turning their heads as she walked by, but she couldn't have cared less. She stopped at traffic lights, and Lily hid behind a large man. She could still hear Sophia, and then she couldn't. Lily glanced round the man and saw Sophia running across the road. The lull in the traffic was short-lived, and she feared she would lose her if the lights didn't change soon. And then she was across the road and turning the corner. Sophia was waiting. She grabbed Lily by the wrist. 'Why you follow me?'

She had ivory skin, high cheek bones and dark brown eyes. She was arrogant and beautiful. Though the harshness of her stare made Lily feel about twelve, she would not show it. She pulled her arm free. She almost laughed when she saw Sophia was wearing the infinity bangle Nathan had bought for her. 'Why was your sister at my door?'

'I do not know what you talk about.'

'Who's Tony?'

There was a hint of uncertainty in Sophia's eyes. She shrugged.

'You can't have Nathan, so you sent your sister to my door pretending to look for someone else.'

Sophia's laughter brought a chill to Lily's blood. She shivered as Sophia leaned towards her. The stench of her perfume was stifling. 'Have him? Are you mad? I don't want your fiancé.' The last word was filled with loathing. 'He is weak and stupid. And you too, if you keep him. He come to me with your brat. He want to stay with me, but I won't have him. So he crawl back to you, and you take him.' She shook her head. 'You are pathetic. You and him. Do not come near me again.'

*

YOU ARE PATHETIC. Sophia's words taunted Lily, keeping her awake. When she threw off the quilt, Nathan stirred. She waited until his breathing settled, then she crept downstairs. She laughed too loudly when she discovered *Ronan* was now Nathan's laptop password. Had he changed it the day Sophia turned him down? There was nothing interesting in his inbox. She checked his contacts list, and she was there. Sophia Lesinska. He'd kept none of her emails, nor any that he'd sent her. But there was something in his trash folder. An email in another language from an Aleksander Bartosz, sent to Sophia and copied to Nathan. There were pictures attached. She flicked through them. Headshots of young women, little more than girls. Not one of them was smiling. When she saw the last picture, her heart leapt. It was Sophia's sister, though there was no resemblance between them. Lily considered forwarding the email to herself, or highlighting the text and pasting it into Google Translate. But it was too risky.

She was about to shut down the laptop when she noticed a folder named *Lily* on his desktop. She clicked on it, expecting photos. He'd taken so many in the early days, especially when they were on holiday. But there were no mementos of better times in the folder. Just Word documents. She read them all, and she wanted to go to the kitchen and get the sharpest, longest knife, and drive it through Nathan's heart.

Chapter 23

DAVID

David fielded his mother's probing questions on the phone. Everything was fine. Yes, he'd take leave and come home soon. Aye, he was looking after himself and eating well. No, he didn't need her to send a parcel of Tolsta beef and machair potatoes. He changed the subject, but it didn't remove the concern from his mother's voice. How come she always knew when something was wrong? A text arrived from Eva. Did he want to see a film? David didn't know what he wanted, other than to get rid of his mother. He'd phone her soon, he said.

David liked Eva. At work, she acted as if nothing had ever happened between them, and he was almost certain she wouldn't make things difficult if it didn't work out. They'd gone for drinks a few times, always at her suggestion, and always ending up back at her flat. There had been no more tears. She took his mind off everything for a time, but he always made an excuse not to stay over. He was a light sleeper, he said. Had to get up early. Didn't want to disturb her. He wasn't sure she believed him, but he couldn't risk staying. Not with the nightmares and something that had felt like a panic attack when he woke one morning the previous week. He'd gone for a sprint round Roseburn Park, leaving the panic behind, although its shadow had lingered all day. Tonight, he was fed-up. Another lonely evening in the flat might make him call his mother back and confess all.

They saw *Bohemian Rhapsody*. It turned out Eva knew everything there was to know about Freddy Mercury and Queen. Though she enjoyed the film, she reeled off a list of factual inaccuracies when they went for a drink afterwards. She seemed particularly aggrieved that 'Fat Bottomed Girls' was actually written four years later than portrayed in the film.

She hinted at going to his place. It was a mess, he lied. He'd be embarrassed. She grimaced. 'Okay. I know exactly what you mean. I have brothers. We'll go to mine this time. And no sneaking out when I fall asleep. Please.'

In the night, he surfaced from a dream of drowning, seaweed wrapped around his ankles, dragging him to the depths of the ocean. He was clinging to Eva, as if she was a life raft.

Chapter 24

SAM

LILY'S RADIANCE HAS tarnished a little. It's subtle. Her smile is bright, but it doesn't reach her eyes. She still stops and speaks. She buys Sam food, and brings him books. Lily has good taste. They're mostly Scottish, a mix of classics and contemporary. Sam doesn't tell her he's read all the classics before, that there was a time when he knew *The Prime of Miss Jean Brodie*, *Sunset Song*, and Hogg's *Private Memoirs and Confessions of a Justified Sinner* inside out. Hogg's novel has blown her away, just as it did him when he first read it. So long ago. Another life. Another world. He smiles at her excitement, takes the book from her, and studies it as if he has never seen it. When he's read it, they debate whether Gil-Martin is Satan or a figment of Wringhim's imagination.

Religion has been on Sam's mind since the other night, when he met Peter again at the soup van. It was no surprise to find the church had been responsible for saving Peter, so to speak. They've tried to ensnare Sam often enough, those eager-eyed street preachers with their pristine clothes and fresh faces. Look like they've been sterilised in bleach. They mean well, but he's always felt it only fair to tell them from the start they're wasting their time. He saw what religion did to his father. Turned him from a

90

happy drunk to a miserable sod, convinced of his and everyone else's sin. Even Sam's mother preferred the drunk to the zealot. But Peter seems different. His way is just to tell, without preaching. He gets Sam's cynicism, his reluctance. He tells Sam the church is not for everyone. Perhaps it's only for those who need it, and perhaps Sam doesn't need anything. Sam needs something, all right. He needs to see a doctor. His legs are giving him gyp, and sometimes he wakes up and he can't breathe. Maybe Peter could help him with that. Maybe he'll ask him next time. Or maybe he'll just drink himself senseless, so he can't feel the pain.

Chapter 25

LILY

Margaret's front door was open, and she was on the step, smiling as she watched Julie park the van. Her hands were clasped, and she was bouncing on her toes. Lily laughed. 'She's so cute.'

Julie smiled. 'Do you think she needs to pee?'

'She's just excited. She was having another counselling session yesterday. Must have gone well.'

Margaret had been busy. The kitchen table was clear and gleaming, and there were three available chairs. There was no space underneath the table, for everything that had been on it was now on the floor.

Lily had read everything she could find about hoarding, from causes and characteristics to risks and reasons. If the psychological causes weren't addressed, the problem couldn't be solved, hence the counselling. It seemed to be working. Margaret had made great progress, but there was still a lot to do. It was going to take time and money. Lily had seen Margaret's bank statements. She could well afford it.

Until now, they'd eaten lunch in the van. Today, Margaret insisted they have it at her kitchen table. She brought out a box of photographs. Father and mother, their sepia fathers and mothers, and everyone's brothers and sisters, aunts, uncles and cousins.

'That's my brother, Tommy.' Margaret pointed to a young boy in a black-and-white photograph. 'He was such a rascal. Father said he wouldn't make it past the age of ten if he didn't stop climbing trees and running along high walls. He made it to twenty-one, and he lived every minute of his life to the full. When he was in the house, his music would be blaring – the Beatles, the Monkees, Pink Floyd. And when he was out, you wouldn't believe how many fathers came to our door looking for their daughters. Father would stare at them over his heavy black spectacles and tell them he did not know the whereabouts of their offspring. They might wish to try a ball and chain in future.

'Tommy died in his bed. They never discovered what caused it. I was glad he'd been a rascal. I should have tried it myself, instead of always doing what I was told.' She smiled at Lily. 'I was quite pretty, you know. I'm sure I could have found someone to marry, but I didn't want to leave Mother and Father on their own after Tommy died. It would have been cruel. I did start university. History. I loved it, but Father took ill, and Mother couldn't cope, so I gave it up. By the time they'd passed away, it was just too late for me. Are either of you married?'

They both shook their heads.

'I expect you're past it, like me,' Margaret said to Julie.

Julie laughed. 'Probably.'

Margaret turned to Lily. 'You're very bonny. It won't be long until someone snaps you up.'

Julie's eyebrows were raised, as if she expected Lily to mention her forthcoming wedding. Lily said nothing. Lunch was done. Julie looked at her watch.

'Sorry, ladies. You have work to do.' Margaret put the handful of photos on the table. 'It's just so good to have people to talk to.'

Julie smiled. 'Why don't you and Lily spend a little more time looking at the photos? I'll make a start on the boxroom.'

When Julie was gone, Margaret smiled at Lily. 'I'm glad it's just us. I wanted to show you a photograph of Tommy and his girlfriend, Isobel.' She delved into the tin, oblivious to the photos that fell around her feet. Lily stooped to pick them up. As she put the fallen photos on the table, she saw a group of girls surrounding a man. Was that Margaret at the front? She was pretty.

'Here it is.' Margaret grasped the photo. 'Isn't Isobel lovely?'

Isobel was lovely. She had cropped dark hair and an elfin face, a short skirt and long boots, a cigarette holder in her right hand, her left hand resting on Tommy's knee.

Margaret smiled. 'I took this picture in Princes Street Gardens. Isobel Fleming. She worked in a baker's shop on Rose Street. She was from Oxgangs. That wasn't good enough for Mother, but Tommy loved her.' Her smile was gone, a shadow of tears in her eyes. 'Do you know if it's possible to find people?' She put the picture on the table and clasped her hands. 'I hear about the webs and the nets and that electrical mail, but I know nothing about that sort of thing. I'd like to find Isobel. I once tried an advert in the paper, but I got no response.'

Lily nodded. 'I could try the internet. If you write Isobel's full name and anything you know about her – addresses, date of birth, family members. I'll have a look later.'

Margaret shook her head. 'I can't ask you to do that. It would be so much work.'

'Not really. I just need to type her name into the search engine, and take it from there.'

'An engine? My goodness.'

'Not that kind of engine. It's hard to explain. Maybe I could bring my iPad with me on Friday and we could do it together?'

'Your eye pad? Whatever good would that do?'

Lily laughed. 'I'll bring it and show you.' She stood. 'Let's see how Julie's doing in the boxroom.'

Margaret noticed the photos Lily had placed on the table. 'That's me in my final year at school.' She lifted the top photo. 'There's Ruth and Susan and Mildred. She had terrible bad breath,

Mildred. Like a dead rat in a sewer.'

'Who's the man?'

Margaret blushed. 'Mr Murray. He was our English teacher, just newly qualified. I liked him. Look.' She pointed at his face. 'He had the loveliest smile and such a gentle manner. He came to the house to tutor Tommy, too. I dreamt of marrying him. I wouldn't have called him Samuel. It didn't suit him. He was a Sam. My Sam.' She put the photo down. 'Silly me. I don't know what became of him.'

Lily looked closer. Those eyes. That smile. She knew exactly what had become of him. It was her Sam.

Chapter 26

LILY

If NATHAN SCRAPED his bitten finger-nails along the edge of the table mat one more time, Lily might start screaming and never stop. Two hours it had taken her to make the chilli, and he'd hardly touched it. Not that there was anything special about it. It just wasn't easy to feed and bath Ronan, and put him to bed while trying to cook a meal.

'Are you all right, love?'

She nodded and tried to force a smile. It was getting more and more difficult to be civil to Nathan. He seemed to be trying. Last week, she'd shrunk his favourite wool jersey in a hot wash. The week before, she'd knocked his phone into the sink when he left it on the kitchen windowsill. Maybe if he'd known neither incident was accidental, he'd have reacted differently, but both times he just shrugged and said it couldn't be helped. His grown-up responses had made her feel childish. But then she'd remembered the folder on his laptop, and she'd started plotting her next petty act of revenge.

Now, it looked like he'd had enough of playing nice. He frowned and pushed his plate away. 'Obviously spending time with me isn't as attractive as spending time with that ... with Julie.'

Lily wanted to take the plate and shove it in his face. See the shock in his eyes, and the chilli sliding down his white shirt. 'You could have spent the last two hours with me,' she said. 'But you sat on your arse watching TV.'

His eyes widened, and she knew the battle that was going on in his head. Lash out? Back down? He reached across the table for her hand. God, he really wasn't himself these days. 'I'm sorry. I've got a lot going on at work. Listen, your work – are you sure about it?'

'Quite sure.' She pulled her hand away. 'I enjoy it.'

'Pardon me for worrying about you.' And now there was an edge to his voice, one she hadn't heard for a long time. It made the hairs on the back of her neck rise. He cocked his head, a nasty smile on his face. 'See when I picked Ronan up today, he didn't want to come with me. Kept saying *Mama, Mama, Mama* in that whiny way of his. You've made him soft. He's not walking. He's hardly talking, except for his whining. I'm not having it. I'll do whatever it takes to toughen him up. Beat a little sense into him if I have to.'

Lily's throat tightened until she could hardly breathe. She shook her head. He laughed. 'Hasn't worked with you, though, has it? I'll just have to try harder with him.'

There was a knife beside the sink. A six-inch blade. She imagined reaching for it. Slashing his face. His neck. His heart. Nathan's eyes followed hers. He smirked. Lily gathered up the plates and went to the sink. She could feel the weight of his eyes, and the expectation of a hand in her hair; her face plunged into the lukewarm water in the sink.

Nothing happened. She tipped the bowl and watched the particles of rice swirl into the sink, caught in the little mesh trap, stopping the last of the water from escaping. She filled the bowl with fresh water, then she reached for the saucepans, the grater, the knife. She didn't hear him move. Just felt his right hand covering hers, pressing the knife into the worktop. His breath was warm on her neck, his hips pushing her against the sink. He was turned on for the first time in weeks.

'I've missed this.' His hands were on her breasts. Her hand

was still on the knife. She wrapped her fingers round the shaft. Glancing down, she saw his right thigh pressed against hers. Just one downward movement. That's all it would take. Wouldn't kill him, but it'd be a start.

'Go on, Lily.' His whispered words caressed her neck, her ear. 'I dare you.'

She slid the knife across the worktop and plunged it into the sink.

He laughed, and let her go, then he picked up his phone and keys from the worktop. 'I'll phone later. Don't let it ring too long.'

*

THERE WAS A chilly wind blowing across the Gardens. On the balcony, Lily shivered and felt all the words jumping and poking inside her head, like birds trapped in a cage, wings flapping against the bars, beaks pecking. She closed her eyes and settled her breathing, then she released the words, imagining their twisted shapes smoothing and relaxing in the wind. She saw them scatter across the Gardens, falling into the fountain, on the train tracks, into cracks and crevasses, disappearing. Gone.

She called Julie. 'It's over,' she said. 'We're leaving.'

'What happened? Did he hurt you?'

'No. He threatened to hurt Ronan, and I wanted to kill him. I'm scared I'll do something to him if I stay. He's … he's been having me followed. Someone has been watching me, reporting back to him. I found files on his laptop. No name, but I presume it's a private investigator.'

Julie took a sharp breath. 'Is he there? Do you want me to come for you?'

'He's at work. Thank you, but I'm going to do this properly. I've been looking at places on the internet. I was thinking maybe Perth or further north. Will you help me move?'

'You know I'll do anything to help, but do you want to leave Edinburgh?'

'No, but renting here is too expensive.'

'I'll call you back.'

Within minutes, Lily's phone rang. 'Philip has a friend with a place in Polwarth,' Julie said. 'James – he's in France for at least a year. Philip just called him. He said you can stay there until he comes back. He just wants enough to cover the bills. Lily, say something. Lily … are you crying?'

She was.

When the call ended, Lily composed herself, went inside, and started planning. It wouldn't be easy. Even when Nathan was at work, he was in the habit of coming home unexpectedly. It would be much easier to leave if he was going on the course.

The phone rang again. 'Hi, honey.' Nathan's voice was warm and soft. 'How you doing? It's quiet here. I'm looking at holidays on the internet. Do you fancy Lapland at Christmas?'

Lately, she'd wondered if he was mentally ill. Now she was certain of it. 'Are you serious?' Her voice sounded hard and bitter.

'Yeah. Ronan would love it. And it would make up for us not having a honeymoon. Listen, Lily, what I said about –'

Someone spoke to him. She could hear his muffled response. She waited, wondering what he'd been about to say. Surely not an apology.

He was back, his voice lowered. 'Sorry, love. The course. I've decided to go after all. I'll be away from Saturday for a week. Do you think you guys will be okay?'

Lily had her hand over her mouth, but the laughter kept escaping around it. She breathed and snorted and dropped the phone.

'What's that noise, Lily?'

She calmed herself and picked up the phone. 'Sorry, I dropped the phone. Next week? It'll be really difficult, but I think we'll manage.'

'Are you sure?'

'Absolutely. Is it Saturday to Saturday?'

'Yeah.'

Lily punched the air. 'That'll be fine.'

Chapter 27

LILY

LILY WAS GETTING used to subterfuge. Pubs and shops with two entrances were handy, especially if the entrances were on different streets, like Deacon Brodies, Jenners and Marks and Spencer. She'd nip in one door and out the other. Once, she went into a shop that sold sex toys, browsed for a while, told them she was being followed by an abusive ex-boyfriend, and they'd let her nip out the fire exit at the back. It was pouring that day, and she really hoped the person Nathan had hired to follow her was standing out in the rain for a good long time, waiting for her to emerge. She wondered if Nathan might drop a hint about her drinking habits and her choice of shops, but he didn't say a word. She'd tried to get into his laptop again a few times, but he'd changed the password. Maybe she was no longer being followed, but she wasn't prepared to take any chances with her new address.

All the way to Polwarth, she kept looking in the side mirror. There was a lot of traffic, and it was impossible to know if they were being followed. They'd made a plan. When they arrived at the flat, Julie would take her clipboard up with her, to make it look as if they were pricing a job.

The flat was tidy and a little sparse. It reminded Lily of the place she'd shared in Aberdeen in third year, with its high ceilings and wooden floors. And she needed to be reminded of that time, a time of promise and awakening. From the living room window, she scoured the street below for signs of the private investigator. No one seemed remotely interested in the van or the flat. She could see straight into another living room. And that was fine. The view from Ramsay Garden was only worth so much. And, though she loved the apartment, she'd never felt at home there.

Julie went to work in the afternoon, leaving Lily and Ronan at her house. While Ronan stalked the cat, Lily looked at nurseries and child-minders on the internet. There was a nursery within walking distance of the flat, and several child-minders. They were all cheaper than the nursery, but how was she to know what was best?

By visiting them, Julie told her when she phoned mid-afternoon. Good idea, but Lily wasn't sure she could even afford a child-minder. Julie said she had to stop worrying. 'You can work at least another day a week with me. And make sure you choose a childminder that's registered with the childcare voucher scheme.'

'I don't know what that is.'

'Google it.'

Lily was doing a lot of googling. She'd considered password-protecting her iPad and netbook. But it would only alert Nathan. Instead, she deleted items from her browsing history – council tax, nurseries, child-minders, contact with fathers, child support, tax credits. She left searches and webpages to do with hoarding and weddings and recipes, fashion and child development.

'Julie, it's scary. I don't how I'm going to afford this.'

'You'll manage. Have you got access to any joint money? You know he's going to stop that as soon as he realises you've gone.'

'I've got a credit card. And there's a joint account.'

'You should think about transferring some of that money into your own account.'

'But it belongs to Nathan.'

'You wouldn't be doing anything wrong. If he was the only one that could touch it, it wouldn't be a joint account. You're going to need it for Ronan.'

She'd think about it when he was gone.

*

MARGARET AND THE iPad were inseparable. Wasn't technology marvellous, she said, and why hadn't she spent her money on this kind of thing, instead of buying all that junk that just took up space? She kept trying to zoom in on things. It didn't always work, and sometimes she looked ready to give the iPad a good shake. Lily would distract her with a new pile of documents or photographs, then she'd hide her device somewhere safe.

Margaret had made tremendous progress. Though there were things she might never part with, she was seeing her hoarding in a whole new light.

'Rubbish. Rubbish. Rubbish.' She'd throw things across the room, and Julie would have them out before she could change her mind.

'Keeping. Mine. Precious.' And no one could take these things from her.

The boxes of legal papers turned out to be university notes, articles and print-outs of reported cases. Whoever had come and taken papers away after Margaret's father's death had done a good job. There were no confidential documents left.

Lily hadn't got far in the search for Isobel Fleming, Margaret's late brother's girlfriend. There were several people with that name on Facebook, but none that matched the age Isobel would be now.

'She was a couple of years older than me.' Margaret's face was solemn. 'Could have pegged it by now. Or changed her name. She probably married. That's what people did in her situation.'

'What situation?'

A tear trickled down Margaret's cheek. She wiped it away. 'She was expecting Tommy's baby when he died. He didn't tell Mother and Father.'

Lily took her hand. 'So, you might have family after all?'

Margaret shrugged. 'They probably didn't tell the child. Poor thing maybe hasn't a clue who he or she really is. I wish I knew. I won't last forever. It would be nice to have family to pass this place to.' Her eyes widened. 'Isobel had a brother. What was his name again? Think. Think.' She opened her eyes and frowned. 'I just can't remember.'

'Let me know if it comes to you.' Lily ignored the look from Julie that said she was mad.

Julie was reversing out of the driveway when Margaret pulled the front door open and ran down the path, arms waving like a windmill. Lily wound down her window.

'Trevor!' Margaret yelled. 'His name was Trevor.'

Chapter 28

SAM

SAM'S GUTS HAVE been taunting him for days, and now there's a pain behind his ribs like he's never felt before. It's his heart. It has shattered into a million pieces, each one sharp and pointy and deadly. They're poking and scratching and tearing, ripping the inside of his chest to bits. He wants to cough, but the blood will spill out all over Lily's fancy sandals. He stares up at her and forces a smile. It feels like the rictus grin on the corpse he once found in a doorway on the Bridges. 'Polwarth?' His voice sounds squeaky. The sharp bits have ripped his throat too. 'Next week? Is it the wedding already? Is that why you're moving?'

She shakes her head and looks behind her, lowers her voice. 'I'm not getting married. He was ... he's ... it's not the right thing for me. We need a new start, just me and Ronan.'

He's swamped with pity for the poor man that's losing her. And there's self-pity too, in buckets. She crouches and puts her hand on his arm. 'I'll still come and see you; I promise. Just not every day. And I'll keep your suitcase, if you want me to.'

He nods. 'I'd like that. I just want you to be happy, Lily. You and the boy.'

'I am happy.'

And she is. There's confidence and hope in her smile. She takes a sandwich and a bottle of water from her bag. He's not hungry, but he smiles and thanks her.

'Sam, there's something I wanted to ask.'

He nods. 'Ask away.'

'Were you ... are you ...?' She shakes her head, and it's clear she's changed her mind. She's searching now for something else to say, and her eyes won't meet his. 'Where are you sleeping now?'

'Here and there. Don't worry about me. You have enough on your plate.'

He waves her off. When she's out of sight, he fumbles for his half-bottle and drains it. He needs more. A bottle. There's enough money in his pocket and he might as well spend it all. The state he's going to be in, it's best if he has nothing left for sticky little fingers to lift.

Sam donates his sandwich to a skinny beggar on the High Street, a young man he hasn't seen before. You'd think he'd been given a nugget of gold, the way he thanks Sam. Off to the shop for a bottle, then he slips into Fleshmarket Close. His mouth waters. This is the way to blessed oblivion. It'll settle his heart and his stomach. An arm from behind stops the bottle. If it's the pig, he'll kill him. And not before time. But it's PC Gunn.

'Sam, what's wrong?'

Sam shakes his head. 'It's the ... it's my friend, Lily.'

There's a dark shadow of terror on the constable's face. 'Has something happened?'

'She's... she's not getting married.'

The terror's replaced by a strange half-smile. It's a little unsettling.

'She's going to live in Polwarth,' Sam says. 'I'll hardly see her. My heart ... it's in bits.'

Chapter 29

DAVID

Lily was leaving Collesso. She wasn't getting married. David wanted to yell in triumph. Instead, he put his hand on Sam's shoulder and tried to ignore the pungent smell of stale urine. To be fair, it probably wasn't coming from Sam. Edinburgh society might have moved on from the Middle Ages, when people emptied their chamber pots out the window, but there were still too many people, mostly men, that couldn't be bothered finding the nearest public toilet when they were caught short. It was a sad fact that one of the highlights of David's job was issuing fixed penalty notices to the culprits.

'Polwarth's not far, Sam,' David said. 'I'm sure you'll still see her. When does she go?'

'Next week.'

'You take care of yourself. Go easy on that stuff, eh?'

Sam tried to smile. 'I know you mean well, but this is all that's going to get me through the next few days. I can't tell you what she means to me. Stupid fool that I am.'

'You're not a fool. We all need good friends.'

'She's the best.'

David nodded. 'I'm sure she is. I have to get off. A plague of shoplifters down in Waverley Mall.'

Sam grimaced. 'Waverley Mall? Is that what we're calling it now? I've a lot of time for Americans, but really?' He shook his head. 'Our language is going to the dogs. You get off, Officer. Take a hike along the sidewalk, why dontcha?'

His attempt at an American accent made David laugh. 'I'll look out for you later if I'm up this way.'

'My apologies in advance for the state you're going to find me in.'

Fleshmarket Close was cut in two by Cockburn Street. David crossed the road and hurried down the steep steps of the close, then through Waverley Station. He expected to see Eva outside Waverely Mall on Princes Street, but two of his male colleagues were waiting for him. He didn't ask where she was.

The shoplifters were a gang of twelve-year-old girls. One of them kicked David in the shins and did a runner. He set off after her, but she was like a bullet darting between shoppers. She was at the top of the escalator, laughing, while he was still at the bottom. He let her go. He wasn't bothered about the stick he was going to get off his colleagues for losing a kid, still bathing in the warm glow from the discovery that Lily was leaving Collesso.

Back at the station, something was going on. He heard Eva's name whispered, and he hoped it was nothing to do with him. They were keeping things quiet for now, rather than have to go through the rigmarole of reporting their relationship and being put on different shifts, not to mention all the leg-pulling.

Turned out Eva was off sick. She'd been on a colleague's hen night the previous evening, and she'd texted David early on, complaining she was sober while everyone else was steaming. Taking it easy, she'd said, because she was working the next day. He'd wondered if she'd be in touch later, but she wasn't. He'd thought of texting her at bedtime, but he didn't want to intrude.

There were a couple of others on duty that had been on the hen night. By the state of them, they hadn't been taking it easy. Alison Blyth, a tiny scrap of an officer with the bravado of a rottweiler, threw up twice before someone persuaded her to eat a slice of toast. It seemed to help, but she looked rough all day. And she kept glancing at David as if she wanted to say something. He wondered if Eva had got drunk after all, and spilled. He'd find out later.

Chapter 30

LILY

THE COLLESSOS WERE coming for dinner. Lily had made a special effort for their last meal. Tomorrow, Nathan would go on his course, and she would be free. While she prepared the meal, Nathan played with Ronan. He fed him and bathed him. He'd have put him to bed, too, but Ronan wanted his mum. She took him from Nathan. 'Come on; we can both do it.'

They were at the bottom of the stairs when someone knocked on the door.

'They're early.' Lily reached for the door. 'Ronan, it's Nana –'

But it wasn't. It was a young woman with poker straight blonde hair. She was wearing a transparent top, short skirt and long boots. She looked ill, her face pale and her body shaking. Lily was certain she'd seen her before, but she couldn't think where. The girl stared at Lily and Ronan, and took a step backwards, a look of disbelief on her face. She spoke, and it sounded like Polish. The only word Lily could make out was *Tony*.

Nathan smiled at Lily. 'On you go. I'll get rid of her. I'll be up in a minute.'

Lily hesitated. On the girl's shoulder, there was a small rose tattoo. 'She looks like she needs help.'

Ronan yawned and leaned his head on Lily's shoulder. 'Bed, Mama.'

Nathan kept smiling. 'Go on up.'

From the landing, Lily heard muffled chat, before the girl's voice rose to a screech. She closed the bedroom door until she couldn't hear a thing, but she couldn't shut out the questions in her head. The girls, the tattoos, Tony. What was going on?

''Is one, Mama.' Ronan had picked *Where's Spot?*

She sat on the floor cushions, Ronan snuggled in her lap, and she let the questions go. None of it mattered any more.

Lily fed her guests until they couldn't take another thing. She drank very little, but she kept their glasses full. Nathan and Rebecca didn't argue. When Nathan and his father went out to the balcony for a cigar, Lily enthused over the sample wedding favours Rita had brought. She liked the personalised candle and the message in a wee bottle, but she couldn't decide between them. When did the order have to be in?

Rebecca couldn't resist a swipe. 'Two months ago.'

'Nonsense.' Rita waved her hand. 'There's time. Let me know by the end of next week. Can you give me the recipe for that chocolate and almond cake? I think I'll make it for the showing of the presents, or maybe the pre-wedding dinner. Rebecca, why don't you spend some time with Lily before the wedding? Maybe she could teach you how to bake.'

The look on Rebecca's face. Lily nodded. 'That's a lovely idea. I'll call you.'

'I can't wait.' Was it alcohol or sarcasm that dulled Rebecca's voice?

'Can't wait for what?' Jonathon asked, as he and Nathan came in from the balcony.

'Lily and Rebecca are going to do some baking. Isn't that nice?' Rita waved her empty glass. 'Nathan, do you have brandy? We could toast our forthcoming nuptials.'

'I do. Are you marrying again, Mother?'

Rita laughed. 'Oh, you.'

There was no brandy left by the time the taxi came. Nathan could hardly stand, and the others weren't much better. Lily helped Nathan up the stairs and into the bedroom. She took off his shoes, but that was as far as she was going. He curled into a ball. 'Sorry, love. Fit for nothing. In the morning?'

Aye, right.

Lily sang as she tidied. It was a song in her own language, a song of hope that her mother used to sing. It wasn't often she allowed a memory of her mother to creep in, but tonight was special. As she dried up, she threw a plate in the air, watched it spin, and considered not catching it. It was one of Nonno Luca's 18th century silver-gilt neoclassical plates. They were family heirlooms. She smiled as she caught it, realising that, for once, Rita hadn't felt the need to remind her of their value tonight.

Nathan didn't stir when she got into bed. He was breathing out fumes that could have paralysed a horse.

*

THE SUN STREAMING through the curtains woke Lily. Or maybe it was Nathan's muttering. A towel round his waist, he was stuffing things into his holdall.

'I'm late, I'm late. Love, I thought you'd wake me. I wanted to say goodbye properly, but my lift's going to be here soon.' He shoved his spongebag into the holdall, then he took it out, followed by a brown envelope and a sweatshirt. 'Did I pack my phone charger? My head's all over the place. Why did you let me drink so much?'

'Mama, Mama, Mama. Dada, Dada.'

Another groan, and he went for Ronan. The unsealed brown envelope lay on the bed. She could hear Nathan pleading with Ronan to stay still. Must be changing his nappy. She lifted the envelope and looked inside. There were three sheets of paper with columns showing sums of money and names. Foreign names. His passport? Maybe he needed it for I/D. She shoved everything back into the envelope.

Ronan's smile was as bright as the morning sun. 'Hey, gorgeous boy.' She took him from Nathan, snuggling her nose into the fragrant folds of his neck.

He squeezed her nose, then Nathan's. 'Pretty Mama. Pretty Dada.'

Their laughter made him giggle, his tummy wobbling. Nathan's eyes were shining and blue. So sincere. He looked at them both as if they were precious. He hadn't done that for months, although he'd been the perfect father and partner, never raising his voice. No animosity, no aggression. But the effort had taken all he had, leaving someone different in his place, a shell of a man. The real Nathan had resurfaced the night of the knife in the kitchen.

His phone beeped, and he stared at the screen, frowning. 'I have to go.' He fumbled in his pocket, then he put a handful of notes on the chest of drawers. 'That should see you through, but there's plenty in the joint account. Bye-bye, my darlings.' As he backed out of the room, he blew kisses. 'I'm going to miss you.'

Ronan waved. 'Bye bye, Dada.'

Chapter 31

LILY

SAM HAD ALMOST finished *The Testament of Gideon Mack*, he told Lily, and a fine book it was too. He'd be needing another one soon. She had a couple in mind, she said. She'd bring them before the end of the week.

He smiled. 'Lily, you look wonderful. This move is the best thing for you, though it's broken my heart. I don't know what your man was like, but I know you wouldn't take the boy away from him without good reason. There are worse things than being alone.'

'That's what Margaret says. She's been alone for a long time.'

'Margaret?'

Lily nodded. 'Margaret Rutherford. She lives in Morningside. We've been working at her house. Her brother, Tommy, died, and she spent her life looking after her parents.' She searched his face. There was something going on behind those dark eyes.

Sam frowned. 'Margaret Rutherford?'

'Do you know her?'

'Should I?'

Lily shrugged. 'Probably not. We better get off. We're going to see some childminders.'

He was still holding her arm. 'Make sure you get a good one.

We don't want any duffers for the boy. That wouldn't do at all.'

*

BY LATE AFTERNOON, the childminders had all blurred into one, until Lily couldn't remember which one smelled bad or had the big garden or the small kitchen or the dodgy looking husband. Her feet were sore and her head was tired, her neck strained from constantly looking over her shoulder. There didn't seem to be anyone following her, but she couldn't relax. And Ronan was grumpy.

Only one more to go, the closest one to the Polwarth flat. The semi-detached house and garden looked immaculate. The woman who opened the door was tall, with short, dark curly hair and a reserved smile. She offered her hand. 'Nina Matthews. Come in.'

There was a toy box in the corner, and Ronan pointed at it. 'Toys.'

Lily put him down on the floor, and he crawled towards it. Through the patio doors, she could see a neat garden with swings, a chute and a climbing frame. There were no toys lying around, not like the garden in Merchiston, where broken dolls and cars without wheels were stamped into the flower beds, as if they'd grown there.

Nina showed Lily her certificates and inspection documents, testimonials and photographs, all kept together in a ring-binder. Lily liked Nina Matthews. She was brusque, but not rude. There would be no nonsense with her, and that was good. Ronan would start there a week tomorrow.

At the doorstep, as she was leaving, Lily swithered over how to word what she wanted to say. 'I'm really sorry if this sounds strange, but if anyone asks about me in the next few days, would you mind saying we're friends and that's why I was here?'

Nina's eyes widened.

'It's just ... his father and I are splitting up, and I don't want him to know where I'm moving to. Not yet.'

Nina smiled and nodded. 'I understand.'

*

PHILIP, JULIE'S NEW partner, was in the armchair by Julie's fireplace. He was reading the Observer, the supplements scattered around him on the floor. He looked very much at home. Cleo was perched on the back of his chair, her eyes closed. Such a scene of bliss. But not for long. Ronan tried to leap from Lily's arms. 'Caaaat!'

Cleo shot up, back arched, hair raised, claws digging into the chair. Lily was glad the cat wasn't sitting on Philip's lap or he might have required intimate medical attention.

Philip glanced over his shoulder. 'Oh dear.'

As Cleo disappeared down the back of the chair, he put the paper down and stood. He had a handsome, kind face, with dark brown eyes, a trimmed beard, and tanned skin. About the same height as Julie, Philip looked at ease with himself. He took Lily's hand in both of his and smiled. She'd been nervous about meeting him, but now she felt herself relax.

Julie came and took Ronan. She had a job for him, she said; he was going to help her shell peas. Lily laughed. 'Good luck with that. If he doesn't eat them all, he can throw them at the cat.'

Philip asked Lily about medical school. He listened intently, leaning towards her. 'Would you consider going back to university here, finishing your degree?'

She shrugged. 'I'd love to, but I can't see how that would work, as a single parent.'

'Where there's a will, and all that. I have some contacts in medicine. Think about it.'

Lily nodded. She'd do that.

Over a wonderful dinner of lamb koftas and minted couscous, Philip asked how Julie and Lily met. They both laughed. He looked from one to the other. 'There's a good story here. I knew it.'

Lily described her first day out with Ronan, and her tiredness as she waited in the queue for the ATM at Waverley Station. Her embarrassment as a pungent scent wafted through the air.

Everyone was looking at her, and Ronan. This tiny silent thing in the pushchair, his face distorted as he kept on squeezing. He didn't even wake up, he was so comfortable in his fragrant, warm bed. Lily wanted to crawl back home, but she needed money and nappies, baby-grows and vests. Exhausted and nervous, she'd made a dash for the baby changing room, leaving her money in the ATM. Julie was behind her in the queue.

Julie grimaced. 'I went to the changing room with her money. Poo was bursting out the sides of the nappy, creeping down his legs and up his back. The smell. I was gagging. And she was just standing staring.'

Lily laughed. 'I hadn't a clue. Julie cleaned him up, and he didn't even waken. We went for coffee, and the smell followed us.'

Julie nodded. 'It was on my hands for days.'

Ronan was looking back and fore between them, as the story was told. When it was done, he banged on the table and laughed.

Chapter 32

LILY

EACH NIGHT, SLEEP was slow in coming, and it didn't stay long. Lily was desperate to be away. Nathan phoned every evening, complaining. The course was boring. His roommate snored. He was missing them. He couldn't wait to get home. She listened and said very little. He'd go mad when he got home and found them gone, but surely he'd see sense, eventually. They weren't right together; they couldn't be. Before long, he'd admit that to himself and his family, and then they could sort out some contact. Maybe.

She borrowed a book of Norse tales from James' bookshelf. At night, she lay in bed and read it, hearing the sing-song, up and down rhythm of her father's voice, telling tales of the gods, Odin, Thor and Frey, and their constant battles with the forces of evil and chaos. She'd fall asleep eventually and dream of her father. It broke her heart to leave him each morning when the alarm brought her round. He'd been gone from her dreams for too long. Was it the promise of her new life that had brought him back? Whatever it was, it was a good thing.

Lily took Ronan to nursery on Friday morning and told the staff she'd collect him early. Back at the apartment, she had everything ready to go as soon as Julie and Philip arrived. She stayed inside while they loaded the van. It wouldn't do to attract the attention of the neighbours or any silent watchers. And though Nathan's family had never shown up without making an appointment, today might be the very day, especially since Lily hadn't contacted Rita about the wedding favours.

When Julie and Philip had left, Lily did a final sweep of the apartment, then she pulled the door closed for the last time. She almost pushed the keys back through the letterbox, but something made her hang onto them, just in case. Nathan wasn't home until tomorrow afternoon, so there was time to come back. Not that she wanted to.

It was exhausting, mistrusting everyone around her. Was that man with the map the private investigator? Might not be a man. Could be that woman posing as a Japanese tourist, or the pretty young girl taking photos. Twice, on the Royal Mile, she darted into a close and exited through the other end, hiding and waiting to see if anyone had followed her. She saw no one. She collected Ronan, and they took a bus to Polwarth. They got off two stops before the flat, and did a few laps of the area, cutting through lanes and hanging around in doorways. They might have gone round for hours if Ronan hadn't got crabbit. He was ready for his nap, and if she wanted it to be a good one, she better get him into his cot soon.

It felt weird to sit in the flat of a man she'd never met, surrounded by his photographs and belongings. His smells. His shape, pressed into the large leather armchair. While Ronan slept, Lily dozed and dreamed of a house beside the sea; the air laden with salt, the constant surge of the ocean on the rocks below. It was home. And its call was stronger than ever. It was hard to leave the dream behind, but Ronan was awake and there was cooking to be done. Julie was coming round soon. Lily was going to try a curry recipe she'd seen on the internet.

She fired up her netbook to check the ingredients, but there was no internet yet. It was going to take a week or two to get it set up. She looked in her bag for the iPad. Not that she'd have much data allowance left after Margaret had been at it. No iPad. Where had she last seen it? In the kitchen at breakfast time.

As she remembered what she'd last done on the iPad, her stomach lurched. She hadn't been sure about it, hadn't really wanted to take Nathan's money, but Julie was right. She had no savings of her own, and she needed it for Ronan. And Nathan owed her, big time. There had been ten thousand pounds in the joint account, and she'd taken half of it. Then she'd put the iPad on top of the fridge freezer.

Chapter 33

SAM

SAM IS STAYING off the grog today. He got a fright in the night. He's still shaking. Demon eyes. Pointed teeth. The breath of a corpse. And claws reaching for him. One pair, and then more and more and more, until he was surrounded. How he had screamed. And then they were kicking him. Vicious blows to a heart that was already bruised. As if the kicking wasn't enough, they grabbed his head and smashed it off the paving stones about a dozen times, until he opened his eyes and found old Johnny Rosco shaking him awake, and telling him to find somewhere else to sleep.

He's all right now. The world must go on. And the feet keep coming. And look, she's back. Lily is back. Has she changed her mind?

'Lily. It's so good to see you. Are you –?'

She looks embarrassed, as if she knows she's raised his hopes. 'I forgot something.'

He nods. 'Where's the boy?'

'He's at the new place with my friend.'

Sam raises his eyebrows. 'A new friend?'

Lily's laughter lightens his mood. 'No. He's with Julie.'

'The clutter buster?'

'The very one. She helped me move my stuff this morning. We took your case. I can't stop, Sam, but I promise I'll be back soon. Maybe need to … maybe leave it a couple of weeks.'

A couple of weeks? Darkness descends again. He forces a smile. 'Can't wait.'

Beyond her smile, there's a shadow of anxiety. She turns and crosses the road. It's busy, but she stays on the outside of the pavement, breaking into a run every now and again. In the gaps between buses and taxis and hordes of people, he watches her until she reaches the corner and the traffic lights. She'll be gone in a moment. Gone again.

His attention is caught by a green van stopping outside the library. When he sees the pig getting out, he spits on the ground. The pig takes off, running along the street towards the traffic lights. He's carrying a holdall, pushing past people and darting onto the road. A car swerves to avoid him, and Sam curses the driver. What he wouldn't give to see that vile beast squashed into the ground. The pig's back on the pavement and almost at the traffic lights. And then he's right behind Lily. Sam can hardly believe his eyes when the pig puts his hand on Lily's shoulder.

'No!' Sam's shout startles a child walking past with her mother. 'Run, Lily. Run!' He's on his feet, stumbling after her, his blanket and cup abandoned.

Sam can smell his own fear as he follows Lily and the pig. Watching that monster pawing at her, arguing with her, forcing her up towards the Castle. It has to be force; Lily can't be going with him willingly.

They turn into Ramsay Lane, and he thinks his chance has come. The pig's looking half-cut and exhausted. He'll get him here, when those three tourists have passed. Lily half turns and he can see her face and it's full of dread. She's looking towards Mound Place, as if she wants to run.

The tourists are gone, but there are more creeping out of the shadows. And then the pig's guiding Lily into Ramsay Garden.

What is going on? Sam follows them to the courtyard. There's no one about now. He's going to take a run at the pig, kick him in the back, knock him over, give Lily a chance to get away. As he prepares to launch himself, a door opens and an older couple come out. They nod at the pig and Lily. The man raises a hand. Something worms its way into Sam's brain. He's not having it. It's shite. It's the drink talking. The couple pass him, and he sees a rock lying on the ground beside the steps. He bends to pick it up, and when he straightens, the door is closing behind Lily and the pig.

Sam races to the door, but he's too late. He slumps against it, weakness washing through him. There's a voice screaming in his head, screaming the truth he's tried so hard to ignore ever since he started following them. The pig. He's Lily's fiancé.

Chapter 34

LILY

LILY THOUGHT THE hand on her shoulder might be David Gunn, but the touch was not kind. A groan rose in her throat and she wanted to sprint across the road, run between the cars and buses and escape. It was too late. Nathan's hand was on her upper arm, squeezing and pulling. He was smiling, but it wasn't real. It was the warning smile, the one that always made her heart beat a little faster. There was whisky on his breath. He had his holdall slung over his shoulder. 'Surprise, honey. Bet you didn't expect to see me.'

Lily stared at him.

'Don't look so happy about it. Have you missed me at all?'

She tried to smile. 'Course I have. Just didn't expect to see you until tomorrow.'

He laughed, and it sounded forced and hollow. Did he know she was leaving? Had the private investigator told him?

'Where's my boy? You haven't left him home alone?'

'Of course not. He's ... he's with Julie.'

'Why isn't he with you? Can't be long since you collected him from nursery.'

'Eh ... they called to say he was grouchy, so Julie and I picked him up early and went back to hers. He fell asleep, and I came

123

out for some shopping. Just heading down to Marks, then I'll get a bus back to Julie's.'

His eyes narrowed. He'd know she was lying. He always did. 'We'll get the car and go for him,' he said. 'Pick up food at Cameron Toll.'

She shook her head. 'You've been drinking. I'll get the bus. I won't be long.'

He frowned. 'I've had one drink. Why do you always make such a fuss? We'll put my bag back and we'll go for Ronan. Okay?'

His voice was too loud, and passers-by were looking at him. Lily smiled. 'Okay.'

The weight of Nathan's arm across her shoulders, guiding her around and between tourists, was unbearable. They were at the corner of Ramsay Garden. What to do? What to do? Go into the flat? Or run? It was tempting. He was half-cut and tired; he'd not bother running after her. But she couldn't leave the iPad.

He didn't say a word as they climbed the stairs. He followed her in and closed the door, but he didn't lock it. That was unusual, but good. She might have to leave quickly. In the kitchen, he dumped his bag on the floor. He ran the cold tap, and Lily's heart somersaulted. Her engagement ring was on the windowsill, and the sun was glinting off the massive diamond. He took a long drink of water. When he was done, he didn't turn. His hands were gripping the sink, and he was silent. Had he seen the ring?

She looked at her iPad, on top of the fridge-freezer. She'd never really liked it. Hadn't needed it, but he'd insisted. Probably easier to use for checking up on her than starting her netbook whenever the fancy took him. No, she'd have gladly left it there if it wasn't for her recent emails. They would lead him straight to her. As soon as he was gone, she'd stopped deleting things. The order for a wi-fi connection at the flat, the Council Tax bill from James, the childminder's emails with her automatic signature that included her address. It had seemed too risky to leave it. And now?

He turned from the sink, and she smiled. 'We don't have to

rush off for Ronan. He's fine with Julie.'

His eyes narrowed. 'So, he's fine with Julie, but not with my family?'

'That was only overnight. You know that.'

His face was twisted with malice. 'Don't tell me what I know, like I'm some kind of imbecile. It's all about you, isn't it? You and Julie and your work. You don't give a shit about me, about what's happening in my life.'

'I don't know why you're being like this, Nathan, but that's not true.'

Big mistake. He smiled as he walked towards her. She could smell sweat. It was so unlike him. 'I'm a liar now? Really?'

Time for a change of tactic. 'You've had a hard week. Do you want to sit down and talk about it? Or ...?'

'Or what?'

'We could go upstairs.' She'd closed the door to Ronan's room, hadn't she? If not, he'd see the cot was gone. 'I've really missed you. We both have.'

His eyes darted back and fore, his head shaking a little, as if he was trying to clear it. Something serious was going on in there. If she could just get him to take a nap. He took off his jacket and put it on the back of a chair. 'Okay. Don't know that I'll be up to much, but we can try.'

She walked up the stairs in front of him, and waited to feel his hands upon her, but he didn't touch her. On the landing, she turned. She wanted to shove him backwards and watch his head smash off each step.

He was frowning. 'Will Julie not be wondering where you are?'

'Probably, but she'll cope.' She kissed him, her lips gentle. 'I've really, really missed you.'

'Me too, love.' There was no feeling in his kiss. Nothing.

He looked upwards, and she did the same. Her heart lurched. The attic hatch was open, the ladder extended. He frowned again. 'Why were you in the attic?'

'I collected the dress. Didn't want you to see it, so I put it up there. Ronan started crying, and I forgot to close the hatch.'

'That's drastic. Couldn't you just have used a protector bag?'

'Hardly. You might have been tempted to look. It's bad luck. Come on. We don't have much time.'

He let her lead him into the bedroom, but he kept turning and looking at the hatch. She pulled him down until they were sitting on the side of the bed. He frowned. 'Lily, there's something I have to ask you first.'

'Yeah?'

'How much was the wedding dress?' That edge in his voice again.

'About seventeen fifty? The accessories brought it to just over two thousand, I think. I know it's a lot of money for a dress for one day.'

He stared at her, his gaze cold and hard. 'I thought it might have been more expensive. Maybe five thousand pounds.'

Run, she told herself. Run. But he was between her and the door. She'd never get past him.

'Are you going to tell me what you did with my money?'

Lily rarely cried unless there was a threat to Ronan, or someone did something very kind for her. She had never cried in front of Nathan, no matter how much he hurt her. It was time for the performance of her life. 'I'm really sorry.' She put her head in her hands and tried to sob. It wasn't easy. 'I just wanted to surprise you.'

His hand was in her hair. It didn't hurt, yet. 'You've done that all right. I thought I could trust you.'

'I was going to repay you from my wages.'

His laughter was loud and harsh. 'At the rate she's paying you? I won't hold my breath.' His hand was tightening in her hair, pulling her head back, exposing her neck. 'You know what happens to thieving little bastards?'

'I'm not a thief. I borrowed it to –'

His hand on her throat, he mimicked her voice. '*I borrowed it.* Taking without permission is not borrowing.' His hand tightened.

'It was for you ... for your wedding present. I ... I paid for it this morning.'

He tugged his hand away. There was spittle in the corners of his mouth, the words forced out through gritted teeth. 'Why didn't you say that earlier? Why do you make me do this? All the time. Why?'

'I'm sorry, Nathan.' She lowered her eyes. They were too dry. He'd know. 'I love you. I wanted it to be special.'

With a groan, his body deflated until he was lying on the bed, staring at the ceiling.

'I'm sorry.' She stroked his face. 'It's probably not too late to get the money back.'

'No. Don't do that.' He frowned and closed his eyes. 'My head. It's so sore.'

'You don't look well.' Her voice was firm. 'I'm going for Ronan. You have a sleep and I'll wake you when we get back.'

He nodded. 'I'm sorry. I'm going to make it up to you.'

'It's okay.' She kissed his cheek for the last time.

Downstairs, her head was thumping, so she ran a glass of water and took some paracetamol. She moved the ring behind a plant pot. He'd find it, eventually. She put the iPad in her bag. A quick text to Julie. *Sorry. Just leaving. Will explain when I see you xx*

His passport was on the kitchen table. She flicked it open. Had he been abroad? There were no stamps on it. A quick look at the back page. It was his photo, but the name was different. Anthony Harris. Maybe it was a mock-up for his course.

Upstairs, his phone rang. She was at the front door when she heard a thump from the lounge. Nathan shouted: 'Lily, what was that?'

Through the door to the balcony, she could see a dazed pigeon. It must have hit the glass door. 'It's just a bird.'

He didn't answer. She heard the floorboards creak upstairs, then his muffled voice.

On the balcony, the bird wasn't moving. She cupped it in her hands and lifted it. There was laughter in Princes Street Gardens. Trains passing through. Trees waving gentle branches. She'd miss this. And though she knew how mad it was, a part of her would miss Nathan and his family. For a time, she'd felt as if she might actually belong somewhere again. She had belonged before. Though life at home wasn't always easy, there were places she could go that filled her heart until it overflowed. She'd wanted to take a job in a shop or a care home, so she would never have to leave her mother and her grandmother. But her stepfather wasn't having it. Not when she was top of the class in everything. It wasn't long before she knew he'd been right to push her. She'd taken a few weeks to get over the homesickness. Lots of phone calls, tears, and a few tantrums. And then, by the end of the first term, it had all fallen into place.

The bird stirred in her hands. A little shake of its feathers, and its eyes focussed. Startled, it stared at her for a moment before taking off. It was time for her to go, too. Time for a new life.

She pulled the balcony door closed. Before she could turn, she heard a sound behind her. The slightest fastest rush of something descending. Something heavy. A sharp pain rang in her head, echoing through her body. She dropped to her knees and heard the clang of metal on the wooden floor. She tried to turn. And everything went black.

Chapter 35

LILY

AFTER THE LONG darkness in her head, the light was slow in coming. Flickering wisps at first. She tried to grasp them, but they were gone. They left the darkness a little less dense, and then the fireflies came, sparking and blinking, lighting the way, just as they had done when she was a child, hiding in a field of corn at dusk. A jar in one small hand, a lid in the other. Pouncing, then holding up the jar. Nothing. And again, and again, while the fireflies blinked all around her. Taunting her until the glass was thrown into the night. Her mother's laughter, and the darkness disappearing. Streaming, dancing lights in myriad colours.

There was a voice, and it made the light brighter. It made her heart soar. The whispered words were like the colours, like her mother's laughter. They were words of love. She didn't open her eyes as someone stroked the back of her hand. She just listened.

Another voice. Harsh. Female. 'You can go now. I'm taking over.'

Don't go. Don't ever go. The colours disappeared along with the reluctant footsteps. She begged them to come back, but they were gone.

'Ms Andersen.' Impatient tones. Cheap body spray, laced with sweat. Lily's eyes opened in protest. She was lying in a bed of white, pristine sheets, and a policewoman was bending over her. She had sharp impatient shoulders, a ruddy face, and distressed wiry hair poking out the sides of her hat. 'I'm Sergeant Rodgers.' Her voice scratched like steel wool. 'I'm taking over from PC Gunn.'

Lily frowned. 'You can't replace him.'

Sergeant Rodgers looked at Lily as if she was a little mad. 'I'll be outside, unless you're ready to talk?'

Lily closed her eyes.

*

WHEN LILY TRIED to sit up, pain and nausea surged through her. She groaned. The nurse frowned. 'Don't move. You've lost a lot of blood, and you're on a drip. No getting up for a while.'

'Where's Ronan?'

'Your wee boy? He's with your friend. She's been phoning. A lot.'

'I need to see him.'

'I'm sorry, but you won't be seeing anyone until they've spoken to you.' She nodded towards the door. 'I've already chased that one out twice. The male officer was all right. He just sat and spoke to you until she told him to go. He seemed very concerned. Do you know each other?'

'A little,' Lily said. 'Not very well. How did I end up in here?'

'You were found in your apartment around seven o'clock last night. Someone called an ambulance. You have a fractured skull, and a broken finger.'

Lily frowned. 'A fractured skull? Temporal? Parietal?'

The nurse grinned. 'I've never had a patient ask that before. You have a linear temporoparietal fracture. You've had a CT scan. No evidence of internal injury, which is fortunate. Are you a nurse or a doctor?'

'I was a medical student. Not now, though.'

'You sound disappointed.'

'A bit.'

'Never too late.'

Lily shrugged. 'Difficult with a wee one. And I'm on my ... on my own. Listen, do you know if Nathan ... if he ...?'

The nurse shook her head. 'I've heard nothing about a Nathan.' She patted Lily's arm. 'I better get ready for the handover. I'm off for the next two days, so I probably won't see you again. You take care.'

*

His HEAD WAS shaped like a turnip, and he had little, weasily eyes. 'I'm Detective Inspector Ford,' he said in a monotonous, nasal pitch. 'You've met Sergeant Rodgers. We have some questions for you, if you feel up to it.'

Lily smiled. 'Don't know how much help I'll be. Post-concussion syndrome can cause odd behaviour. But then I've always been odd, even without a fractured skull. I once told someone I met in a toilet that –'

The frizzy one was scowling. Lily hadn't meant to be flippant. There was a disconnection somewhere between her brain and her mouth. Probably wasn't the best time to be questioned, but DI Ford had looked so desperate, she went along with him. 'What do you want to know?'

He made a sound that might have been a laugh. 'Let me think. Yesterday, you move out of the apartment you shared with your fiancé, Inspector Nathan Collesso. Apparently, he knew nothing about your move. You return to the apartment because you've left your iPad. Your friend and your son are waiting in your new flat at Polwarth, but you don't come back. There's an anonymous 999 call. You're found with a head injury, and your living room looks as if Mohammed Ali and Mike Tyson have gone ten rounds together. Inspector Collesso is missing. What do you think I want to know?'

'Did you like Nathan?'

DI Ford raised his eyebrows. 'Do you know what happened to him?'

Lily shrugged. 'I think he was probably dropped on his head at birth.'

Another voice. Male. Authoritative. 'Ms Andersen is not up to questioning. She needs to rest.'

DI Ford turned away. 'Doctor, we have a missing officer who has lost a great deal of blood. Ms Andersen may be the only person who knows what happened to him. We have to find him as soon as possible.'

The doctor came into view. He looked to be in his late sixties, with a stern face and wild grey hair. He didn't quite smile at Lily, but his features relaxed a little. 'Ms Andersen, you are not obliged to speak to the police. If you wish to do so, I would strongly advise you to have a solicitor present.'

'Doctor, this is not a formal interview.' A hint of desperation in DI Ford's voice. 'We need to find Inspector Collesso.'

The doctor sighed. 'Ms Andersen, there is a missing person: Inspector Collesso. He may be bleeding. Do you know where he is?'

Scenes tumbled through Lily's head. Meeting Nathan in the street. Going upstairs. The attic and the ladder. Five thousand pounds. Nathan lying down. And nothing else. 'I don't know.'

The DI leaned over the bed, his weasel eyes staring into hers. 'But you asked me if I liked him, past tense. What did you mean?'

What did she mean? She remembered the knife, the hatred, the temptation. Had she …?

'Enough.' The doctor raised his hand. 'Please leave.'

Chapter 36

JULIE

THERE WAS A greasy, scruffy detective sitting at Julie's kitchen table. He took notes, but he showed little interest in her answers, and he wouldn't tell her anything. His phone rang, and he went into the hall to answer it. Julie listened at the door, but she couldn't hear what he was saying. In minutes, he was slouching back in, sitting down. 'Ms Ross, you ever been concerned about Ms Andersen's mental health?'

Julie shook her head. 'Why do you ask?'

He shrugged. 'You're sure she said Inspector Collesso was away on a course?'

'He was away. He told her he was going on a course.'

He picked at his grubby fingernails. 'Did you ever see him hit her?'

'No, but I saw the aftermath one morning a few months ago.' The detective looked sceptical. Julie's voice rose. 'He took Ronan away in the middle of the night; locked Lily in the flat.'

'Why would he do that?' He was biting his thumbnail. If he dropped even a sliver of himself on her table ...

Julie shrugged. 'Because he's evil. Maybe you should ask your colleague, Sophia. That's where he took Ronan.'

He leaned towards her, grinning. 'What do you know about him and Sophia?'

'Just that they worked together, and they were having an affair.'

'Aye?' He looked dead chuffed. Probably fancied himself the winner of an office sweepstake on Nathan's love life. He tugged, detaching a bit of nail, and he started grinding it between his front teeth. The noise made Julie shudder. He smiled, his tongue flicking the delicacy further into his mouth so his back teeth could have a go, then he fished the piece of nail out of his mouth and rolled it between his fingers. 'The boxes and bags in the living room at Polwarth – the rucksack and suitcase – you and your partner brought those over yesterday?'

Julie nodded.

'Did you open the old leather suitcase?'

'Why would I? As you know, I called the police when I became worried about Lily. After I'd given a statement, I lifted Ronan and took him here with his cot and a few bits and pieces. I left everything else there.'

He nodded. 'I'm going to take your prints, then I'll speak to your partner. Where is he?'

'He's upstairs with Ronan.' Julie stood. She really didn't want this man leaving anything of himself in her home, but better to know exactly where it was. She lifted the wastepaper bin and held it out towards him.

'What?'

'Your nail. In here, please.'

He shoved his hand in his pocket. 'I'm keeping it for later.'

*

PHILIP LOOKED BEMUSED as he washed his hands. 'I've never been fingerprinted before. What's going on?'

Julie shrugged. 'I phoned the hospital again. All they'll tell me is she's stable.'

'Did you tell them he was hitting her?'

As she spread butter on toast for Ronan, Julie nodded. 'I had to. I was worried he had come back early and caught her in the flat.

By the time I phoned, I think she was already in hospital. Coffee?'

Philip nodded. 'Please. He was very interested in that old battered leather suitcase, and whether I'd opened it.'

Julie put a cup of coffee on a mat on the other side of the table, then she sat beside Ronan and cut the toast into fingers, and the boiled egg into slices. Ronan grabbed a finger of toast, waving it in the air. 'Where Mama?'

'She'll come back soon, darling.'

'Okay, Doolie.' He shoved the toast in his mouth.

'What did you tell him about Lily's mental health?' Julie asked.

'Nothing.' Philip stirred the coffee. He looked at Julie, a slight smile on his face. 'I know nothing about her mental health.'

'You must have formed an opinion.'

He shook his head. 'I don't go around analysing people I meet outside the clinic. Well, not all the time. And even if I had formed an opinion, I wouldn't tell him.'

'Would you tell me? Please.'

'Are you suggesting staying in an abusive relationship is a sign of poor mental health?'

Julie shrugged. 'I guess not. It just makes no sense. She's so bright and clever. He's a creep. They had nothing in common. I don't think she even liked him, and she certainly couldn't have cared less that he was seeing someone else. So why did she stay?'

'I don't know why she stayed.' Philip shrugged. 'It sounds like she successfully compartmentalised what was going on. It's a psychological defence mechanism. We all do it. Leaving the pressures of work behind so we can enjoy time at home, or shutting out an argument with a loved one, so we can function at work. It's a way of getting temporary respite from a hostile situation. Maybe when Lily decided to stay, she detached herself emotionally from the relationship as a way of protecting herself from the hurt.

'It's not a healthy, long-term strategy. The danger is you begin to generalise, believing all relationships are hostile and detaching emotionally from everyone. That doesn't seem to have happened with Lily, but it could have, if she'd stayed much longer. She probably got out just in time.' He frowned. 'There could still be repercussions. Depression, PTSD, flashbacks. I doubt she's going to get away without some psychological trauma. She needs counselling. I could recommend someone.'

Julie nodded. 'That would be great, if she'll agree to it.'

The doorbell rang. Julie opened the door to a tall woman with long, dark hair and a solemn face. 'I'm Janice Morgan, social worker.'

Janice Morgan wasn't giving much away. Ms Andersen was recovering in hospital. Mr Collesso was missing. His family had asked that Ronan be placed with them.

'His family?' Julie tried to keep her voice even. 'Ronan won't settle with them. Last time he was there, they had to bring him back early because he wouldn't stop crying. Have you seen Lily?'

'No. I'm going there now. I wanted to see how Ronan was first.'

Ronan had finished his breakfast. He and Philip were sitting on the floor doing a puzzle.

'He's fine,' Julie said. 'I'll keep him as long as necessary. He's safe here.'

The social worker nodded. 'I can see that.' She lowered her voice. 'Have you ever been concerned about Ms Anderson's parenting?'

'Never. She's a wonderful mother.'

'Her mental health?'

'No.'

'That's good. The nurses asked if you have any clothes for Ms Andersen. The ones she was wearing when she was brought in are … em … they're probably going to be used as evidence.'

'Evidence of what?'

'I'm sorry, Ms Ross. I can't say any more. Do you have anything?'

'I have a couple of things I bought her for Christmas. They're flimsy. What does she need?'

'Everything, I think.'

'There's a jacket in the van, and a pair of jeans. Some trainers. Just give me a few minutes.'

Chapter 37

LILY

LILY HAD NEVER liked fairground rides. They made her sick. And though the raising of the head of the bed could only have taken seconds, it felt like a never-ending rollercoaster. She vomited on the consultant, leaving streaks of yellow bile on his shirt and tie. She apologised. He smiled. 'Happens all the time. I should have stood well back or worn an apron.'

When the spinning stopped, she found it was better to sit up. She could see the door without turning her head. The frizzy one was still there. Lily slept, and her sleep was deep. There were no dreams. When she woke, there were two figures by her bed. Her eyes focused, and Lily smiled. 'David. You're back.'

David Gunn nodded, his face flushing. 'This is Janice Morgan. She's a social worker.'

Lily had thought her head was much clearer, but Janice Morgan's words made no sense. Nathan had told his colleagues he was concerned about her mental health several times before he went missing. His mother had told Social Work she wasn't fit to look after Ronan on her own. They wanted to look after him.

'Never.' Lily tried to keep her head still, despite the desire to shake it first, then Janice Morgan. 'They can't have him. He doesn't even like them. They give him chocolate.'

Janice Morgan nodded. 'Would you agree to a psychiatric assessment?'

'I'd agree to a heart, liver and lung transplant if it meant Ronan wouldn't go to those people. And if you can find a spare heart for Nathan, he's in dire need. His sister, too.'

The social worker almost smiled. 'I'll speak to the staff. See if we can get an assessment arranged.'

David watched her go, then he turned to Lily. 'I know I shouldn't ask, but did he, Collesso, did he do this to you? Your friend said …'

Lily tried to remember. It was hopeless. 'I … I don't know what happened.'

David nodded. 'I'm sure it'll come back to you eventually. Is there anything I can do?'

'No, thanks.'

He frowned. 'If you think of anything, ask to see me, and I'll get whatever you need. I'll –'

Janice Morgan was back, along with the consultant. He'd changed his shirt and tie, and he was raging. He leaned towards Lily. 'This … this person says you've agreed to a psychiatric assessment. Is that correct?'

'I didn't think I had a choice, if I want to keep my son.'

He shook his head and pushed his white fringe back from his eyes. 'It's entirely unnecessary. There's nothing wrong with your mental state. And even if there was, no psychiatrist in their right mind would do an assessment the day after a patient incurred a significant head injury. It's her that needs her head examined.'

As he stamped out of the room, Janice Morgan's face was scarlet. Lily felt a little sorry for her.

'Okay, we'll leave the assessment for now,' the social worker said. 'I saw Ronan this morning with your friends, Julie Ross and Philip Munro. He's very settled. Ms Ross said you'll probably both stay with her until you've recovered. I'm satisfied Ronan is not at any risk of harm.'

They watched her leave. David was still frowning. 'DI Ford is going to want to talk to you as soon as you're fit. Do you have a solicitor?'

Lily shook her head. It hurt like hell.

'I can arrange a duty solicitor for you.'

'Thank you.'

*

WORDS WERE COMING out of the solicitor's young mouth like little sharp missiles. He had the strangest eyes. One brown. One green. Lily leaned towards him. 'Heterochromia iridum.'

The strange eyes widened. 'I beg your pardon.' He had a little pointy chin with a dimple in the middle.

'You have different coloured irises.'

'And?'

Lily shrugged. 'It's unusual, that's all. Are you qualified?'

'Yes, I'm qualified.' A fragment of spittle landed on his notebook. He wiped at his lips. 'My firm doesn't send unqualified people to hospitals on a Saturday morning to assist suspected criminals.'

'But they send kids?'

'Kids? I'm three years older than you.'

'That makes me feel so much better. Listen, all I want is to see Ronan, my son.'

He shook his head. 'You can't see anyone. Your partner, a police officer, is missing under suspicious circumstances. The police want to question you. It doesn't get much more serious than this. Do you want to tell me what happened?'

She shrugged. 'I don't know. We were in the flat. Nathan wasn't feeling well, and he went for a rest. I came downstairs and went into the kitchen. And then I woke up here.'

The solicitor looked peeved. He'd see her tomorrow, he said, at the police station.

There were no more colours and no light. Asleep or awake, everything was dull and grey, like the unrelenting pain in her head and her finger. She tried to remember, and the effort exhausted her. There was a constant stream of medical information running through her brain, as if she was reading from a textbook. Facts and figures about traumatic brain injury and post-traumatic amnesia. In forty-five per cent of cases, the memory loss lasted more than a month. Funny how she could remember that, and every word Nathan had said before she went downstairs.

She didn't want to eat, and she didn't want to talk to the nurses that fussed around her. David Gunn didn't come back. Just a succession of faceless figures sitting outside the room. Watching. Waiting.

Chapter 38

LILY

THE DISCONNECTION BETWEEN Lily's head and her mouth was back. Her mouth kept smiling, and DI Ford and the frizzy one were looking at her as if she was completely mad. The doctor had offered to keep her in if she didn't feel up to being interviewed. She didn't feel up to it, but she had to see Ronan.

Nathan was missing, they told her. He'd lost a lot of blood. Her fingerprints were on a brandy bottle, along with his blood. His fingerprints were on a metal fire poker, along with her blood. Did she want to tell them what had happened?

'I handled the brandy bottle the night before Nathan left. He and his family drank it. As for Friday, I bumped into Nathan and went back to the apartment. I remember nothing else.'

DI Ford looked sceptical. 'Were you in the attic?'

'No, I'd left the hatch open that morning, and the ladder was down. Nathan asked why. I … I told him I'd put the wedding dress up there so he wouldn't see it.'

He started tapping his pen on the table, and the noise was excruciating in Lily's fragile head. 'Were you on the balcony?'

'I don't remember.' She frowned, the pain growing. 'Maybe I was. I … it's so hazy. Do you think you could stop tapping that pen? It hurts my head.'

DI Ford slammed the pen down. 'How about I make a few suggestions? Inspector Collesso discovers your things are gone. He confronts you, and you fight. He hits you with the poker. You hit him with the bottle. He's knocked out. It goes too far. Maybe you have some friends with you, and they help you dispose of his body.'

'What happens next?' Lily leaned towards him, as if she was asking about the plot of a TV drama. 'I return to the apartment, hit myself over the head, call an ambulance, and collapse.' She sat back in the chair. 'Doesn't sound very believable, does it?'

The frizzy one looked at her notes. 'Your friend claimed Inspector Collesso has beaten you before. Perhaps you'd had enough. Saw red. Wanted to get back at him.'

'I don't think so.'

They wanted to know about the old suitcase. What was in it? Whose clothes and books?

'They belong to my friend, Sam Murray.'

DI Ford nodded and smirked. 'His address?'

Lily rubbed her forehead. 'My head is broken. I'm not up to much more of this. I think you know who Sam is. I'm guessing you know where he 'lives'. Why not just come to the point?'

How they laughed about her and her 'friend'. She stared at them until they shut up. The frizzy one's face was redder than ever, and the DI wiped at his weasily little eyes. 'What is it with you and the homeless?' He glanced down at his pad. 'Last time you came to our attention, you'd been assaulted on Princes Street while helping a beggar.'

'Is this really relevant?' Lily's solicitor asked, looking at his watch.

DI Ford frowned. 'I'll decide what's relevant. So, where is your dear friend, Sam? He left his pitch on Friday afternoon, and he hasn't been seen since.'

Lily shook her head. 'I spoke to him on my way back to the apartment. It was just before I met Nathan. I –'

'Truth is, you arranged for your homeless pal to follow you to the apartment. You both assaulted Inspector Collesso. Maybe you had the help of others, maybe not. It went further than you meant it to, and you and your pal disposed of the body.'

'No.'

'Has Sam ever visited you at Ramsay Garden?'

Lily shook her head. 'He doesn't know where I live.'

DI Ford looked unconvinced. 'Really? Not a close friend then?'

Lily ignored his question. She tried to read the notes on his pad, but her head could make little sense of the upside-down scrawl. He put down his pen. 'Why would Inspector Collesso tell so many people that you were mentally unstable?' He glanced down at the pad. 'Over a long period.'

She shrugged. 'I can't answer that, but you both know him. He had … has a nasty side. Maybe he was hoping to get custody of Ronan. Who knows?'

'And this course he was on. Tell me about that.'

'He didn't say what it was about. I'm not even sure there was a course. Maybe he was abroad. He had a false passport.'

DI Ford's eyes widened.

'It was in the name of –'

He held up his hand. 'The interview is over. Don't leave the country, Ms Andersen. We'll be in touch soon.'

His colleague stared at him with narrowed eyes. 'What's going on, Sir?'

'Interview's over. Like I said.'

The name Lily had been about to say was still in her mouth. Anthony Harris. Anthony. Tony.

Of course. Tony. The man the girls had been looking for. It was Nathan.

Chapter 39

DAVID

THE FLIMSY BLUE top had slipped off Lily's left shoulder, exposing the lace strap of a navy vest. There was a price tag on the vest at the back of her neck. David wanted to remove the tag so it wouldn't scratch her pale skin. The wind was chilly, but she was carrying her jacket. She looked so thin and young, in tight jeans and trainers. She turned her head to watch another taxi drive past. She looked washed out, with a shadow of tears in her eyes. He cursed the officers that had sent her out into the cold with a head injury, leaving her to find her own way home.

'Lily, how are you? I saw you from the car park.'

'David.' She tried to smile. 'You're not stationed here, are you?'

He shook his head. 'Had to drop something off.' It wasn't a complete lie. The desk sergeant at his station did have something to be delivered to Howdenhall, and he'd jumped at the chance, knowing Lily was there. He'd used up most of his lunch hour, waiting, hoping he'd see her. 'I'm going back into town. Can I give you a lift? You don't look well.'

She frowned, then she nodded. 'Thanks.'

He was glad she'd walked down the road, out of sight of the station. 'Wait here. I'll get the car. Going to put your jacket on?'

She smiled and shrugged herself into her jacket.

In minutes, he was back. Neither of them spoke until they reached Mayfield Road. 'Can I ask you something?' Lily said. 'Was Nathan on a course last week? He phoned me every night, told me how it was going, but now I wonder if he was up to something else. I think DI Ford suspects it too.'

David frowned. 'I shouldn't say anything. I …'

'I swear I won't tell anyone.'

He sighed. 'There was no course. Nathan told his boss he had to take time off to look after you. He said you … you were …'

'Mad?'

'Emotionally challenged, and finding it difficult to look after Ronan on your own.'

'It's not true.'

'You don't have to tell me that.'

Lily directed him to Julie's house, a semi-detached Victorian villa. 'Thank you,' she said. 'It was kind of you.' She reached for the door handle, then she turned back. 'Why do they call him Bruce?'

David's stomach lurched, his face reddening. 'You know about that?'

'I do now.' She smiled. 'Sorry. I overheard it at a retirement dinner a while ago. I didn't know if they were talking about him, but lots of things have since fallen into place. Why Bruce? And don't spare my feelings. I was leaving him, remember.'

'Bruce is a bent cop with several other unsavoury characteristics, in Irvine Welsh's book, *Filth*.'

'You think Nathan's bent?'

David didn't let his eyes meet hers. 'I don't really know him.'

Someone appeared at the window. It was her friend, Julie, and she was holding Lily's son. Lily's smile widened as her son started bouncing and laughing. 'Thank you again.'

'Can I give you my number?' David reached into the glove compartment, pulled out a pad and a pen, and scribbled. 'If you need anything, please, please get in touch.'

Chapter 40

SAM

IT'S COLD IN Greyfriars Kirkyard. The wind is whipping up the trees and bushes, so they dance and moan like dervishes. Sam tries to get into the Covenanters' Prison, but the gates are locked and it's impossible to climb over them. The plaque on the wall tells him prisoners were held there in 1679 for over four months, getting only four ounces of bread each day. What he'd give for some bread now. His stomach is rumbling loud enough to raise a body or two. He should have gone further while he had the chance, but he couldn't leave without knowing how Lily was.

A couple of police officers gave the cemetery a cursory once-over on Friday afternoon. He thought he was done for, but they weren't taking it seriously. Didn't even look inside the enclosures. There's been a steady stream of tourists and locals parading through the cemetery. Young girls on their own in the dusk. Are they mad? He'd not be here himself if he had any choice.

He's slumped behind a gravestone, his body shaking and shivering, his mouth as dry as the bones below him. He tries to plan. Maybe he'll go west, lose himself in Glasgow. He'll need to toughen up if he's to survive there. He should have toughened up long ago, taken the advice of the pig and found another pitch.

Lily and the pig? It makes no sense, and it's taunted him since Friday. His head is in his hands, his eyes closed, when he feels something brush against his upper arm. It's nothing. Just a gust of wind. It happens again, only this time there's a hint of icy fingers. He stops himself from crying out, but the swallowed scream echoes in his head. It's so loud, he doesn't hear the voice at first.

'Hey, you; I said are you all right down there?'

Fool. He opens his eyes. He hasn't seen the boy before, but he looks like so many others in the city. Gaunt pitted cheeks, eyes dulled by a cocktail of chemicals. Skin and bone. Clean and well-dressed, though.

Sam smiles. 'I'm fine, son. You gave me a fright there. Thought MacKenzie had escaped his mausoleum.'

'MacKenzie?' The boy frowns, his eyes screwed up. 'Don't know him. I'm looking for a fat guy, bald.'

'A tramp?'

He shakes his head. 'He's respectable. Said he'd meet me in here. Make it worth my while. Might be more work in it. He's got mates. They have parties; that kind of thing.'

A hint of nausea races up Sam's gullet. The boy's wearing a warm jacket with a hood. And it's too big for him. 'What if I was to give you fifteen quid for that jacket? It's all I've got. Would you not just take the money and go?'

The boy's laughter is too loud as he peels off the jacket. 'It's worth a lot more than that, but you can have it. I'm not going anywhere. You soon switch off, as long as they don't hurt you.'

Sam pulls out his money. Two fivers and the rest in change. He counts it into the outstretched hand, noticing the boy's long, delicate fingers. He might have played the piano as a child. 'You can have this.' Sam offers the jacket he's been wearing. It's not a bad jacket, but it's got no hood, and it's thin.

'No thanks, pal. The punters aren't too fussy, but … you know.'

Sam nods. 'Listen, son, if anyone asks, you haven't seen me.'

'Sound. Take it easy.' The boy shivers, then he walks away,

winding his way between tombstones. He disappears behind the church. There are voices. He's found his punter.

Sam lied. There's money in his trouser pocket. Enough to last a few days. Hood up, eyes down, and he's in and out of the shop in seconds, the girl behind the till too busy with her phone to bother looking at him. On the Meadows, he scoffs a cheese roll, washing it down with water that tastes like nectar. Shame they didn't sell booze; if he doesn't get some soon, he's in for a rough time with the DTs. If he hadn't got that bottle on Friday afternoon before he headed for the cemetery, he'd be up Shit Creek by now. He drinks too much of the water and feels sick, but it's not coming back up. No way. His hands shaking, he opens the newspaper.

Fears continue to grow for the safety of an Edinburgh police officer. Inspector Nathan Collesso has been missing since Friday evening. His luxury apartment at Edinburgh's Ramsay Garden remains under police cordon. Scene of Crime Officers have been removing items from the property, where, it is believed, a disturbance took place. The signs of a violent incident have left the police with significant concerns for the safety of Inspector Collesso. The missing officer's fiancée, Lily Andersen, was found unconscious in the apartment. At the time of writing, she was stable in Edinburgh Royal Infirmary, with her discharge expected today. The couple has a young son, and they are due to marry this month.

Inspector Collesso's father, a prominent Edinburgh wine merchant, Jonathon Collesso, said: 'We are devastated that Nathan is missing in such horrific circumstances. We would urge anyone with information to get in touch with the police.'

The police are keen to speak to Samuel Murray, a homeless man often seen sitting close to the National Library on George IV Bridge.

Lily's safe. Sam's not, though no one's going to recognise him from that mugshot. It's well out of date. Must be ten years since he was arrested for being drunk and disorderly. He shoves the paper inside his jacket and hurries on. He's got an idea.

Chapter 41

DAVID

PLEASE, PLEASE GET in touch. Could he have sounded any more desperate? As he drove away from Julie's house, David feared he was losing it. He felt dragged down by his work and his after work and all the shit that came with both. Eva, his only distraction in recent weeks, was still off sick, and she wasn't returning his texts and calls. He'd gone by her flat a couple of times, and there was no answer. He missed her laughter, and the easy way between them. And yet, he was glad she hadn't been around for the last few days. He wasn't sure he could have looked her in the eye and acted as if he was worthy of her. As if he wasn't consumed with thoughts of Lily, and what might have happened if someone hadn't called that ambulance.

And more. He'd been summoned to the Dumbiedykes flat, and he was dreading it. Maybe he'd say he was only there to talk business. In a hurry. No time or need for any 'bonus'. It was tricky. They had to trust him, and he had to do whatever it took to ensure that happened.

The afternoon was long and dull, nothing to break the monotony of paperwork but the constant whispering and speculation about Collesso. Though one or two of his colleagues thought Collesso had done a runner, most of them were certain of his death, and no one was in mourning. They hadn't quite started a sweepstake on the identity of the perpetrator, but it was only a matter of time, and Lily was odds-on favourite.

David didn't go home after work. He ate in a pub, though he had little appetite, then he walked to Dumbiedykes.

Same old routine. Jakub answered the door. The same lackeys were sprawled on the couch playing cards, but only two of them this time. Jakub took David into the kitchen. It was a stinking mess of dirty crockery and mouldy take away containers. His voice was low as he brought David up to date with developments, and filled him in on requirements. It didn't take long.

'You want bonus now?'

David looked at his watch and shook his head. 'No time tonight.'

Jakub laughed. 'Not even quickie?'

'No.'

He shrugged. 'Okay.'

The men didn't look up from the couch. In the hallway, David heard laughter and the creaking of a bed. Jakub nodded towards the door at the end of the corridor. 'You sure? Your friend, Aneta, she is waiting.'

'Quite sure, thanks. Next time.'

Jakub checked the peephole, then he turned the key and opened the door. David had almost escaped when he heard a cry. 'What was that?'

Jakub shrugged.

It came again. And then a man's voice yelling something in Polish.

'Go,' Jakub said, his hand on David's back, trying to push him out.

Though he wanted nothing more than to run, David turned and shook his head. 'I'm not leaving until I find out what's going on.'

Jakub laughed and held up his hands. 'Okay, Mr Policeman. You go see.'

The noise was coming from the last room. David pushed open the door. The missing lackey was on the bed, his body pinning Aneta down. She was crying and struggling. The man turned and stared at David, anger in his dark eyes. He yelled something in Polish and gesticulated with his arm, obviously telling David to close the door.

'Get off her,' David shouted.

The man laughed and gave David his middle finger. His eyes widened as David lunged at him, grabbing him by the back of his hoodie and dragging him from the bed. He was taller and bulkier than David, but he was half-cut and hampered by the jeans around his ankles. Thankfully, his boxers were still on. He threw a punch, missed, overbalanced and hit his head off the corner of the dressing table. He crumpled on the carpet, blood oozing from a wound on his forehead.

Behind him, David heard Jakub laughing. 'So, you want your bonus now?'

He didn't, but he wanted to be sure she was okay. He nodded. Jakub shouted something and the other two lackeys appeared. They pulled their mate to his feet, one of them dragging his jeans up over his thick, hairy legs. He looked dazed, though it didn't stop him from uttering words that sounded like a threat, as his friends helped him from the room.

It was an hour before David escaped, and only because Jakub came knocking on the door. 'Your time is up.'

In the hallway, David told Jakub their arrangement was over unless he kept his men away from the girls.

Jakub shrugged. 'Okay. I tell Henryck before. I tell him again.' His eyes narrowed. 'But remember, you are not the boss man here. You be careful.'

Chapter 42

LILY

THREE NIGHTS IN a row, Lily dreamt she'd stabbed Nathan, and he was dead. She'd woken with an overwhelming sense of relief, followed by guilt. She didn't want him dead, and she really didn't want to have killed him. And then, in the early hours of the fourth morning, there was a new dream. And this one felt more real.

In the kitchen, Julie's smile was warm. 'You're up early. How are you feeling?'

'Weird. I'm remembering things.'

'That's good, isn't it?' She put the kettle on.

'Maybe. I was on the balcony. There was a dazed pigeon, and I held it until it could fly. It's blank again after that, but I think … it makes no sense, but I feel as if Sam was there. And Sophia. I could smell her, feel her fingers touching my neck. I tried to open my eyes, but I couldn't.'

'Will you tell the cops?'

Lily shrugged. 'It's all so vague and patchy. I'll wait and see if anything else comes back to me. I hope you're going to work today. I'm taking Ronan for a walk. We need to get out.'

Julie's hand was poised above the toaster. 'Are you sure? The doctor said to rest.'

Lily nodded. 'Certain.'

Julie dropped the bread into the toaster. She opened a drawer beside the sink and rummaged, pulling stuff out. A couple of phone chargers, small binoculars, a wi-fi router. 'I know it's here somewhere.' Two plug adaptors, a broken clock and three glasses cases. 'Bingo.' She pulled out a mobile phone. 'Better charge it.'

The police had Lily's phone, netbook and iPad. Her solicitor had said there was no chance of getting them back any time soon.

'Take this with you wherever you go.' Julie looked so worried. 'Please.'

Outside, everything looked different. Brighter. False. The grass on the Meadows was too green and the sky too blue. Noises were amplified to unbearable levels. The shouts of boys playing football. Barking dogs. The hum of distant machinery. There were only pigeons in the play park, rustling among the wind-blown litter and leaves that had gathered by the fence, the scrunching sound, along with the creaking chains of the swing, piercing Lily's head. A constant dull pain throbbed in her finger, and Lily wondered again where Nathan was. Had she harmed him? Would he come after her? Would he take Ronan?

At last, Ronan began to tire. He held out his arms to be lifted from the swing. 'Home, Mama. Bed.'

She was almost back at Julie's when she saw a man walking towards her. He had a bag over one shoulder, a camera over the other, and a broad grin on his face. Lily put her head down.

'Lily Andersen?'

She shook her head and kept walking.

'I'm Joe Lucas. *Evening News*. Can I talk to you?'

'No.'

'Please?' He darted in front of the pushchair, and she was tempted to ram into him. 'I just want to ask you about today's news. Just a comment, that's all.'

He was young and desperate. She knew she should say nothing, but she couldn't. 'What news?'

He looked surprised. He tapped his pen on his notebook. 'You haven't heard? Could we go somewhere to talk?'

'No. Just say what you have to say, and go.'

He nodded. 'The other girls. The allegations. Are they true? Did you know what kind of man your fiancé was? Do you know where he is?'

'I know nothing. Please leave me alone.'

He lifted his camera. 'Can I get a picture?'

Lily took the phone from her pocket, pressed some random buttons, and held it to her ear. 'Police please.'

His eyes widening, he backed away. 'No need for that. I'm just doing my job.'

She stayed where she was, phone at her ear, until he was gone, then she hurried to the house. As she waited for Julie's computer to start, Lily's heart hammered. There was sweat on her brow, and the wound on her head tingled as she clicked on the news website. It flashed up on the screen, the words crashing into her eyes.

FOUR WOMEN.
DATE RAPE DRUG ALLEGATIONS.
THE LAST ONE LESS THAN TWO WEEKS AGO.

Chapter 43

SAM

IT'S THE BEST gaff Sam's had in years. It's cold at night, but there are piles of newspapers and black bags full of clothes. Plenty to cover himself with. And books, heaps of them. There's a tweed cap, and he sticks it on and sneaks out in the evening, round to the corner shop for some grub, then he fills the water bottle from the garden tap and empties his bucket behind the shrubs. In the morning, the sun warms up the shed until he's roasting. He bought a litre of vodka the first night and he's making it last. Difficult, but there's not much money left. If it wasn't for the threat of the DTs, he'd have tried to go without.

He doesn't know when he last slept so well. He should have tried this long ago. How many garden sheds are there in Edinburgh, ignored by their owners? And this one's in good nick. He's almost finished the thriller when the torch flickers and goes out. Bugger. Just a few chapters left. He'll have to go to the shop for batteries.

The batteries are behind the till, and he almost gasps when he sees the price. He'll not be getting those today. He picks up the evening paper. *Missing cop allegations; page 4.* Can he read it without buying the paper?

'Don't even think about it.' The shopkeeper holds out his hand.

Sam leaves the shop with a pasty, the newspaper and twelve pence. He reads page four in the street, standing under a lamppost. There are tears in his eyes as he makes his way back to the shed. Those poor girls. He should have helped them. And Lily. She didn't know what that pig was really like; she couldn't have. Those marks on her cheek? Was that him? Bastard.

The shed's cold, and the pasty tastes sour. Probably days out of date. He washes it down with a slug of vodka. And another. He shakes the bottle. Why not? He's going to have to find money tomorrow. The vodka slips down like velvet. An early night tonight, with nothing to read, unless there are batteries in one of those drawers in the old chest.

There are batteries, but they're the wrong size. There's a box of long kitchen matches. A long match doesn't last all that long, but half the box sees him to the end of the book.

Chapter 44

JULIE

THE HOUSE WAS dark and cold. Julie put on the kitchen light and called out again. Nothing. She checked the front porch. The pushchair was there, along with their shoes and jackets. They must be in. She put the kettle on, then she sat at the computer and tapped the mouse. The screen came to life. Julie groaned as she read the news story. Her mobile phone rang. It was Philip. 'Have you seen the evening paper?'

A soft light shone under the bedroom door. She could hear Ronan babbling. She pushed the door over and saw Lily curled up on the bed, asleep. Ronan was sitting on the floor in a nest of shredded tissue paper. Squiggly red lines covered his face. In one hand, he had the mobile phone Julie had given Lily. In the other, a lipstick with only a chewed red stump. His clothes were covered in a collage of sanitary towels, plastered this way and that. He smiled, his mouth and teeth bright red, then he laughed into the mobile phone. 'Hi Doolie.'

Lily groaned and opened her eyes. 'What's the time?'
'Almost five.'

She shot up, her eyes red and puffy. When she saw Ronan on the floor, she leapt off the bed. 'Shit.'

Ronan laughed. 'Shit. Shit. Shit.'

*

RONAN WAS IN his feeding chair, eating haddock and peas. Julie put a cup of tea in front of Lily. 'He came to no harm; stop beating yourself up.'

'I should have put him in the cot, but I was so tired, and we fell asleep on the bed. I didn't think I'd sleep so deeply. The paracetamol tablets in my bag: he could have taken them all.'

'He didn't. Was the lipstick expensive?'

'Probably. Nathan bought it, but I didn't like it. Do you think he'll be sick?'

Julie shrugged. 'He doesn't look any the worse for it. And it is for putting on your lips, so it can't be too toxic. Probably just wax and … stuff.'

'Wax and chemicals and shit.'

Ronan banged his fork on the table. 'Shit.'

Lily frowned. Julie smiled. 'I guess it's always funnier when it's someone else's kid. How did the journalist know where to find you?'

Lily shrugged. 'Nathan's father has friends in the police. Maybe they told him, and he passed it on to the journalist. Don't know how he knew it was me, though.'

The phone rang. Julie answered. It was Margaret, and she sounded frantic. She had to see Lily, she said. She wasn't mad, she really wasn't, and only Lily would understand.

'Lily's … she's not really … she's busy,' Julie said. 'I could come.'

'I don't want you to come,' Margaret said. 'I only want Lily. Let me speak to her, please.'

Lily took the phone from Julie. She frowned as she listened. 'Okay,' she said at last. 'I'll be round soon.'

Chapter 45

LILY

FOOTSTEPS WERE RUSTLING in the leaves, Nathan's hands reaching out to grab her. Lily turned. There was no one there. Plenty of hiding places, though. When she began stepping onto the road to give lanes and driveways a wider berth, anger seethed through her. Just let him try. She gripped the small can of hairspray Julie had persuaded her to carry. It'd do for starters. And when he was down, she'd find a rock and smash his head in. She smiled and exhaled. A hooded figure emerged from a driveway. Lily screamed.

'Soz.' The pock-marked youth shuffled away. Lily's only consolation was his headphones. He wouldn't have heard her, would he?

Julie had urged Lily to wait until Philip arrived in an hour, when one of them would take her to Margaret's. Lily had been adamant. She had to go now. Margaret needed her. Lily hadn't told Julie the truth. She was running from the recent news and the thoughts in her head. If she kept moving, they wouldn't catch her.

The next street was wider and better lit, with dog walkers and couples and cyclists. Still, she had that feeling of being watched, the hairs on the back of her neck tingling. And then she was in Morningside.

Margaret opened the door. Her cheeks were flushed, and her eyes full of fear. 'Lily; thank God you've come.' She ushered her in. 'Quick. Quick. Close the door. Come through here.'

Lily followed her into the kitchen. The light was off, but the blind was open. Margaret stood at the window. 'Do you see it?'

She could see the outline of the trees and bushes, the compost bin, the shed, the wooden bench. She could see the moon hiding behind the clouds. 'Can you give me a clue, Margaret?'

'I never come in here without putting on the light, but my hands were full. And the moon was bright and I saw it.' Margaret's fingers gripped Lily's upper arm. 'Can't you see it? The shed. The light.' She frowned. 'Oh, it's gone now. There was a flickering light before.' Her grip tightened. 'I don't want to phone the police. They'll say I'm mad. I had a social worker round yesterday. She wasn't very nice; kept asking me about my mental health. I don't want to go to the asylum. I'm not mad.' There were tears in her eyes. 'I'm not.'

Lily smiled. 'I know that.'

Margaret looked at Lily's hand. 'What have you done to your finger?'

'It's nothing. Just a sprain.'

'Julie said you hadn't been well. I've missed you so much.' She gestured towards the back door. 'What will I do?'

'Is the shed locked?'

Margaret shook her head.

They only had three working hands between them, so Lily armed herself with an empty cordial bottle, and Margaret brandished Lily's mobile phone, with 999 keyed in. All she had to do was press the green button if Lily gave the signal. In her other hand, Margaret had a torch. The moon had slipped out from behind the clouds, illuminating the garden. At the shed door, they stopped. There was a loud noise from inside.

'Is that snoring?' Margaret said. 'Who the heck is sleeping in my shed?' She shoved the phone into Lily's pocket, pulled the door open, and grabbed a garden fork. 'No need for the police. I'll sort him out.'

Sam's sleepy face peeped out from under a blanket of newspapers.

'It's okay, Margaret,' Lily said. 'He's a friend. I'll explain.'

The voice that answered was not Margaret's. 'I look forward to hearing your explanation.'

It was DI Ford, with two uniformed policemen. Lily stared at the detective. 'You were following me?'

He laughed.

Chapter 46

SAM

IT'S QUITE SIMPLE. Why can't the solicitor understand? Sam hadn't even wanted a solicitor, but a young policewoman had persuaded him otherwise. There was a duty solicitor, she'd said, just a phone call away. It would protect Sam. Probably another of these fancy protocols. An office full of solicitors waiting for a homeless person to call. This one doesn't exactly look happy to be here. She advises Sam to say nothing, but he can't see the point in that. He just wants to tell the truth and get out of here.

'Get out of here?' She's looking at him as if he's quite mad. 'You think you're getting out after what you've done to a cop?'

He shrugs. She advises him again to say nothing. He's not going to take her advice.

The DI has a head like a vegetable; a giant potato or a neep. His colleague's a frizzy-haired sergeant. Looks like she's chewing a wasp. They start off polite enough, encouraging Sam to tell them what happened last Friday afternoon. He's relived it so many times, and each time, his heart has thumped just as it did then. Just as it's doing now.

He's got to the bit where Lily and Collesso have disappeared into the flats. Sam considers leaving, but he can't. It's the top buzzer.

He presses the bottom one, and summons a voice from decades past, the one he used when he started teaching, to convince the pupils and himself that he knew what he was doing. 'Delivery for your neighbour.'

'Okay.'

He sneaks up to the top floor and leans against their door. He hears light footsteps, as if on stairs, and then on a wooden floor. It's her. She's okay. There's a tap running. The footsteps again. A thump followed by a shout, but he can't hear the words. A sliding door. And nothing. He thinks of leaving. Maybe he's being stupid. Maybe she's fine, and it's none of his business. He turns away and then he hears something else. Heavier footsteps on the stairs.

It's not there, I'm telling you. Such anger and fear in the pig's voice. *It's not ... I don't know ... maybe she took it. Bitch. I bet she took it. I'll call you back.*

A pause. Doors opening. Closing. A heavy clanging sound. Metal falling on wood. And a groan.

He's never going to break the front door down on his own. He'll get a neighbour. Aye, and who's going to help him break into a luxury flat? He wastes so much time trying to decide what to do. He almost doesn't try the door, and then he laughs when he finds it open. The mingling smell of Lily and the pig is so wrong. The kitchen door's open, so he goes there first. Sees a brandy bottle in a recycling bag. That'll do. Back down the corridor and he can hear hissing, like a venomous snake. He slips into the living room. The sofa is white, stained with patches and trails of blood. The hissing is coming from outside. A sliding door is open, a trail of blood leading towards it and out. And the pig's there, and he's forcing Lily backwards over the balcony ...

Sweat is pouring down Sam's forehead into his eyes. He's wiping it away and hoping they don't see the tears mingling with it. The DI laughs and starts clapping. 'What a performance. You've missed your vocation. Get yourself along to the Festival Office. Bound to be an opening for an actor with your skills.' The smile slips away and he leans towards Sam. 'Shame you're looking at a life sentence for murder.'

'Murder? He was still alive after I hit him with the bottle.' He ignores the touch of his solicitor's hand on his sleeve. 'What was I supposed to do? Let him kill her? Should have taken a knife and butchered the bastard.'

'Maybe you did. A lot of blood in that flat.'

'Aye, and most of it Lily's.'

'You're very fond of Ms Andersen. Care to tell me more about that?'

Sam shrugs. 'Nothing to tell. She's my pal.'

'Did she ask you to hit him?'

Sam laughs. 'Ask me? She wasn't capable of seeing me, far less asking me to do anything.'

The DI sits back, his arms crossed. 'What then?'

'I carried Lily to the sofa and covered her with a blanket. Picked up the phone to call an ambulance, then I heard footsteps thundering up the stairs. Thought it was you lot. I dived behind the sofa, and they stormed in. Three huge guys and a woman. They didn't look like police. More like Special Branch or the SAS, come to get him at last.'

The female copper laughs. 'Special Branch? The SAS? I would say you've been watching too much TV, if I didn't know you were living on the streets.'

The DI laughs too. They make a strange sound between them, their laughter forced and unnatural.

'You can laugh,' Sam says. 'If there was any justice in the world, that's exactly what would happen to your colleague. He's a sick bastard.'

Sam leans towards them, and they both lean back. He laughs. 'Collesso was never that fussy. My personal hygiene, or lack thereof, didn't keep him away. Oh, no. He liked to get really close. Whispering in my ear. And more.' Sam pushes his hair back from his face, exposing his right ear.

There's shock on their faces, but it's momentary. The DI shakes his bald head. 'Could have been anyone.'

'Could have, but it wasn't. When you get him, I bet you could match this to his teeth.'

There's silence. He takes advantage of it. 'The man is an animal. He put me in hospital when he should have been working. Night shift was just play time for him. A car and a uniform and he thought he was invincible.'

The lassie's wee face is red. 'Why have you never made a complaint about him?'

Sam shrugs. 'Someone like me, making a complaint against someone like him? I knew someone like you would never take it seriously. Get yourself a mirror, Sergeant. Have a wee look and see exactly what I see.'

Neither of them like that. Good. There's fire in Sam's veins. He should have stood up for himself long ago. It's taken Lily to make him do this. She's the only good thing in his life, and he'll make damn sure she doesn't go down for something she hasn't done, for something he should have done.

The frizzy one is stumped. In her mind's eye, she's still looking in that mirror. Neep-head leans forward. 'Tell us more about the people you say took Inspector Collesso away.'

Sam nods. 'The woman had long, black hair. The men were big. Shaved heads. Doc Martin boots. Leather gloves. They were searching for something. A couple of them went upstairs. I couldn't see them properly, but they sounded angry. I think they were speaking a Slavic language.'

'They were from Czechoslovakia?'

Ignorant bastard. Sam smiles. 'Where's that?'

The frizzy one whispers in the detective's ear. He reddens. 'Where do you think they were from?'

Sam shrugs. 'I'm no linguist, but they sounded Eastern European.'

'Could have said that in the first place, instead of ...' The

DI's voice tails off, and his eyes don't meet Sam's. 'What about the woman?'

'She spoke their language. He ... Collesso ... he was coming round then. Moaning and crying like a baby. She put a bandage on his head, then the men helped him up and out of the flat, with the holdall he'd been carrying earlier.' He frowns. 'The woman was last to leave. She bent over Lily, checked her pulse, and pulled the blanket up around her. Then she called an ambulance on her mobile phone.'

'Why didn't you stay with Ms Andersen? She could have died between your call and the ambulance arriving.'

Sam nods. 'I've spent the last few days asking myself that question. I was a coward. But when you live on the streets, and a member of the local constabulary regularly uses your head as a football ... and that's when he's in a good mood ... it's hard to have any trust.' He shrugged. 'To be honest, there wasn't much more I could have done for her.'

'Have you and Ms Andersen been in contact with each other since this happened?'

'No. I was surprised to see her tonight.'

'You expect us to believe it's a coincidence that you end up in the shed of someone for whom Ms Andersen has been working?'

'It's no coincidence. Lily told me she knew Margaret Rutherford. I didn't let on that I knew Margaret a long time ago, before I married. I taught her. Tutored her brother too, and I remembered where they lived. I kind of hoped it might be a way of reaching Lily, finding out if she was okay.'

Sam's sitting on his hands, trying to keep them from shaking. He knows what's coming if he doesn't get some booze inside him. Disorientation, hallucinations and fever. Sweating and a racing heart. And then the nightmares.

They want him to look at some pictures, see if he recognises anyone. They look like a shower of bad bastards, but he shakes his head at each one. Looks like they might be about to wrap things up. No way. He's not finished. 'See those girls that made the complaints, the ones in the newspaper? I can help you with that.'

DI Ford looks uneasy. He glances at his colleague and pushes his chair back. 'Give me a minute.'

No way. 'I want to make a statement. I want …'

He stares at Sam. Something has changed. 'You'll make your statement.'

The frizzy one gets up, but the DI puts out his hand. 'Not you, Sergeant Rodgers. Please stay here.'

Her face is like a burst tomato.

When he returns, the DI smiles at Sam. It's almost scarier than the other pig's smile. 'That's enough for tonight, Mr Murray. Sergeant Rodgers will take you to Margaret Rutherford's, and she'll pick you up at quarter to ten tomorrow and bring you to the station. You can make your statement then.'

'Me?' The sergeant glares at the DI. 'Take him? Pick him up?'

'Aye, you.'

'But I'm out on the beat tomorrow morning.'

'That's fine. You won't be required to interview Mr Murray and neither will I.'

Mr Murray, eh? And the DI's still smiling at him. Weirder and weirder. 'I don't suppose I could speak to Lily before I go?'

DI Ford shakes his head. 'Not tonight.'

Chapter 47

LILY

AFTER A LONG wait, Lily was interviewed by two female detectives. Good cop and good cop. Way too much smiling. A quick run over how Lily came to find Sam in the shed. No challenges to her story. A couple of questions about the night of the attack. Did she remember anything else? She told them of the vague feeling that Sophia Lesinska and Sam might have been in the apartment.

'That's it from us, Ms Andersen.' The younger of the two closed her notebook and slid Lily's phone towards her. 'We'd like you to speak to some colleagues.'

'At this time?' Lily's head was sore, and she was exhausted. 'What about my solicitor?'

'We could make it tomorrow and you can bring your solicitor if you wish, but it might help you to know you're no longer a suspect in this case.'

'Then what do they want to talk about?'

'Nathan Collesso.'

Great. She shrugged. 'Might as well get it over with.'

It was gold star treatment from then on. A different room. Comfy chairs. Hot tea in a proper mug. Chocolate biscuits. Two officers from Professional Standards. Their questions should have been easy enough to answer. Who were his friends? What did he do in his spare time? She hadn't a clue. Didn't remember ever meeting a friend of his, and when he wasn't at home, he was at work. Or so he said.

What about lengthy phone calls?

There were lots of those, she said, but he always left the room. She told them of the call where he'd sounded scared and said someone was watching him.

Foreign trips?

Not that he'd told her. But all those courses and the false passport ... who knew? She told them about the email from Aleksander Bartosz, with the photos of girls. She shook her head as she realised. 'I've just remembered – a girl came to our door the night before Nathan went away. I wondered why she looked familiar. Her picture was in the email.' She described the girl and told them about Sophia's sister. 'Both said they were looking for someone called Tony. Though I was suspicious of Sophia's sister, I didn't realise it was Nathan they were after. You know about Nathan and Sophia, don't you?'

The tall one, DI Hammond, nodded. 'Lily, do you remember anything about the Thursday night that week? Was Nathan out?'

Lily thought back. She nodded. 'I was expecting him home for dinner, but he didn't come. I was in bed, asleep, when he got home, and he left early in the morning. I think he said the next night that something had come up at work.' She shrugged. 'It wasn't unusual.'

His eyes were like lasers. 'So, you didn't see him that night?'

She shook her head.

'Did you do the laundry? Anything unusual about the clothes he'd been wearing that day?'

A sudden burst of nausea rushed through her. 'Is this ... it's not anything to do with the allegations in the news, is it? One of those attacks was recent. Was it that night?'

The man's eyes didn't meet hers. 'Let's leave it there for now.'

Chapter 48

DAVID

EVEN WITH THE light on, the first bedroom in the Dumbiedykes flat was gloomy and cold. It smelled of sweat and sleaze, and there was an aura of desperation so thick David could almost taste it. It made him shiver. Jakub seemed unperturbed by any horrors that might lurk in the rumpled bedding. He lounged on the bed, his eyes on David, standing with his back against the door. David felt something tickle the back of his neck and he almost jumped. It was a red nylon robe, hanging on a hook. There was a scattering of cheap body sprays and make-up jars on the dusty dressing table, a pair of high heels in the corner. The drawer of the bedside cabinet was open. Inside, something long and pink glittered. David looked away. He wanted to open the curtains, open the window, run.

'You okay for Tuesday?' Jakub asked.

David nodded. A burst of laughter came from the living room.

Jakub shook his head. 'Henryk, he is ... what you Scottish people say? Hammered. Guttered. Pished. What is right?'

David smiled. 'Any of those will do.'

'That's why I take you in here. Best you stay away from him. He don't like you much after last time.'

David shrugged. 'Same here.'

'Be careful. I cannot keep him on chain always. But I keep him from the girls, from Aneta.'

'Can I see her?'

Jakub smiled and pushed himself from the bed. 'She is not here. All the girls are out. Aneta, well, she like to be going out and doing her thing.' He winked. 'She do it good, eh?'

David didn't bother to hide his disgust. 'You too?'

Jakub's laughter was loud and cold. 'I have ears, but I don't touch your little bonus. She don't have what I like.' He stood a little too close to David, and there was something unfathomable in his dark eyes. He lifted his hand, as if he was going to touch David's face, then he let it drop to his side, and he shrugged. 'I don't think Aneta have what you like, eh? But you take it, because you can.' He nodded towards the door, dismissing David.

Back home, David tried Eva again. Her phone went straight to voicemail. He'd been tempted earlier to ask her friend, Alison Blyth, what was going on. But he wasn't certain Alison knew about their relationship, and he didn't think it was his place to tell her. Looked like there was nothing to tell, anyway, when Eva was ignoring his calls and texts.

He was getting ready for bed when an email arrived from his mother. She was one of the few people that emailed him these days, everyone else preferring the brevity of texts and messages. She'd have a hard job fitting her regular island news bulletin into a text. She wrote like she talked, with scarcely a pause for breath. Tonight, he was glad of her ramblings. His brother-in-law's sciatica. His sister's job interview. The death of Jessie Bheag, in her late eighties. He'd known Jessie all his life, and she'd always seemed ancient. His old school friend caught drunk-driving. The weather, the sheep, how the hens were laying, and the price of fuel. And then the grand finale. There was a sergeant's post coming up in Stornoway in the next few months. His mother's best friend, Myra, had a third cousin that worked in the station. Myra was keeping his mother informed. It would be great to have him home, she wrote. He could work the croft in his spare time. Though he had no interest in working the croft, the thought of going home was more tempting than he'd ever admit to his mother. The island wasn't quite crime-free, but the chance of getting embroiled with an organised crime group from Eastern Europe was non-existent. Maybe he'd think about it, after all.

Chapter 49

SAM

MARGARET HAS PUT on weight, and wrinkled a little, but she still has those kind eyes and a bonny face. She seems unperturbed at seeing Sergeant Rodgers and Sam. She wasn't in bed yet, she tells them; it's been an exciting night. Are they coming in? Cup of tea?

Sergeant Rodgers shakes her head. 'Just dropping him off. Can he sleep in your shed again?'

Margaret's frowning. 'No, he can't sleep in my shed.'

The officer nods. 'I'm sure he'll find a spot somewhere.' To Sam. 'Do you want to make your own way to the station tomorrow for ten?'

'A spot? What do you mean a spot?' Margaret's reaching for Sam, grabbing his arm, pulling him towards the door. 'He'll sleep in my boxroom. It's clean and clutter-free now. Do you want to come and check? In fact, if we moved the bed, he could sleep in the front room and have a window. With the help of a sturdy lass like you, we'd have it moved in no time at all.'

Sergeant Rodgers looks peeved. 'Not my job.' She's backing away at speed. 'See you at quarter to ten, if you're still here.'

Sam's feeling cold and awkward, and all he wants is to find that spot and get some sleep. 'I'll get off.'

'You will not.'

He's inside. And then he's sitting at the kitchen table. Something to eat? A cup of tea?

A wee sherry or six would go down well, but he doesn't ask Margaret. He keeps his shaking hands beneath the kitchen table. 'It's kind of you, but I'm not one for eating at this time.'

'Nor at any time by the looks of you.'

He shrugs. 'I don't have a great appetite. I wake up hungry some mornings. Maybe tomorrow?'

Margaret nods. 'I've got organic eggs and bacon from happy pigs. Are you going to sleep in the boxroom?'

'I like the shed.'

She looks confused. 'Are you sure?'

He nods and smiles at her. She smiles back, and he sees a shadow of the girl he taught.

'You'll need a quilt and a pillow.' She bustles out of the room, muttering to herself.

She'd been a bright girl, and the brother had been quite a character. Did Lily say he'd died? He'll ask another time. He's tired and shaky, and he wants to sleep before the DTs catch up with him. But if they don't get him tonight, they'll get him in the morning, and he'll be no use to the cops. He eyes up the kitchen cupboards and wonders if she has a stash somewhere. But she's not a drinker. Her eyes are too bright.

She's back with the bedding. 'I'm sorry about the roses. I'm sure there's a manly set somewhere.'

'Roses are perfect. Margaret ... you wouldn't ... you don't have ...'

'How about a brandy before you go out? It's been quite a night. I don't drink very often, but I think it might help me sleep. And it'll keep you warm.'

Sam's heart is threatening to jump out of his mouth and dance across the table. 'That sounds nice.'

'It was Father's.'

Shit. The alcohol will have evaporated years ago. It'll be like cough mixture by now. A thick sugary syrup, no use to man or beast.

'It's in the den.'

'The den?'

'The cupboard in the hall. Father always kept his unopened bottles there. It's cold, you see. I won't be long.'

Unopened bottles. Sam's hands are drumming on the table, heart fluttering, stomach clenching, mouth watering.

A 1943 brandy. The bottle is a work of art. It would fetch a fortune at auction, but he can't tell her that. The ghost of the brandy is already in his mouth, warming his gullet, seeping through his stomach and his small intestine into his bloodstream. Bottle's not even open and he can feel that heat spreading through him, worming its way to his brain. His whole body, his whole being, is lighter and lighter, higher and higher, melting into warm oblivion.

'Sam?'

He shakes his head. 'Sorry?'

'Do you want anything in it?'

That'll be right. 'No. Straight as it comes, please.' He's sitting on his hands. Doesn't trust them not to wrestle the bottle from her and neck it in one go.

It's a decent measure, and he's willing his hands not to give him away. Willing his mouth not to gulp. Watching her take a delicate sip. And then his hands are on the glass, and he doesn't know if they're shaking or not, and he doesn't much care. One gulp and it's down.

Oh, my sweet Lord.

He's almost running down the path. Quilt, pillow and hot water bottle under one arm, brandy bottle in the other hand. She's not daft, Margaret. Would he like to take the bottle with him? Have another before he settles down for the night? She's seen him for exactly what he is, and right now, he couldn't care less.

*

176

SAM LIKES A good ankle. And two of them are such a bonus. He'd have put money on a bit of oedema, the classic pitted skin that holds the indentation of a finger pressed against it or the circle of an elasticated sock. But not Margaret. Her ankles are shapely and slim and he can't take his eyes off them as she flips his organic eggs.

'Sam?'

His face is burning and he can't look up. It's not sexual, he wants to tell her. That kind of urge left him along ago, around the same time as his wife and children. He rubs his face. 'Yes?'

'Two eggs or three?'

'Two, thank you.'

Happy pigs make bloody good bacon. And the eggs slip down like the oysters Sam ate on his honeymoon, a million years ago, when life was perfect and the future held only promise. Sam can't remember the last time he used proper cutlery, but he hasn't forgotten how to place it when he's done. At 12 o'clock, like his mother taught him. Knife edge pointing in. Fork tines pointing up.

Margaret's in her element. Smiling and humming and loving every minute. And he is too. She's very easy to be with. No questions, except how did he sleep and would he like a shower and a toothbrush? She's left a new one in the bathroom for him. She's left out some of Father's clothes too, but if he doesn't want them, that's fine. They're on their way to the charity shop as soon as Lily and Julie come back.

He remembers Lily's drawn pale face in the moonlight, before the officers hustled her away. Will she hate him when she learns he attacked the pig, and left her like a coward?

Margaret looks thoughtful. 'I'm going to call Julie. Ask her to send Lily over. Maybe tonight or tomorrow.'

He nods. 'The daytime would be better, and she can bring the wee one.'

Margaret's smile is gone. 'The wee what?'

'Her son. Wee Ronan.'

'She has a son? Does she have a man?'

There's a blue tit on the bird feeder at the window, clinging to the wire cage with delicate claws as its little beak pecks and pecks. 'She had. She … that's why the police were here. Did you hear about the missing policeman a few days ago?'

'Inspector Cornetto? I felt for his poor parents. What they must be going through.'

Sam nods. 'Indeed. But things are not always what they seem.'

'No, they are not. I didn't say I felt sorry for him, did I? Those poor girls. The man must have been a fiend. One of those sex beasts. And he had a fiancée and a child. Some men are incorrigible.' It only takes a moment for the penny to drop. 'Our Lily? Engaged to that monster? Oh, the poor darling. She's brought such light into my life. You wouldn't believe it.'

A spark of jealousy taunts Sam. He smiles and squashes it. 'Me too.'

She puts her hand to her mouth. 'The homeless man they wanted to question … was that you?'

'Aye, but I didn't kill him. Just a wee tap on the head before he killed Lily.'

'Good for you.' She frowns. 'There was a photo in the paper. Quite the handsome lad.'

'Aye. Never have I seen such a case of deceiving looks.'

She's still frowning as she waves him off in a pair of Father's trousers, a white shirt and a sports jacket. And brogues that pinch his feet.

Chapter 50

SAM

SHE'S A NASTY wee piece of work, that Sergeant Rodgers, with her mocking sneer.

'What's that you're modelling? Vintage 60s? You didn't take long to get into her old man's pants. It'll be hers next.' She sniffs. 'Did you raid her booze cabinet when she was sleeping?'

Nose like a bloodhound, and that face; he's seen better looking roadkill. He doesn't answer. Not worth it. He's showered and dressed, his hair combed, teeth brushed, and he's feeling pretty damn good.

The feeling doesn't last. An hour in, and Sam feels sick. He wants to clutch his knees and pull them up to his chest. He wants to be somewhere else, but there's no escaping. At least the officers from Professional Standards are taking him seriously, and they're courteous. They started off asking for descriptions of the girls he saw with Collesso. He has a good memory, but they all seemed to morph into one. Young. Probably legal, but only just. Short skirts and tops. Long skinny legs. Dark eyes and olive skin. Sometimes Collesso was alone with one of them, and they'd be so out of it, they could hardly walk. Other times, there might be a few of them with him. They were on the game, and it looked like Collesso was their pimp.

It's bad enough to talk of those girls, but this tale … it fills him with fear and dread and shame. He can see it all, as if on film. The moon shining. The air still and warm. He shouldn't have been there. Not in World's End Close. The very name still sends shivers down his spine. It was a combination of drink and yobs on the street that had seen him escape into a close that he usually avoided. He wouldn't get a good sleep, for he couldn't stop thinking of the two teenage lassies last seen in the World's End Pub, at the head of the close, in 1977. They'd left with two men, and their bodies were found in East Lothian the next day. It had taken decades to convict anyone of their murder, by which time one killer was dead, and the other responsible for a catalogue of sadistic crimes.

He must have drifted off, and he woke to the sound of grunting and moaning. The moon was shining down on the pig and a girl. Sam had stayed in the shadows and watched the pig roll off her, pull up his trousers, and spit on the cobbles. He'd picked something up off the ground, something red, and shoved it in his pocket. He'd walked away, smiling, without a backward glance at the girl. She'd groaned and rolled over onto her knees. The state she was in. Vomiting and crying, her skirt round her waist. Sam had covered her with his coat and held her hair back while she retched. The vomiting stopped. She'd looked at him, her eyes glazed, and asked why he'd done this to her, and where were her knickers.

Sam had grabbed his coat and sleeping bag, ran from the close. For days, he'd waited for the cops to lift him. His DNA would be all over her, from his coat. Maybe he should go to the cops and tell them everything. But they'd never believe him. He'd been accused before. He wasn't going through that again. And then the pig told Sam he'd seen him in the close that night. If he wanted to stay alive, the pig said, he'd say nothing. So, he said nothing.

The officer asks twice before Sam can find the words to answer. At last, he nods. Aye, he'd know the girl, even now. The desolation on her pretty face is etched on his brain, and he can still hear her words, slurred in a local accent.

The other man leans across the table. 'Were you watching Inspector Collesso? Were you following him?'

As if. No, he says. He'd slept in closes and courtyards off the Mile for years. It was fear of the pig that made him move to Old Calton Burial Ground. They want every detail of the attacks on Sam. He hadn't realised there were so many until he starts to recount them. He wipes at his mouth, but he can't erase the unpleasant taste of the memories, even after they're all out. And then it hits him. Although the pig had been a nasty piece of work for years, the assaults only started after Lily befriended Sam. The pig had been watching. That's why he hated Sam so much.

The thin veneer of wellbeing from the morning is gone. He's a useless, alky bastard, just like the pig always said. He did nothing for those girls, nothing to stop that monster, nothing to protect Lily.

He can't go back to Margaret's afterwards. Can't face the chat and the cheerfulness. He considers going to his pitch, but he's awkward in Margaret's father's clothes and he doesn't want to have to explain himself to his regulars and fellow beggars. He wanders down to the dry hostel at the Cowgate, where he has a meal and a chat with Peter. The man understands. He knows what Sam means when he says a part of him just wants to get back to the life he knew. But that life will never be the same. He'll be constantly watching over his shoulder, waiting for the pig to get him. And he's tasted a bit of luxury now – the soft pillow and quilt, the hot water bottle, the brandy, the fine clothes. Hard to turn away from that. His head is so mixed up; he doesn't know what to do.

'You don't have to decide right now,' Peter tells him. 'Go back and get a good sleep. Think about it tomorrow.'

Sam gives Margaret's door a timid knock, and she pulls it open immediately, as if she's been waiting behind it. She smiles. 'You look like you need some rest. A good book, and a big torch.'

There's a box of books in the cupboard. He picks up the top book, a hardback, and he gasps. 'I can't take that to the shed. It's worth a fortune.'

'Away with you. What's so special about it?'

'Careful. It looks as if it's never been read.'

'But it has. I carried it back and fore to school every day for weeks while we studied it in your class. Then my dad and my brother read it. We knew how to look after books in my family.'

It's a signed first edition, second print copy of *To Kill a Mockingbird*. On the back, there's a picture of Harper Lee, taken by Truman Capote. The dust jacket alone would triple the value of the book. He tells her, but she's not interested.

'Here.' She shoves it at him. 'It's not worth much in a box. Go on. Off to bed with you. Have a brandy to help you sleep.'

A few slugs of brandy and less than half a page of the book, and he's asleep.

Chapter 51

LILY

Ronan stared at the man that held Margaret's front door open. Lily did a double-take. Sam looked so different. Clean-shaven, in smart clothes, his hair tidy. She could have passed him on the street. When Sam spoke, Ronan laughed. 'Sam!'

Sam waved at Ronan, then he took Lily's hand. 'I'm sorry.'

'No, I'm sorry.'

He frowned. 'What for?'

'Dragging you into this. I wouldn't have mentioned you if they hadn't found the suitcase. And then leading them to you like that. You?'

'For not finishing off that … that lowlife when I had the chance. Leaving you alone and injured. Everything.'

'So, you were there, in the flat?'

'They didn't tell you?'

Lily shook her head. 'Didn't tell me anything, and my memory's been bad. It's like trying to join the dots, but they keep jumping about, then they fade to nothing. Was I on the balcony? Did you carry me to the sofa?'

He nodded. 'Just before –'

There was a shout from the kitchen. 'What are you two doing out there?'

'Come in, come in.' Sam took the pushchair from Lily and wheeled it into the kitchen. 'Margaret, meet Prince Ronan.'

'Your Majesty.' Margaret knelt down and tickled Ronan's chin. He grabbed the tie of her blouse and tugged, laughing as he pulled out the bow.

Margaret laughed too. 'Cheeky monkey, aren't you? Lily, oh Lily. Come in. Sit down.' She turned to the cooker, humming as she added some bacon to the pan.

Lily kept her voice low. 'Do you know where Nathan is?'

'Dada Naishan.' Ronan banged the table. 'Where Dada?'

Lily took a wee farm animal board book from her pocket. It was on a twisted plastic cord. Ronan pulled it straight and let it go, laughing as the cord curled up again. He opened the book.

Sam shrugged. 'Some men took him away. Big foreign lads. Eastern Europeans, I think. There was a woman with them. Long dark hair. She phoned an ambulance, then she left with them.' He shook his head. 'Still can't believe it, Lily. You and that –'

'Pig,' Ronan said, pointing to a picture in the book.

Sam nodded. 'Exactly.'

Lily laughed.

'What are you two whispering about?' Margaret's smile beamed across the room. She had an egg in her left hand, a plastic spatula in her right. There was a smear of oil shining on her cheek. 'Would you like an egg, Lily? Some bacon? Sausages? They're from happy pigs.'

Lily shook her head. 'No thanks; I ate earlier.'

'Shauthage.' Ronan banged his hands on the table.

Margaret put a brimming plate of food in front of Sam, then she passed a small plate with a sausage to Lily. When it had cooled, Ronan chomped into it with gusto. Lily's head was buzzing. Eastern Europeans? Those Polish girls at the door. The photos attached to the email. Was Nathan involved in trafficking girls from Poland to Scotland?

'You're a very handsome little boy. Yes, you are.' Margaret took Ronan from Lily.

He was grinning, his little white teeth shining. 'Mo shauthage.'

'Another one, Mummy?'

Lily smiled. 'Maybe just a half, or he'll never eat his lunch.'

'Half it is. Lily, there's something on the hall table. It came in the post today. I couldn't believe my eyes. That engine of yours must be good. Go and have a look.'

There was an envelope addressed to Margaret, with photos and a hand-written note from Isobel MacLean. A widow, she lived in Haddington. Three of a family: a boy and two girls. The boy, her first-born, Tommy MacLean, lived in London. His date of birth was four months after Margaret's brother died. It had been so easy once Lily knew the brother's name. Only one Trevor Fleming from Edinburgh on Facebook. He'd taken a while to answer Lily's message.

'Splendid news, isn't it?' Margaret was there, Ronan in her arms. 'I'm going to phone Isobel later. I'm so excited.' She glanced at the kitchen door and lowered her voice. 'I'd like Sam to stay in the house, but he doesn't want to. Can't be good for him in the shed. What do you think?'

'He's been on the streets for a long time. That shed is like a mansion to him. You know he has a drink problem?'

'I guessed. What could have changed his life so? I don't like to ask.'

'Nor me.'

'The winter's coming. What then? If he came in as a lodger, he'd have an address and he could claim his pension. He wouldn't have to beg.' She passed Ronan back to Lily. 'I'll make myself scarce. You have a word.'

*

SAM NODDED. 'You've got me there, Lily. I did say the thing I missed most about not having an address was being able to vote. I'd dearly love to have a say if we ever get another independence referendum. We can't carry on like this. And just wait until Brexit. We're fucked.'

He put his hand over his mouth. 'Sorry. I'll have to clean up my act.'

Ronan wasn't listening. He was sitting on the table, making a buzzing sound as he waved a travel hairdryer around his head.

Lily smiled. 'Margaret only wants what's best for you. If you say you want to stay in the shed for now, she'll accept that. She'll probably want to insulate it and put in heating.'

'I take it she's a woman of means?'

She nodded. 'Her father left her well provided for.'

'I'd never take advantage of that.'

'I know.' She put her hand on his. 'No one thinks that.'

'Will you tell her I'd like to stay in the shed for now?'

She smiled. 'Of course. Can I give you some money?'

He shook his head. 'No. I've got food and books and everything I need.'

'Drink?'

He blushed and looked away. 'There's brandy in the shed, and plenty more where that came from, apparently. Don't like to take her booze, but if I don't, I'll know all about it. Maybe that pension idea is a good thing. I could buy stuff for myself.'

'I'll look into it next week, get you a form.'

He smiled. 'You're a darling. But are you all right? You're so pale.'

'I'll be fine. Just want to get moved into our own place, and back to work, but I've to wait for the all clear from the doctor. Careful.' Lily ducked as Ronan started waving the hairdryer around her head.

There was a shout from Margaret. 'Lily, come and see what I've done with the boxroom.'

Sam reached for Ronan. 'You can dry my hair.'

Lily's stomach lurched as Sam slid Ronan across the table. There was a voice in her head shouting at her to take her child away. A memory … She tried to grasp it, but she couldn't. It was so vague, but she had to heed it. She lifted Ronan. 'We better go. I need to rest.'

Ronan wriggled. 'No, Mama. Sam's hair.'

'You can do Sam's hair another day.'

Chapter 52

SAM

Sam drains the last of the brandy and wipes his mouth. That look in Lily's eyes as she pulled Ronan away from him. How did she know? Was it Margaret that told her? But he wasn't living in Edinburgh then. They were in Perth, and the case never made the papers. His father-in-law saw to that. Anything to protect his precious daughter and his grandchildren. Sam's children. His daughters. His son. The only photo he had of the three of them had been safe in his pocket until the pig found it and tore it into shreds while he laughed in Sam's face. He spent hours trying to put those fragments back together, tears and snot dripping all over them until all that was left was a sticky pile of nothing, and a fading memory of their wee faces. Didn't take long for their faces to disappear. The pig must have told Lily about the investigation. That's the only way she could know.

He has to get out of here. Get money and booze. He's pulling off Margaret's father's clothes. Scrabbling in the corner of the shed for the rags he discarded. Idiot. What was he thinking? That he could go back to who he was? He is who he is. No amount of happy pigs, organic eggs or posh clothes can change that. As he turns, his elbow knocks the book to the floor, the cover fluttering after it. He wants to stamp all over it, all over the stupid dream that things could be different.

But why do that, when he could make good money from it? He'll take it to Geordie's pal, the one who deals in antiques and asks no questions. He won't even have to fight for his pitch. No need to beg for a good long while. There's a pang of guilt as he slips it into his pocket. He's never stolen anything in his life, but where has honesty ever got him?

Chapter 53

LILY

Lily listened to the faint sounds of Philip and Julie's Saturday night. The clinking of dishes and cutlery, laughter, the news on the radio. Philip getting a bottle of wine from the cupboard under the stairs. All muted, for Lily's benefit. So normal, warm and real. She felt safe for the first time in a long time. That pristine, soulless apartment. The empty relationship. Nothing but their child in common. Nathan incapable of love and closeness and honesty. Lily so desperate to make it work, whatever the cost. Such a sham.

Lily had gone to bed at the same time as Ronan. She was exhausted and her head was sore from going over and over the incident with Sam, and wishing she'd reacted differently. He wouldn't have hurt Ronan; she was certain of it. But it was too late now, and she couldn't get his look of utter dismay out of her head.

And then, on the edge of sleep, something else came into her head. Though she'd strained so hard over recent days to recapture the memory of the day she was injured, when it came, she didn't want it. But it was going nowhere. Just playing over and over, like a film in her head.

She's on her knees on the floor in the lounge, Nathan's mouth pressed against her ear. 'Where is it, you bitch? Tell me, or I swear I will kill you.'

The poker for the fire is on the floor, discarded and bloody.

'Nathan.' Her voice is slurred. A warm stream of blood trickles down her neck, and her vision is blurring. 'I don't know what you –'

He drags her to her feet and throws her on the sofa. He straddles her, his hands in her hair, shaking her. There's blood on the white furniture. The thought of his mother's face when she sees it makes Lily laugh. He explodes, hitting her on the face, on her head. She puts her hands up to protect herself, and there's a dull crack and a sharp pain as he bends her finger backwards.

'The money.' He's slavering as he shakes her. 'Where is it?'

'Five thousand?'

'I don't give a shit about that. Where is the suitcase?'

'Sam's case?'

'What has that kiddie-fiddler got to do with anything?'

She shakes her head and winces as a bolt of pain shoots through her. 'Not Sam.'

His laughter is loud and his voice mocking. 'Not Sam, your poor homeless little friend? He's a pervert. Lost his wife and his family and his home because he couldn't resist touching up children. And you, sitting on the ground beside him, touching him, reading to him, letting him slaver all over my son. Do you know how much I hated you when I saw that? The way you looked at him, like you never looked at me. Like you really loved him. You respected him. You cared.' His voice breaks. 'You cared more for an alky pervert than you cared for me.'

He's ranting as he pulls her towards the balcony door. The money, the suitcase, Sam. She's a whore, a thief, a bitch. They're on the balcony, her feet scrabbling on the metal treads, trying to stop him as he drags her towards the railings. It's hopeless. He's bending her backwards over the metal rail, his words hissing in her ear. 'Tell me where it is. If I don't kill you, they will. They're on their way, and you don't know who you're messing with. I'm going to give you one last chance.' His voice drops to a whisper. 'Where is the money?'

There's a soft breeze, the song of birds, the sound of traffic. As the blood oozes down her neck, a shape looms behind Nathan. Her eyes drift closed.

Even her perception of the attack was a sham. She'd thought he'd discovered she was leaving him. But it seemed he hadn't even known. All he was worried about was the money in Sam's suitcase. Had he put it there, thinking the suitcase belonged to the Collesso family? Just an old case that no one used for anything other than random books? How much money was in it, and where had it come from? She hadn't looked in it for ages, not since she'd started giving Sam books of her own. And Sam: was there any truth in what Nathan had said? She had to find out.

Ronan stirred when she put on the bed-side lamp, and then he settled. She called the phone number she'd been given by the officers from Professional Standards. They asked her to come in on Monday afternoon to give another statement.

One more call to make. In her bag, she found a scrappy piece of paper with a phone number.

'Hello.'

That voice. She wanted to close her eyes and ask him to keep talking. Didn't matter what he said.

'Hello. Who is this?'

'David. It's Lily. Are you at work?'

'Lily. It's lovely to hear from you.' He sounded as if he meant it. 'I'm off for a few days.' She fancied she heard the strains of a Runrig track fading as he turned it down. 'Why are you whispering?'

'Ronan's sleeping.'

'How have you been?'

'Okay. I wanted to ask you something. Not on the phone, though. Can we meet?'

'Of course. Tomorrow?'

Chapter 54

DAVID

'MY FATHER WAS a fisherman too.' As she spoke the words, Lily's smile slipped away. She hunched her shoulders, almost folding in on herself. It was such a contrast to earlier. While they'd walked along the waterfront at Cramond, watching the boats swaying in the swell, she'd been so animated. She'd asked David if he minded talking about his father. He'd shaken his head, and questions had poured from her. What size of boat did he have? Had David gone out with him as a child? What did they catch? Who was waiting for them at home?

He'd been a wonderful dad, he told Lily, as they walked. A little stern, but never unkind. He sometimes seemed lonely, in a house with one quiet boy and three females who were loud and confident and opinionated. David went out in the boat with him as often as he could, and he loved that time away from his mother and his sisters. Just the boys. His father would talk more then. He loved fishing and the sea, but he tried to discourage David from following in his footsteps. There was little money to be made, and the risks were too high. He should find himself a good solid job on land. Probably best to leave Lewis. There were more opportunities on the mainland. His father had almost choked on those words, torn between his love of the island and its heritage, and his belief that success and prosperity for his son could only be found elsewhere.

Brought up in the Free Church, his father never questioned the strict doctrine passed down to him by his parents. He went to church twice on Sunday and a couple of prayer meetings during the week. Lily had laughed when she heard that this pious man had married a humanist who wouldn't allow their children to be indoctrinated.

'They never argued about it.' David smiled. 'He'd be sitting reading the Bible on Sunday afternoon, and we'd be at the beach. There were evening visits from the minister and the elders of the church, desperate to save us from eternal torment. My mother would smile and offer them tea. When their talk strayed into matters of religion and Sabbath observance, she'd change the subject. Without shouting her down, they didn't stand a chance. And my poor dad would just sit there. I know it concerned him. If you believe in an eternal hell, and you know that's where your loved ones are heading, it must be torture. Still, he never preached at us. The closest he got was singing psalms when I went out in the boat with him. He had a wonderful voice, and I loved to hear him sing. Sometimes I thought I might have liked to go to church with him, but I didn't want to upset my mother.'

It had been a long time since he'd talked of his father. Though he went home as often as he could, his mother and his sisters didn't like to talk about their loss. He'd felt the same for the first few years, while his head and his heart had railed against the cruelty of fate, but eventually the pain had eased into acceptance, then gratitude.

Lily had gone quiet, so he'd suggested they go for a coffee. And then she'd told him about her father. He wondered why she'd said it when the words seemed to cause her such pain.

'Where did he fish from?' David asked.

'Hamnøy. It's a fishing village in the Lofoten islands in Norway.' She stared into the swirling foam in her mug.

A Norwegian father. That explained the spelling of her surname.

David watched as she struggled with the memories, waiting while she sorted her words into something coherent, something bearable.

'We moved to Norway when I was five. He died six years later, and my mother and I came back to Scotland.'

He leaned towards her. 'Tell me about Hamnøy.'

What a picture she painted, when at last the words came. It was the oldest fishing village in Lofoten, surrounded by huge, jagged mountains. She spoke of long summer nights, and daytime trips to sheltered inlets, their shoreline rich with puffins, sea eagles and cormorants. Dark nights when the northern lights danced across a land strewn with tiny fishermen's cabins perched on stilts above raging winter seas.

Winter was a season of excitement, when the men fished for the cod that migrated south from the Barents Sea, spawning in Lofoten. The thrill of waiting for the first catch. The delight in her eyes. 'Google it,' she said.

He did, and the images took his breath. 'It looks amazing.'

'Can I see?'

She clutched his phone, flicking through the pictures. When she looked up, there were tears glistening in her eyes. 'It's so long since I've talked of it or seen it. Thank you. Do you mind if I look up something else?'

He shook his head and watched as her thumbs tapped and then her eyes grew wider, and a tear spilled from her right eye and trickled down her cheek. He almost lifted his hand to stop it, but she rubbed it away and held the phone up. It was a picture taken at dusk, of a simple wooden church, a gentle floodlit glow stretching across snow-covered graves.

'It's the church at Flakstad.' Her voice was low, and he had to lean forward to hear her. 'That's where he's buried. Among the fishermen that lost their lives at sea. Those that the sea gave up.' She looked up, her brow creased. 'Was your dad …?'

David shook his head. 'He wasn't found.'

She put the phone on the table. 'I'm sorry. That must be so hard.'

He smiled. 'It's okay. I've had a long time to get used to it.'

'My father would have given his life to the sea if he'd had a choice. Far better, far more honourable, he said, than shrivelling to a shadow at the mercy of his own mutant cells.'

'Do you speak Norwegian? Are you fluent?'

She shook her head. 'Not now. I remember some, but not enough.' She frowned. 'I would love to go back and see my family. Maybe one day.'

David smiled. 'It's important to go home, back to your roots.'

She leaned towards him, excitement on her face and a touch of apprehension. 'Norway's not really home.'

'No? Where then?'

She fiddled with her scarf, rolling the tasselled ends between her fingers. She smiled. 'It's –'

His phone vibrated and pinged as a text came in. A wave of dread poured over him and he wanted to snatch it away before she could look at the screen. He'd let himself be lulled into behaving as if they were friends. He'd let her think she could trust him, as if he hadn't already betrayed her a dozen or more times.

She looked at the screen, then up at him, her eyes wide and wounded. She shoved the phone across the table. He looked down.

I must see you tonight. Sophia.

'I … it's not what you think. It's just … I'm not … we're not …'

She laughed, and there was a chilly edge to it. 'None of my business. Makes a change for her to be involved with someone that's not about to marry someone else, presuming you're not.'

She put on her coat and glanced at the door. Looked like she was thinking of leaving without asking him whatever it was she'd come for. He almost prompted her, but then she'd know just how desperate he was for her to stay.

At last, she spoke, her tone brisk. 'That thing I wanted to ask: it's Sam. I've remembered some of what happened the night I was attacked. Nathan said Sam was a pervert, that he lost his family because he interfered with children. Do you know if it's true?'

David frowned as he considered what he could tell her without breaking any more rules. 'I don't know much,' he said, at last. 'Didn't know anything until Collesso told me after we'd been to the hospital to see Sam. I looked into it a bit. There was a significant amount of anecdotal evidence to suggest Sam was innocent. There was no prosecution and no conviction. He's not on the sex offenders' register. I don't think Ronan is at risk from him. The allegations came from a female much older than Ronan, but still a child. Does that put your mind at rest?'

She nodded. He wished he could tell her more. That the girl was fifteen and troubled. That after Sam had lost his family and an impeccable teaching career, after he'd taken to the bottle and the streets, the girl had accused two lecturers and a janitor at the local college of the same thing. There were undoubtedly girls that attracted a series of abusers, girls that might just as well have their vulnerability tattooed across their foreheads, girls that would never escape the cycle. But no one believed this girl was one of them, and none of her complaints had resulted in prosecution. It seemed Sam may well have fallen prey to one of the occupational hazards of teaching as a young man.

Lily looked at her watch. 'I have to go. I'll get a bus.'

'Please let me take you back.'

She shook her head. As he watched her walk away, David felt as if he'd been hollowed out. Nothing left inside but self-loathing.

Chapter 55

LILY

SAM WAS GONE, and so were his old clothes. Margaret was distraught. He'd die. Starve to death. Freeze. Spontaneously combust. Or drink himself senseless and fall in front of a bus. Julie had listened to Margaret's fears over and over during two phone calls, she told Lily. 'I tried to tell her he looked after himself for years on the streets, but she wouldn't listen. She wants you to call her.'

Lily had no more success than Julie at calming Margaret down. The conversation went round in circles until her head was buzzing. 'I'll let you know if I see him,' Lily said. 'No, he doesn't have a mobile phone. No, I don't think you should call the police. No, I don't think you should go out looking for him. No –' She looked at the handset. 'Charming. She just put the phone down on me.'

Julie laughed. 'Me too. How did it go with David?'

Lily hesitated. No point in telling Julie about David and Sophia. She repeated what David had said. 'I wish I'd reacted differently yesterday. I'd hate to think that's what's put Sam back on the streets, if that's where he is.'

'Will we look when Ronan wakes up? Philip invited us over for dinner. We could take a detour, drive around and see if we can find him.'

They found a girl in Sam's pitch on George IV Bridge. She was well-settled; been there for days, she said in her slow rasping voice, her eyes half shut, head nodding. Aye, she knew Sam, but she hadn't seen him. Didn't want to. She wasn't giving up this spot. Did Lily have any money? No? Fags? No? Fuck's sake.

They looked in some closes off the High Street and the Canongate. Not a homeless person to be found. Lily didn't want to go any further up than St Giles. Even that was too close to Ramsay Garden; it made her head ache. It was getting late when they drove past the Old Calton Burial Ground. She would have gone in, but Julie wouldn't let her.

'I'll maybe come back tomorrow morning,' Lily said.

Julie shook her head. 'You're going to the police station in the afternoon. You need to rest. Sam will be fine.'

*

LILY HARDLY SLEPT, fear snaking up inside her at the thought of her interview. No doubt they were going to ask about Nathan's violence. How could she talk of it without trying to explain why she'd stayed? She hadn't the first clue, other than her stupid dream they might one day be a happy family.

And it wasn't just the interview that was bothering her. It was David. She'd trusted him. More than that. She hadn't forgotten the things he'd whispered in hospital when he thought she was unconscious. He'd begged her to wake up, telling her how much she meant to him, saying he'd always be there for her. She'd believed him. When they'd walked at Cramond, she'd felt a hint of excitement that she hadn't felt for a long time. It had made her open up to him. Now she just felt stupid.

In the morning, Lily showered and dressed and put her makeup on before Ronan was awake. When he came to with his usual grin, she lifted him, changed him and dressed him, then she fixed on a smile and they went downstairs.

Julie was ready to leave for work. 'I'll see you at lunchtime,' she said.

'Are you sure? I could try Nina, the child-minder.'

Julie shook her head. 'It's fine. I'm not busy today.'

Ronan was sitting on the kitchen floor with a pile of bricks. He waved goodbye to Julie. Lily turned to the sink. Through the window, she could see Cleo sitting on the fence below a big birch tree full of sparrows. Her tail was wagging back and fore as the birds flitted from branch to branch, taunting her. Lily felt a touch on her leg. It was Ronan. He was standing. She put him in the same spot and walked backwards to the sink. He smiled, then he bent forward until his hands were on the floor and his bum was in the air. Lifting his hands, he took off, bowed legs wobbling, body swaying. He didn't fall. One shaking wonderful step at a time, he made his way towards her, his grin growing wider and wider. She held him, tears falling on his silky head.

*

DI HAMMOND INTRODUCED DI Miller. The female officer was in her fifties, with a firm handshake and steely blue eyes that softened when Lily began to answer their questions. Lily felt as if she was talking about someone else, a weak, timid person who let others walk all over her. By the time she'd told them everything, she scarcely recognised herself.

'We'd like to get some photos of the scars on your cheek,' DI Hammond said. 'Are there any other scars?'

Lily shook her head. No visible scars, anyway.

DI Miller stood. She gave Lily a tight smile. 'Come with me. There's just one more thing after the photos.'

Lily swallowed a groan. They knew. That thing she'd been running from ever since the news of those other girls in the paper. The one thing she hadn't told them.

The photographer was around Lily's age, and she had a bright smile. She gave Lily wipes to clean the make-up off her face. 'Sorry you have to do that. It's a bummer.' She tilted Lily's head from side to side until she got the light just right. 'The marks are very faint. Not necessarily the best evidence for our purposes, but definitely good for you. You don't really need make-up to cover them.'

Lily nodded. 'I don't wear it often. Felt in need of some armour today.'

'That's understandable. Are you almost finished?'

'I hope so.'

Back in the interview room, there was a tension that made Lily shiver. Neither officer made eye contact with her as she sat and pulled her chair in. When, at last, DI Miller looked at Lily, there was something new in her eyes. Sadness? Shame? Lily couldn't tell. DI Miller pushed an evidence bag across the table.

A pair of knickers from Marks & Spencer. Navy with spots and a little bow at the front. Regular, every-day, ordinary knickers. Size ten. From a set of five pairs, variations on a blue and white theme.

'Are they yours?' DI Miller asked.

Lily tried to stifle the groan, but it escaped through her pursed lip.

'Ms Andersen?'

She shrugged.

'They were in the attic of the apartment, in a small holdall with several other pairs. Your DNA is on this pair. None of the others.'

Lily hugged herself, but she couldn't stop her body from shaking. There was no way to avoid it. Not now.

Chapter 56

LILY

EDINBURGH WOULD BE buzzing, Lily's flatmates had said. A great way to celebrate the end of their third-year exams. She'd declined. Told them she'd be fine on her own. She didn't tell them just how much she'd enjoy having the flat to herself. It wasn't easy for an only child to share a flat with four others. They were all fine in their own way, but together ... sometimes it was too much for her. She relished the thought of a night alone ... or maybe not quite alone.

She'd met Andy at a party five weeks before her exams. He was a marine biologist, a post-graduate. They'd chatted for ages about the sea and wildlife and conservation. When he was leaving, he'd taken her hand, stared deep into her eyes and thanked her. She didn't want his thanks. She just wanted him to kiss her.

They met up twice after that, and still he didn't kiss her. She convinced herself he wasn't interested in her in that way; he obviously just wanted to be friends. He asked her to come and hear his band playing in a pub. She almost said no. Her exams were only two weeks away. But she went. There weren't many in the musty stone vault of the pub. Mostly family and friends of the band. They sounded good, but the words were lost in a morass of drums and bass. In front of her, the drummer's mother danced in fishnet tights, like a knock-kneed chicken with one leg tethered to the floor. Lily wanted to leave. And then Andy sang the Cure's "Lovesong". Their eyes locked, and everyone around them disappeared.

He kissed her that night, outside the pub. As her heart threatened to leap from her chest, she pulled away. She told him she couldn't see him again until the exams were over. He'd smiled, and in his eyes, she saw a promise of things to come. She'd gone out with a few guys over the years, but, though most of them seemed keen, it never went further than a couple of dates. She just wasn't that interested. There were no secrets in the flat, and the others laughed at Lily's chastity. Who was she saving herself for? When she met Andy, she knew the answer.

But there was plenty of time for him, her flatmates said. He'd wait. It was only one night. She'd never been to Edinburgh? No way. She was coming, and that was that.

And so she went. And it was fun, at first. They were staying with a flatmate's cousin in a place off Leith Walk, all bunking down in the living room. They dumped their stuff and headed out. Cocktails in Harvey Nichols. Shopping in the shadow of the Castle, and Lily could hardly take her eyes off the Princes Street skyline. Food in an Indian restaurant at the West End. Lots of pubs. Lots of *craic*. And too much drink.

Lily remembered the party up to a point. It was a dingy place. Two of her flatmates slipped into dark bedrooms with guys they'd only just met. She wanted to leave, but she couldn't find the cousin whose flat they were staying in. Exhausted, she wanted to lie down, but the other bedroom doors were locked. She phoned Andy. It went straight to voicemail, and she left a stupid message. Something vaguely suggestive. Something that would embarrass the hell out of her in the morning.

Lily didn't want any more to drink, but someone gave her a plastic cup of something, and everything changed. She remembered throwing up in a stinking bathroom, then fighting the urge just to sleep there, her head resting on a sticky toilet bowl, until someone lifted her from the floor.

A smile. Perfect teeth. A drink of water, and a sleek car. Stumbling feet and powerful arms, helping her up so many stairs. And then nothing until the following afternoon.

*

THE BLACK SILK sheets felt horrible on her skin. She pushed them away. Tried to get up, but her head was spinning and aching and broken. There was an en-suite, and someone came through the open door. A policeman? What?

Terror gripped and twisted her stomach. She scrambled into a sitting position and heaved. He shoved a basin under her chin. 'Here.'

When she was done, he brought her a towel. He kept his distance while she wiped at her mouth. 'Poor you,' he said. 'I didn't think you had anything left to throw up. I've cleaned up the kitchen and the en-suite. I'll have to leave the sofa until I get home from work.' He looked at his watch. 'This is awkward, but I'm already late.'

'Who are you?' With every word, her stomach lurched.

He smiled. 'You don't remember? Not anything?'

She shook her head.

'That's a first.' He sat on the side of the bed. 'I'm Nathan. We met at the party … in the kitchen. You were … eh … let's just say I stopped you making a fool of yourself on the kitchen table. The guy with the beard? Dirty dancing?'

No. No way. 'The police were called?'

'Your dancing wasn't that bad.' His smile was so broad, his teeth so white. 'No, Lily; I wasn't on duty. Police officers have private lives too. You jumped off the table, right into my arms. It was quite romantic, really. Ordered me to take you home. Do you not remember anything?'

'No.'

He frowned and looked at his watch again. 'Listen, I have to go. I could give you a lift somewhere, but my car ... well ... it's quite new.'

She wiped her mouth, then her brow. 'I don't think I can walk.'

'Okay. I'll go to work and try to get back here in an hour or so. We'll get you sorted out then.'

He was on his way down the stairs before she realised she was naked. And sore. So very sore. Everywhere. A vice gripped her lower abdomen. She scrambled off the bed, and it turned out she could walk. Run, even. She only just made it. Whoever planned the layout of the en-suite had done it well. You could use the toilet and spew into the sink at the same time.

Lily had never felt this bad in her life. There had been sickness – the usual childhood plagues. There had been period pains that had kept her off school. But nothing like this poisoning of her body and her brain, so that each nauseous thought brought on spasms of guilt and pain and confusion. If someone had handed her an easy way out, a gun, say, she would have been tempted.

When she thought it might be safe to leave the en-suite, she scanned the bedroom for her clothes. They weren't there. Just a white t-shirt on a chair. She put it on and inched her way downstairs, supported by the wall and the banister. Halfway down, she had to sit and wait for the world to stop spinning. But she couldn't wait, because sitting was painful, and she didn't want to have to think about why that might be.

The flat was white and pristine throughout, spoiled only by a stain on the sofa. Her clothes were scattered around the lounge. She put them on and they felt sticky and grubby and cheap. They were for the bin as soon as she got home. She searched for her knickers, but she couldn't find them. The contents of her handbag were spilled out on a white rug of the softest wool. She snatched up her phone. It was switched off. Her jittery hands could hardly hold it, far less turn it on. At last, it came to life. Four missed calls and six texts from her flatmates. And a voicemail from Andy.

Hey Lily. I'm so sorry I missed your call. You've no idea. I had such a boring night. All I wanted to do was call you, but I didn't want to disturb your fun. Then you call when I'm fast asleep and my phone's switched off. Let me know as soon as you're back. We have so much celebrating to do. And Lily ... I ... God ... I can't wait to see you.

The phone rang. It was Anna. They were getting the bus in two hours. Where was she? Lily groaned. 'I'm sick. Really sick.'

'Jeez, you weren't that bad. You should have seen the state of Leanne by the end of the night, and she's tucking into a fry-up as we speak. Disgusting – bacon fat dribbling down her chin.'

Lily ran to the kitchen. There was nothing left to come up. Just dry boaking, wringing her stomach. She wiped her mouth on a dish towel. 'Sorry, Anna. You still there?'

'I really didn't need to hear that. Listen, we'll take your things. Meet you at the bus station at four thirty.'

Lily had been to mindfulness classes. The others had laughed, their derision so typical of many in the medical profession. Though studies had shown the benefits of mindfulness training, both to patients and medical staff, if it didn't come in an injection, a tablet or a capsule, and cause myriad horrible side-effects, it couldn't be up to much. But she'd enjoyed it, focussing on the present moment, acknowledging her feelings, her thoughts, the sensations of her body.

On the balcony, wrapped in a coat she'd found hanging in a hall cupboard, she closed her eyes and tried to meditate. It was almost impossible, with her head and her heart racing, and that constant dull ache between her legs. As she focussed on exactly what her body was doing, she felt her breathing settle, her heart rate slow and the nausea subside, just a little. She could live with this. It couldn't last forever. When she heard a key in the door, she felt the panic rise. She stopped it.

She took a cup of tea from Nathan, and it stayed down. She listened to what he had to say about the previous night, and, though she felt the safety of the world as she knew it slip a little, she didn't show it. He offered her a lift to the bus station, and she accepted.

'You've got my number,' he said. 'Let me know if you're in Edinburgh again. Maybe we can have another night of fun.'

Lily had no memory of exchanging numbers, or of any fun. She wouldn't be calling him again. Her face scarlet, she told him she couldn't find her knickers. He shrugged. As far as he remembered, she wasn't wearing any. Must have lost them at the party before they met. Maybe it was that guy, the one she was dancing with. The one he'd saved her from.

*

IN THE INTERVIEW room, tears and tangled words poured from Lily. It was her fault the other girls had suffered. Drink had never affected her like that. She should have known he'd drugged her. She should have seen a doctor, had a blood test. And those flashbacks over the next few months, those hideous flickering moments in black and white, alien scenes from a triple-X-rated movie that had made her heart race and her face burn. They weren't real. They couldn't be.

Before long, she knew she was pregnant, and that could do strange things to the brain. When Ronan was born, there could be no more thought of it. How could she even consider that her precious boy was conceived that way?

DI Hammond crouched beside her, his eyes glistening. He put a box of hankies on her knee and squeezed her arm. 'It is not your fault. He did this to others before he met you. We're going to get him, Lily. He's going to pay. And you need to see someone, a professional. For your sake and Ronan's.'

Chapter 57

JULIE

Julie kissed Ronan's cheek and pulled the quilt over him. Big Bunny clutched tight, his long eyelashes flickered and closed. She could have stayed there, just watching, if it wasn't for the memories that took her back to the life she might have had, if things had turned out differently. She'd put it all behind her long ago, hadn't spoken of it in years, and didn't intend to start now. But the memories had been inching closer since Lily and Ronan came to stay, and her house had taken on the feel of a family home. Ronan's smell and his laughter. The soft tread of Lily's footsteps in the dead of night. She'd tried to fight the memories off, but they poked at her, keeping her awake when everyone else slept. It was easier during the day. So much to do. She kissed Ronan again and left him and Big Bunny to their sleep.

In the back garden, the pots were looking tired, the straggling remnants of annual bedding plants sprawling over the edges. She'd clear them out and get some winter pansies. Her hands and her jeans were covered in compost when she heard the front doorbell. She went round the side of the house. There was a green van parked beside her van, and two men were looking up at her roof. They were tall, with shaved heads, sallow skin, and dark eyes. She'd heard about these guys going round telling people they needed work done. They usually targeted the elderly, and she hoped they weren't about to put her into that category.

Julie smiled. 'Can I help you?'

One of them returned her smile, but she wasn't taken in. They had 'thug' written all over them. The other one pointed upwards. 'You need work.' His Eastern European accent was thick and harsh. 'Your roof.'

'No, I don't.' She didn't look up.

'Yes. Come. I show you.'

'No need to show me anything. I don't want any work done.'

'But, Mrs –'

'It's Ms. I'm more than happy with my roof, so why don't you find another mug to target.'

'That's not very polite.' A Scottish accent. Smooth and mocking.

Julie turned, and he was holding Cleo. They'd only met that once, and he'd been handsome and well dressed, not a skinny hobo, with darting bloodshot eyes. 'Nathan?'

'The very same. Alive and well. Were you worried about me? Was Lily? Nice cat.' Cleo struggled, and he held her tighter, his gloved hand stroking her neck. 'We don't have much time, Julie. Where's the suitcase? The one Lily removed from my apartment.'

Julie's heart thumped. 'I don't know what you're talking about.'

Cleo's yowl sent chills through her. The cat struggled, growling and scratching. Nathan let her go, laughing as she leapt to the ground. There was blood dripping from her flank, and a razor blade in his hand. 'Don't go far, cat. We might need you.'

A hood dropped over Julie's head. She felt deft fingers tying something at the back of her neck, then she was lifted and thrown into the van. Any time she'd imagined a random attack, usually after hearing of a stranger rape, she'd been certain she'd at least put up a good fight, get in a few kicks and scratches as she was dragged off the street. She hadn't figured on being picked up from behind, arms pinned to her sides, so it was impossible to fight back.

She struggled to a sitting position, her back against the wheel arch of the van. She could smell him getting closer, and then one hand was on the top of her head, the other holding something sharp against her throat. It was much more substantial than the razor blade.

'I have nothing to lose, Julie. If I don't get that suitcase, you and your cat, Ronan and Lily … well … I'll leave it to your imagination.'

'The police have it.' The words sounded muffled inside the hood.

He yanked the hood up. 'You what?'

'The police took it.'

'From where?'

'The flat. Lily's flat.'

'What do you mean? She doesn't have a flat. It's my flat. Mine.'

The rage in his voice. What would he do when he learned the truth? Her mind scrabbled for something to tell him, but she could find nothing. She felt him press harder against her throat. 'She was moving to another flat, the day you came back from your course.'

The noise he made. Like a wounded animal. 'This is your doing. She'd never think of leaving me without your encouragement. You are going to pay. You are –'

One of the thugs spoke. 'We must go.'

She felt a tremor run through Nathan's body before he shoved the hood back down. He grunted as he straightened up. He took a step backwards and a deep breath. She knew what was coming, but not where it was going to hurt. It was her shoulder, and the kick sent her tumbling sideways, her head banging on the wheel arch. 'You're dead, bitch. Dead.'

She scrambled to her knees. Through the hood, she could see light, and she crawled towards it. Someone grabbed her and dragged her further into the van. Her hands were tied and clipped to the wall, her ankles to the floor. There was no chance of making a noise by kicking at the metal. But she could shout. And she did.

The hood was tugged off, a good handful of her hair going with it. Something damp and foul-tasting was shoved in her mouth and covered with tape. The hood was tied tighter. Nausea surged up to her throat. And panic. What if she couldn't breathe?

'See if she has a phone.'

She felt a hand thrust into the pocket of her jeans, pulling out her phone.

And then his voice. 'You go ahead. I'll see you soon.'

The van door was slammed shut.

Despite the gag, Julie could breathe. She tried to calm her racing heart. She needed to concentrate, keep track of where the van was going when it left her street. They turned left, and right, and left again. She knew they were on Melville Drive. When the van stopped, she thought they were probably at the lights on Brougham Street. She might have kept track after that, but she became aware of muffled crying close by. She wasn't alone in the back of the van. Was it Lily? The thought terrified her.

There were traffic lights and junctions for around fifteen, twenty minutes. Every time the van stopped, she heard the other person struggling and moaning. The van speeded up, swerving out into another lane, swerving back in. Sudden braking, and her body was jolted against the hard floor of the van. She was sore all over, the ties on her hands and ankles tight, her shoulder throbbing.

And then the van slowed. Around twenty miles an hour. Must be a built-up area. It stopped, and she heard a door opening and closing, possibly on the passenger side. The muffled crying turned to groaning. The van pulled forward and stopped again, the engine still running. The passenger door opened and, in the pause before it closed, she thought she heard the thunder of a train. They were on a winding road, their speed slow. After a few minutes, the van turned to the left and stopped.

When the back doors opened, she heard the sea, waves rolling onto a shore, and the calling of birds. There were thumping footsteps inside the van, laughter and a struggle, the moaning growing louder. And then it was gone.

Someone lifted Julie, as if she was as light as a child, and threw her over their shoulder. She could smell the sea now. There was a mechanical hum in the background. A short walk and they were inside, the men talking in their own language. It was rapid and harsh, and her jaw and her body ached.

She heard a key turn in a lock. She was dropped to the ground, pain coursing through her shoulder and down her arm. Julie heard the key turn again, footsteps receding. She tried to pull her hands apart, to loosen the ties, but it was hopeless. She could hear the other person crying and moaning. And there was another sound. Soft whispering. It was close, and closer, someone shuffling towards her. A hand on her arm.

Chapter 58

SAM

Sam's not alone. It's his mother. He's certain of it, though his brain tells him she's nothing more than a pile of bones in the cemetery in Linlithgow. His brain can tell him what it likes; he knows his mother's hands. She doesn't speak; she just holds him and listens.

'I didn't go through with it, Mum. When I saw the greed in that man's eyes as he offered me a small fortune, and probably less than half of what the book was worth, I couldn't do it. It's with Peter. He'll see it gets back to Margaret. I hope she'll just think I borrowed it. I'm a fool, Ma. I thought those thugs in the van down the Cowgate wanted directions, and I made it so easy for them. But I'm ready to go. Hasn't been much fun. Not these last few years. Not since … well, you know. Actually, I hope you don't. I'm glad you're here, but I hope you weren't there. Meltdown of the century. A poor wee lassie tells a lie. Of course they're going to investigate, and some people are going to believe her. Just didn't expect one of them to be my wife. Says a lot about the marriage. Couldn't have been up to much as a husband, a father, could I, if she was willing to believe it without question?

'Before that, I was sober and respectable. Wife, three beautiful kids, a job I loved. And in a few seconds, on the word of a daft girl, it was all gone. One night on the bottle, and I fell to bits. Let it all go. I doubt the marriage could have been saved, but I could have fought for my kids, for my job, for my life. Ma, I'm sorry I'm so weak. Don't go. Don't leave me, Ma …'

There's a noise at the door. Maybe he can knock them over, make a run for it. Laughter cascades through him. Run for it? He can hardly move his little finger. Through a narrow slit in one eye, Sam sees two of the Poles, each with a body over their shoulder. The bodies are dumped on the floor like pieces of meat, and the door is locked again. It's two women, and they're hooded, wrists and ankles bound. They're moving. Still alive. For now.

The one closest to him has skinny legs, a short skirt, and high heels. She's whimpering and moaning and wriggling. The other one is more solid. Not overweight, just real and shapely. She's wearing a checked shirt and jeans. They're stained a little around the thighs. Looks like earth. Maybe he can help them, if he can just get these useless hands to work. If he can just move this stupid body.

'Any chance of some help, Ma? You were always the strong one.' And his mother's listening. No doubt about it. Strength trickles through his wasted legs, his bruised back, his left arm. The right's no use. Not even his mother can fix it. Three breaks, at least. He'd counted them. Blacked out for a while after the third.

He's like a caterpillar, rippling across the wooden floor. The closest one, she smells of sweat and fear. 'Don't be scared, lady; don't be scared. Not of me.' That's what the words in his head say, but what comes out of his swollen mouth is just mumbling nonsense, and a little blood. The fingers of his left hand struggle with the knot behind her hood. At last, it loosens, and he pulls the hood upwards.

Sam knows this girl. He's seen her before, with her dark curls and her thick make-up. He's seen her with the pig, and too many other drunken, pawing men. She was different then, with her brash laughter. Now, her eyes widen in terror. When he reaches out to remove the tape from her mouth, she shakes her head and shuffles backwards. Sam turns to the other one. She's hardy. Not a whimper or a cry. She's trying to pull her hands apart, but it's hopeless. She smells of soap and earth. Clean, like Lily. He shuffles towards her, then he puts his left hand on her arm and tries to squeeze. It doesn't work, so he pats, as if she's a puppy.

Chapter 59

JULIE

THE PERSON SMELLED bad, but the touch was gentle. The patting stopped. There was muttering and groaning and shuffling as they moved behind her. Julie felt fingers fumbling at the back of her neck. There was a lot of grunting and moaning and tugging. And the hood was off. She was in a small, bare room. There was a window with padlocked wooden shutters, and through a slim gap down each side of the shutters, light flooded in. Close by, there was a girl with dark curls and wide eyes. More shuffling and Julie could see the person who had helped her, and he looked like the victim of a road crash. There was dried blood all over his head and face, and fresh blood trickling from his mouth. One eye was closed, and the other was just a small slit. The hand that reached towards her taped mouth was swollen and bruised; the fingers crusted in blood.

The tape was coming off a millimetre at a time, and it hurt like hell. He tried to mutter an apology, but only blood came out. Julie nodded, and he tugged. There was a tearing noise, as the tape and the top layer of her skin and her lips, and any lurking hint of a moustache, came off. She tried to force the cloth out of her mouth with her tongue, but everything had seized up. She sat back and let the bloody fingers do their slow work. The gag was gone, and her jaw was frozen, her mouth half open, pain pulsing through her face. At last, the pain eased, and she could close her mouth. 'Thank you,' she said.

There were footsteps in the corridor. The girl let out a moan, and the man shuffled away. He settled against the far wall, where he slumped into sleep, his breathing laboured and his body twitching. The footsteps faded. Julie sat and stared into space, waiting.

Chapter 60

DAVID

THE FLAT AT Dumbiedykes was strangely quiet. The kitchen had been cleaned. It wasn't perfect, but the surfaces were clear. There were three black bin bags lined up beside the door. The living room was bare. No overflowing ashtrays, no empty bottles or glasses. Looked like they were clearing out.

'Is Aneta here?' David asked.

Jakub shook his head and frowned.

'What's wrong?'

'Last night, we get ready to leave the flat. The girls, they are going to another place. Aneta … she find her passport and she go. The men, they look for her. I wait to hear from them.' He put his hand on David's shoulder. 'She will be okay.' He scribbled on a notepad. It was an address. 'This is for you. Under railway bridge. Through white gate.' He waved his left hand. 'On this side. You reach castle, you go too far. I see you there tomorrow, early.' He looked over his shoulder, though David was certain there was no one else in the flat. His voice was hushed. 'Your phone. The boss man, he will look at it. You don't want him to see a thing, you lose it. Understand?'

David nodded. He wasn't stupid, but he appreciated the warning.

Jakub ripped the page from the pad and passed it to David, along with a small key. 'You need this for the gate. And you must be careful with Henryck.' He put his hand on David's forearm. 'I don't want you …' He hesitated, searching for the word. He shook his head and pulled an imaginary knife across his abdomen.

'Gralloched,' David said.

'Gralloched? What is this?'

'Disembowelled. It's what you do to deer, after they're shot.'

'Deer?'

David had the Google Translate App on his phone. Aneta's English was good, but sometimes she'd used the app to tell him things. He punched in *deer* and passed the phone to Jakub.

'Ah,' the other man said. '*Jeleń*.' He held an imaginary gun at shoulder height, one eye closed. 'You do this?'

David nodded.

'Then this?' The imaginary knife was back again, pulled across Jakub's abdomen.

'Aye. Gralloching.'

Jakub shook his head. 'We don't want this gralloching for you.'

*

SHE WAS STANDING outside Frankenstein on George IV Bridge. Smiling at David, she pushed her hair back from her face. She smelled of cheap body spray and cigarettes.

'Aneta?' he asked. 'Where is she?'

The girl shrugged. He remembered his shock at seeing just how young she and the girl in the next room were that first night, when they'd opened the bedroom doors in the Dumbiedykes flat. Now, pale and shivering, her top had slipped off her shoulder and he saw the same rose tattoo as Aneta's. It was a brand. They all belonged to the same person. The boss man. The man he would meet tomorrow.

'Do you speak English?' David asked.

The girl held her thumb and forefinger almost touching. 'Little bit.'

He took out his phone and used the translation app to ask if she'd seen Aneta yesterday. She nodded.

Are you worried about her?

She shook her head again and took the phone from David. She typed something and passed it back to him.

She has many men. She makes much money.

The girl put her hand on his arm. Her nail varnish was chipped, the nails ragged and grubby. She smiled and gave him her little bit of English. 'I be good girl for you. I do anything.'

'No thanks.' He took a twenty-pound note from his pocket and gave it to her. She stared at it, then at him. 'For nothing?'

'For you.'

She smiled and walked away.

David crossed the busy road and made his way towards Sam's pitch. He had photos of Aneta on his phone. Maybe Sam had seen her. But Sam wasn't there. David walked the length of the Royal Mile, showing the photo to shopkeepers and a few homeless people he'd got to know, but no one had seen her. With aching legs, no money left in his pockets, and no idea of where else to look, he gave up. Hopefully, Aneta was far away, well out of reach of the Polish thugs.

At home, he soaked in a hot bath, then he ordered a pizza. He was settling down to watch a film when a text came in. It was Eva. He'd given up trying to contact her a few days earlier. It seemed pointless.

Can we talk?

No kisses. No smiley emojis. Either he'd really pissed her off, or she wasn't well. He called her. She was at home with her parents in Kirriemuir, she said, her voice flat. She was sorry she hadn't returned his calls and texts.

'What's wrong?' he asked. 'Was it … did someone say something? I swear I haven't told anyone. Alison Blyth's being weird. She keeps looking at me funny.'

'I told her about us, at the hen night,' she said. 'Don't know why. I wasn't even drunk. She was. I didn't think she'd remember. And no, you did nothing. It's not you.'

He'd used that excuse too often. It's not you. It's me. I'm not ready. It's bad timing. Maybe if …

'I was raped.'

The mug lurched in his hand, spilling hot tea on his thigh. Pepperoni flavoured nausea surged from his stomach. 'What?'

'That night. I was raped.'

She spoke in the same flat tone. He wanted to shout. He wanted to ask her who, where, how? Had she reported it? And if she had, how come there had been no mention of a rape at the station? He stopped himself from howling his rage down the phone, from threatening to kill the bastard. 'I'm sorry, Eva. I'm so sorry. Can we … do you want to meet up?'

'No. I just wanted you to know I'm not ignoring you. It's difficult. I'm sorry. The doctor gave me something. Valium, I think. I'm not really dealing with it very well. I guess you're wondering why you haven't heard there was a rape, why no one is talking about it at the station?'

'Eh … no … well … maybe …'

'I have reported it. I've been interviewed and examined and tested. My drink was spiked. I was drugged.'

As the truth dawned on him, David felt a cold surge of rage. He knew why it was being kept quiet, and who had done it. He didn't trust himself to speak.

'Thing is … well, I'm not supposed to tell anyone,' she said. 'But I know you'll keep it to yourself. It was Collesso.'

Chapter 61

LILY

ANDY, THE ALMOST-BOYFRIEND at the end of third year, was on Lily's mind as she sat on a bench in Princes Street Gardens. He'd given up after leaving a few desperate voicemails. The loss she'd felt as she listened: she thought she might drown in it. She couldn't bear to see him again. She'd betrayed him by sleeping with Nathan. She wasn't worthy of him.

Throughout the summer holidays, her mother kept asking what was wrong. Lily didn't know why she was so tired and low. Even her favourite places couldn't lift the gloom that surrounded her. She'd been offered a summer job in the local shop, but she didn't take it. She couldn't face people. And she couldn't get that night in Edinburgh out of her head, nor could she understand why it had affected her so much. Her flatmates got drunk all the time, and it seemed like a badge of honour if you were so guttered you forgot how you got home or who you were with. Whenever she thought of that night, she felt shameful and nauseous. Soon, she was nauseous every day. By the end of the summer holidays, she knew why.

Her mind turned things over endlessly, trying to find a solution. She could stay at home and have the baby. Take a year out. Return to medical school as a single parent. She told her mother. There was no anger, no recrimination. Just shock and a touch of fear. Lily knew what scared her mother: having to tell her stepfather. Within an hour of her mother telling him, Lily left home for the last time.

Her stepfather's insults echoed in her head all the way back to Edinburgh. He hadn't called her anything she hadn't already called herself, but hearing the words spoken aloud from his pious mouth, in front of her stunned, silent mother, somehow made them real.

As the bus approached Edinburgh, she'd taken her phone from her bag. There were three texts from her mother. She deleted them. She scrolled back to find the last text from Nathan. He'd sent her several over the summer, and she hadn't answered.

Hey Lily. Wish you'd get in touch. I'd love to meet up. Nxx

She called him. They met in Café Royal. His face when she told him. Would she do a DNA test when the baby was born? And she really had nowhere else to go?

She realised now she'd made a crucial mistake at the start. Nathan was a hunter. It was important for him to do the chasing. Her refusing to answer his texts had only made him keener. If she'd come to Edinburgh and found somewhere else to stay, let him pursue her, he might have treated her differently. Trouble was, she'd had no money to find somewhere else to stay, nor did she have the devious nature required for that kind of subterfuge. She wasn't Nathan.

It hadn't all been bad. She didn't doubt he had feelings for her, but he wasn't ready to be forced to settle down, and he took that out on her. It was just words at first. Perhaps if he'd attacked her physically in the early days, while she was pregnant, she would have left. That came later, after Ronan, and it was so gradual, she almost didn't notice it at first. The odd shove, holding her arm too tight to stop her from walking away, pinning her shoulders against the bed until he'd said what he wanted to say. Perhaps it would have stopped at that, had he not got mixed up in whatever chaos was going on in his life. It had pushed him to the edge. Maybe if …

She laughed out loud. A woman walking past gave her a wary

glance. What was she doing sitting here trying to rationalise it, making excuses for him? How could she still be in denial about a truth she'd just been forced to confront?

He was a rapist. A monster. And she'd been a fool. Panic threatened to engulf her, as everything he'd taken from her paraded through her head. Looking up at Ramsay Garden, she could make out the balcony of their apartment. She remembered the hope she'd felt as she stood there that last day, on the cusp of a new life, moments before he had tried to force her over the edge.

To hell with Nathan Collesso. He wasn't taking anything else from her. Though her hands shook, and she wasn't sure she could keep her voice steady, she googled the University of Edinburgh School of Medicine, and then she made a call.

*

LILY'S GREETING ECHOED in the hallway. No one answered. She heard a noise upstairs, and she called out again. Nothing. Half way up the stairs, and the noise came once more. It sounded like a baby's cry. The third time she heard it, she knew it wasn't human. And it was coming from the airing cupboard on the landing.

'Cleo?'

The door was ajar. She pulled it open and saw the cat sitting on the floor, licking her flank.

'Are you hiding from Ronan?' She reached out her hand, and Cleo bolted from the cupboard. She left behind a dark stain on the floorboards.

Downstairs, Cleo was sitting in the middle of the hallway. Lily knelt beside her and saw that the cat's fur was matted with congealed blood. Bile rose in her throat. She could smell the blood and something else. It was dark and suffocating. There was a movement behind her, a creaking, a footstep on the wooden floor. She stumbled to her feet and spun round.

It was the kitchen door, creaking in the wind. The back door was open, and there was some mess in the kitchen. Julie wasn't the tidiest of people, but she rarely left the drawers open and their contents spilling out onto the worktop and floor.

Lily checked the front of the house again. Julie's car and van were there, but Ronan's pushchair, jacket and shoes were gone. She took her phone from her bag and called Julie. It rang for a while before it was answered. No one spoke.

'Julie, where are you? Cleo's hurt.'

She heard laughter, and it wasn't Julie. The phone fell from her hand and landed on the table. She must have hit the loudspeaker button, for tinny laughter filled the kitchen. She wanted to sweep the phone onto the floor and stamp on it, so she would never have to hear that laugh again. Or the voice that was taunting her now.

'Lily? Talk to me.'

She shook her head. It was an illusion. It was the head injury. They'd told her this might happen.

'Answer me. I know you're there, Lily.'

Lily cut the call and turned off her phone. Victims of domestic abuse often imagined their abuser was following them. They saw their abuser's face transposed upon that of a stranger. They heard the voice of their abuser whisper threats in their ear, over and over, long after the abuse had ended. But not her. She would not be held captive by the ghost of Nathan Collesso. She thought it through. Julie had taken Ronan out for a walk. She'd lost her phone, and someone had found it. Lily's name had come up on the screen when she rang. The person who found it was having a laugh, and her broken head was convincing her it was Nathan. At her feet, Cleo was rubbing against her. Lily looked down, and her tights were covered with Cleo's blood.

She was certain the cupboard under the stairs hadn't been this untidy before. The cat basket was at the back of the cupboard, resting on top of a heap of canvas shopping bags. Cleo didn't struggle as Lily placed her in the basket.

'Good girl.' She closed the basket and tied the leather strap.

Inside, Cleo was still licking her flank. Lily opened the drawer in the hall table. More mess. She found Julie's address book, and she used the house phone to call the vet and a taxi.

Chapter 62

JULIE

THE PAIN IN Julie's shoulder was growing. Her mouth was dry and her back sore. She was desperate to use the toilet. She heard someone unlock the door. The sight and smell of Nathan, a warped grin on his face, was terrifying. He crouched beside the girl. 'You're a mess, aren't you?' He yanked the tape off her mouth, and she cried out in pain, followed by an angry burst of what sounded like Polish.

Nathan laughed. 'Speak English, darling.'

'Tony, I don't try to escape. I promise. I don't.'

'No? And you didn't wind up the other girls, either? Didn't tell Olga to attack Councillor Mason on the High Street?'

'That pig. He hurt Olga.'

'And you didn't take your passport and try to run away from me? Didn't say you were going to the police?' There was rage in his voice. 'After all I've done for you?'

'No. I don't do that. I promise, I don't.' Her voice wavered. 'You must help me, Tony. I love you. You say you love me too.'

'Shut up.' He pushed her, and she stumbled sideways to the floor.

The man slept on. Nathan looked down at him. 'Another mess.' He turned to Julie. 'Had you met before today?'

She shook her head. 'Why would I have?'

Nathan laughed. 'You've never met Lily's dear friend, Sam? A treat for you. Fragrant, isn't he? I'm guessing he removed your hood and gag?'

Julie said nothing. Nathan turned and booted Sam in the stomach. He came to, groaning and retching. 'Shouldn't have done that, Sam.'

Nathan pulled Julie off the floor and pushed her against the wall with one hand, reaching into his back pocket with the other, and pulling out a knife. The blade was five or six inches long, and shining. He stroked it down her cheek, smiling, his breathing heavy. Over his shoulder, Julie saw the girl's eyes widen, then she groaned and curled herself up. Sam tried to stand. Julie willed him not to make a sound, not to attract Nathan's attention. He must have realised his efforts were useless, and he slumped back against the wall.

Nathan trickled the knife down Julie's throat, his eyes gleaming. He slipped it between the buttons on her shirt and sliced downwards, laughing as the buttons popped off. Thank God she was wearing a t-shirt. Her eyes followed the knife across her stomach and down her right leg. She felt a spasm of fear running through her, squeezing her bladder until she thought she might just let go.

He stared into her eyes, then he smiled and winked. 'Think I'll save you for later.'

As Julie's legs gave way and she slid down the wall, he turned and waved the knife between Sam and the girl. 'Eenie meenie miney mo.' He stopped at the girl. 'You'll do first.'

He sliced through the rope on her ankles, then he turned her and released her wrists. She threw herself at him. 'You don't hurt me, Tony.' The shake in her voice belied her words. 'I know you don't. I love you always.'

He laughed as he pushed her from the room, locking the door behind them. Julie listened to their retreating footsteps, the ominous threat of his silence, and the fading sounds of the girl's desperation. She concentrated on the birdsong outside the shuttered window. Such a range of pitches and melodies. High and sweet. Low and insistent. Rising. Soaring. Resting. And then the occasional frantic calls of seabirds, echoing across the gentle waves that whispered on sand.

When the first scream came, Julie told herself it was a bird. It had to be. The next scream woke Sam. Startled, he struggled into a sitting position. The last scream was wild and terrifying, filling every corner of the house, ricocheting and tearing. Even after it stopped, it left an echo lodged in Julie's ears and in her heart.

By the time Nathan came for her, half an hour or so later, Sam had slumped back into sleep, and Julie was so scared, she doubted she could stand. Nathan pulled her to her feet, shoving her against the wall, then he knelt and sliced through the rope around her ankles. He winked. 'You didn't think I was going to carry you, did you?'

He shoved her out of the room, and her steps were weak and slow until she felt the knife scratching between her shoulder blades. He pushed her down a long corridor. 'First right. Nice and gentle. Wouldn't want any accidents, would we?'

It looked like an office. Two desks with computers and printers. The blinds on the small window were closed. He pushed her towards a door in the corner. 'In there.'

It was a boxroom, dark and stinking of blood. There was more. An aura of fear and pain, the faint rumbling echo of that last scream. He put on the light and sniffed the air. 'Could do with your cleaning services in here. I reckon I've got it covered, though. Can't do much better than fire for disinfection and general destruction of evidence.' He smiled. 'Fire's not pleasant, Julie. Think barbecue; char-grilled meat; cremation. Think, Julie. Think carefully. You have information that I need. We can do this the hard way or the easy way. Doesn't make much difference to me. I'll be out of here tomorrow. You can walk away, or you can burn.' He shrugged. 'Up to you.'

His words gave her hope that she wasn't about to meet the same fate as the girl. There were two chairs. He nodded towards one. Before she could sit, he stopped her. 'Wait.' He took a hankie from his pocket and mopped at the seat. A smear of blood coloured the hankie. 'Sit.'

There was a wild and eerie gleam in his eyes. His hair was greasy. He'd changed his clothes since he'd taken the girl, but still they were dishevelled and loose on his skinny frame. There was blood spatter on his shoes. He leaned towards Julie, and he smelled bad. 'Does Ronan miss me?'

'Yes.'

'Was Lily worried about me?'

She nodded. The slap was unexpected. It stung. Julie cursed the tears that welled in her eyes.

'Liar. She was leaving me. Where was she going?'

Julie hesitated too long. He kicked out, and the chair overturned. She was on the floor, and he was sitting on top of her, pressing her shoulders into the ground. The pain in her injured shoulder was unbearable. She thought she might throw up. And then he was gripping her chin in his hand, squeezing and muttering and mumbling. She was a bitch, a whore, a cow, a dyke. What was going on between her and Lily? That was it, wasn't it? He didn't have what it took to keep Lily happy, but Julie did. She shook her head.

'What then? Why wasn't I enough for her?'

This wasn't the time to break it to him just how fucked up he was, so she said nothing. A phone rang. Still sitting on her, he reached into his pocket. He frowned before he answered, his voice terse. 'Yeah? What is it?' He listened, his face reddening. 'Just do something with him. Distract him. It's not rocket science. What? Rocket science? You know … Oh, forget it. I'm busy. Just make sure he's got the rabbit. He'll be fine.'

He was talking about Ronan, but who was the boy with? Someone that didn't know what rocket science meant. Sophia?

Nathan cut the call and put the phone in his pocket. He stared into space for a moment, then he shook his head, as if the caller had brought him back to reality. He stood and lifted the chair, helped Julie up, and sat her down. Settled on his chair, sorted his shirt, cleared his throat, and smiled. 'You were saying, Lily was moving to …?'

'Portobello,' she lied. Her heart raced. Perhaps he already knew it was Polwarth.

'How did she get this flat?'

Julie shrugged. 'I presume she saw it advertised somewhere.'

'And I'm guessing you helped her move. So, you'd have seen the old leather suitcase.'

Julie nodded. 'We just loaded it into the van with everything else.'

'We?'

'Lily and I.'

'Did Philip not help?'

He knew about Philip. Had he been watching her house? Was Philip safe?

Nathan was tapping his foot on the wooden floor. 'Which one of you took my money?'

'Can I go to the toilet?'

'When you tell me who took the money.'

Julie shook her head. 'We left everything at Lily's flat and went to work. I came back later on my own. When the police told me Lily was in hospital and that I had to leave with Ronan, I took his toy box, his cot and some of his clothes. I left everything else there, including the suitcase. Really, if we were going to look through Lily's bags for something to steal, that would have been the last one we'd have thought of looking in.' She shrugged. 'I don't know what else I can say, except that the police were extremely interested in the suitcase, too. Can I go to the toilet now, please?'

He reached into the pocket of his jeans and pulled out Julie's phone. 'Let's try your pal again. She wasn't for speaking to me earlier, but if she knows what's good for her, she'll answer now.'

Lily's phone must have been switched off. Nathan kept cutting the call and trying again. He stared at the phone, and Julie knew he wanted to throw it to the ground and stamp on it. He shoved the phone in his pocket, then he stood and turned away from her, and she could hear his breathing, loud and ragged. He left the room, slamming the door behind him.

Julie looked up at the ceiling. There was blood on the lampshade. The door opened, and a woman came in. Small and dark, young and skinny and scared, she was carrying a plastic bucket. There was a small tattoo of a rose on her shoulder. She didn't look at Julie. Just put the bucket in the corner and left.

Was he having a laugh? How was she supposed to open her jeans with her hands tied behind her back? She groaned, her full bladder, her sore shoulder and her aching head taunting her until she felt the threat of tears. Bastard. She wouldn't give him the satisfaction.

'Need some help?' He was back.

'No thanks.'

'Thought you were desperate.'

'Not that desperate.'

He laughed and turned her round. With rough hands, he tugged at the rope, pulling at her shoulder. She bit her tongue, rather than cry out. When her hands were free, she felt the blood rush through her arms and her fingers. She squeezed her hands until the pain eased.

'You have one minute.' He pulled a couple of tissues out of his pocket and threw them on the floor. 'Don't say I'm not good to you.'

He only gave her a minute, but it was enough. When he returned, he used duct tape to bind her wrists at the front. It relieved the strain on her shoulder. Just as he finished, the phone in his pocket rang.

Chapter 63

LILY

A WOUND THAT was too regular and straight to be accidental. A blade or a scalpel. A deliberate cut. The vet's words sliced through the fickle bubble Lily had surrounded herself with. There were no taxis to be seen, so she ran. In Julie's house, she took the stairs two at a time. She hadn't noticed earlier that the attic hatch at the end of the hallway was open and the ladder was down. In her bedroom, the contents of the drawers had been tipped out on the floor, and her mattress and Ronan's were upended. The toys had been thrown from the toy box. Julie's room was a mess too. She turned on the mobile phone. Several missed calls from Julie's number. It only rang once before he answered. 'Lily. At last.'

'Where's Ronan?'

Nathan laughed. 'You're very calm. This isn't what I expected. Thought for once you might actually show some emotion. Cry a little. Beg. That knock on the head seems to have turned you into even more of an ice maiden than you were before.'

'Where is my son?'

'*Our* son is safe. As long as you do what I ask, he'll stay safe. You got that?'

'What do you want?'

'The money from the suitcase.'

'There was just clothes and books in it.'

'I don't believe you. You were ... you were leaving me.' He took a sharp breath. 'You took that money to set yourself up.'

'I took nothing except my own belongings, Ronan's furniture and toys, and Sam's suitcase. The police took the case.'

'Aye, so your friend said. Here, why don't you have a word?'

The timid voice did not sound like Julie. 'Lily? Is Cleo okay?'

'She's fine; she's at the vet. Is Ronan there?'

'No,' Julie said. 'He's with someone else ...'

'That's enough.' Nathan was back. 'Trouble is, I don't believe either of you. Someone took it. So, here's what you're going to do. Tomorrow, you're going to meet me with the money. Every penny. And I might consider giving Ronan back to you.'

Lily was silent.

'Did you get that?'

'I got it, but I don't have a clue where the money is or how much there was. How am I supposed to get it for you?'

'This is getting tiresome. Ask Philip if he took it. Julie tells me he helped you move to Portobello.'

Portobello? Julie had lied? That was brave.

'I thought it might have been Julie, but she's denying it under significant pressure. You really don't want to make me apply too much pressure, do you? You know I can.'

Lily tried to keep her voice steady. 'Please don't hurt her.'

Nathan laughed. 'I'll think about it. Not making any promises about your other friend. He's not doing too well, but I had a few scores to settle with him.'

'You have Sam?'

'However did you guess I was talking about Sam? Of course. You only have two friends in the whole world, and I have them both. So, how much are your friends and your son worth?'

Everything. Anything. 'You ... you tell me, because I don't know how much you want.'

He sighed. 'I don't believe you, but I'll indulge you. A hundred and twenty thousand pounds. By tomorrow morning. Don't call me. I'll be in touch. And Lily … no police, or you never see Ronan again. And your pals die.'

*

PHILIP HAD HIS elbows on Margaret's kitchen table, his hand over his mouth, fear in his eyes. Every so often, he'd stroke his hand down his beard, and then it was back, covering his mouth. Lily hadn't known where to go, what to do, after Nathan's call. Then Margaret had phoned to ask if there was any news of Sam. Lily had said she'd be round shortly. She'd phoned Philip and asked him to meet her there.

Margaret and Philip had listened to Lily's tale in silence. When Lily was done, Margaret started rummaging in the small chest freezer in the corner of the kitchen. What next? A fry up?

'Here it is.' She pulled out a large flat Tupperware box covered in frost and took it to the sink, where she ran it under the hot tap. She dried it with a towel and took it over to the table, where she prised off the lid. Beef burgers. Three packets. Only, they weren't packets. She'd cut the fronts off and laid them on top of piles of banknotes.

'Father said you should always keep money in the house, and what better place for it?' She scooped out a couple of handfuls of notes and passed them to Lily and Philip. 'Get counting.'

There was forty-two thousand pounds in cold twenty and fifty-pound notes.

Lily frowned. Even if it was enough, she couldn't take Margaret's money. She said as much, and Margaret jumped up from her chair. 'You'll take it, and more. Just a minute.'

In seconds she was back with a battered, faded box that had once housed a Kenwood food processor. Lily remembered Margaret snatching it from her when they were clearing a bedroom, saying she needed it; she was going to use it one of these days. It had felt too light for a food processor.

Margaret opened the box, and her hands delved inside, displacing chips of polystyrene. They scattered onto the table and dropped to the floor. She took out two smaller Tupperware boxes. This time, Margaret counted every note herself. She scribbled a sum on a notepad and checked her calculation. 'Seventy-six thousand, four hundred. Just as I thought.'

Lily shook her head. 'Why do you have all this money in the house?'

Margaret shrugged. 'Precisely for this kind of emergency.'

Philip had been quiet, but that made him laugh. 'We can't take it, Margaret. Lily, do you really think we shouldn't go to the police?'

'We can't. You don't know what he's like.' She didn't tell them just how terrified Julie had sounded. 'He's involved in something bad. He'll …' She shook her head.

Margaret nodded. 'You don't have a choice but to take my money. Now, do you think I should get along to the bank first thing tomorrow and get the rest?' She didn't wait for an answer. 'It's difficult getting large sums without notice. They don't keep much on the premises. Believe me, I know. Why do you think I've been hiding a bit here and there for the last few years? And before you ask, none of it is out of date. I keep a good watch on expiring currency, always make sure I exchange it in good time. Father did that too.'

'I could go to the bank in the morning,' Philip said. 'Get my savings out. It wouldn't be enough, but it'd be a help. But as Margaret says, you need to give them notice.'

Margaret drummed her fingers on the table. 'There was that man around Tollcross a few years ago. He gave a good price for a bit of jewellery. One of Father's clients used him from time to time. I wonder –'

'No.' Lily's voice was firm. 'You are not pawning your jewellery.'

There was only one option left. Lily sent off a text. In seconds, she had an answer. 'Will you give me a lift, Philip?'

*

JONATHON COLLESSO LOOKED wary as he approached the car, parked a few doors down from his house. He got in to the back seat beside Lily. 'What's going on?' he asked.

'Have you heard from Nathan?'

Jonathon hesitated. 'Rebecca has. Just today.' He sighed. 'We were so desperate to hear he was all right, and then all those stories in the press, the questions the police have been asking.' He shrugged. 'I don't know what to think. He told Rebecca he has Ronan. Said he's safe with a friend. Warned her not to tell anyone, but I overheard her, and she admitted it, made me swear I wouldn't contact the police. How did he get Ronan?'

Lily told him about going to the police station and returning to find Ronan gone. About Nathan's calls and his demand. Philip stayed silent in the front.

'You know I have friends in the police,' Jonathon said. 'I should contact them.'

'No. You can't.' Lily's voice shook. 'He's … I don't think you know what he's capable of. We'll never see Ronan again.'

Jonathon nodded. 'A hundred and twenty thousand?'

'We have almost seventy thousand. We just need the rest.'

'Where can I find you?'

Lily told him Margaret's address.

'Give me a couple of hours.'

*

MARGARET HAD FOUND her jewellery, and she'd been calculating. First thing in the morning, she'd contact the Tollcross man. If she didn't get what the jewellery was worth, they'd make up bundles a little short of a thousand. These criminal types, they wouldn't count every note, would they? She seemed disappointed to hear it wouldn't be necessary.

Two hours later, Jonathon Collesso texted Lily, and she went out to his car. There was a rucksack in the passenger footwell. 'It's all there,' Jonathon said. 'A hundred and twenty thousand. I can't let someone else pay for what he's done.'

Lily thanked him and promised she'd be in touch the next day. She went inside and broke the news to Margaret that her money wouldn't be needed after all. Margaret looked gutted.

Chapter 64

JULIE

Without a word, Nathan led Julie to a door that opened into a cellar. His hand on her back, he guided her halfway down the steps. From above, a man spoke. Julie kept going into the musty darkness. A step wobbled. Or maybe it was her legs. With her hands tied, there was no way she could steady herself, and she stumbled down to the concrete floor. His laughter echoed around the cellar.

'Couldn't wait to get away from me? That's not very polite. I was going to join you, but something's come up. I'll be back soon, and you and I are going to get to know each other a lot better.'

The door slammed, and she heard a key turn. Though she could see nothing now, she knew there was a mattress on the floor, a wooden chair, and a table. She'd glimpsed them in the gloom before the door shut. She wouldn't be going near the mattress of her own accord.

Something rustled in the corner, and it wasn't small. Too much noise for a mouse, and not enough for a person. Julie made a dash for the chair, then she pulled her legs up and hugged them. Leaning back, she groaned as her shoulder pressed against the spars. Was it broken? She hoped not. She was going to need all her strength and both arms to get out of here.

It was an hour or more before she was brave enough to leave the chair and make her slow way around the cellar. At the top of the stairs, there was a chink of light down the side of the cellar door, but the further she got from it, the light disappeared and there was nothing to be seen. She felt the walls, desperate to find a door or a window, or even just a gap in the brickwork that would allow contact with the outside world. There was nothing. When something scurried across her foot, she yelled out and ran back to the chair.

There was someone outside the cellar door, slowly turning the key. Julie's heart thumped, her stomach twisting. The door was pulled open, and the light hurt her eyes. There was a shape in the doorway. It was the woman who had brought the bucket earlier. She crept down the stairs, her arms full, and she laid some things down on the bottom step. She went up the stairs backwards, her eyes on Julie.

It looked like a quilt. And the bucket. It was kind of her, but Julie wouldn't be able to use it with her hands tied. And there was something else, and it made her heart race even more than her fear of Nathan. Every bit of her body ached as she stumbled towards the steps. It was a small bottle of water, and the top had been removed. Could she lift it with her bound hands? What if she knocked it over? She inched her hands towards the bottle, spreading them as far as the tape would allow. Her fingers shook as they closed round the bottle, her shoulder aching as she raised it to her mouth. Water had never tasted so good. She forced herself to stop and save the rest. She looked up. The woman stepped back and reached for the door.

'Thank you.' Perhaps the words were lost as the door creaked shut and the key turned.

Julie stayed on the third step from the bottom. She pulled the quilt around her as best she could. It smelled damp, but it felt dry, and she soon warmed up. On the edge of unexpected sleep, she remembered. The stories in the paper. The date rape drug. The water. She was a fool. How long before the drug took effect? She waited and waited, and nothing happened.

Sleep came, and it went. Awake, she listened for noise, and there was nothing. No movement in the cellar, and none in the house. Asleep, she dreamt of Philip and Lily; her sister in Australia; her dead parents. She dreamt of Ronan, his little arms squeezing round her neck. *Night night Doolie.*

Chapter 65

SAM

Sam's mother is gone, and she isn't coming back. There's no one else in the room with him now. Just the echo of that scream. It's hair-raising, blood-curdling, spine-chilling. He'd discouraged his pupils from using such words and phrases. They should think about what the cliché represented, he'd told them. Find another way to say it, a different, more interesting way. But in the end, they were clichés for a reason. And there were no better, more interesting words to describe the effect of that last scream.

Hard to tell if the DTs have been and gone, but that's the least of his worries. The fear of them has always been worse than the reality. That's often the way, isn't it? You build something up in your mind, giving it all your energy and focus, feeding it until it's so big, everything good is swamped. And then the thing happens, and it's fine, and you're fine, but when you look back, all you can remember is the fear, and the fear becomes the thing, so that next time, you fear it even more.

So, he's just waiting. And he's broken and uncomfortable, sore and sad, but look what he's got inside his head, where no one else can go, not even the pig. He watches the brief clips of Lily over and over. And they bring him light and love and, if not laughter, at least the memory of it. That smile. That smile.

Chapter 66

DAVID

DAVID MISSED THE sharp right as he drove under the approach viaduct, so he continued along the main street and turned. All was quiet in South Queensferry, scarcely a soul to be seen. The red steel cantilevers of the Forth Bridge were gleaming in the early morning sun, and a train was crossing. He wished he was on it, heading north. Heading home. Leaving this shit behind. It was a crisp, cloudless day, the sun casting a golden hue across the Firth of Forth. He drove under the viaduct and took the narrow road that skirted the shore. Half a mile, and he came to the locked gate. He got out to open it, and the morning smelled fresh and peaceful. Not a hint of what was to come.

There were trees on either side of the winding road. Between the branches, he saw a tanker moored at the Hound Point oil terminal. Further on, he glimpsed an oil rig rising from the water, then an island. When he first came to Edinburgh, he'd fancied taking a boat trip from South Queensferry, cruising under the three Forth bridges, then out to the islands to photograph puffins. Now, he couldn't imagine doing anything normal again. He was exhausted, kept awake most of the night raging against Collesso.

At the cottage by the shore, David parked between a green van and a small jeep. The back doors of the van were open, and a man was scrubbing the interior with a long-handled brush. At the sound of David's car, the man turned. It was the youngest of the men from the Dumbiedykes flat. He nodded towards the cottage.

It was a squat, single-storey building with small windows and woodwork that needed painted, missing slates and broken guttering. An established garden that might once have been someone's pride and joy was now overgrown and neglected. It was dismal, and David didn't want to go in. He was standing by a rickety gate, looking out over the water, when a hand gripped his shoulder. He almost cried out.

'My friend.'

It was Jakub. David was embarrassed at the rush of relief, as if he really had bumped into a good friend. Fool.

'You are worried.'

David swallowed and shook his head. 'Wasn't sure I was at the right place.'

'This is the place. Your other friend, he sleeps inside. Always sleeping. Or this.' Jakub curled his left thumb and forefinger into a hole, slipping his right forefinger in and out in a crude gesture. He spat on the ground and muttered something in Polish. 'Forget him. You have come at right time. We get Aleksander off the boat.'

There was a yacht anchored in the water, and a dinghy dragged up on the shore. David nodded. He could do that. Wouldn't have a clue how to sail the yacht, but handling an inflatable dinghy was second nature to him. He followed Jakub to the shore. It was a small dinghy with a couple of bench seats and an outboard motor. Jakub looked nervous as they pushed it towards the water.

'You want me to do it?' David asked.

Jakub smiled and nodded.

The water was choppy, but it was nothing compared to the swells in the Minch. Maybe if both his brothers-in-law hadn't been fishermen too, David would have feared and avoided the water after losing his father. It wasn't an option. Though the fate of his father made them all more respectful of the ocean, his brothers-in-law had young families to feed and when they needed weekend or holiday help onboard, it was David they asked, and he was always keen to earn some money.

In minutes, they were alongside *Tatiana*. She was a small boat, about thirty feet long, and well maintained.

'Tatiana – this is his wife,' Jakub said. 'She will not get off. Just Aleksander.'

While David scanned the boat for the best place to disembark, a tall, lean man emerged from the hatch. Aleksander Bartosz had the same shaved head as his men, a long, hooked nose, deep-set eyes that were almost black, and thin, impatient lips. Behind him, a woman appeared. Her beauty took David's breath. High cheek bones, dark glossy curls, brown eyes framed by the longest of lashes, and lips shaped into a perfect cupid's bow. Her eyes met David's, and she smiled. Bartosz saw David nod in response to the woman. His eyes narrowing, he directed David towards the stern with grouchy gestures. David awaited a rope to harness the dinghy to the yacht, but Bartosz wasn't bothering with any such nonsense. In seconds, he was reaching for Jakub's hand, and he was over the side and in the dinghy. As they greeted each other, their voices were loud and harsh above the sound of the outboard motor. Bartosz didn't give David a second glance as they made their way towards land.

Ashore, David followed the men to the cottage. In a dark room, Jakub's men lounged against the wall. They saw Bartosz, and they straightened up. He greeted them one by one with a handshake and some questions. Their answers were brief. No one smiled. Bartosz turned to David and held out his hand. Did he want to shake hands? Thankfully, Jakub's curt voice put David right. 'Your phone.'

David passed his phone to Bartosz. The man flicked through it, lingering over the photos, a sleazy smile on his lips. There were some photos of David's friend Zoe. She lived in Edinburgh, and they'd been at North Berwick a few weeks earlier for a walk on the beach. And a smiling Eva, on a night out that seemed so long ago. The last few were of Aneta. She'd made David take some pictures of her posing and making silly faces. She looked like a child. With a sudden rush of guilt, David realised he hadn't remembered to ask Jakub about Aneta. His head had been too full of Eva and Collesso.

Bartosz laughed a dark, humourless laugh, followed by some comments, the gist of which would have been identifiable in any language. He thrust the phone at David.

Jakub looked embarrassed. 'He say I must tell you he know why you stare at his beautiful wife, if this is all you can get for yourself.'

'Is that right?' David's words were slow and deliberate. He saw apprehension in Jakub's eyes, a slight shake of his head as if to warn David against letting his emotions get the better of him. Jakub was right. David needed to curb the dark rage that was growing inside him.

Another volley of Polish from Bartosz, and it seemed as if the entire room held its breath. At last, Henryck said something. Behind David, Jakub gasped. David didn't turn. He couldn't. His eyes were fixed on Bartosz. The colour had slipped from the man's face, his lip curling like a snarling dog. First, his eyes pinned Henryck to the wall, then his hand. He gripped Henryck's throat, squeezing.

'*Nie, nie, nie,*' Henryck shouted, his arms waving. 'Tony. Tony Harris.'

Bartosz loosened his grip, and Henryck slid to the floor, his hands fluttering around his throat. David turned to Jakub. There was a shit-load of rage in the Polish man's eyes.

'What's happened?' David asked.

Jakub shook his head. 'I tell you later.'

Bartosz pointed at David. 'You, bring Tony Harris. Now.'

Jakub hustled David out of the room. There was a young woman in the corridor. She looked tired and scared, with skimpy clothes hanging from her skinny frame.

'Tony?' Jakub said.

The woman pointed to a door in the corridor. It was half open, and David could hear a vicious, bitter voice, one he'd hoped never to hear again.

Chapter 67

JULIE

It had been niggling at Julie's mind throughout the night. Mingling with the fragmented dreams of her loved ones. Something she'd seen on YouTube. Or was it television? Something she'd laughed at, confident she would never need. Each time she almost grasped the memory, it was gone. A banging door brought her round, followed by shouting. Several voices. The creaking and dragging of heavy things across floors. Doors opening and closing, inside and outside. Getting ready to leave?

As a spasm of hunger gripped her belly, she remembered. It was a video of a man, his wrists bound with duct tape. Pulling them apart was impossible. But raising his arms over his head and backwards, then bringing them downwards and outwards with all his force. Simples. Unless you had an injured shoulder.

She could straighten her arms out in front of her, but trying to raise them – it was agony; worse than anything she'd ever known. Or was it? She shook her head. She wasn't going there. Though the memories had been dangerously close to the surface since Lily and Ronan and Philip, she was determined not to let them get any closer. But maybe there was something from that time that could help. Maybe she could use the breathing exercises. She closed her eyes, and she was back in the clinic with all the others, focusing on the rhythm of her breathing. In and pausing before she exhaled. Out-breath longer than in-breath, to relax the muscles. Practising and learning to maintain the rhythm, so that when the pain came, she wouldn't tense up. She wouldn't let her breathing get faster and faster and turn into panic.

She took a deep breath through her mouth and tried to raise her arms, blowing away the pain in short bursts as if she was blowing out a candle, the pain supposedly disappearing with every puff. Only it wasn't disappearing. It was worse than the worst of the long-ago contractions and the everlasting pushing and squeezing, worse than the pain that had made her grunt and swear and crush her husband's hand.

With tears trickling down her face, breathing and blowing, she tried to force her arms upward, but she couldn't do it. Anger simmered at the edge of her reason. She hated Nathan Collesso, and if she was to meet the same fate as that girl, she wouldn't make it easy for him. But most of the anger was from the past. The same anger that had consumed her for years. She let it come.

That pain had been much worse than the labour or this. Worse than anything she had ever known. The pain of seeing her silent baby bundled up and rushed from the room. The agony of waiting. A nurse whispering to her husband and then the sombre return of the tiny wrapped daughter. Gazing down at perfect lips that would never take a breath or blow out a candle. Her head and her heart filling with a rage that would be with her for years, ending her brief marriage and sabotaging her subsequent relationships, so she would never have to feel that pain again.

Fuelled by the anger, she forced her arms downwards as fast as she could, at the same time pulling her hands apart. For a fraction of a terrifying, pain-filled second, there was nothing, and then she heard a faint ripping noise, and it was louder, and three of the four layers of tape were breached, and her teeth were tearing at the fourth layer. And then the tape was gone.

The table didn't stand a chance. Three kicks and the leg came off. In the brick wall, she felt a small ledge, and she forced the table against it, so it would stay upright. She used the bucket, hiding it under the stairs, then she drank the rest of the water. She dragged the quilt to the chair, sat, and pulled it over her. She didn't have to wait long.

Nathan left the door at the top of the stair open. He stretched and yawned. 'Morning. Sleep well? I did, thanks. I was going to come and say goodnight, but I figured you'd be keener to please me after a night in here.' His feet were light on the stairs. As he got closer, the hammering of Julie's heart grew louder. 'I see someone felt sorry for you. She'll pay for that. But first, it's your turn.' He reached out his hand and ran it down the side of Julie's face. He cocked his head as he cupped her chin in his hand, tilting her face towards the light. 'Lily was right; you probably scrub up well. Maybe you and I … maybe in different circumstances.' He ran a finger over her collarbone, pushing her shirt aside so her shoulder was exposed. 'A small tattoo here; a rose.'

Julie swallowed hard as nausea and plastic-tasting water surged up from her stomach.

Nathan frowned. 'I still think the wedding photos would have looked daft. A forty-something bridesmaid for a twenty-three-year-old bride?' There was anger in his eyes as he dropped his hand. 'Is she seeing anyone?'

Julie almost laughed. 'I doubt she'll feel that way inclined for a long time.'

'And that's my fault? How?'

Anger and adrenaline made Julie reckless. 'Are you serious? You beat her. Left gouge marks on her face. Plunged her head underwater. Locked her in and took her son to your mistress in the middle of the night. And that was just one night. There were others, but she didn't tell me the details.'

'So?' He shrugged. 'She liked it rough. Do you, Julie?' His breath was foul. 'I bet you do. The old ones are always so grateful for attention, they'll do anything.'

She said nothing. He reached out and pulled away the quilt. Julie willed her hands not to shake, not to dislodge the broken tape she'd reapplied.

'Get up.'

She stood.

'Over there.' He nodded towards the mattress.

Julie sat on the edge of the mattress and felt the springs digging into her flesh. She couldn't see his face, just his outline, his hand moving. She heard his zip opening.

'Lie down.'

She made as if to lift her legs onto the mattress, at the same time lowering her hands to the floor, grasping the end of the table leg and pulling it out from under the mattress.

The sound he made when she drove the table leg into his crotch was so satisfying. He bent double, and she was off the mattress and hitting him over the head. Again and again, and he was on the floor. Adrenaline had numbed the pain in her shoulder. She wanted to smash the table and chair over his head. She wanted to kill him. Instead, she ran for the stairs, the chair leg still in her hand. She didn't look back as he yelled: 'I'm going to kill you, bitch.'

Two steps to go. One. His hand closed round her ankle, tugging her backwards. She tumbled down the steps and lay dazed on the cellar floor, the chair leg gone. And then he was sitting astride her, the knife in his hand. 'Killing you is going to give me much more pleasure than shagging you.'

The knife glinted in the light from the open door, and Julie thought of the silent baby and how much she'd have welcomed a quick end then. Not now. Not with Philip and Lily and Ronan. But she had no strength left. Madness gleamed in his eyes as he grinned and pulled back his arm.

'No, Nathan.' A hand gripped his wrist. 'Aleksander is asking for you. Go. I'll deal with her.' It was a soft, island voice.

Nathan stood and pulled up his zip. He pressed the blade back into the handle of the knife. 'She dies. Stick her back in with the tramp. They can burn together.'

The man helped Julie up. At the top of the stairs, she recognised him. He'd been watching Lily that day at the Grassmarket. David, wasn't it? She stared into his eyes. They were dark with anger, but there was more there. Was it kindness? It was impossible to tell.

Chapter 68

LILY

THROUGHOUT THE LONG night, the flames in Margaret's hearth had curled and swirled in a twisted frenzied dance, taking Lily back to the warmth of childhood fires, and laughter and stories. To nights when the storm raged outside, and the hiss and crackle of salt-laden wood sent sparks flying out of the fireplace, making her jump and dance and stamp. There were no sparks from Margaret's smoke-free coal, but the flames were mesmerising. She couldn't sleep, not when she didn't know where or how Ronan was, but her eyes had fallen closed from time to time. That was when the memories of her mother came. The firelight sparkling in her mother's eyes as she toasted bread in front of the fire; arms holding Lily close in the big chair, whispering words of love until she slept. Each time the memories came, she shook her head and opened her eyes, chasing them away.

It was fine to remember the other fires. The smile on her father's face and the curl of smoke from his pipe; the clicking of her Hamnøy grandmother's knitting needles; the stories from her uncle. Sitting on the knee of her mother's father while he sang, feeling the words vibrate deep in his chest. Her maternal grandmother and her wise words. What would you have to say about this, Granny? What would you do? There were no answers in the flames, but the memories had calmed her heart a little, as long as she kept her mother at bay. She had tended the fire all night, while Philip dozed in the opposite armchair. Sometimes she'd glanced over at him and found him awake and watching her. He said nothing. Just tried to smile before his eyes drifted closed again.

Now, they were sitting at Margaret's kitchen table drinking coffee, and ignoring the pile of toast Margaret had made. Lily's eyes strayed to the silent television in the corner, and it took a moment for her brain to process what she was seeing.

Suspicious death. Body found in the Waters of Leith.

There was an artist's sketch of a young woman. It was Sophia's sister. Lily excused herself. In the bathroom, she tried to hold back tears, as her imagination ran wild. She stopped it. The girl was … she'd looked like she was on the game. It was a dangerous occupation. Nothing to do with Nathan.

The phone in her pocket rang. The voice was foreign. Male, cold and hard. Lily swallowed her fear and listened to the instructions.

*

IN WAVERLEY STATION, Lily felt as if she was made of glass. One bump from a rushing traveller, and she might disintegrate. The next train was leaving in eight minutes. There was a queue for tickets. It moved quickly, leaving her two minutes to get to the train. Lily made it without bumping into anyone, without falling apart. She eased the heavy rucksack from her shoulder, and she sat, hugging it. All around her, people were fiddling with their phones and their laptops, reading their papers, snoozing. As if it was just another day. As if her son hadn't been abducted by a madman.

It took fifteen minutes to reach Dalmeny. Off the train and down the tree-lined ramp towards the car park. Through the bare trees, she could see several cars idling. There was a green van parked in a disabled space. She got closer and saw two thugs in the front seats. The driver opened the window. 'You have the money?'

'Where is my son?'

He shrugged, then he nodded towards the other side of the van. 'Out, Henryck.'

The passenger opened the door and got out.

'Get in, Ms Andersen.'

'I need to know my son and my friends are safe.'

'You not come, you not know.'

In the van, Henryck sat far too close. Lily moved away and felt the handbrake against her thigh. Henryck laughed. The van stank of disinfectant. She wondered why they hadn't put her in the back, why they were letting her see where they were going. They took a left turn towards South Queensferry, down the brae, and they were at the waterfront. They drove along the water's edge to a white wooden gate. It was padlocked. The driver drew to a halt, and Henryck got out and unlocked the gate. There was a man outside a building by the shore. He shouted a greeting, waved his hand, and Henryck waved back.

They drove alongside the forest on one side, the Forth on the other. At last, the van stopped at a cottage by the shore. Lily got out and she could hear the constant surge and pull of tumbling water, and beyond that, the hum of machinery from Hound Point oil terminal. There was a side gate, where a skinny, scruffy man stood looking out to sea. He turned. It was Nathan.

Chapter 69

DAVID

STICK HER BACK in with the tramp. They can burn together. Collesso's words made David's heart race as he followed Jakub down the corridor. Was it Sam? David had been certain Collesso was responsible for attacking Sam in the cemetery. Had he taken him now? Jakub stopped at a door and turned a key. He pushed the door open, lifting his other arm and burying his nose in the crook of his elbow. The smell hit David, nausea surging from his stomach. He swallowed a dry boak. Julie grimaced and turned her head, but she didn't try to run. No point, with Jakub in front and David behind her. Jakub nodded his head, and Julie went in. Though he hated himself, for a moment David willed Jakub just to shut the door, let them walk away without having to look. But Jakub followed Julie in, his nose still covered. David heard Julie gasp. By the time he entered the room, Jakub was poking with his foot at a huddled shape in the corner, and Julie was on her knees crouching over the shape. It was Sam. His breathing was loud and shallow, and there was an ache of sorrow in David's heart.

Julie stroked Sam's arm. 'You're going to be all right, Sam. We're going to get you help.'

David crouched beside her. He felt for a pulse in Sam's wrist.

It was faint. Only proper medical attention was going to bring him round. Julie looked at David, her eyes full of tears. 'You have to help him.'

'Come,' Jakub said. 'We must go.'

David looked at his watch. As he rose, he gave Julie a slight nod. Jakub pulled the door closed and locked it. From the other end of the corridor, David could hear Bartosz yelling, and Collesso answering in weak monosyllables.

'What's going on?' he asked Jakub.

Jakub shook his head and gestured towards the front door. Outside, he stared at the water, his eyes troubled.

'Did they find Aneta? Is she all right?'

Jakub was silent for too long. At last, he spoke. 'They don't find her. Come. We have much to do.'

There were bags and boxes beside the front door. They carried them down to the shore, leaving them close to the dinghy. When Jakub turned away, David opened the top of a small box and glanced inside. Passports. Too many of them.

Back at the cottage, the green van was pulling into the parking space. Henryck and the young Polish man that had been cleaning the van got out. And someone else.

David gasped when he saw Lily. Collesso was standing at the side gate. He waved and called to her. She had a rucksack on her shoulder and it looked heavy. Her footsteps seemed reluctant as she made her way towards Collesso. What was going on?

'What is wrong?' Jakub asked.

David shook his head, scarcely daring to speak, but he had to know. 'Why is she here? Is she part of this?'

'No. She is fool. Must be, if she is with him. She has Aleksander's money. That's all.'

'What will happen to her?'

Jakub shrugged. 'Aleksander will decide.'

There was a movement behind them. It was Henryck. He was watching Lily as she followed Collesso down towards the shore, a lewd grin on his face, hands cupping his crotch. He turned to David. 'I have her after Tony. She need real man. You want to fight me for this one? Maybe you want Jakub instead? He like pretty boys.'

Big mistake. Both of his hands at his crotch like that. Left his face wide open for David's fist. As blood spurted from Henryck's nose, he bellowed like a wounded beast. He lashed out with his right fist and caught David on the chin, sending him staggering backwards into Jakub. For a second, David wondered if Jakub would help his colleague, if they would both turn on him. Jakub laughed and pushed David back towards Henryck. David hit him on the side of the head, the impact sending a wave of pain up his arm. Henryck's giant hands reached for David's throat. David ducked and drove his head into Henryck's chest, pushing him backwards until he was jammed against the door of the cottage, arms flailing, his feet trying to gain purchase on the loose stones of the path. David drove his fist into Henryck's stomach, again and again. The large man dropped to the ground. David felt Jakub's hand on his shoulder.

'Enough.'

Henryck was crumpled in the doorway, gasping. He spat out a mouthful of blood, then he looked up at David. 'I will kill –'

Behind Henryck, the door opened. He sprawled backwards into the cottage. Bartosz stooped and lifted Henryck by the shoulders, forcing him into a sitting position. He slammed the door shut.

Chapter 70

LILY

Nathan's face was covered in scratches and red marks. He smelled of sweat and alcohol. He was jittery, almost bouncing on his toes, his pupils wide.

'Where's Ronan?' Lily asked.

He tutted and shook his head. 'Ronan's fine. Have you got the money?'

She nodded and eased the rucksack off her shoulder. The relief on his battered face as he took it. 'Thank God. You've saved my life. I don't know how you did it. You're a star.'

So, he knew fine well she hadn't had the money; that she'd had to find it somewhere.

He tucked the rucksack behind a bush by the gate. 'Come and look at the view. You like the sea.'

He took her arm and led her away from the cottage, down onto the sand. She kept looking back, hoping to see Ronan. There was a log, and he straddled it, pulling her down beside him. He smiled, and, beyond the bruising and the grazes and the hint of madness in his eyes, she saw the little boy from a school photo in his parents' lounge. He must have been about ten, and he was gorgeous. Those blue eyes and his white teeth. The dimples in his cheeks. Who could have foreseen what he would become?

'It's nice here, isn't it?' he said. 'When I was recovering from my head injury, the sound of the water was so soothing. We should have lived somewhere like this. Maybe things would have been better.'

'What happened to your face?'

He rubbed at his cheeks with shaking fingers. 'Your pal's fiery. I'll give her that.'

'Is she all right?'

The smile of the ten-year-old was gone, replaced by a more familiar peeved look. 'She's fine. For now.'

'And Sam?'

He shrugged. 'Dunno. He wasn't too good last night.' He leaned towards her. 'Why do you care so much? He's an alcoholic beggar. He smells.'

Lily leaned away from him. 'When did you last have a wash?'

A flush crept up his neck. 'I've been busy. I'll get a shower before I … before we go.'

We? Go where? She didn't ask.

'Sam's a pervert. I don't get it. What was with him and that other beggar down on Princes Street? Why would you get involved with people like that?'

How could she even begin to explain common decency to someone with his morals? 'Where's Ronan?'

'I told you, he's fine. He'll always be fine. I'll make sure of that.' He frowned. 'Did you have to love him so much? Why couldn't I have had some of your affection? Just a bit. That's all I asked. Just a little love.'

She had tried. Told herself over and over how lucky she was. A gorgeous boyfriend and a beautiful apartment. Money and fancy clothes. It must be love. She'd whispered the words to him in the dark, trying to force some feeling into them. If she said it often enough, it might come true. And then Ronan was born, and she knew what love was. She knew she'd never feel that for Nathan.

Out in the water, a moored yacht rolled and shifted with the waves. A dinghy had been pulled up on the sand. There were trails of footsteps from the cottage to the shore and back again. Was he leaving on the yacht? She couldn't see it. Nathan at the mercy of the seas. Something so much bigger than him; something he could never control.

'Why did you tell your colleagues and your family that I was mad?' Lily asked. 'That I couldn't cope with Ronan?'

'Had to tell them something to explain all the time I was taking off.' He poked at the sand with his finger. 'Let's face it, you are a bit weird.' He ran his hands through his greasy hair, leaving it sticking up. 'I've been going through hell for the last few months with this lot.' He nodded towards the cottage. 'And you didn't even care.'

'I didn't know. You wouldn't talk to me.'

He shrugged. 'What was I going to say? I'm involved with a gang of Polish criminals? How would that have gone down with Saint Lily, protector of the weak and the poor? You wouldn't have believed me. They threatened to kill me if I didn't do what I was told. That girl coming to the hotel, and the two of them coming to the door: they were sent to scare me. You didn't even tell me Aneta came to the door. Why wouldn't you tell me?'

'Sophia's sister? She's dead. It was on the news.'

'She's not Sophia's sister.' He laughed. 'She's a tart. That's what happens to tarts that don't do what they're told.'

An icy fear swept through her. Despite everything, she'd believed there was a line he wouldn't cross. 'You didn't kill her. I know you didn't.'

He laughed again, and it felt like a knife in Lily's heart. 'Nice that you have such faith in me, but it's none of your business.' His smile was gone. 'What was I thinking, getting mixed up with you? Not that I had much say in it. Didn't ask you to get pregnant, to move in with me, to have my child. It was all your doing. I asked for none of it.'

The knife twisted in Lily's heart, and it brought a surge of rage.

She nodded. 'You're right. You didn't ask for anything.'

'I'm glad we agree.'

Lily launched herself at him, pushing him backwards off the log. He sprawled on the sand, and she straddled him, punching and slapping at his head and face. 'You didn't ask. You just took. Everything. A life I loved. A promising future. You took it all.'

He didn't even try to protect himself. She wanted to gouge at his eyes, his face. Leave marks just like he'd done. But she couldn't. She didn't have it in her. Her rage subsiding, she pushed herself off him and sat on the sand with her head in her hands. She felt him touch her arm.

'I never meant to hurt you, Lily. I thought you were happy.'

Lily let out a dry, humourless laugh. 'Happy? The way you treated me?'

'No one forced you to stay.'

Lily nodded. 'It's going to take me a long time to work out exactly why I did. Perhaps I wouldn't have stayed, if I'd faced up to the truth at the start.'

'What truth?'

She shook her head. 'Who'd have thought? A good-looking guy like you having to drug and rape women, and then keep the trophies in a bag in the attic.'

There was fear in his eyes. His voice sounded like a child. 'Drugs? Date rape? I'd never do that.'

'Date rape?' She laughed. 'I can't speak for any of the other women, but there was certainly no date with me. Just rape.'

'That's shit. I took you into my home. You spent the night. I left you there alone. As if I'd risk that if I'd drugged you.'

'Am I supposed to feel grateful for the preferential treatment? Where did you attack the others? In a close or a cemetery?'

'You are mental.' His eyes narrowed. 'How long had you been planning on leaving me?'

'Since you threatened to beat Ronan.'

His laughter sounded false. 'So easy to wind you up. I would never hurt him. There's someone else, isn't there? You haven't got the guts to leave me and make a go of it on your own. Who is he? Or is it a she?'

'There is no one else. Just me and Ronan.'

'Just you and Ronan? That'll be right.'

Fear gnawed inside her. He stood and looked down at her, his face breaking into an enormous smile, one she knew too well. It was the precursor to a level of mental cruelty that had always confounded her. His smile deepened. 'You're not having Ronan. No one but me is bringing up my son.'

Chapter 71

LILY

A PLAINTIVE CRY rang out. Lily knew the tragic sound. She looked up and saw a herd of curlews flying towards the sea. Her grandmother had told her the sound of the curlew represented the cries of a mother who had lost her child and would mourn forever. Like Lily's mother. Perhaps this was payback. The sky darkened, and the sound of the birds faded. Everything went quiet as a rush of fear swept through her.

Lily stood, her body shivering. 'You said …'

He smiled. 'You didn't really think I was just going to let you walk away from here with my boy, did you? Let you and him walk into the arms of someone else? You should have seen his face when he woke up at Julie's and saw me. He was so excited. And then he walked. He took his first steps.'

'No, he didn't.' Lily's voice was weak.

Nathan laughed. 'Don't be jealous. He's mine too. He'll be fine with me.'

She grabbed his arm. 'Take me with you. We can be a family somewhere else. Please. I love you. I always have.'

He frowned, as if he was trying to work out whether she meant it. As if he was tempted.

'Please, Nathan.'

He shook his head. 'I can't trust you now. Not when you were leaving me. Sophia will be a good mother to Ronan.'

'Sophia?' Lily's voice rose. 'She called him a brat and said you were weak and stupid.'

'That's just her way. She didn't mean it. We're good together.' He said it with force, as if he was trying to persuade himself. 'She gave up her work to look after me. Nursed me back to health. You wouldn't have done that. Anyway, you've only yourself to blame for how things turned out. The week away was to be the last time. I was going to hand over the money on the Friday, and that would have been an end to it. You and I would have married, and everything would have been fine. If you hadn't moved out; if the money hadn't gone missing; if the police hadn't become involved and everything hadn't fallen apart. You opened Pandora's Box when you made that stupid decision. You threw me and Sophia together.'

Lily couldn't speak. He patted her shoulder. 'You'll be fine. Look at you; you're gorgeous. There's someone else out there for you. You can have more children and forget about us. I'll try to send photos to my parents. Might not be easy, but I'll try.' He scuffed the sand with the toe of his shoe, then he looked at her and smiled. 'Did you bring the present?'

Present? She stared at him.

'The five thousand pound present. My five thousand pounds.'

Lily shook her head. 'It's in the apartment,' she lied. 'A vintage pocket watch. Top drawer in the bureau in the lounge.'

'Fat lot of use that is to me now. What about the ring?'

'It's on the kitchen windowsill.'

He tutted. 'Sophia will not be pleased.' He shrugged. 'Just have to get her another one.' He took her arm. 'Come on, we'll give the money to Aleksander, then one of the guys will take you back to the train station.'

'What about Julie and Sam? Are they in the cottage?'

'No. I'm sure you'll hear from them soon enough, but you

really should get some new friends.' He held out his hand. 'I need your phone.'

She took it from her pocket and handed it to him. He laughed. 'What the hell is this antique? Did you sell the iPhone I bought you?'

'The police have it.'

He scrolled through her messages, then her address book. 'Who's David?'

Lily swallowed. 'Just a … a friend.'

'Is he a tramp?'

'No. He's a … the brother of a mother at Ronan's nursery.'

He laughed. 'You are a useless liar. Always have been.' He shoved the phone into his pocket. 'Come on.'

The birds in the trees mocked her as she followed Nathan towards the cottage. Her heart was expanding in her throat, and soon she wouldn't be able to breathe.

Nathan stopped at the gate. He looked behind the bush, then at Lily. 'Where is it?' He hit himself on the side of the head, then he kicked the bush. 'You brought it, didn't you? You gave it to me? Where is it?'

Lily shrugged. 'You left it there.'

'Hey!'

There was a man perched on a windowsill beside the cottage door, phone to his ear, smoking a roll-up, and barking out monosyllabic foreign sounds. The rucksack was at his feet. Nathan should have been relieved, but he looked terrified. The man was tall and thin, his head shaved. He was wearing waterproof salopettes, a fancy sailing jacket and deck shoes. He looked up, and he had the darkest, coldest eyes Lily had ever seen. Sunken cheeks, a hook nose and thin cruel lips.

The door opened, and Henryck came out carrying a petrol can. His face was battered, worse than Nathan's. It hadn't been like that half an hour ago, when they'd picked her up from the station. What was going on in there? He held up the petrol can.

The thin man nodded and watched him go round the side of the cottage. He cut the call and stared at Nathan with a look of disgust. 'You leave my money, as if it was nothing? And you call yourself police?' He pushed himself off the windowsill and moved towards them. 'Get rid of her.'

Nathan nodded. 'I'll ask someone to take her to the station.'

Aleksander laughed. It was loud and harsh and terrifying. 'She is going nowhere. You had choice. Why you not go to Edinburgh to get the money? Why you so scared to be seen, Inspector? Is it because everyone will know what you are?' He spat on the ground. 'Bringing your problems and your tramps to me. Using my men and my van for your dirty business. You know I cannot let her go.' He gestured to someone behind Lily. 'You. Put her with the others.' He lifted the rucksack and went into the cottage.

The colour had disappeared from Nathan's face. 'Lily, this isn't what I wanted. I …'

She felt a hand on her shoulder. She turned, expecting Henryck or the van driver. When she saw David, an overwhelming sadness replaced the terror in her heart. She shrugged his hand off her shoulder. 'You're involved in all this? With him?' She shook her head. 'I trusted you.'

David's eyes wouldn't meet hers. Nathan's did. They darted between Lily and David, then he reached into his pocket and took out her phone. He scrolled and hit a number.

David was looking towards the shore when his phone rang. Was he smiling? He took his phone from his jacket pocket and answered it. 'Lily. Or should I say Nathan? What can I do for you?'

Nathan's hand shot out and pulled Lily towards him. There was a knife in his other hand. 'Round the back. You too, you bastard.'

Chapter 72

JULIE

PERHAPS IT WOULD have been better for Julie if David hadn't stopped Nathan from killing her. Death by knife might be preferable to being burned alive. She'd read that most people trapped in a burning building died from inhaling smoke and toxic gasses. She sure hoped that was true. They hadn't tied her arms or legs when they put her back in the room, and she soon understood why. There was no way she could force the padlock on the shutters. Her fingers were sore from trying. The house had quietened down, just occasional footsteps, and the odd muffled conversation.

Sam's chest sounded like someone sucking the last of a glutinous milkshake through a straw. His limbs were cold and his skin grey. As Julie held him close, trying to force some heat into his body, there was a slight smile on his face. She envied him. At least he wasn't sitting here wondering what it would be like to die in a fire.

Was it worth having another go at the window? Giving up didn't come easy to her. Never had. The angry years had made her independent and strong. She'd been happy by herself. Hadn't expected or needed anything more than the odd casual liaison until Philip came along. The last few months with him had been wonderful. She'd had good friends and family, and work that gave her satisfaction. And she'd had Lily.

Julie understood Nathan's incredulity about their friendship. That day at Waverley Station, she'd helped a girl who could have been the daughter she lost. A girl who looked washed out and anxious. When Lily asked her to go for a coffee, she'd almost said no, she was busy, had to get on. But something in Lily's weary eyes had gripped her. There was a hint of desperation, and a slight social awkwardness, but so much strength. By the time they'd drank two coffees each while Ronan slept on, she wanted to get to know Lily better.

Over the coming months, they'd met often. Lily had listened to Julie's tales of growing up with an older sister that she'd loved and hated in equal measure. How she resented her mother for being a nurse and missing so many important events. And how much she'd loved her father, though she never told him. Lily told Julie a little about her family. Losing her beloved father. The pious stepfather that could never replace him. Her fear that she would never see her home or her mother again. Just saying the words seemed to hurt Lily so much, Julie didn't ask for more.

She knew Nathan wasn't good for Lily. But abused? If anyone had suggested it before the day of the gouges on Lily's cheek, she would have laughed and told them it was nonsense. Not Lily. It was her own strength that had provided the cover for Nathan.

A raised voice from outside startled her. It was Nathan. 'You were leaving me for him? You bitch. And you, Gunn. No wonder your reports were so bland. Innocent little Lily, doing nothing but mothering and working. I was paying you, and you betrayed me. I'll kill you both. She's first.'

Julie pressed her face against the shutters. 'Don't hurt her,' she whispered. 'Please.'

Chapter 73

DAVID

THE LOOK ON Lily's face shattered any illusions David might have had that he could salvage something of the bond he'd once imagined between them, when this was all over.

'It was you?' Her eyes were wide, her voice angry. 'You were reporting to him? The night we met on the High Street, and the first time I went to work with Julie. You told him.'

David shook his head. 'Not the ... not the High Street.'

'But you told him I was working with Julie.'

David nodded.

'Thanks, David. He beat me both times.'

Collesso moved the knife to her throat, and David stifled a gasp. 'Shut up, you lying bitch. I've never beaten you. I should have. What's this about the High Street?'

'We ... we met on the High Street the night I came back from Julie's and went out for a walk, before you came home.'

'And you exchanged phone numbers?'

'Not then.'

He pointed the knife at David. 'When did she get your number?'

David shrugged. 'I can't remember. It was a while back. I wanted her to trust me, so I tried to get close to her. She didn't

268

want to take my number, but I insisted.'

There was anger and insanity in Collesso's narrowed eyes. 'Why didn't you tell me she was leaving me? Your reports that week were just the same as ever. All she was doing was working and shopping and speaking to her wee pal, Sam.'

David tried to swallow the anger that was creeping through him. He had to keep calm. Keep Lily safe. Get help for Sam. 'That's all I saw. I couldn't watch her every minute of the day, could I?'

The knife was back at Lily's throat. Nathan's eyes swivelled between them. 'You're liars. She got this phone after I disappeared, so you've been in touch since then. You've played me, both of you.'

David laughed. 'That's shite. I gave her the number on a bit of paper long before you went missing. She must have put it in her phone. I'm not interested in her. Never have been.'

'Was Aneta more your type?'

David shrugged. 'Maybe.'

'Or wee Eva Hunter?'

Cold, hard rage pounded in David's head. Adrenaline surged through him, his hands curling into fists. It had taken all his self-control not to take the knife from Collesso in the cellar, and plunge it between the bastard's ribs, feel it slide into his heart. But he couldn't, then or now. He had to keep it together.

'You and Eva. You shouldn't have hidden that from me,' Collesso said. 'Not when I was paying you. I needed to know everything you were doing. Fortunately, I was in the pub that night, and her drunken pal couldn't keep her mouth shut.' He grinned, and it was dark and malicious. 'Tasty, Eva. Isn't she?'

David swallowed a groan, and it felt like ground glass in his gullet. 'You're a bastard.'

Collesso laughed. 'Is that right?'

A car drew up at the cottage, and Sophia got out. 'Nathan?' she shouted. 'What are you doing?'

'Hi honey. Wasn't expecting you.' Nathan folded the knife and stuck it in his pocket, then he shoved Lily towards David. 'Know what? You two are welcome to each other. Don't think you've got long together, though, unless Aleksander has a change of heart.'

Lily stumbled and almost fell. David caught her and pulled her to him. She tried to shrug him off, anger and fear in her eyes, but he held tight. Sophia stood in front of Collesso, her eyes avoiding David.

'Where's Ronan?' Collesso asked.

'He … he fall. I take him to hospital. It is okay. He has two stitches on his knee. They tell me collect him in one hour.'

Lily shook her head. 'You're a liar. You don't just leave toddlers in hospital and go back for them later, like a sick pet. What have you done with him?' She tugged against David. He felt a sharp burst of pain as she stamped on his foot, but he didn't loosen his grip.

There was a sad look on Sophia's face, tears in her eyes. 'Nathan, Aneta is dead. She was found in a river early this morning.'

David groaned. So that was why Bartosz was angry, and Jakub evasive. How could this have happened? He should have kept looking for her, protected her.

Collesso's laughter seemed to push Sophia backwards. 'What? I should care about some dead Polish slut?'

'But it is Aneta. She was our friend.'

Collesso shook his head. 'She wasn't my friend. She was a whore. That's what happens to whores. Especially ones that don't do what they're told.'

Sophia gasped. 'Nathan, did you kill her?'

'Does it matter? She was no one. The bitch was stirring up the other girls. Told one of them to attack a councillor. She took her passport and ran. Spent the night with a punter, then I found her at the bus station. She threatened to go to the police.' Collesso's face was flushed with anger, spittle in the corners of his mouth. 'Her life was shit before I rescued her. She should have been more grateful.'

Sophia nodded. 'Okay. So you …?'

'I had to kill her. She'd have ruined everything.'

David leapt at Collesso. He punched him on the side of the head and Collesso fell to the ground. David landed a kick on his chest and pulled his foot back for another.

'No, David,' Sophia yelled. 'Leave him!'

David backed off, his breathing ragged, pain gripping his heart. Collesso was on his knees, groaning. Sophia yelled again, a volley of Polish fury. Lily had her by the hair, pulling her backwards. 'Where is my son?' Lily shouted. 'Tell me!'

Sophia's feet stumbled, her hands reaching for Lily's. David grabbed Lily and disentangled her fingers from the other woman's hair.

Collesso was on his feet. 'Crazy bastards,' he said. 'You two deserve each other. Come on, love.' He took Sophia's hand, and they walked away.

'Nathan. Please!' Lily struggled in David's arms, as Nathan and Sophia got into the car. It pulled away, and she turned to him, her voice frantic. 'You've got to help me. We have to find Ronan.'

At last, David let his eyes stray across the road to the forest. There was movement. Shadows getting closer. It would soon be over. He put his hand on the button on the collar of his jacket and whispered, 'Ronan's safe. I promise. You'll see him soon.'

As the shadows became running shapes storming towards them, a sudden light illuminated the cottage. Before he could make sense of what he was seeing, David felt a pulsing sensation beneath his feet, the fastest slightest current passing through the soil, drumming, warning. 'Lily …'

She followed his gaze, their eyes fixed on the cottage, their ears already primed for the blast as the cottage exploded.

Chapter 74

LILY

Leaves and debris and shards of stone were falling around Lily. She brushed them off and sat up. Flames were shooting from the roof of the cottage. She scrambled to her feet and saw David battering with a rock on a back window. The glass smashed, and she heard a whoosh. It knocked her backwards, and she felt the breath forced from her body as she hit the ground again. Above her, slow powdery clouds drifted across the sky like any other day. For a moment, she watched them. Perhaps they would have held her attention for longer had she not heard a shout. It was Julie.

Behind the glass, there were wooden shutters. David and two black-clad men were thumping at them, and nothing was happening. Lily remembered she'd seen an axe beside a heap of logs. She'd fancied she might pull it from the wooden block that held it, and beat Ronan's whereabouts from Sophia. Too late for that, but she scrambled to her feet and ran. She pulled on the axe. Nothing. Her foot on the block, she tugged again. It gave a little. Another tug, and she heard a creak. It was free.

In seconds, David had demolished the shutters with the axe, and he and the men were climbing through the window. Lily followed them. The heat in the room was stifling, and the smoke was thick and black. She could see nothing, but she could hear Julie. 'Over here. Get Sam. He's in a bad way. Get him out.'

Lily tried to move towards the voice, but someone knocked into her, and she fell. Coughing, she rolled over and tried to stand. She was on her knees and there was shouting all around her. So many voices. The air was too hot to breathe. The membranes in her mouth were dry and her throat was aching. She felt someone grab her, pulling and dragging her across the floor towards the window. She tried to pull away, to go back for Sam. She tried.

Lily must have blacked out. She came round and there was something tight on her face. She opened her eyes and tried to lift her arms, but they were wrapped in a crinkly foil blanket. David was leaning over her, his face black. 'Lily; thank God. I ...'

Someone asked him to move. It was a paramedic. Such reluctance and so much more in those grey eyes as he backed away.

'Wait.' She forced her arm out of the blanket and pulled the mask away from her mouth. Her voice was hoarse and scratchy. 'Is Ronan really safe?'

David nodded. 'You'll see him soon.'

'Were you undercover?'

He didn't answer. A man appeared behind him. He had a shaved head and a leather jacket. He took David's arm. 'Come on. Time to get you out of here.' If he hadn't spoken with a broad Glaswegian accent, he could have passed for one of the Polish thugs.

David's smile looked forced. 'Take care, Lily.'

And he was gone.

Chapter 75

LILY

DANGER LURKED IN quiet streets and play parks, in busy shopping centres and buses, in the empty flat across the road, at nurseries and childminders. Everywhere. It had been two months since the incident at the cottage, and Nathan was still on the run. The police had tried to persuade Lily to go into witness protection. Her evidence would be crucial to getting a conviction. She refused. He'd taken enough. She wasn't prepared to lose herself again. She was moving to Polwarth and getting on with her life. At least, that was the plan. In reality, she was tempted to stay inside, her door locked and her windows shuttered. Anything to keep her son safe. But she had to take Ronan out. They went to a mother and toddler group three times a week. There was no leaving him with anyone, and no visiting Julie. The thought of being in that house from where Nathan had taken Ronan – it was too much, while there was still a risk he might return.

Julie came to the flat at Polwarth, and sometimes Philip took them all out in the car. Julie wasn't driving yet. She'd suffered a scapular fracture, but she hadn't needed surgery. Just a sling and some painful exercises that she had to be reminded to do. Lily hated to think of Julie alone in that house. She'd offered her the second bedroom in the flat, said she'd take Ronan in with her, but Julie refused. Philip stayed with Julie at night, and she was fine during the day. She would not let Nathan Collesso drive her out of her own home, she told Lily. Just let him try to come back. She had an arsenal of weapons cunningly disguised as household implements planted in strategic places. She was ready for him.

They'd hardly spoken of what had happened. Lily swung between wanting to know everything and nothing. She was still trying to piece things together. She remembered the explosion. Going into the cottage and coming round on the grass outside, and the place swarming with armed police. Being taken to hospital. Janice Morgan bringing Ronan to her later. 'Silly Mama,' Ronan had said, when she held him so tight, he couldn't move. 'Leave me.' She'd put him down and he'd gone in search of the cat.

When she gave a statement about what had happened at the cottage, Lily asked the officers about David, but they wouldn't tell her anything. She presumed he'd been brought in to get close to Nathan and the traffickers. She'd heard on the news that a woman had been found injured two miles from the cottage, so she'd asked them if it was Sophia and was she undercover too? Was that how Ronan came to be with social work? The officers had changed the subject.

They arranged an alarm in the Polwarth flat, and the address was flagged to ensure a quick response to any emergency call. They told her they'd be watching. She saw them sometimes. A patrol car passing, slowing, officers looking up. Shadows in the opposite street as she left the flat. A prickle between her shoulder blades, as if she was being watched.

*

THE TAXI DRIVER smiled at Lily as he took the pushchair out of the boot. She paid him and he gave her a card. 'Call me any time, love.' He was cute and she couldn't help returning his smile. He winked before driving off.

Margaret had lost some weight and gained some colour in her cheeks. She laughed as Ronan toddled towards the kitchen. Lily scooped him up in her arms and sat at the table. Margaret made tea. She sat opposite Lily. 'I spoke to my nephew last week. He sent me photos, and he looks so like Tommy. He's coming to Edinburgh next month. I'm so excited. I'm …'

Lily heard the front door opening and a car pulling away. Her heart raced.

The kitchen door creaked open. Ronan peeped over her shoulder. 'Sam!'

Tears welled in Lily's eyes as she heard the creak of a wheelchair on the linoleum. Sam touched her arm, and she turned, brushing the tears away. He looked good. New teeth. Short hair. Colour in his cheeks to match Margaret's. He smelled of soap and coffee. He frowned, his eyes staring into hers. 'Don't cry, please.'

'I'll try not to. How are you doing?'

'Great. Started helping down at the shelter, teaching two boys to read, and chatting to anyone that wants to talk. And I've been quite good with the booze, haven't I, Margaret?'

Margaret nodded. 'Not bad. Two or three of an evening. That's all. Might even manage without it one of these days.'

Sam winked at Lily. 'Maybe, but it'd be a shame to waste all your father's bottles. You know what Philip said about moderation management. He thinks it's better than total abstinence. More achievable. A bit like yourself and the collecting. Not easy to give it all up at once.'

Margaret looked a little shame-faced, and Lily wondered what was going on in the other rooms, and whether all the clutter busting had been in vain.

'Come out to the shed, Lily.' Sam started wheeling himself towards the back door.

Lily stared at Margaret. 'He's back in there?'

Margaret laughed. 'Not for sleeping. He's in my spare room. The one at the front. He's a proper lodger, no matter what the neighbours might say. He's got his books in the shed. He likes to sit in there sometimes. Often. Too often.'

Sam winked at Lily again. 'Come on. Ronan will be fine with Margaret.'

Chapter 76

SAM

Despite the sadness and the fear she's trying so hard to hide, Lily still brings light. Sam takes her hand. 'We hardly see you. I miss you more than I can say.'

She's still smiling, but it's forced now. 'I miss sitting beside you on George IV Bridge. I miss the Old Town. I miss everything except him.'

Sam nods. 'We need to go back one of these days. I hear there's a bird in my pitch. Let's go and harass her.'

Lily laughs. 'You want to hear her cheek.'

'She'll not get much if that's her attitude.' He smiles. 'You're only a short walk away now. You can come round any time.'

'I know, but I hate seeing you like this. It's my fault.'

'You blame yourself for this?' He gestures to the stump of his right leg and the wheelchair. He shakes his head. 'It was nothing to do with him. No one but myself to blame. I told you in the hospital. It's peri … peri something or other.'

She nods. 'Peripheral neuropathy.'

'That's it. Caused by the drinking and the diabetes. You were always telling me to get help. I should have listened. But I was lucky to keep the top half of my leg. I'm being fitted for a peg-leg when the stump heals. Not sure I'll make anything of it. I've got lazy.' He leans towards her. 'If it makes you feel any better, my right arm's fucked, and that is down to him. But I'm going for physio, and they say I might get some use back in it.'

'Sam, you nearly died from internal bleeding.'

He shook his head. 'It'll take more than a few kicks from Collesso to finish me off. Everything's fine. It's you I'm worried about, with that nutter on the loose. Do you think he's still around?'

She shrugs. 'Who knows? I tell myself he'd never come back and risk being caught. And then I look at Ronan and I can't see how he could stay away.'

Sam takes his mobile phone from his pocket. 'I have this thing, and no one to call. Margaret makes me take it everywhere, in case he gets me, or I'm abducted by the Poles again, even though one of them ended up as mince on the shore and the others are inside. Lily, I hate not seeing you, not talking to you. And I hate that you blame yourself. You've never done anything to hurt anyone. From the day we met, my life changed for the better.' He thrusts the phone at her. 'Put your number in there. And ring yourself, so you have my number. If you need to talk, or cry, or shout, call me. Please.'

The sun is shining on the window of the shed. Margaret and Ronan are in the garden. The boy's holding Margaret's hand as he toddles round the edge of the lawn. Lily's smiling as she watches them. There's a question in Sam's mouth, one he's wanted to ask her so often, but the time has never been right. Probably isn't right now either, but he's going to go for it. He takes a breath. 'Do you have any family you could stay with? What about your mother?'

Her smile fades. She shakes her head, and he wants to cut out his tongue.

Chapter 77

LILY

LILY FELT LIKE her heart might leap from her mouth if she opened it. She looked through the shed window. Ronan and Margaret were gone. She should go after them, make sure they were safe.

'Don't worry,' Sam said. 'There's a new double lock on the front door. No one's coming in without a battering ram.' He smiled. 'There they are.'

They were at the kitchen window. Ronan was laughing as he reached for a small, hanging stained-glass sun-catcher.

Sam's smile faded. 'I'm sorry I asked. None of my business. Will we go in?'

She wanted to jump up from the old wooden chair and wheel Sam into the kitchen, pretend he'd never asked. But something kept her in the chair. A sudden urgent need to tell him. She couldn't ignore it.

'My mum wouldn't want to know.' Deep in her chest, the words were poking, scratching, hurting as they came out. 'Not now.'

He nodded. 'You're not close?'

A shaft of afternoon sun was beaming through the window. It seemed to lose its brightness, blurring into a shaky column of muted light, against the memory of her mother's smile. 'We were.'

'Tell me about her.'

'She was … I'm sure she still is … beautiful.' Lily smiled. 'She actually looks like Julie. I think that's why I wanted to be friends with her. Mum's small and dark and nothing like me. I took after my father's side. The height, the hair. Skinny and ungainly.' She ignored the look that said he didn't see her like that. 'My father was Norwegian, from the Lofoten islands, and we lived there for a while when I was a child. He died, and me and Mum came home. We were so close after that. Though I was devastated to lose my dad, it felt good to have Mum to myself. I thought it would always be like that. And then *he* came along and spoiled everything. Always talking of the devil and sin.'

The hand on her arm tightened. 'Who was he?'

She groaned. 'The minister; my stepfather. My mother married him three years after my dad died.'

Sam took his hand away, and she wanted it back. He leaned towards her. 'Did he harm you?'

She shook her head. 'Not like that. He wasn't a bad man. Just stern and repressed, and much older than her. They married, and all our laughter was gone. I don't think my mum was unhappy. She just became introspective and obsessed with his religion. He had his good points. Without him pushing me academically, I wouldn't have gone to medical school. It wasn't what I wanted.' She frowned. 'I didn't want to leave at all. My Granny was frail, and she didn't get on with my stepfather. I wanted to move in with her and look after her, but she died suddenly, and I knew it was probably best for me to go. I fancied studying literature or art, but he wasn't having it. I should have a proper career, he said. Turned out I loved medicine, but I wasn't street-wise enough for city life. Maybe if he'd let me be a proper teenager, I'd have known how to look after myself.'

'When did you last speak to your mother?'

She stared out the window. 'At the end of the summer holidays after third year, when I discovered I was pregnant.'

'You told her?'

Lily nodded. 'I think she would have helped me, but he called me for everything. Said I had to leave, that I couldn't shame him and my mother. The minister's stepdaughter having a bastard child, and bringing it up in their home? That couldn't happen.' She shrugged. 'There was nowhere else for me to go but to Nathan. Mum phoned and texted for a while, but I didn't answer. I was so hurt. Eventually, I blocked her number.'

Sam took her hand again. 'What about contacting her now? Maybe things would be different.'

She shook her head. 'I thought about it after Ronan was born, and again after our engagement. Maybe I would have, but he … Nathan … he called her.'

The memory made her want to curl up and cry. She'd broken one of his rules, the ones she could never grasp, no matter how hard she tried. They were fluid and sketchy and changed from hour to hour. The consequences were much the same, with subtle variations on a brutal theme. No matter how brutal it got, her reaction didn't change; she would not cry in front of him. So that day, he took her phone, locked himself in the bathroom and made a call to her mother. She shivered as she remembered his voice, so loud and confident.

Sam stroked her arm. 'What did he say?'

Nathan's words had been shoved down into a deep place. Maybe best to leave them until they'd crumbled away to nothing. Until they couldn't hurt her.

'Lily?'

Maybe it would have been best, but the words flooded up and spilled out, rapid and stuttering and devastating. 'He said he was a social worker in Glasgow, and I was a drug addict. He told her I'd turned to drugs after having an abortion. And that I'd said the baby was my stepfather's; that he'd raped me.'

The devastation on Sam's face. She smiled to try and chase it away. 'I know my mother wouldn't have believed anything like that about my stepfather. She knew I got pregnant while I was away, so she'd just have thought it was me being vindictive, and she'd have been really hurt. Though the truth was nowhere near as bad as Nathan had told her, I still couldn't get it out of my head that my stepfather had been right about me all along. I was stupid and weak and cheap. I had got so drunk, I couldn't even look after myself. Or so I thought.' She shrugged. 'The longer I've left it, the more difficult it's become to even contemplate contacting her. My stepfather wasn't fond of me to begin with, and I didn't make life easy for him. I doubt he would let her have anything to do with me now.'

'You don't think they'll have seen your name in the papers?'

'Doubt it. They're not big on reading papers. Too much sin in the world.' She shivered. 'I'm not used to being scared, Sam, even when I was with Nathan. Now I feel as if I'm on the edge of something that might swallow me up, destroy me.'

'You're strong.'

'Everyone says that, but I don't feel it. And if I was strong, why did I stay? Why did I put up with that?'

There were tears in his eyes as he squeezed her hand. 'With your upbringing, it would never be easy to walk away from the father of your child, monster or not. You were so young. I bet he promised you the world.' He frowned. 'I'm no psychologist, but maybe you thought if you married him, you'd be respectable. Then you could get in touch with your mother.'

She nodded. 'I used to lie next to him at night and imagine the life we were going to have after we were married. We'd have more children. Be happy. We'd go home, and I'd show my stepfather how wrong he was, make my mother regret the years she'd missed with her grandchildren. And when the voice came, as it inevitably did, poking and reminding me of all the things Nathan had done, telling me he'd never change, I'd shove it along with all the other crap in a box deep in my head, lid firmly closed.'

Sam stared out the window, then he swallowed. 'You said you

thought you had drunk too much that first night. You don't have to tell me, but did he … was it the same as for those other girls … the drugs … the rape?'

She couldn't stop the tears. 'Just the same.'

He pushed his wheelchair close and pulled her to him in a one-armed hug.

*

AT THE FRONT door, Margaret thrust something at Lily. It was a personal attack alarm – a small box with a cord. Lily pulled the one Julie had given her from her pocket. It was an aerosol that emitted a loud sound accompanied by dye and a noxious smell.

'Very good,' Margaret said. 'But you can clip this one on.' She fixed it to the handle of the pushchair. 'You just pull the pin out with one hand.'

Lily smiled and thanked her. 'I'll see you soon.'

Sam rolled his wheelchair down the path and joined her at the gate. 'Will you think about contacting your mum? She knows you better than anyone; she'll understand. Where is she? You didn't say.'

Lily shook her head. 'Nowhere near here.' She tried to smile and felt the tears lurking again. 'Thanks, Sam.'

He nodded. Ronan waved. 'Bye Sam. Bye Maggot.'

Chapter 78

DAVID

THE WHITE SANDS stretched out before him, and David held his breath, anticipating the familiar surge of calm and well-being. It didn't come. He zipped his jacket up to his neck and started walking. He'd feel better by the time he reached the caves; he always did. Not today. As he turned to go back, the rain started. It felt oppressive and doom-laden. Before he reached the car, the rain was gone, the sun was back, and a rainbow arched across the Bridge to Nowhere. Typical island weather. Another day, and he'd have followed the shimmering bow onto the moor, his boots crunching through the glistening heather as his eyes scanned the sea.

There was a strange car at his mother's house, and he couldn't face a visitor. He went in the back door and sneaked up the stairs. Sitting on his bed, he watched the sunlight on the waves, and Lily was back in his head, along with a dozen fears and questions. What if Collesso returned? What if he found her and Ronan? What if ...?

David hadn't wanted to leave Edinburgh, with Collesso still on the run. He'd wanted to stay on in his post. No chance, his hander, MacPhail, had told him, as they debriefed after the explosion at the cottage. MacPhail had hurried him away from the scene, away from Lily. Back to the gloomy portacabin on an industrial estate, the same portacabin he'd visited for a debrief after each trip to the Dumbiedykes flat.

'You've been undercover often enough,' MacPhail had said. 'You know the score. It was never going beyond today.' He'd cocked his head to the side, observing David with suspicion. 'You done well, son. Very well. Might be a promotion in this. But …'

'What?' David was short on patience, his body still flooded with adrenaline and hatred. He wanted to kill Collesso.

'Lily Andersen. You got a thing for her?'

He shook his head. Had MacPhail heard him tell Lily that Ronan was safe? David had been wearing two listening devices. One was concealed in a pen in his pocket. The other was in the button on the collar of his jacket. He'd tried to cover it up before whispering to Lily.

'Why'd you attack the Pole?'

David shrugged.

'Though it was a stupid move, I can understand you attacking Collesso,' MacPhail said. 'All the Pole did was say he'd like to shag Collesso's bird.' MacPhail smirked. 'And questioned your sexuality. I'm assuming that wasn't what got to you.'

'Maybe it was,' David said, desperate to shift the focus from Lily.

'Whatever. You'll be back here soon enough when the bastard's caught and tried. You'll have to give your evidence from behind a screen.'

That was two months ago, and Collesso was still on the run. Surely he'd have left the country by now, the case against him watertight since the Poles had pleaded guilty to human trafficking and exploitation, abduction, involvement in serious and organised crime, and benefit fraud. Henryck had blown himself to bits. The others had left the cottage seconds before the explosion, and were caught on the shore. Bartosz's wife had jumped overboard. She didn't get far before she was picked up by officers from Border Policing Command, on standby at the nearby oil terminal. Bartosz claimed to have known nothing about Henryck setting fire to the cottage. Said he thought the can of fuel was for the van, and though David was certain Bartosz knew fine well what was going on, and would have had no qualms about Julie, Sam and Lily dying in the fire, he couldn't prove it. There was no pleading guilty to rape or assault or murder for the Poles. That was all down to Collesso, they said, and the girls had backed them up, desperate to tell their stories. If it wasn't for the court order that restricted publication of anything relating to Collesso's case while he was on the run, their stories would be all over the newspapers.

Collesso had been under suspicion for a while before David was brought in. His role was to get close to Collesso, and get enough evidence to convict him. It wasn't easy. Collesso trusted no one at the station but Sophia, and he wasn't about to make friends with a teuchter constable from the sticks, even one that had been in London for the last few years. It was Sophia that manipulated Collesso, with whispers about David. Street girls and debts, gambling and association with known criminals, a disciplinary matter at the Met. Before long, Collesso made sure they worked together as much as possible. It didn't take him long to recruit David as his lackey and introduce him to the Polish gang. Collesso wanted David to keep him and the gang informed of anything of interest that came up at the station, and to turn a blind eye to the activities of the street girls. In reality, Collesso was far more interested in having someone keep an eye on Lily.

There had been nineteen Polish girls in Edinburgh, each of them branded with the same rose tattoo. Most of them were of Roma origin, living in slums in Poland. They'd been brought over to Scotland with the promise of work, and then forced into prostitution and benefit fraud. There were only eighteen girls now, and David couldn't shift the feelings of guilt he felt over Aneta's fate. If only he'd found a way to warn her, let her know it would soon be over. But he couldn't risk blowing his cover. That first night in the Dumbiedykes flat, he'd been relieved she wasn't as young as the other two girls. She'd asked him, with a sullen look, what he wanted her to do. Just talk, he'd said. She was disbelieving at first, then grateful. With the help of Google Translate, she told him, over a few visits, how she'd come to be there. Though she loved her family, she'd been desperate to escape her life of discrimination and squalor. She and her cousin worked in a hotel in Kraków. That was where she met Tony Harris. A Scottish wine merchant, he was handsome and sophisticated, and she couldn't believe it when he took an interest in her, and eventually asked her to marry him.

Tony bought her clothes, arranged her passport, and sent her a plane ticket. She flew from Kraków to Amsterdam to Edinburgh. Expecting to see Tony at the airport, she was surprised to be met by Jakub and Henryck. They took her to the flat in Dumbiedykes, mostly keeping her in the one room. She could hear what was going on in the other rooms, and she knew what was expected of her. The first man they brought to her left with deep scratches down his face. She wasn't fed for three days. It was Jakub that persuaded her to see sense. He told her Tony had disappeared. Aneta asked for her passport, and Jakub said the boss man had taken it. She would not get work or benefits, he'd said, without a passport. She could not go home. This was the only way.

In time, when she'd proved herself, and agreed to the rose tattoo on her shoulder, they let her out with the other girls, a lackey always close by to collect the money. Sometimes he'd let the girls go off with men in cars, as long as the men paid upfront. One night, she was in a car in an industrial area in Leith, when a police car pulled up in front of them. The driver of the car panicked and pushed her out before taking off at speed. But the police weren't there for him. Someone had broken into a warehouse. Aneta stayed in the shadows and watched the policeman in charge send two young officers into the building while he waited by the car. It was Tony.

When she tried to attack him, he'd held her off, begging her to let him explain. She calmed down, and he told her he'd been working undercover in Poland, trying to infiltrate the gang of traffickers. He'd gone along with their plans to get her over here, intending to free her from them, to marry her. But the gang had told him she'd changed her mind and hadn't come. Now he'd found her, everything was going to be okay. He couldn't take her home with him, or the gang would kill them both. But he'd come and see her. He was a regular visitor to the Dumbiedykes flat, with his promises that she'd be free soon, that he was almost ready to expose the gang. First, he had to prove himself, and that meant sometimes he was the one watching over the girls, collecting the money. He told Aneta it broke his heart to see her used in that way, but he had no choice.

Then Aneta met Olga. She was in a brothel in Muirhouse, and she told Aneta she too thought she was coming to Edinburgh to marry Tony Harris. For reasons Aneta couldn't understand, Jakub sent her to a hotel one night, where she first saw Tony's fiancée. Then Jakub gave both girls Tony's address, and they discovered he and his fiancée had a child. Eventually, she found out Tony wasn't even his real name. She was going to make Collesso pay, she told David. She had a plan. He couldn't say too much, but he'd urged her to be careful.

On his third visit, she'd told David it was no good just talking. 'We must do something,' she said. He'd frozen, conscious of the listening device he was wearing and the back-up team positioned in the van outside. She'd shaken her head and laughed. 'Don't worry. We don't do the sex, just make the noise. I don't tell them nothing.'

She jumped on the bed a few times, banged the headboard off the wall, groaned and moaned and yelled, until someone knocked on the door and told David his time was up. Aneta had laughed. She looked so young and pretty, and he'd wanted to take her away. How he wished he had done something before she found her passport and made a run for it. Her fate would haunt David forever.

There was a book on David's bedside table, a novel his sister had given him. He picked it up and opened it where he'd left the bookmark late last night, before he'd turned the light off for the last time. He scanned the page, then he flicked backwards in the book, searching for something he recognised. Nothing. He'd almost swear he had never started reading it. This was no use. He put it down and dug his phone out of his pocket. One call and he was set for a night out in Stornoway. That'd take his mind off things for a few hours.

Chapter 79

DAVID

THE PUNTERS AT the bar in McNeill's were three deep, their voices loud and the mingling stench of their perfume and aftershave overpowering. By the time David had been served, Constable Angus MacLeod was ensconced in the furthest, darkest corner, facing the wall. David passed Angus his pint. 'You been at that married woman in Coll again?'

Angus took a long drink, then he wiped his mouth on his sleeve. 'That was a misunderstanding. I didn't touch her.'

David raised his eyebrows. 'Word on the croft was you were shagging her in the back of the patrol car down at the Braigh.'

His friend's face paled. 'Keep your voice down.' He glanced around. 'You're kidding, right? If that gets about, my promotion's down the tubes. Seriously, I didn't shag her anywhere. Wouldn't have said no in different circumstances, but her man's a nutter.'

'But it is about a woman.'

Angus smiled. 'You know me too well. She's not married, not even spoken for. And she's gorgeous.'

'So, what's the problem?'

He shrugged. 'Her sister works here. If she sees me, she'll let her know, and there'll be no more boys' night out. She'll turn up with her giggling pals, drinking shots and dancing on the table. Does my head in. I've got a reputation to uphold.'

David laughed and shook his head. 'Nice try. D'you think I'm stupid? You don't want her to meet me.'

'Haven't a clue what you're talking about.'

'The Castle Grounds, Hebcelt 2007, Tracey Ferguson. About time you were getting over it.'

Angus shrugged. 'Steal a pal's bird. What do you expect? Like I'm ever going to trust you again.'

'She wasn't your bird. She didn't even like you.'

'She would have, given the chance.' He smirked. 'One look into 'Davie's beautiful grey eyes' and she was lost.'

'Do you ever see her?'

Angus shook his head. 'Nah. She left the island years ago. How's the *craic* in Edinburgh?'

'I'm done there. It was a secondment. I've been back in London for a couple of months.'

'My head's spinning trying to keep up with you. Anyone on the scene?'

There wasn't. He and Eva had spoken on the phone a few times, but they hadn't met, and it wouldn't happen now. To his shame, he was relieved. She still sounded broken, and he couldn't face seeing her. He felt responsible. Collesso may never have targeted her that night if it wasn't for him. 'No.'

'I'm not convinced, Davie; I've seen that lovesick look once or twice before. Want to talk about her?'

'No.'

'Thank God for that.' Angus drained his pint and shoved a tenner at David. 'Go on up.'

'We could just go to another pub, without the sister.'

Angus shook his head. 'She's got spies everywhere. This'll do me.'

They were on their fourth pint, and they'd talked fishing, crofting, football, barmaids, the career path of every boy in their year in school, and a few of the girls. Angus looked around, then he leaned towards David. 'See that Collesso ...'

David's heart thumped. 'What about him?'

'Were you working with him?'

David nodded.

'And no one knew what he was up to?'

He swirled his pint glass, watching as a slight head of foam built up. He put the glass down. 'Some suspected he was dodgy. Maybe not that dodgy.'

'And he's on the run?'

David nodded. He thought for a moment, rearranging the story in his head. 'They nearly had him. Just about to move in when the cottage he'd been hiding in exploded, and caused chaos. He burst through a cordon, him and a Polish girl. She was found a few miles down the road, thrown from the moving car. Broken arm and leg.'

'He took her hostage?'

'No. You didn't hear this from me, but she was an undercover officer from Poland, doing an administrative role at the station. She was in hospital for a couple of days, then gone. Rumour has it she was wired and got Collesso to admit to murder of ... of one of the trafficked Polish girls. If they hadn't been waiting for her to get his confession, the armed cops would have moved in much sooner. They'd have got him before the Polish dafty tried to start the fire, and blew the cottage and himself up instead.'

Angus sat back. 'And I thought it was wild here. Three cases of sheep rustling this year, and a riot with weapons in the Narrows.'

The Narrows was a paved street outside the pub. David looked out the window, but the only excitement was two seagulls squabbling over half a bread roll. 'Weapons?'

'Stiletto heels, a golf umbrella, and a sausage supper. You'd be surprised at the injuries.'

David laughed. 'Sounds like heaven to me.'

Angus narrowed his eyes. 'You're not thinking of coming home, are you?'

David smiled and drained the last of his pint. He looked at his watch. 'Past your bedtime, mate.'

'Never mind my bedtime. Are you?'

David put his glass on the table and shrugged. 'Dunno.'

'Shit.' Angus stood and pulled his hood up. 'Don't even think about going for the sergeant's post. That's mine.' He stared at David. 'You've already put in for it? My job and my bird. Is nothing sacred?'

David smiled and shook his head. 'I thought about it, but I haven't done anything. Maybe next time.'

Outside, the moon was high and full over Lews Castle, sparkling on the water in the harbour, where the masts of the fishing boats shifted in the cold breeze. David phoned his mother. She was more obliging these days than she'd been when he and his childhood friend had walked to Ness. She'd be there in twenty minutes.

'Fancy another pint while you're waiting?' Angus nodded towards the Crit. 'No chance of seeing the bird or any of her mates in there.'

'No thanks. I'm going out in the boat with Gordy early tomorrow. I think I'll start walking; clear the head.'

'Fair enough.' Angus shivered and blew on his hands. 'Cold, eh? You'll need your thermals tomorrow. Right, give me a shout at the weekend. Might let you meet the bird and her pals after all. See if we can get rid of that lovesick air that's hanging around you.'

David laughed. 'Worth a try.'

'I've got just the one in mind.'

'Just the one?'

'Don't be greedy. One will do, for starters. See you, mate.' He walked away, then he turned back. 'I meant to say in the pub.' The breath of his voice steamed out in little white tendrils around his face. 'Lily Andersen.'

David's heart thumped. 'What about her?'

'Collesso's bird. Is she from the west side? From Valtos?'

David shook his head. 'She's not from here.'

Angus shrugged. 'Must be a coincidence. There was a Lily Andersen in my cousin's year in school. Father was Norwegian. They lived in Valtos, then they moved to Norway. Her father died, and they came back just before she started secondary. Must have been the year after we left the Nicholson. Her stepfather's a minister. He's ill, in hospital; has been for a while. According to my cousin, she was odd at school. Insisted on speaking to everyone in Gaelic with a Norwegian accent. She left the island to study medicine. Must be someone else.'

David waved Angus off, then he sat on the wall, all thought of walking to meet his mother gone. He remembered Lily's smile in the café at Cramond, as he'd talked about his father and home, and then her excitement when she'd started to tell him about her home, before Sophia's text changed everything. He hadn't for a minute imagined she was going to tell him she came from Lewis.

And she had Gaelic. The words he'd whispered in the hospital when he'd thought she might not come round echoed in his head. Never had he imagined she would understand him. He felt sick.

Chapter 80

LILY

THE PHOTOS OF Nathan were gone. Rebecca's photos were still in her parents' house, but she wasn't there. Just Rita and Jonathon, looking lost and old. Rita was all over Ronan, hugging and kissing him. Lily asked after Rebecca.

'We don't really know where she is.' Jonathon sounded weary. 'Staying with a friend, we think. She was in hospital for a while – the Royal Edinburgh. We saw her then, but now she rarely answers our calls. I think she blames us for failing to … to protect her from him.'

The Royal Edinburgh? It was a psychiatric hospital. And failing to protect her from what? The arguing? Nathan's temper? Hardly. Rebecca gave as good as she got. Lily watched the grey pallor in Jonathon's cheeks give way to pink. He looked embarrassed. Lily's eyes strayed to a photo of Rebecca, wearing an off-the-shoulder dress. She had a rose tattoo on her shoulder. It made Lily shiver.

She'd been tempted to ignore the letter the Collessos had sent to Julie's, asking her to bring Ronan to see them. But it wasn't fair to keep him from them. She'd checked with the police first, and she'd been advised not to take him until officers had visited and had a look round the house. They'd let her know today that it was safe to come.

'Ronan, how about some photographs with Nana and Grandpa?' Rita combed his hair, brushed crumbs from his clothes, and shoved her iPad at Lily. 'Make sure they're good ones.'

Afterwards, they took a ball out into the garden. Whenever Ronan fell, Rita would run to comfort him, but he'd pick himself up before she could reach him, and he'd take off. He was tough. He never cried unless he was really hurt, and even then, it didn't last long. Not like his father. Lily remembered Rita telling her one night, in a drunken whisper that everyone heard, what a cry-baby Nathan had been. Rita had to go into the classroom with him every day for the first two years of school and stay until he was settled. In primary three, he was bullied, and they had to change his school. Lily had asked no questions and made no comments. She'd seen the simmering rage in Nathan's eyes, and she'd known she was going to pay later for his mother's indiscretion. She'd tried to change the subject, but Rita wasn't finished. In the new school, Nathan discovered the only way to avoid being bullied was to become the bully. How proud Rita had been then. Her boy. No one was going to get the better of him.

As Lily walked down the path towards the gate, a passing police car slowed down. There were two officers. Lily's heart beat a little faster, but David wasn't there. She hadn't seen him since the cottage and the explosion. It was like he'd disappeared off the face of the earth. One officer nodded at her. She opened the gate and felt a hand on her upper arm. It made her jump.

'Sorry, I didn't mean to frighten you.' It was Jonathon. 'I just wanted to thank you for coming. You don't know how much this means to us. I feel responsible for everything, for Nathan, for –'

She shook her head. 'It's not your fault.'

Jonathon gave her a weak smile. 'I'm not so sure about that. We tried for a family for years before he was born. He was so longed for, he was always going to be spoilt.' He shrugged. 'That shouldn't have turned him into a monster. Even as a child he was cruel and manipulative. Charming and plausible too, when he wanted to be.

We couldn't have a pet. Wouldn't have trusted him with it. And then poor Rebecca came along when Nathan was six, and he was so jealous. Rita covered up for him. The pushchair that almost went in the burn at The Hermitage. It wasn't Nathan's fault, according to his mother. He'd got over-excited pushing her. Or the times she almost choked on her food. He was just trying to help feed her. And all those insults and put-downs as she got older. Anything to knock her confidence, and it worked. I was glad I was often away on business, Lily; I couldn't bear it. And then he asked to come and work with me, and I didn't want him, so I pulled strings to get him into the police. I thought it would be good for him. Turns out it was the worst thing I could have done. I put Nathan in a position where he could abuse others, and I'll never forgive myself.' Jonathon frowned. 'I was so pleased when he met you, and when we heard he was going to be a father. I thought everything would be all right. Is it true he was abusing you?'

Lily nodded.

'I'm so sorry. Please, Lily, let me know if I can do anything to help, anytime. You've given us a beautiful grandson and a reason to keep going. I'll always be here for you.' He hesitated. 'I know it's unlikely, but if you see Rebecca, please tell her we love her and want her to come home.'

*

ON GILMORE PLACE, the clouds were dark, and wind-swept debris danced along the pavement. She should have taken a taxi home, or even the lift offered by Jonathon. But Lily wasn't ready for them to know where she lived. They'd assumed she was still with Julie and she hadn't enlightened them. The street was quiet as the last of the day's light faded. As she approached a stretch of tall tenements with shops and businesses on the ground floor, Lily saw a recumbent shape in the doorway of an empty shop unit. She got closer and saw a leg sticking out of an old beige woollen blanket.

Her Lewis granny had blankets like that, with three blue stripes at the top. She'd kept them in a chest at the bottom of her bed. They smelled of peppermint and mothballs, and Lily remembered sick days, when she would curl up on the old green sofa in front of the fire, wrapped in blankets, while her granny told stories in her soothing, melodic voice. Tales of their shared Norse heritage. The grain mills above the beach at Valtos. The Lewis chessmen carved from walnut tusk, discovered in the sand dunes near Ardroil after a storm. The Norse mill and kiln at Shawbost. And then Lily would tell a tale from Norway, one of her father's tales of the fin folk: dark, sorcerous shapeshifters that lured their human victims –

There was a groan, and the leg moved. The blanket shifted, revealing a tear in the grubby denim and a glimpse of skin so pale it was almost translucent. The foot wore a flimsy slip-on plimsoll, and it was too small to be a man.

Ronan was asleep. Lily wedged the pushchair tight against the wall and put the brake on. She knelt by the shape and reached to where she thought an arm might be. 'Are you all right?'

The shape groaned and twitched.

'Can I get you something? Food? Water?' She heard creaking, and she looked up. A *To Let* sign was shuddering in the wind. Steadying herself with a hand on the low window ledge, she turned to check on Ronan. He was in a deep sleep, his plump cheeks pink and his features relaxed. It was too late in the afternoon for such a sleep; she should have tried to keep him awake.

She felt the cold trail of fingers on her hand. She didn't turn immediately, for her mind was still on Ronan and how she'd have to rouse him when they got to the flat. When the fingers wrapped themselves around her wrist, she felt fleeting relief that the person was conscious.

Conscious and strong. The hand hauled her upwards and inwards, pulling and dragging her over the blanketed shape. She heard a muffled yell as her foot caught something soft. She tried to grasp the wooden frame of the door, but the person who pulled from inside the shop was too strong. Behind her, Lily was aware of the shape coming to life and darting from the doorway, grabbing the pushchair.

Chapter 81

LILY

'No!' LILY's SHOUT was muffled by a hand over her mouth. She was dragged backwards into the darkness of the shop. She heard the squeak of the pushchair's wheels on the floor and relief flooded through her.

'Don't wake him.' Nathan's whispering voice was no surprise to Lily. 'Put him through the back. Stay with him.'

The other person said nothing. Lily felt a bracelet of cold steel around her right wrist, heard a click, and then another. Her hand had been cuffed to something. Nathan's hands were on her shoulders, forcing her body against the wall and down to the floor. Behind her, she could feel the cold metal ridges of a radiator.

'Sit, won't you?' The words were soft and pleasant. His hands slid into her pockets, removing her phone and the personal alarm. He turned her phone off. 'I'm sorry, Lily, but I have to take care of Ronan. Me and ... well, you don't need to know that. We'll be a family. He'll be fine, I promise.'

'You didn't even want him.' Defeat had dulled Lily's voice.

He laughed. 'I wanted him very much. Otherwise, I'd be far away by now.'

She shook her head. 'Why ask me to get rid of him so many

times? You even made an appointment for me at a clinic.'

'I was testing you. I wouldn't have let you go through with it. So, were you working with the cops? You can tell me now. You and Sophia?'

'No.'

'Don't know how I didn't see through that Polish bitch. Pretended to be so in love with me, but a good Catholic girl couldn't have sex before marriage. Couldn't have sex with a suspect, more like. And the bitch was wired. Tried to arrest me. I hope her injuries are serious. As for you, I really wanted that weirdness of yours to be an act. The missing family, the bizarre friends, the cleaning job, the perfect mother, the suffocating virtuousness ...'

The real Nathan was surfacing. Lily heard him swallow. A tight cough. 'Don't you want to know where I've been?'

She shook her head. It didn't matter.

'I was hiding in plain sight. Those officers watching you didn't even see me. They really let you down today. Not that you've helped yourself any, taking the same route every time you went out. And your inability to resist a tramp. You made it so very easy for us.' He laughed. 'You all underestimated me. The cops thinking Bartosz was the mastermind. That fool. He's only got himself to blame for his greed. Coming ashore and getting caught for a hundred and twenty thousand pounds? Idiot. The cops haven't even scratched the surface. Why else would they all plead so quickly? That's how it goes in this game. You get caught, you cough, to avoid a full investigation. Nineteen women? Big deal. You've no idea of the size of the enterprise, the level of depravity, the appetites I'm catering to.'

The touch of his fingers on her cheek made bile rise in her throat. 'Don't think I haven't considered how much I could get for you. I could have you disappeared from here within the hour. No one would ever find you.' He moved closer, put his other hand on her shoulder, letting it slip beneath her clothes. 'I'd make sure you had the mark of the rose first, so everyone would know you were mine. It hurt me that you wouldn't do that for me, Lily. It was so small, it was nothing.

'But I'm not a monster, so I won't sell you. In fact, I want to help you.' His words dropped to a whisper. 'You said at the shore that I took everything from you. If I could give you one thing back, what would it be?'

Her voice was weak. 'You know.'

'I don't.' His words tickled her ear. 'Tell me.'

'Ronan.'

'I can't do that. He's mine. What else?'

There was nothing else. Lily couldn't stop her tears. He wiped them away, and pulled her to him. 'At last. It wasn't healthy to be so controlled. Come on; there must be something.'

She shook her head.

'I know.' He sounded excited. 'I know what I can give you. Your mother. I lied. I didn't speak to her. Never. See, I'm not as bad as you think. You go to your mum. She'll help you. You'll meet someone else. Have more kids. You'll forget about us.'

The weirdest sound erupted from Lily's mouth. Strangled distorted laughter, and she couldn't stop it. Nathan gripped her chin, squeezing. 'You could thank me.' He squeezed tighter. 'Freak. As if I'd leave my son with you.'

Lily heard a click, and a beam of light lit the room. Nathan was holding a torch. He looked healthier than when she'd last seen him. His hair and eyebrows were black, and he had a moustache and a goatee beard. He was wearing a suit.

'Not bad, eh? You could have passed me in the street.' He smiled. 'You did. Several times.'

He rested the torch on a chair and gripped her right foot. He fixed a small box to her ankle, securing it with velcro. 'You move too much or try to stand, they'll be scraping what's left of you off what's left of these walls.'

From his pocket, he took a roll of parcel tape and another two black boxes. He taped one of them to the front door. It looked like a small digital alarm clock. It was 16.45. Time for *Bob the Builder*. He did the same with a side door. 'At 3pm tomorrow, I'll deactivate the devices and you're free to go. Well, you will be, if you can remove your gag and alert someone to release you. Sorry I can't stretch to refreshments or toilet facilities.'

From the next room, she heard the snuffling, shuffling sounds of her son awakening.

'Mama.' Low groaning. Rustling covers. 'Mama.' Louder. Little fat belly straining against the pushchair straps.

'Does my head in, that whining.' Nathan turned off the torch. The room was black. 'Come on,' he shouted. 'We're going.'

Lily heard wheels on the floor. Ronan banged on the bar of the pushchair. 'Mama!'

'Ronan.' A normal voice. She had to keep a normal voice. 'I'm here.'

'Mama, where are you?'

Nathan kicked her thigh. 'Don't speak to him. Don't you dare.' Over his shoulder. 'Get him out of here. Go straight to the car. I just need to sort the door and gag her, then I'll be with you.'

'Okay.' A muffled voice. 'I'm going.'

It was Rebecca.

Chapter 82

LILY

LILY HADN'T ALWAYS been the saint Nathan proclaimed her. She'd made her stepfather's life a misery, taunting him with superstitious tales and talk of spirits and selkies and séances. His face would turn crimson, his breathing shallow, and she would pray for his sanctimonious heart to explode in his skinny pigeon chest. She wasn't sorry for it, other than the upset it had caused her mother. She rarely chastised Lily. Just that look, and the occasional plea for kindness and understanding. Perhaps her mother knew Lily would get bored with it eventually, that age and maturity would bring an end to her nonsense. It had, but still she hadn't accepted him.

And then the way she'd treated her mother. It was inexcusable. She should have kept in touch. Her mother deserved to know Ronan and she shouldn't have let her childish pride keep them apart.

As for Rebecca, Lily hadn't stopped to consider what had made her so surly and resentful. It was time to put things right. 'We visited your parents today, Rebecca. They're desperate to hear from you.'

The wheels stopped. There was a burst of childish laughter. 'Mama. You there.'

He sounded so normal and happy. 'Clever boy,' Lily said.

'Shut up.' Nathan's face was in hers. 'Don't say another word.'

'Your parents are broken.'

His hand shot out and grabbed her hair, twisting her head to the side, then slamming it against the wall. His breathing was shallow. 'Stop. Just shut up.' He let go of Lily and backed away. He pulled the side door open. 'Get him out of here.'

There was a bright light in the lane. It seeped into the room.

'Funny Dada.' Ronan giggled. He turned in the pushchair. 'Becca. Funny Becca.'

In the weak light, Lily saw that Rebecca had changed out of the tramp's clothes. She'd lost weight. Her cheeks were sunken and her hair dull.

'Get out.' Nathan took a step towards Rebecca. 'Now.'

She didn't move. 'What else did they say, Lily?'

'They love you and want you home,' Lily said. 'They told me to tell you if I saw you.'

'Don't listen to her lies, Rebecca,' Nathan said. 'We have to go.'

Rebecca shook her head. Her eyes didn't meet his. 'I ... I don't think I want to.'

'There's nothing for you here.'

'There's Mum and Dad ... Lily ... Ronan.'

'Mum and Dad don't want you; they never did. Lily hates you. And no one else is having Ronan.'

'That's not true, Rebecca,' Lily said. 'I don't hate you. And your parents said they're sorry they didn't protect you from him.'

Nathan pointed at Rebecca. 'Protect her? It's me that needed protecting. Always nipping my head, clinging to me, following me. And not just as a child. Why do you think it couldn't work between us, Lily? Because she was always there, whispering and criticising and making herself available.'

And then Lily knew why Jonathon had looked embarrassed. It wasn't just resentment she'd felt from Rebecca. It was jealousy. Rebecca was in love with Nathan. She had the rose tattoo, the same as the Polish girls. They were going to live together as a family. Lily shivered. He had no boundaries. 'Rebecca, your dad said Nathan was a danger to you ever since you were born.'

Nathan laughed. 'Since she was born? Proves you don't have a clue what you're talking about. We didn't know her when she was born.'

That was what Jonathon said, wasn't it? *And then poor Rebecca came along when Nathan was six.* Of course, there was only three years between them. Rebecca was adopted.

Nathan's words were tinged with an edge of hysteria. 'You think I'd shag my sister? What do you take me for? She's not a Collesso. She's nobody. A discarded little runt from some flea pit. They don't love her. No one could. Why do you think she's so messed up?'

Rebecca lowered her head, a hand on her eyes, squeezing. On her wrist, Lily saw the infinity bangle. She almost laughed.

'I'm the one they love.' Nathan had the voice of a child. 'Me.' He pulled the door open further. 'Come on, Rebecca.'

Rebecca looked at Lily, then at Nathan. There was indecision and fear on her face.

'Becca, I'm sorry for what I said. You know it's always been you.' Nathan sounded desperate. 'Please, let's go.'

Rebecca took a step towards him, pushing Ronan closer to the door, further from Lily.

'Always been Rebecca?' Lily said. 'Just a couple of months ago, you and Sophia were planning to leave with Ronan. You were talking about getting married, giving her my engagement ring. You were going to leave Rebecca then.'

Rebecca's eyes widened. 'Nathan, tell me that's not true. You said Sophia meant nothing.'

'See that bangle you're wearing?' Lily said. 'He bought it for me. Then he gave it to Sophia. Now you.'

Rebecca tore the bangle from her wrist and threw it on the ground.

'I've had enough of this shit.' Nathan patted his jacket pockets, then his trousers. He frowned. 'Where's my phone?' He hit himself on the forehead and glared at his sister. 'I gave it to you. Where is it?'

'Tell me the truth about you and Sophia,' Rebecca said, putting her right hand in her pocket. 'Maybe then I'll give you the phone.'

'Fuck this.' Nathan lunged at Rebecca, then he stopped and took a step backwards. Lily couldn't see what was going on between them.

Ronan laughed. 'Bang bang gun.' He rocked in the pushchair. 'Becca's gun.'

'You took that out of my suitcase?' Nathan sounded incredulous. 'You?'

'Trust no one, you said.' Rebecca's voice was stronger. 'I took your knife, too. Hid it in a safe place. I bet the police would love to have it. That poor Polish girl …'

Nathan shook his head. 'You wouldn't turn me in, and you wouldn't shoot me.'

'No?' Rebecca took a step to the side and Lily saw the pistol in her right hand. With her left hand, Rebecca edged the pushchair closer to Lily.

'Careful.' Nathan sounded out of breath. 'Do you want to see him blown to bits?'

Rebecca's laughter was scornful. 'Blown to bits? I'm not stupid. I heard you on the phone to your mate, making sure they weren't real. *I just want to give her a fright*, you said. *I don't want to blow anything up*. As if you'd handle explosives. You're a coward; you always have been.'

Nathan turned to Lily. 'Don't listen to her. They're real. Same as the cottage. You saw what happened there.'

Lily shook her head. 'The cottage went up because your daft Polish pal poured petrol round it, and lit a cigarette beside a leaking gas pipe.'

Keeping the gun pointed at Nathan, Rebecca knelt beside Lily and removed the device from her ankle. With wild laughter, she chucked it at her brother, then she followed up with the device from the front door. Nathan didn't flinch, and Lily knew they weren't real.

'He's full of shit,' Rebecca said. 'He's been nowhere near your flat; he wouldn't dare. I found you. I followed your friend from Sciennes. And all that talk of the crime network he's involved in. It's rubbish. It was just him and Bartosz. He's been hiding with a couple of dealers in Wester Hailes who owed him a favour until I gave in and agreed to rent a caravan for us in Mortonhall.'

Nathan snorted. 'Gave in? You begged me, you crazy bitch. You wouldn't have survived after getting out of the nuthouse if I hadn't been there for you. Who else would sit up with you all night and talk you out of topping yourself? What a waste of time that was.'

Rebecca leapt at him, pressing the gun against his chest with both hands, backing him against the wall. 'And whose fault is it I'm messed up?' Her voice wavered, but her hands were steady. 'You raped me. I was fifteen. And not just me. All those girls in the paper. You're a monster.'

Nathan held his hands in the air, desperate words pouring from his terrified mouth. 'I haven't raped anyone. I love you. I'll do anything. And you can't kill me in front of my boy. Think what it would do to him. If you shoot me, you'll deafen him for life. You wouldn't do that, Becca. I know you wouldn't.'

'I'll let them go,' she said. 'Then I'll shoot you. Where's the key for the cuffs?'

'In my left trouser pocket.'

Lily could see the uncertainty on Rebecca's face. There was no knowing if the key was really there, and to find out, she was going to have to take a hand off the gun. Unless she let Nathan reach for it himself, which would be madness.

Ronan strained against the pushchair straps. 'Mama. Out!'

The yell made Rebecca glance sideways, just for a fraction of a second. It was enough for Nathan. He grabbed the barrel of the gun with both hands, forcing it upwards, and turning it back towards Rebecca, then yanking downwards, breaking her grip. And her trigger finger.

Chapter 83

LILY

LILY KNEW JUST how dangerous it was to cross Nathan. A perceived insult or criticism, an annoyance, even just a wrong glance. They could send him over the edge. She'd seen it so often. And yet, she had never seen him look the way he did now. Not the night he almost punched her when she'd been out late. Nor the night he held the dumbbell over her head. When she compared those nights to this, he'd looked almost angelic. Now, as he stared at Rebecca, he seemed possessed. The hands that held the gun were shaking as if he had a serious neurological disorder. Not just shaking. They were clenching and unclenching the grip of the gun, and she feared he might discharge it involuntarily. His eyes were bulging, his nostrils flaring, and there was spittle in the corners of his mouth. She could hear his breathing, and it was ragged and shallow.

Ronan lifted his arms to Lily. 'Out, Mama.'

With one hand, Lily pulled the pushchair closer. Nathan seemed oblivious, so she undid the straps, and Ronan launched himself onto her lap, wrapping his arms around her neck.

Rebecca was clutching her right hand with her left, her face twisted in pain. 'You broke my finger.'

'You broke your own fucking finger, you idiot.' Nathan's voice shook. 'On the ground. Face down.'

Rebecca did as he said. He took a thin plastic cable tie from his pockets and bound her wrists behind her back.

'Get up. Now.' His voice was heavy with venom. 'Get up, you bitch.'

Rebecca didn't move. With the gun in his right hand, he reached down and hauled her up by her hair until she was on her knees. 'Who do you think you are? After all I've done for you.'

Rebecca was silent, her eyes closed.

'Answer me!'

Nothing.

He pressed the gun into his sister's lower abdomen. 'Do you know how long it takes to die from a bullet in the guts? Hours of torment as the poisons seep into your body.' He cocked his head to the side. 'Or maybe not.' He moved the gun up to Rebecca's mouth. Her eyes shot open, and she shook her head, pursing her lips. He forced the muzzle of the gun into her mouth. 'If I was careful, avoided the blood vessels and the spinal cord, you could live for hours. In agony. While I watched. Nothing would please me more.' He shook his head. 'You? You dared to take my gun, to threaten me? You?'

A sliver of blood trickled from Rebecca's mouth.

'I'm going to make you wish you'd never been born. I'm going to –'

Ronan's laughter was high and bright. He pointed at the window. 'Look, look, look. What is it, Mama?'

There was a small dark shape outside, peering in. The shape moved, and the door rattled. 'Police. Is anyone in there?' It was a woman.

'Don't make a sound.' Nathan's voice was low and harsh. He pulled the gun from Rebecca's mouth and pointed it at Lily. 'Don't you dare.'

There were footsteps in the lane. Nathan swivelled the gun towards the side door. It creaked further open and a female officer came in. She looked about twelve. She was small and slim, with short brown hair and a big smile that slipped from her face as she surveyed the room. Her eyes rested on Nathan and widened. 'Sir?'

'For fuck's sake, Blyth.' Nathan spat the words out. 'Are you alone?'

She shook her head, raising her hands. 'A neighbour called it in – strange light in the empty shop. We were passing. Graham's in the car. He'll come looking for me any minute.'

Nathan gave a humourless laugh. 'Or not. Lazy bastard. Letting you come in here alone? What was he thinking? What were you thinking, walking into an unknown situation?'

'Not this. That's for sure.' She shrugged. 'He is a lazy bastard, but he's going to figure out something's going on before long. Or maybe he'll get stuck with a crossword clue. Either way, he's coming in.' Blyth glanced at Rebecca. She was kneeling in front of Nathan, a streak of blood on her chin. 'You all right?'

Rebecca gave a wee nod, her eyes wide and scared.

Blyth smiled at Lily. 'And you?'

'I'm okay.'

The officer winked at Ronan and wiggled her raised fingers. He giggled. Blyth looked at Nathan and raised her eyebrows. 'What now, sir?'

'Lower your left hand and turn your radio off.'

The radio was clipped to the top left of Blyth's high-vis vest. She pressed a button on the radio. It beeped, and Nathan nodded. 'Get your cuffs, and put them on.'

Blyth sighed. 'Sir, really? My own cuffs? I'll never live it down.'

Nathan laughed, and it was a genuine laugh. 'Sorry, but I remember you in training. A feisty wee thing. We don't want any heroics. Just do it.'

As the officer unclipped the cuffs from her vest, a sudden voice yelled from the lane. 'Blyth! Where the hell are you?'

Footsteps approached the side door. Blyth glanced at Nathan. He shook his head in warning, pointing the gun at her. She looked at the door, back at Nathan, and she shrugged. 'Sorry, sir.' She took a sharp breath. 'Don't come in!' she shouted, her voice loud and clear. 'It's Collesso. He's armed.'

To Lily's surprise, Nathan showed no anger towards Blyth.

Instead, he had a wry smile on his face, as if he'd expected no less. Outside, the footsteps retreated at speed.

'So, not just a lazy bastard,' Nathan said. 'A coward too.'

Blyth shrugged. 'You told us often enough. Don't go putting yourself in danger. Not for anyone.'

'Aye, but.' He motioned to the cuffs. 'Put them on, then sit down against the wall.'

Blyth hesitated, then she did as she was told.

'Okay, here's what's happening,' Nathan said. 'Me and Lily and Ronan are leaving.'

Lily's heart almost leapt from her mouth. He was taking her? Why? It dawned on her, and she almost laughed. He couldn't cope with Ronan on his own. First, it was Sophia, then Rebecca. He'd run out of options now, so he was taking Lily.

He pointed the gun at Rebecca, his eyes narrowing with spite. 'I would like nothing better than to put a bullet in you. If it wasn't for Ronan, I'd have done it. Ungrateful bitch. You ruined it for me and Lily. You disgust me.'

There was hatred in Rebecca's eyes. She spat, and it landed on Nathan's cheek. His eyes fixed on his sister, he lifted his forearm and wiped his face with the sleeve of his jacket. His steps were slow as he walked towards Rebecca. The rage was no longer apparent, but Lily knew this sudden calm was worse. If he had any sense, he'd run now, before more police arrived. But she knew Nathan. He simply couldn't let such an insult pass. Maybe Rebecca knew that too, and she was playing for time. He stopped in front of his sister and she kicked out at him, catching him on his shin with the heel of her boot.

'Well, well, well,' he said. 'The worm really has turned.' He laughed, swivelling the gun in his hand until he was holding it by the barrel. Lily knew what was coming. She held Ronan tight to her, so he wouldn't see.

Blyth cried out just before Lily heard the crunch of the gun hitting Rebecca's skull. When she looked up, Rebecca had slumped into unconsciousness. On the top of her head, the glisten of blood seeped through her hair.

Nathan crouched beside Lily and unlocked the handcuffs. 'Put him in the pushchair, quickly.'

Lily's legs were weak as she pushed herself to her feet. Hungry and tired, Ronan squirmed and struggled as she tried to tie the straps of the pushchair.

'Hurry up. That stupid cow's already delayed us.'

Lily tied Ronan in, but he began to cry. 'Let me give him something to eat. It's in the bottom of the pushchair.'

Nathan kept the gun on Lily. 'Be quick.'

Lily crouched and took a banana from the bag below the pushchair. She unpeeled it. Ronan grinned and grabbed it. 'Ta, Mama. Go.'

'Out the door, and turn right,' Nathan said. 'I'll be behind you.' He waved the gun. 'With this, so don't try anything stupid. The lane goes along the back of the shops. You'll come to another lane on the right. Down there, and the car's parked across the road.'

A sudden image of Sophia pushed from Nathan's car, lying injured in the road, came to Lily. She shoved it away. She'd have climbed into a hearse driven by the devil as long as Ronan was with her.

Lily wheeled the pushchair to the side door. She breathed in the cold air, and felt exhilaration at the thought of escaping the confines of the cold, dark shop. Ronan turned and smiled, his face impish in the light from the lane, his voice a wee whisper. 'Nee naw, nee naw, nee naw.'

He was right. There were sirens, and they were close.

'Run,' Nathan yelled.

There was another sound overhead. It was loud.

'Hebicopter, Mama.'

A bright light hovered above them.

'How the fuck?' Nathan cried. 'How the actual fuck?'

'You are like the most wanted person in Scotland,' Blyth said, from behind them. 'Maybe even the UK.'

'Get back in! Now!'

Lily and Ronan were back in the room, the door slammed closed.

Chapter 84

LILY

NATHAN TURNED ON the torch. Scanning the room, he held each of them in the spotlight, as if to make sure they hadn't suddenly found a means of defending themselves against his gun. He hovered the light back over Rebecca. She didn't move.

Ronan laughed. 'Becca sleeping. Ronan wants the big light, Dada.'

The torch moved on to Blyth. 'Sir,' she said, squinting her eyes, 'you thought this through?'

Nathan shrugged. 'Short answer? No. I didn't expect this level of competence from a force that couldn't arrange a shit fight in a farmyard.'

'Probably just luck, sir. Or not, depending which side you're on. In the area at the right time. It happens. So, what are you going to do? You realise if you fire that gun in here, you're going to damage –'

'My son's hearing? And everyone else's. Aye. I know that.'

Outside, cars squealed to a halt, doors opening and closing.

'And if you don't give yourself up, they'll send the armed unit in. They won't know the child's here. Probably think it's just you and me. It's going to be chaos. Distraction devices. A lot of noise. Maybe some firing.'

Nathan sighed. 'Okay, Blyth. You're not dealing with Joe

Bloggs. I do know the routine.'

'Maybe best just to give yourself up, sir.'

'I like you, Blyth, but you're starting to annoy me.'

'Okay, sir. I'll shut up. But –'

He pointed the gun at her.

'Okay.'

Nathan paced the room, gun in one hand, torch in the other. Outside, another vehicle stopped. There was the sound of a sliding door and shuffling feet. Nathan closed his eyes. 'Don't even think of telling me what that is, Blyth.'

'No, sir.'

A mobile phone rang. It was Blyth's.

'Where is it?' Nathan asked.

'Right trouser pocket.'

'Lily, get her phone.'

Lily was reluctant to take her hands off the pushchair, but the threat of his gun persuaded her. As she bent to take the phone from Blyth's trouser pocket, the officer whispered an apology.

Lily handed the phone to Nathan. He took the call, a smile hovering on his lips. 'Sorry to disappoint you, sir, but it's not Blyth. She's otherwise engaged. No, she's not injured. Just a little tied up, so to speak.' He listened, then he sighed. 'I can't, sir. It's too late.' He shook his head. 'No, there are others. Three of them.' He was silent for a while. At last, he nodded, his eyes on Blyth. 'Okay, sir. You're right. She is a good officer, and she doesn't deserve this. I'll send her out.'

He cut the call. Blyth shook her head. 'Sir, let the others go. Think about it. You'll get more mileage from me as a hostage.'

Nathan smiled. 'Best offer I've had in a long time, Blyth, but I don't think so. I've no scores to settle with you. You're safer out of here.'

'Do you want me to give them a message?'

'What? Like I want a getaway helicopter, a speedboat, a lump sum, a new passport?'

'An ambulance for her?' Blyth said, nodding at Rebecca.

'That bitch doesn't deserve any help. Just go. Slowly, though. Wouldn't want you getting shot by Police Scotland's finest, would we?' He slipped her mobile phone into her pocket. 'Be more careful in future.'

'Yes, sir.'

Nathan pulled the side door open. Blyth's gaze lingered on Rebecca, then Lily. She looked as if she might apologise again, then she shook her head and raised her cuffed hands before stepping out into the lane. As the door swung shut, Lily heard shouting outside. It roused Rebecca. She stared at Nathan, her face twisted with something that might have been pain. Or disgust. He didn't seem to notice. He began to pace the room again, the gun dangling in his right hand. Still clutching the pushchair, Lily considered ramming him, trying to knock him over, but she'd seen how quickly he could react, and she didn't dare put Ronan at risk. She pulled the pushchair over beside Rebecca and crouched down.

'Are you okay?'

Rebecca nodded. Her face was pale, and she was shivering. It was cold in the shop, and it would only get worse. 'You should go,' Rebecca said, her voice weak. 'Take Ronan and go.'

Nathan stopped pacing. 'No one is going anywhere. I'm in charge here. I'll decide what's happening.' He sounded weary, as if all the fight had left him. He tucked the gun into his pocket, then he knelt in front of Ronan.

The child smiled and lifted his arms. 'Hey, Dada.'

Nathan hugged Ronan, nuzzling into his neck. Ronan yawned and cuddled close. 'Sleepy. Home, Dada.'

Nathan nodded. He gestured towards the side door. 'Push him out into the lane,' he said to Lily.

Light-headed with relief, Lily walked towards the door.

'Just Ronan,' he said. 'I need him out of the way before I end this.'

Dread pulsed through Lily. It wasn't fear of what Nathan would do to her. It was the thought of Ronan being left alone. She turned. 'Who's going to look after him?'

'My parents. Maybe your mother. It's time they met.' Nathan shrugged. 'He'll be fine.'

'He'll be fine?' The dread turned to rage. 'You really don't give a shit about him, if that's what you think. Your mother had to go into class with you every day for the first few years of school, yet he'll be fine on his own. You're a selfish murdering bastard, and you never deserved to be his father.'

Nathan smiled. 'A selfish murdering bastard with a gun,' he said, raising the pistol and pointing it at her. 'Push him out. Now.'

When Lily pulled the door open, she could feel the down-draught from the hovering helicopter. Poised at the doorway, the front wheels of the pushchair just over the threshold, she felt the gun caress the space between her shoulder blades.

'Go, Mama,' her son said. 'Ronan's hungry.'

The back wheels caught on the threshold as Lily pushed her son out into the lane, the cold harsh touch of the gun on her back. She swivelled the wheels, so the pushchair was facing down the lane. Facing safety. Ronan turned and waved his pudgy fingers at Nathan. 'Bye bye Dada.'

'Bye bye Ronan.' Nathan's voice wavered. 'Dada loves you. Always.'

Lily's hands were tight on the pushchair handle, her knuckles white. She would never be able to let her son go. Nathan must have known it too, for one of his hands covered hers. She waited for his fingers to prise hers off the handle, but his touch was light. His whispered words on her neck made her shiver. 'Did you ever love me?'

Without turning, she nodded and felt no guilt at the lie. 'Very much.'

'I couldn't reach you. Why not?'

Lily shrugged. 'Maybe I am a weirdo, like you always said.'

He was silent. When at last he spoke, his voice was heavy with emotion. 'I don't think so.' He lifted his hand. She felt the touch of the gun, pushing her forwards, out into the lane. 'Look after him, Lily. Tell him I loved him.'

As she walked towards a wavering figure at the end of the lane, Lily's shoulder blades were hunched in anticipation. Each step felt like a mile. She had almost reached the figure when gunshot split the air.

'Bang bang, Mama.' Ronan turned. He was grinning.

Lily's legs felt like they might give way. She waited for the pain, the bleeding, the weakness. There was nothing. She exhaled and kept walking.

She stepped out into the street, and someone took the pushchair from her. Someone else enfolded her in a blanket and hustled her towards an ambulance. A wave of armed officers rushed past, storming down the lane, as a second shot rang out.

Chapter 85

LILY

THE SUN WAS flickering through the branches of the bare blossom trees on the Meadows. Underfoot, the paths were slippery, and Julie took Lily's arm. Their breath steamed out into the frozen day as they walked back towards Sciennes. They'd been looking at a job in a flat on Lauriston Place. The flat was minging, but they both felt an inordinate excitement at the thought of getting back to work. They stopped at the traffic lights on Melville Drive.

'You look happy,' Lily said. 'Something going on?'

Julie shrugged. 'Just glad to be getting back in the saddle.'

'Is that all?'

Julie smirked. 'Not quite. Philip asked me to marry him.'

Lily shrieked, and an old woman standing beside them almost jumped onto the road. Lily put her hand on the woman's arm. 'I'm sorry. It's just that he asked her to marry him.'

'That right?' The woman didn't look too impressed. 'And did she say yes?'

Lily shrugged. 'I hope so. You did, didn't you?'

Julie shook her head. The woman tutted.

'Don't worry.' Lily smiled. 'She will. She'll not get a better offer.'

The woman nodded. 'No' at her age, anyway.'

Julie watched the woman walk up the other side of Livingstone Place. 'Can't get over that cheeky bitch.'

Lily laughed. 'She's right. And she doesn't even know how wonderful he is. You can't let him get away.'

'No chance of that, but I don't have to marry him. Not yet, anyway. I tried it before and I didn't much like it.'

Lily stopped, her mouth dropping open. 'You've been married?'

'Did I not tell you?' Julie smiled. 'You're not the only one with secrets.'

Back at Julie's house, Philip was mortified to be caught dozing with Ronan asleep on his chest. 'I'm sorry.' His voice was hushed, and Ronan slept on. 'I meant to put him in the cot, but he wore me out playing football.'

'In this weather?' Julie shivered. 'It's freezing.'

'The beautiful game is an all-weather sport.'

'If you say so. Tea?'

Philip nodded. He tried to sit up, but he was stuck. With Julie in the kitchen, Lily was tempted to tell Philip not to give up, to keep asking until she said yes. He was a star, the way he'd looked after the three of them, making sure they had a lovely Christmas Day and a quiet start to the new year. He'd taken Ronan to every childhood activity he could find. Now, Ronan was besotted with him.

Philip smiled at Lily. 'You're having a night out?'

Lily nodded. 'I've forgotten how to socialise. Probably have two drinks and head for home.'

Julie was back. 'You better not. And don't come for Ronan too early tomorrow. We're all having a long lie. If you get lucky and fancy a day in bed with some handsome chap, we'll amuse ourselves.'

*

ALTHOUGH THEY HADN'T yet returned to work, Ronan had spent some regular time with Nina, the childminder, and she and Lily had become friends. It was Nina's birthday, and she'd invited Lily to join her and her friends on a night out. It was fun. Lily was chatted up in the pub by a cute vet student from Northern Ireland. He was the soberest of his rowdy group, but that wasn't saying much. Had he been less inebriated, she might have been interested.

They moved on to a club, where they drank and danced and shouted at each other. Just after one o'clock, Lily decided to leave. Yes, she assured Nina, she'd get a taxi; she wouldn't walk. Outside, Lily was tempted to go against her promise. It wasn't far, and she enjoyed walking, but something inside her had changed. She'd become timid, turning and looking behind her on quiet streets, her heart racing at strange noises in the night. It was only to be expected, her counsellor said.

There was one couple at the taxi rank. The woman had her head on the man's shoulder. His arm was around her waist. Lily's heart jolted. She backed away, but he turned. His smile faded. 'Lily?'

'David. How are you doing?'

'Fine, thanks.' He didn't look it. A cab drew up. His partner reached for the door handle and lost her balance. David caught her before she hit the ground. The state she was in, she probably wouldn't have felt a thing if he hadn't caught her. Not until tomorrow morning, anyway. He opened the back door, and she scrambled inside.

David turned to Lily. 'We can't leave you here on your own. Could be ages before another taxi comes along. We're going to Corstorphine. We'll drop you off first.'

She hesitated, but it made sense. David got in the front, so she slid in beside his partner in the back. The taxi took off, and the drunk girl sidled across the seat towards Lily, her eyes still shut. She let her head rest against Lily for a couple of seconds, then her eyes shot open. 'Who are you with your bony shoulder?' She had a Lewis accent, too.

'I'm Lily.'

'Zoe.' She smiled and whispered to Lily.

Lily laughed and shook her head. 'No.'

'Go on. Give him a laugh.'

Lily reckoned David would probably pass out if she mentioned his truncheon.

'Spoilsport.' Zoe's eyes drifted closed. No one spoke until they pulled up outside Lily's flat. She thanked David, and told him she'd pay, but he wouldn't hear of it.

He got out of the car and opened her door. 'Look after yourself.' He looked a little sad. As the taxi pulled away, she swallowed her own sadness.

*

THE MASSIVE FLAT screen TV had always seemed incongruous beside the bookshelves in James's flat. Lily had spent the early part of the evening flicking through films and programmes, but nothing could keep her attention. She'd watched a little of a DVD Julie had lent her when she'd picked Ronan up that morning, but it was in Danish with subtitles and it required a level of concentration that was lacking. She turned off the TV and thought about going to bed. It was early, but she'd read for a while. Her phone buzzed.

Can we talk? David

He'd been hovering at the back of her mind all day. And every day. She hadn't had the chance to thank him for saving her life at the cottage, and last night hadn't seemed like the right time. She should ignore him. Nothing good could come of talking to him. He knew too much. And he had a partner. She'd ignore him. At least until tomorrow.

But those grey eyes plagued her while she changed into her pyjamas and brushed her teeth. There would be no sleep for her tonight if she didn't reply.

*

THROUGH THE PEEPHOLE on the door, Lily saw David rubbing his face. He looked nervous. Her hand was shaking as she turned the key. She should have gone to bed instead of asking him to come round and then getting dressed again. Could have met him somewhere tomorrow. Could have just ignored him.

His smile was a little wary. She showed him into the living room. His hair was damp at the back, and there was a hint of aftershave.

'This is nice.' He looked round the room. 'I like the lights.' She'd strung fairy lights around the bookcases and alcoves to brighten up the place. 'Lots of books.'

'They're not mine. The flat belongs to a friend of a friend. Would you like tea or coffee? Wine?'

'Tea, please. I'm driving, and I had double my weekly quota of alcohol last night.'

Lily nodded. 'Me too, but I think I'll have a glass of wine.'

She returned from the kitchen with their drinks. She sat at the opposite end of the sofa, the space between them heavy with anticipation. At last, he put the mug on the table and turned to her. 'I'm sorry I wasn't there to protect you from him. It's haunted me ever since.'

Lily smiled, cradling her wine glass. 'You couldn't be everywhere. You saved my life once already, and I didn't get a chance to thank you.'

He shrugged. 'I didn't do much. If it hadn't been me, someone else would have got you out.'

'Still. Thank you.'

'How have you been?'

Lily's smile slipped away. She gulped at her wine, then she put it on the table. 'Up and down. According to my counsellor, I'm doing better than I should be. Ronan's getting on great. I love this flat, and I've got it for at least another year. Julie and I are going back to work next week.'

'But?'

'It's going to take time, isn't it?' She shrugged. 'One day I feel completely numb. The next, I'm raging. Mostly with myself. I was so stupid.'

He shook his head. 'You weren't the only one taken in by him.

324

People that should have known a hell of a lot better trusted him.'

'I bet you didn't.'

David smiled. 'No, but, without saying too much, I knew a lot more than they did when I met him.'

Lily shrugged. 'I don't know if I can even claim to have been taken in by him. Maybe at first, but it wasn't long before I knew he was bad news. Didn't know just how bad, but bad enough. I guess I was trying to make the best of the situation, for Ronan's sake. Maybe thought I could change him eventually. Like I said, so stupid.' She thought for a moment. 'Can I ask a couple of things? Then I don't want to talk about him anymore.'

He nodded.

'Were you looking for me on the Royal Mile that night?'

'No. I was looking for him.'

'Did you know I was moving to Polwarth?'

'Aye. Sam told me. I was delighted. No way was I telling Collesso.'

Lily smiled. 'Thank you, again. Where are you now?'

'Back in London. And hating it. I'm just up for the weekend to see Zoe.'

'How was she this morning?'

'Rough, but she's made of strong stuff. She's got a new job. We were celebrating.' He frowned, colour flushing his cheeks. 'She's not … we're not … she's a friend from home. We've been close since we were kids. It might have looked like more at the taxi rank, but I was just holding her up. She's got a partner. He's on the rigs.'

Lily bit her lip to stop the smile of relief and to hide her amusement at his protestations. 'Do all your friends make lewd comments about your truncheon?'

He rubbed the back of his neck. The flush had reached the tips of his ears. 'Just Zoe.'

Lily grinned. She drank the last of her wine. 'Can I get you anything else?'

'A glass of water would be good.'

Chapter 86

DAVID

DAVID LEANED HIS head back and closed his eyes. He felt as if he'd just run a marathon. He thought back to the day they met, all those months ago, on Princes Street. Before that, he'd seen pictures of Lily, taken on the Royal Mile by covert officers. They'd already ruled her out as Collesso's accomplice before David was brought in, and she wasn't under suspicion, probably because of intelligence from Sophia. Though he knew she wasn't a suspect, he'd wondered what kind of person would be engaged to a man like Collesso. Hiding his feelings about the man was one of the hardest things David had ever done. Collesso didn't have a single redeeming quality.

Meeting Lily was a shock. She was bright and funny and she'd looked at David with questions and a hint of laughter in her eyes, as if she could read his thoughts. He really hoped she couldn't. He'd taken her statement. They hadn't known each other, Lily and the homeless man. She'd just been passing when a girl grabbed his cup of money and ran. Lily went after her, returning with his money and a swollen eye. A passer-by had called the police. They found Lily sitting on the ground, talking to the man. She didn't want any fuss, she'd told David, and the description she'd given of the girl was laughable. When he said there was no chance of finding the girl, Lily had smiled as if she'd been given a precious gift. David suspected she might even have paid the girl to get the money back. Collesso's fiancée had a social conscience. The whole thing made no sense.

Back in the car, David's colleague had asked him to guess who she was engaged to. He'd feigned ignorance, trying to ignore a silly stab of jealousy. 'No idea.'

'Collesso. Met her and their wee one on Lothian Road once when I was out with him. Collesso gave her the third degree. What was she doing? Where was she going? Who was she meeting? He tried to make a joke of it, but I wasn't fooled. How does someone like him get someone like her? There's no justice in the world.' He'd rubbed his hands together. 'Wait until Bruce hears about this.'

'Do we have to tell him?'

'Too bloody right. Can't wait to see the look on his smug face.'

The look on Collesso's face had been anything but smug. From that day, David had worried about Lily, desperate to keep her safe. Hadn't worked out that way, though.

At New Year, Zoe had invited him to Edinburgh, but he was undercover on a drugs case in Wolverhampton. As soon as it was over, he'd taken a long weekend off and headed north. Though he longed to see Lily, he'd had no intentions of contacting her. Until he saw her at the taxi rank. He'd lost count of the number of times he'd taken his phone from his pocket to text her today. When he finally did, he couldn't believe her response. He'd had a mad rush to make himself presentable. Fool. He'd have been fine as he was.

He heard a stifled laugh. He opened his eyes. She was sitting cross-legged, watching him. Their drinks were on the table, and he hadn't heard or sensed a thing.

'Some policeman, eh?' He sat forward and took a sip of his water.

Lily picked up her mug and cradled it in her hands. 'Are you tired?'

He shook his head. The nightmares were gone, and he was sleeping well. He hadn't got up until mid-morning. Zoe had gone out with friends for round two of her celebrations, leaving him her car keys. He'd been up Arthur's Seat, then he'd driven out to Falkirk to see the Kelpies. And all the time, Lily was on his mind.

'Are you going to stay in London?' she asked.

'Not sure. I've got a meeting next week. I don't really know where I want to be.'

He didn't tell her the Edinburgh job had taken more from him than he'd expected. It was the first time his target had been a police officer, and that had brought its own challenges. But that wasn't it. Most of his undercover work had involved drugs, and though he pitied the people he got involved with, they were often the authors of their own misfortune. The trafficking case had been different. The plight of the girls, and his inability to save Aneta, had really got to him. Though he'd only been doing undercover work for a few years, it was long enough to see what happened to his older colleagues, burned out, addicted to the thrill, ending up with PTSD and other mental health issues. It was terrifying and lonely, living a lie, manipulating people, pretending to be someone else, making false friendships. It was exhausting, and it was time to get out.

She put her mug on the table. 'I've got some news. I'm going back to university this autumn, here in Edinburgh, to complete my medical degree.'

That smile and the light in her eyes. She was glowing. 'That's wonderful, Lily. Great news.'

He knew then exactly where he wanted to be. 'I might come back here,' he said, his mouth a little dry. 'I'd do it properly this time. A transfer to Police Scotland.'

Her eyes widened. She leaned towards him. 'I'd love that. Could we –?'

He drew back. 'Lily, there's something I have to tell you.'

Chapter 87

LILY

Lily felt her smile fade. Her mouth turned dry and her heart sped up. David looked uncomfortable. Was it something about Nathan? But what could it be? Nathan was dead, and she was glad. She felt for the victims that would never see him brought to justice, but he couldn't hurt her now, and Ronan was safe. Was it Rebecca? Lily had been certain Nathan had killed his sister that day, before turning the gun on himself. Why else would there be two shots? Turned out it was just Nathan being manipulative to the end, trying to mislead her and the police officers, trying to make everyone think the worst. Lily heard later that he'd pressed the gun to Rebecca's head and told her she was going to die. He'd thought for a moment, laughed, and said he reckoned she'd suffer more if she had to live without him. He'd shot the wall, and then himself. Straight through the heart. Rebecca had suffered some temporary hearing loss. After being treated in hospital for her injuries, she'd been charged with abduction and possession of a firearm. Her father was hopeful the charges were going to be dropped, but maybe David knew differently. Lily hoped not. Rebecca was doing better than anyone had expected. She was back home with her parents, and she and Lily were getting close. That couldn't be what

David was going to tell Lily. He wouldn't know anything about Rebecca's charges. Not when he was based in London.

Maybe it was just that Lily had given herself away with her excitement when David talked about coming back to Edinburgh. She'd been about to ask him if they could be friends, but he'd no doubt realised she hoped for much more than friendship. He was probably in a relationship. She remembered Nathan mentioning someone called Eva, and the anger and pain on David's face. Disappointment taunted her, and she wished she could go back to that earlier moment when she'd replied to his text. She wished she'd deleted it.

David's shoulders were stiff. 'It's ... I want you to know I didn't go looking for any information about you or your family. That wasn't part of my remit. If others knew, no one told me. It was when I was last home. A friend mentioned you might be from Valtos.'

Relief bubbled inside her. It made her want to laugh out loud. She wanted to kiss him. She realised she'd wanted that since the day they first met. Calming herself, she smiled. 'I was going to tell you at Cramond. Only Julie knew. I didn't like speaking about home and my mother, and Julie respected that. Nathan wasn't interested. He knew I'd lived in Norway, and that I wasn't on speaking terms with my family. I think he just assumed they lived somewhere near Aberdeen, and I didn't bother telling him otherwise.' A sudden wave of emotion threatened. She tried to smile. 'I felt as if I was living the wrong life. Someone else's. The island, my heritage – they mean everything to me, and I didn't want to share that with him. It was too precious. I couldn't have him polluting it. Does it sound silly?'

David shook his head. 'Not at all.' He looked apprehensive. 'So, you have Gaelic?'

'Yes.'

'I really hoped that bit wasn't true, after what I said in the hospital. Maybe you didn't hear me. You were still asleep.'

Lily held her breath. She could lie. Tell him she hadn't heard him. She was unconscious. She had a brain injury. She didn't remember.

Or she could whisper the words of love back to him in their native language, as if she was saying them anew and meaning every word.

As she looked into his grey eyes, she made her choice. His eyes widened, and he reached for her hand. When their fingers met, she felt a jolt of electricity. They kissed, and all the disordered bits of her life settled into place. It felt like coming home.

*

IT WAS MUCH later that David asked her if she ever thought about going back to the island. Lily stared at the fairy lights. Since Nathan's revelation, her mother had been constantly on her mind. She should have been relieved to know her mother hadn't tormented herself, believing Lily was a drug addict who had lied about her stepfather. She was relieved. But she'd also had to face a disturbing truth. Although her devastation when Nathan made the call was genuine, recently she'd questioned why she hadn't contacted her mother to put her straight. She wouldn't even have had to speak to her. A letter would have done it, with a photo of Ronan. Why hadn't she? Because there was a small, hidden, spiteful part of her that had wanted to punish her mother and stepfather, and let them believe Nathan's words. And she hated herself for it.

'I wish I could,' she said, at last. 'I miss it so much. I'd love to bring Ronan up there, after I've finished my training, but my mother and I, we've lost touch.' Lily shrugged. 'And it's not just her. It's my stepfather. We were never close. He wouldn't want me around now.'

David opened his mouth to say something and closed it. He frowned.

Lily sat up. 'What is it?'

'My mother sends me the Stornoway Gazette. I saw recently ...'

Fear darted through her, jolting her stomach and encircling her heart. What if … what if her mother …?

'Your stepfather … the minister … he died.'

*

FOUR TIMES LILY punched the number into her phone, each time stopping just short of the final digit. She remembered an evening in the depths of a Hamnøy winter, standing with her parents on the wooden decking of their home, the sea boiling beneath their feet, as they watched the Northern Lights. Her father said the lights were the glow from the armour of Valkyrie warriors, bearing dead heroes home to Valhalla. Lily had asked what Valkyries were. They were warrior maidens with the power to choose who would live and who would die in battle, her father had said.

'Will I be a Valkyrie when I'm bigger, Mammy?' she'd asked.

Her mother had shaken her head. 'How could you be a Valkyrie, Lily? You are the kindest, gentlest person in the world, and you would let everyone live.'

She punched in the full number. The phone rang several times. Perhaps her mother had changed her habits and now went to bed early. Maybe she was staying with a friend or a neighbour, too lonely in that big old manse. Perhaps …

'Hello.'

That voice. Hushed with the residue of grief, yet so unchanged. And Lily was certain then that her mother's love would be the same. Unchanged and deep and enduring.

'Mammy … it's … it's me.'

Acknowledgements

To MY READERS, I can't thank you enough for your support. Special thanks to my exceptional beta readers, Ishbel, Anne, Connie and Clare. Thank you to my editor, Lynn Curtis, for her wonderful editing skills and helpful suggestions. Many thanks to Hannah Linder at Hannah Linder Designs and Kate Coe at Book Polishers for the excellent design and typesetting work, and for their friendly, helpful service. Thank you to Jim Smith for his expert police advice. Apologies for any artistic licence used in dealing with aspects of police procedure. All mistakes are mine. And to my family and friends, thank you for still believing.

✷✷✷

IF YOU LIKED *Deception*, you'll enjoy *In the Shadow of the Hill*, *Madness Lies* and *Unravelling*.

Check out my website www.helenforbes.co.uk and sign up to my mailing list for news, views and more. Be among the first to hear when my next novel is due out. And please do leave a review. They are a great help to me and other readers.

About the Author

HELEN FORBES IS a lawyer and author of the DS Joe Galbraith novels, *In the Shadow of the Hill* and *Madness Lies,* and the standalone psychological thriller, *Unravelling.* She was born and brought up in the Highlands of Scotland, and lives in Inverness.